LAST HOPE
FOR SURVIVAL

UNOFFICIAL GRAPHIC NOVEL
#1 FOR FORTNITERS

LAST HOPE
FOR SURVIVAL

UNOFFICIAL GRAPHIC NOVEL
#1 FOR FORTNITERS

NATHAN MEYER
ILLUSTRATED BY ALAN BROWN

Sky Pony Press
New York

This book is not authorized or sponsored by Epic Games, Inc. or any other person or entity owning or controlling rights in the Fortnite name, trademark, or copyrights.

Sky Pony Press books may be purchased in bulk at special discounts for sales promotion, corporate gifts, fund-raising, or educational purposes. Special editions can also be created to specifications. For details, contact the Special Sales Department, Sky Pony Press, 307 West 36th Street, 11th Floor, New York, NY 10018 or info@skyhorsepublishing.com.

Sky Pony® is a registered trademark of Skyhorse Publishing, Inc.®, a Delaware corporation.

Visit our website at www.skyponypress.com.

10 9 8 7 6 5 4 3 2 1

Library of Congress Cataloging-in-Publication Data is available on file.

Cover design by Brian Peterson
Cover illustration by Alan Brown

Paperback ISBN: 978-1-5107-4520-9
E-book ISBN: 978-1-5107-4522-3

Printed in China

LAST HOPE
FOR SURVIVAL

UNOFFICIAL GRAPHIC NOVEL
#1 FOR FORTNITERS

CHAPTER 1: CODY

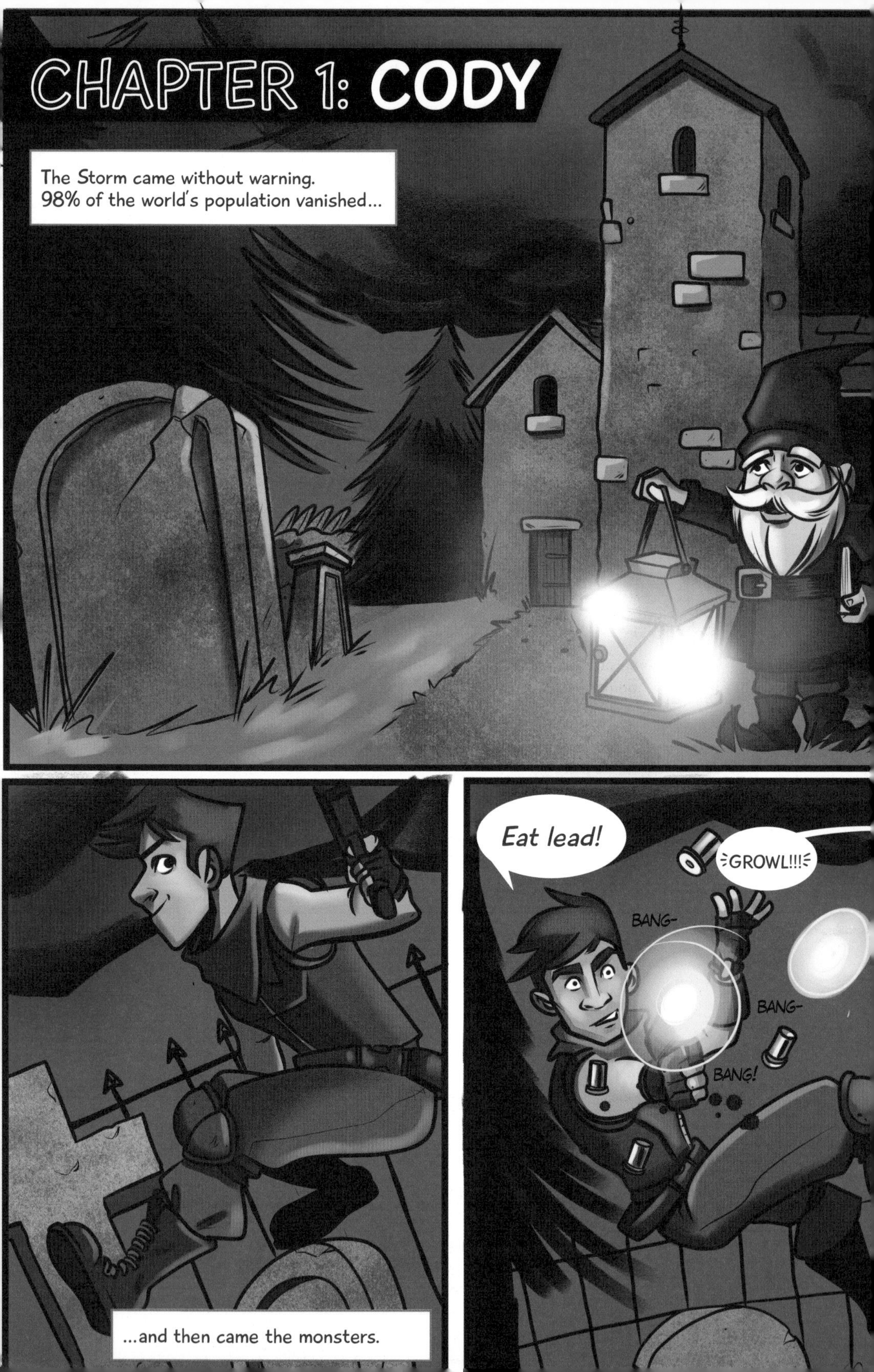

The Storm came without warning.
98% of the world's population vanished...
...and then came the monsters.
Eat lead!
GROWL!!!
BANG-
BANG-
BANG!

I've always wanted to say that.

Cody Valdez spent high school at the Chilton Military Preparatory Academy. He's used to running five miles, doing push-ups, and climbing rope. So far, the End of the World has presented many challenges, but physical obstacles aren't a problem for Cody. When the Storm came, he was ready, even if he's about as far from home as he can get--

KA-BOOOM!!!

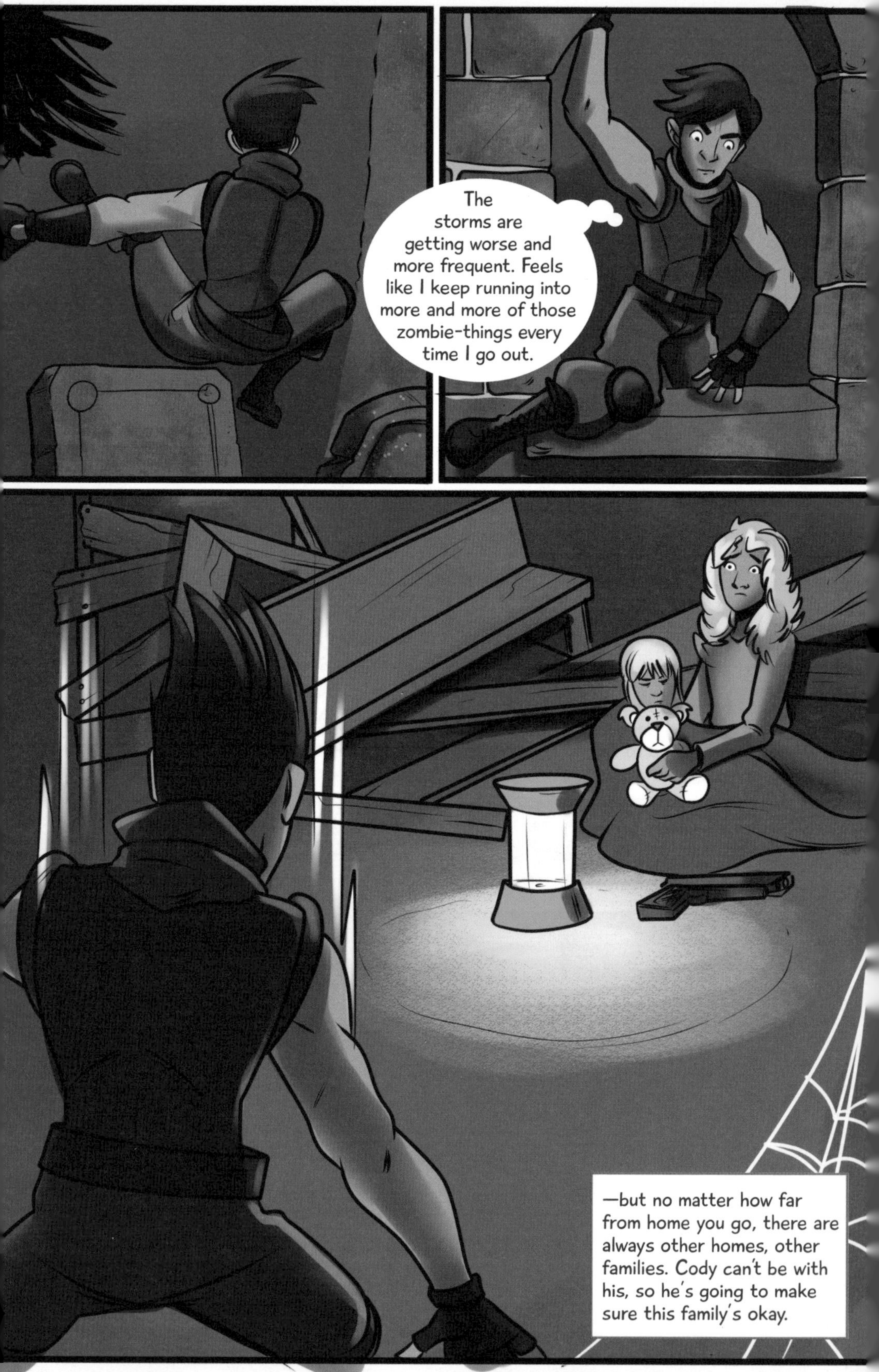
The storms are getting worse and more frequent. Feels like I keep running into more and more of those zombie-things every time I go out.
—but no matter how far from home you go, there are always other homes, other families. Cody can't be with his, so he's going to make sure this family's okay.

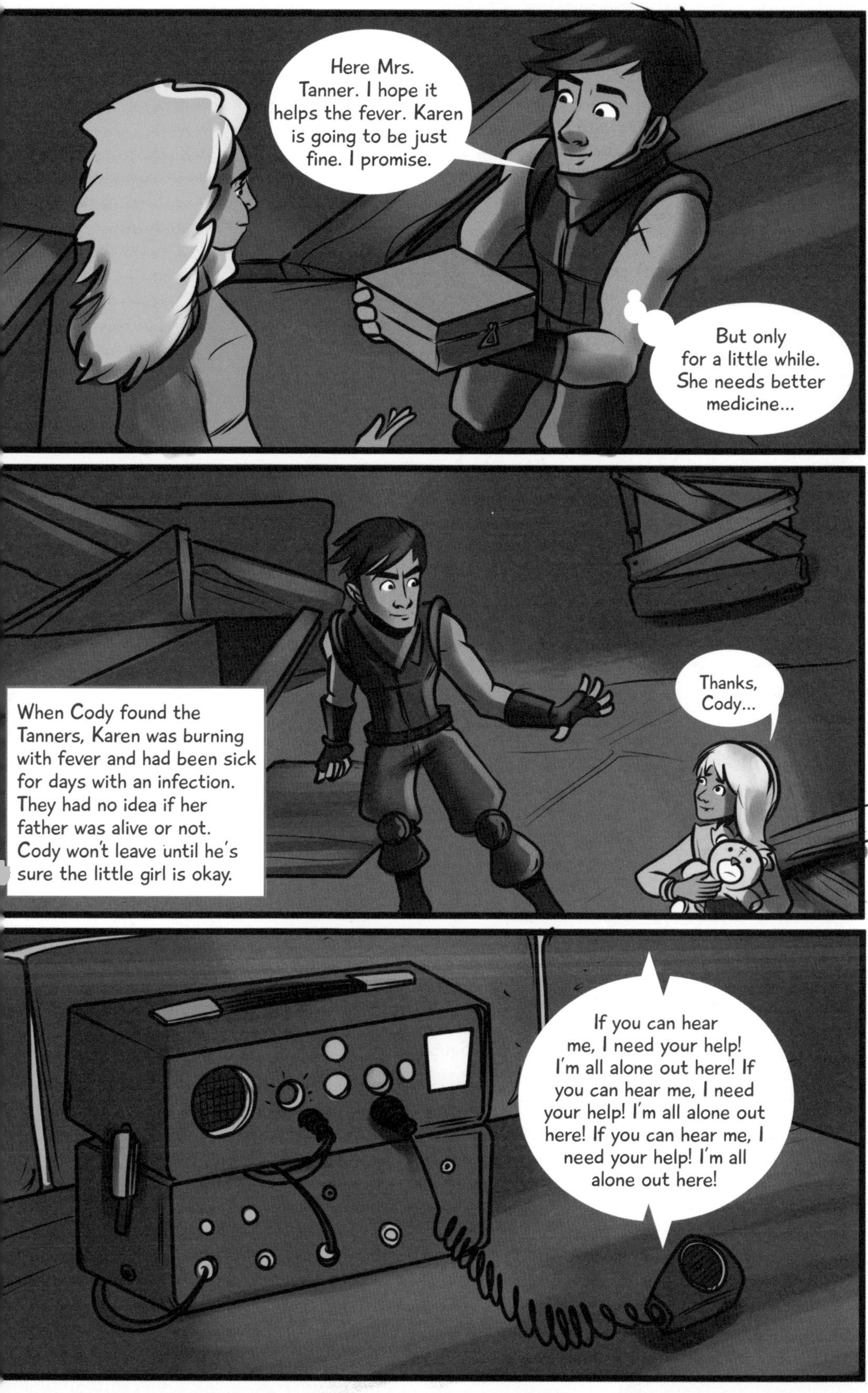
Here Mrs. Tanner. I hope it helps the fever. Karen is going to be just fine. I promise.
But only for a little while. She needs better medicine...
When Cody found the Tanners, Karen was burning with fever and had been sick for days with an infection. They had no idea if her father was alive or not. Cody won't leave until he's sure the little girl is okay.
Thanks, Cody...
If you can hear me, I need your help! I'm all alone out here! If you can hear me, I need your help! I'm all alone out here! If you can hear me, I need your help! I'm all alone out here!

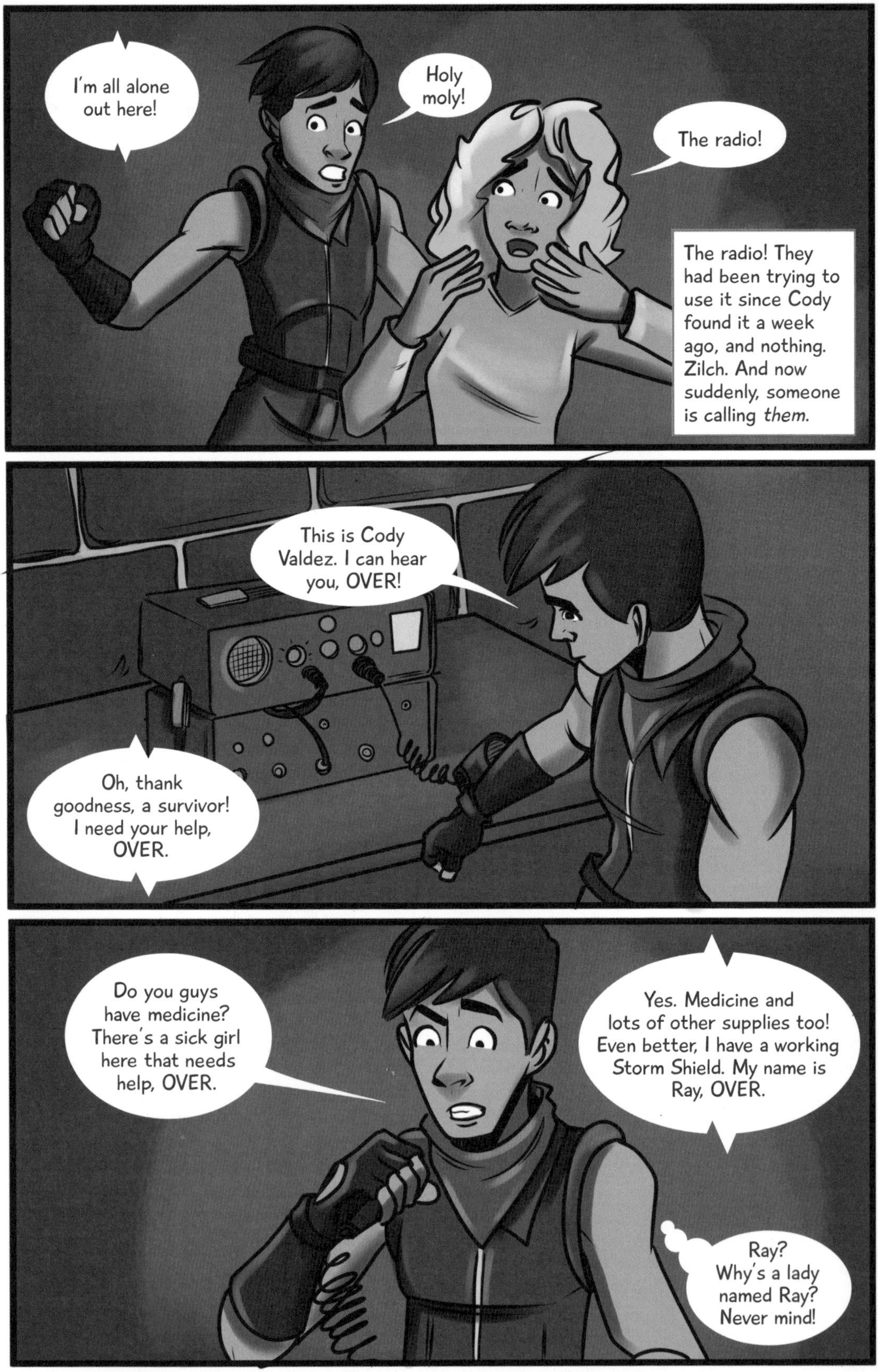
I'm all alone out here!
Holy moly!
The radio!
The radio! They had been trying to use it since Cody found it a week ago, and nothing. Zilch. And now suddenly, someone is calling *them*.
This is Cody Valdez. I can hear you, OVER!
Oh, thank goodness, a survivor! I need your help, OVER.
Do you guys have medicine? There's a sick girl here that needs help, OVER.
Yes. Medicine and lots of other supplies too! Even better, I have a working Storm Shield. My name is Ray, OVER.
Ray? Why's a lady named Ray? Never mind!

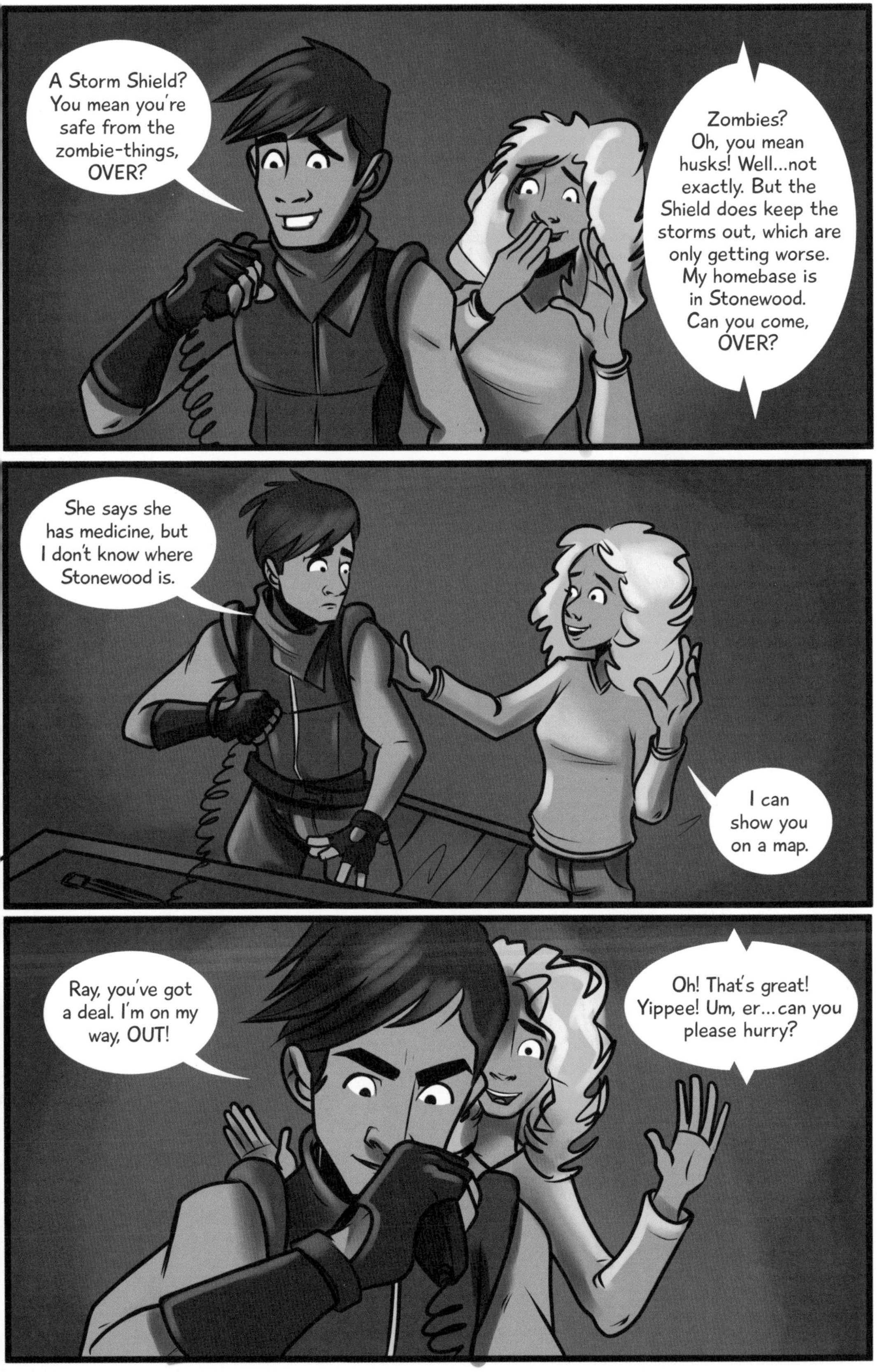
A Storm Shield? You mean you're safe from the zombie-things, OVER?
Zombies? Oh, you mean husks! Well...not exactly. But the Shield does keep the storms out, which are only getting worse. My homebase is in Stonewood. Can you come, OVER?
She says she has medicine, but I don't know where Stonewood is.
I can show you on a map.
Ray, you've got a deal. I'm on my way, OUT!
Oh! That's great! Yippee! Um, er...can you please hurry?

CHAPTER 2: SARAH

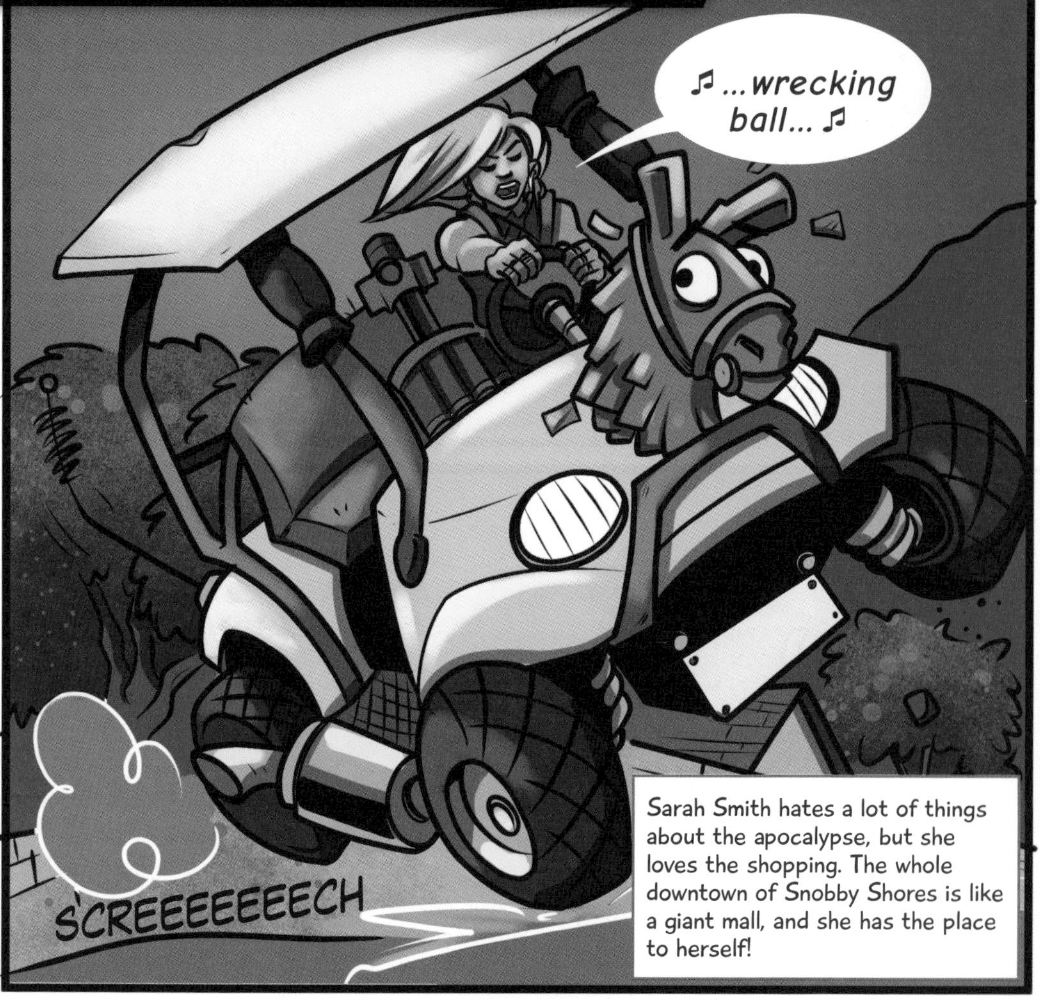
♫ ...wrecking ball... ♫
Sarah Smith hates a lot of things about the apocalypse, but she loves the shopping. The whole downtown of Snobby Shores is like a giant mall, and she has the place to herself!
SCREEEEEEEECH

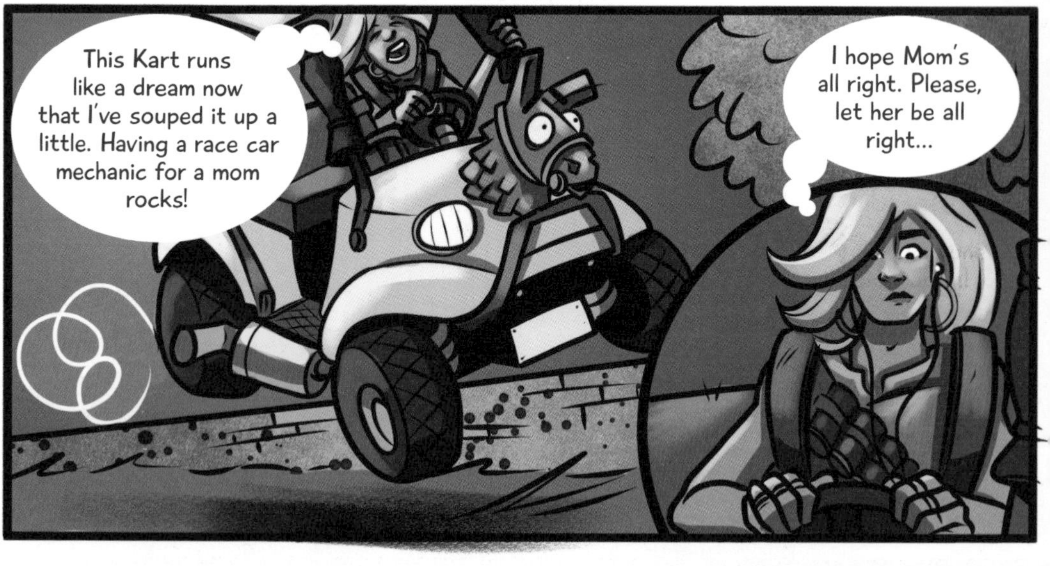
This Kart runs like a dream now that I've souped it up a little. Having a race car mechanic for a mom rocks!
I hope Mom's all right. Please, let her be all right...

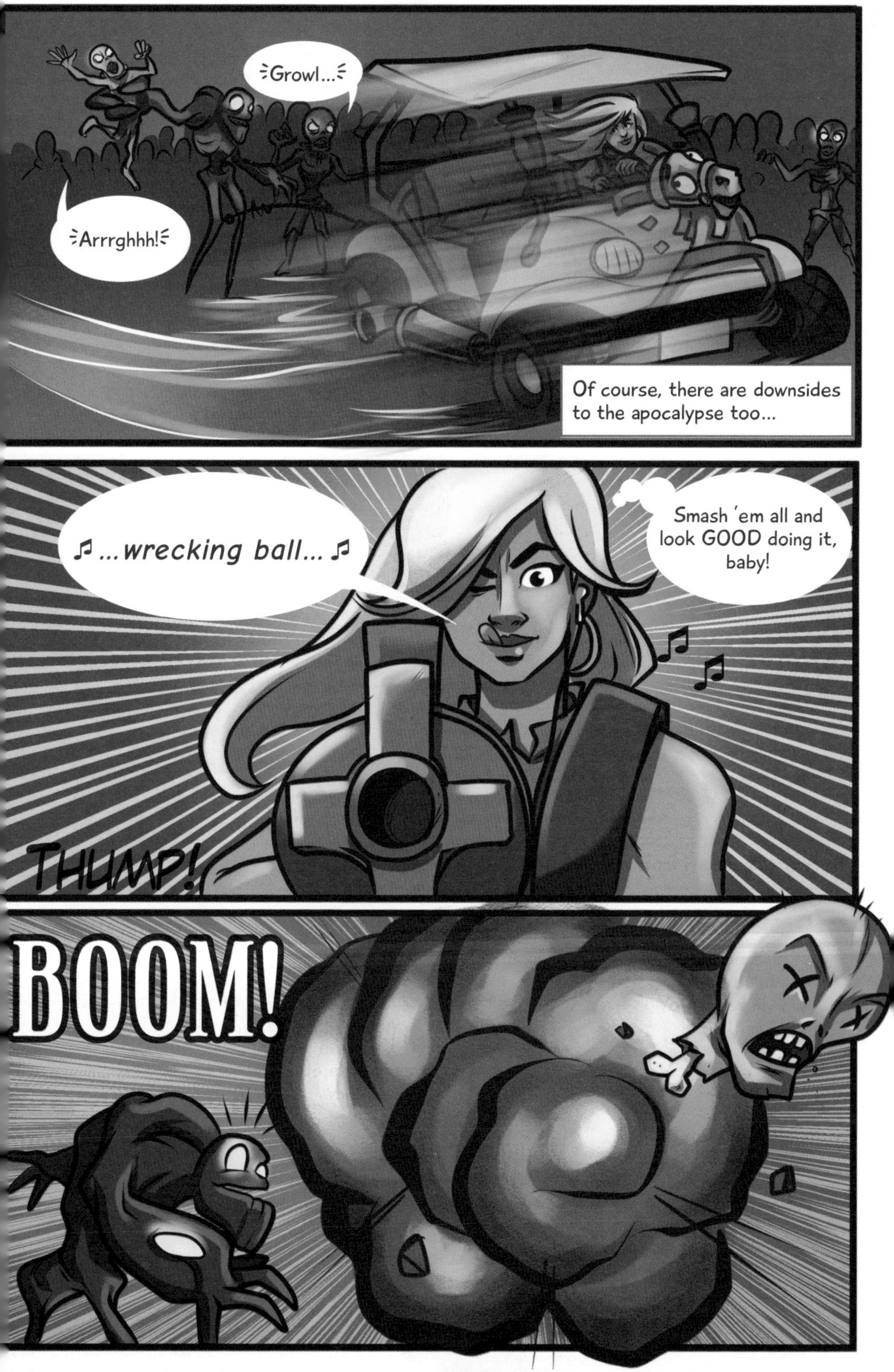
Growl...
Arrrghhh!
Of course, there are downsides to the apocalypse too...
♫ ...wrecking ball... ♫
Smash 'em all and look GOOD doing it, baby!
THUMP!
BOOM!

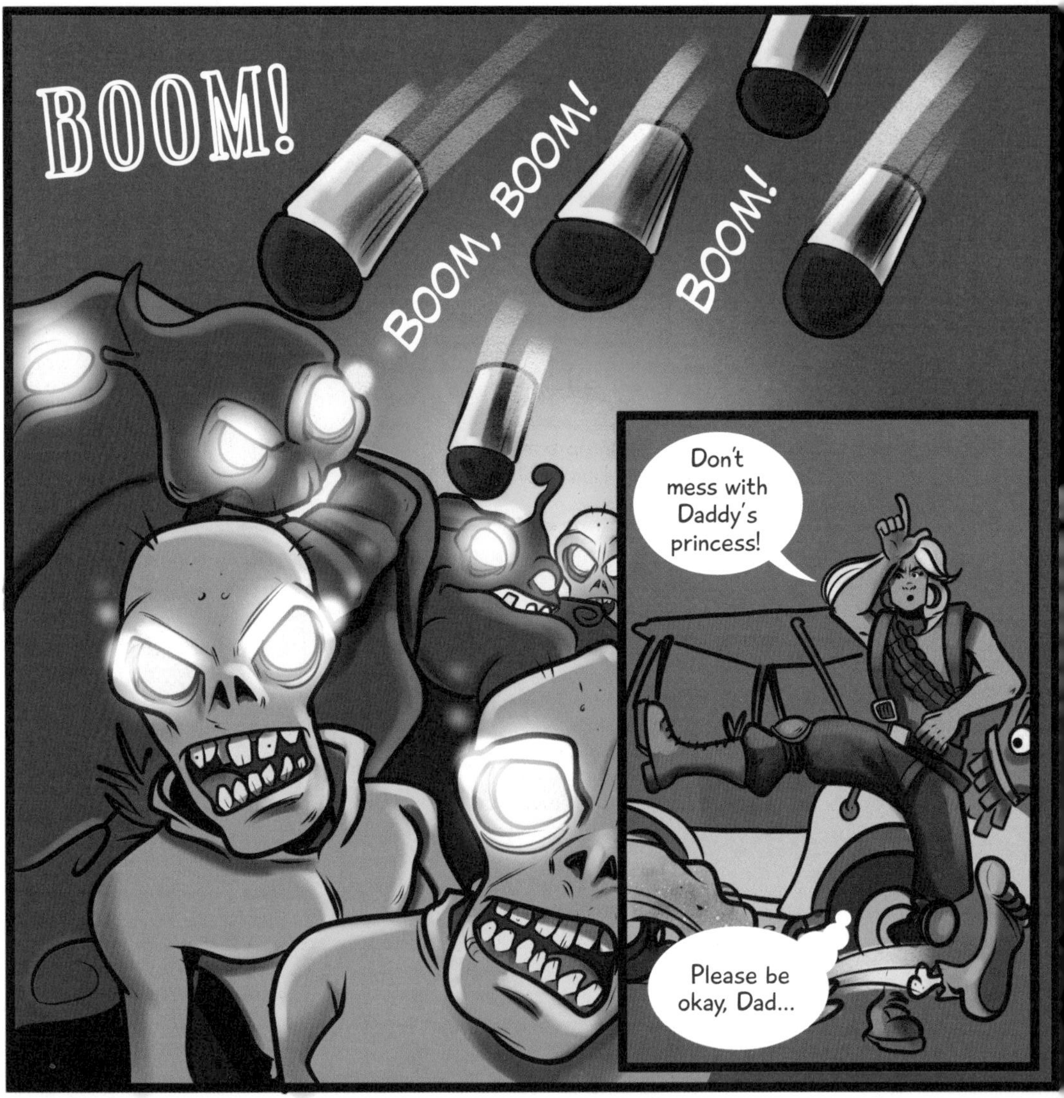
BOOM!
BOOM, BOOM!
BOOM!
Don't mess with Daddy's princess!
Please be okay, Dad...

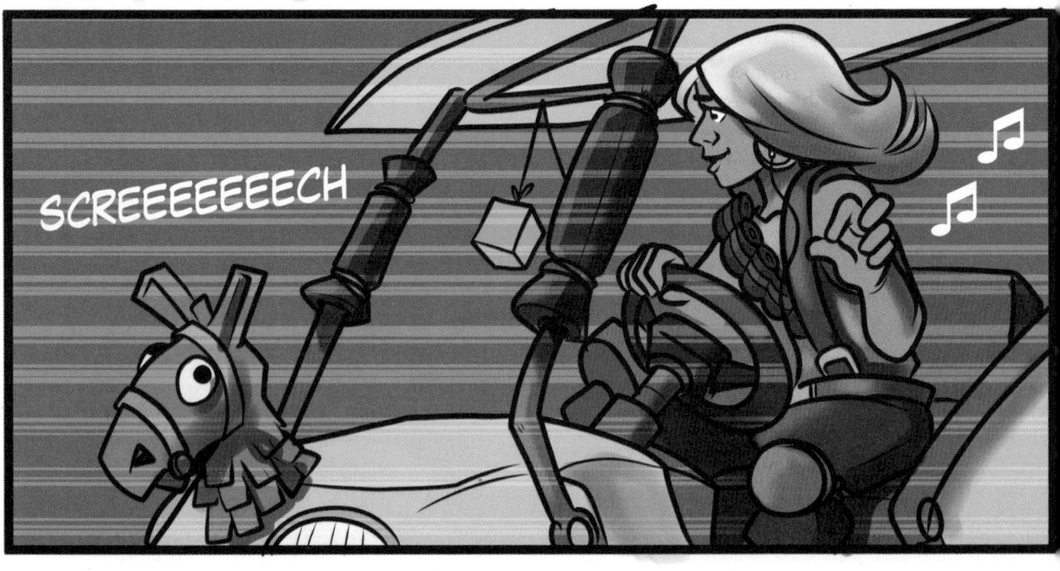
SCREEEEEEEECH

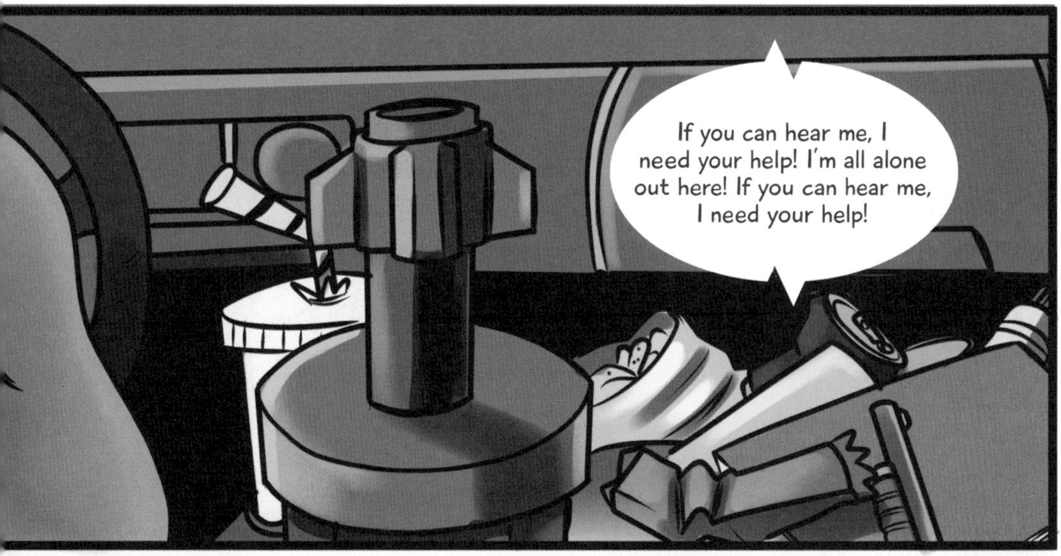
If you can hear me, I need your help! I'm all alone out here! If you can hear me, I need your help!

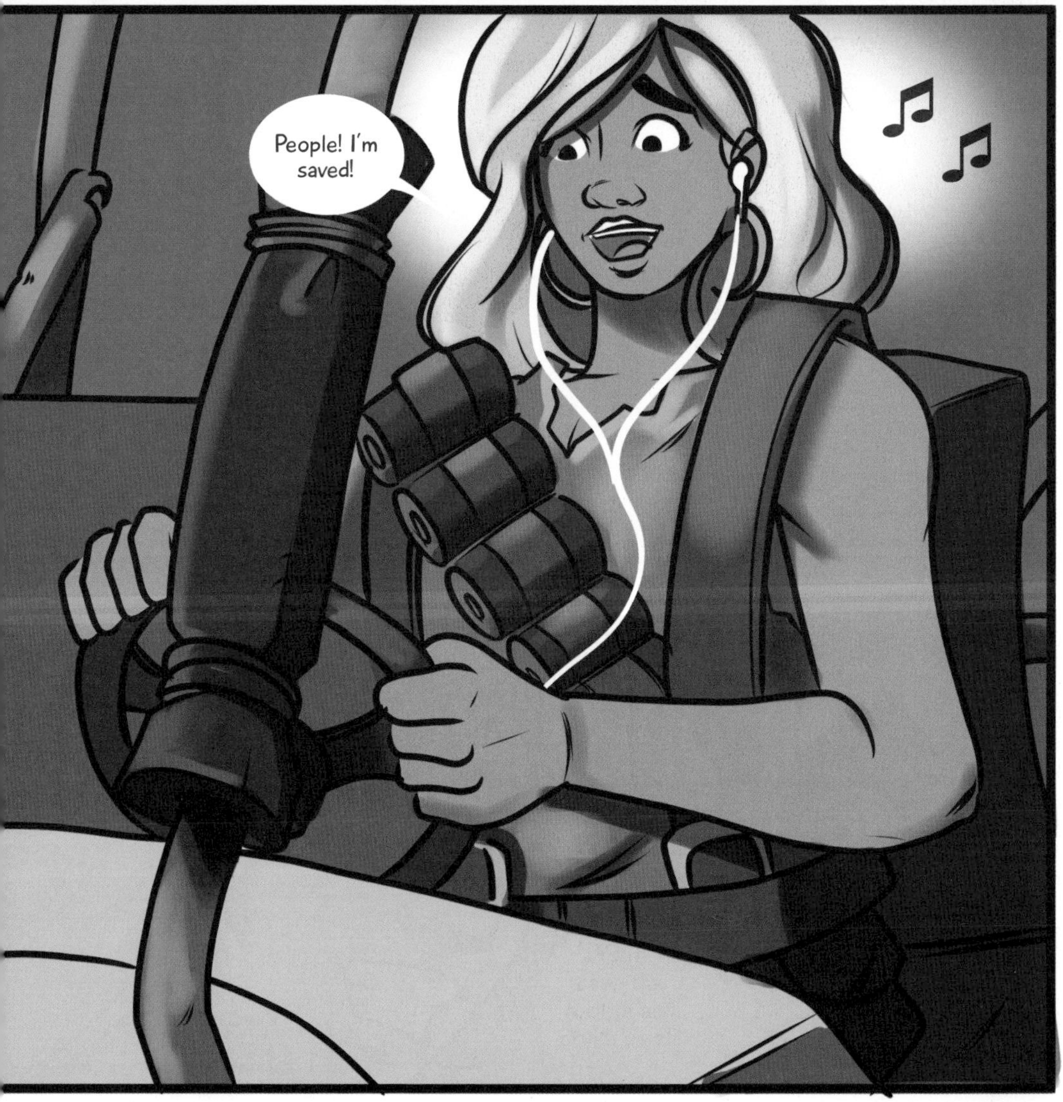
People! I'm saved!

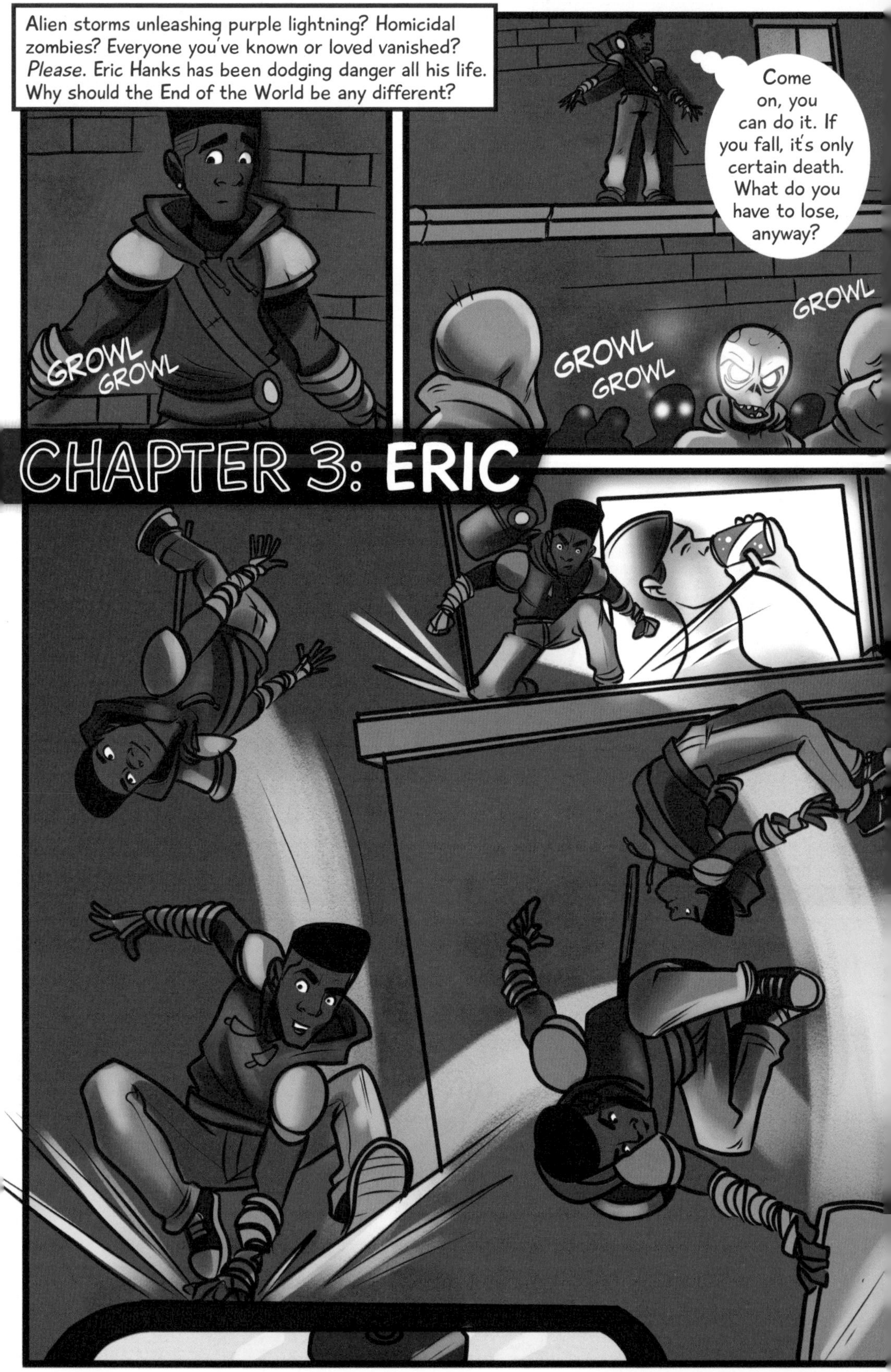
Alien storms unleashing purple lightning? Homicidal zombies? Everyone you've known or loved vanished? *Please.* Eric Hanks has been dodging danger all his life. Why should the End of the World be any different?
Come on, you can do it. If you fall, it's only certain death. What do you have to lose, anyway?
GROWL
GROWL
GROWL
GROWL
GROWL
CHAPTER 3: ERIC

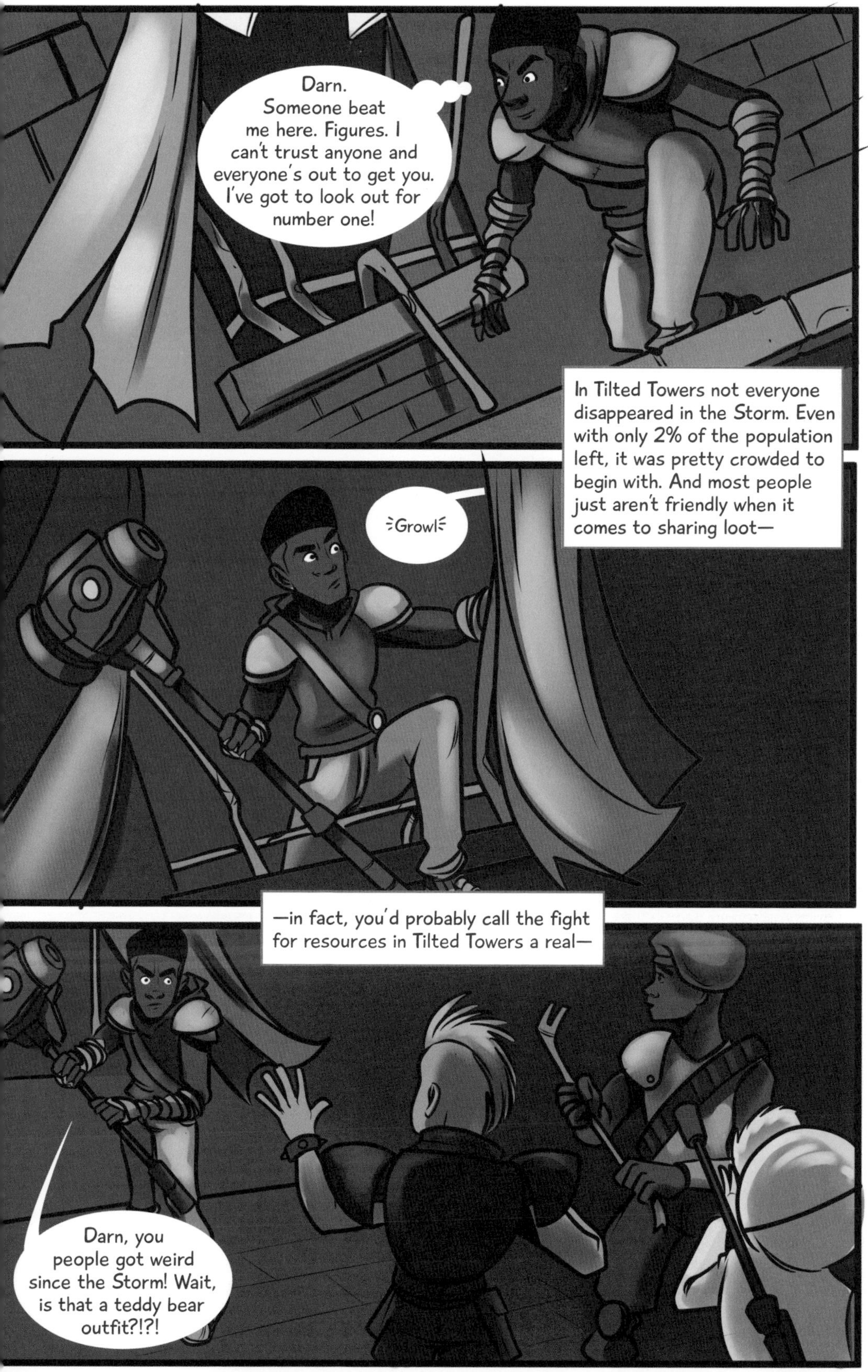
Darn. Someone beat me here. Figures. I can't trust anyone and everyone's out to get you. I've got to look out for number one!
In Tilted Towers not everyone disappeared in the Storm. Even with only 2% of the population left, it was pretty crowded to begin with. And most people just aren't friendly when it comes to sharing loot—
Growl
—in fact, you'd probably call the fight for resources in Tilted Towers a real—
Darn, you people got weird since the Storm! Wait, is that a teddy bear outfit?!?!

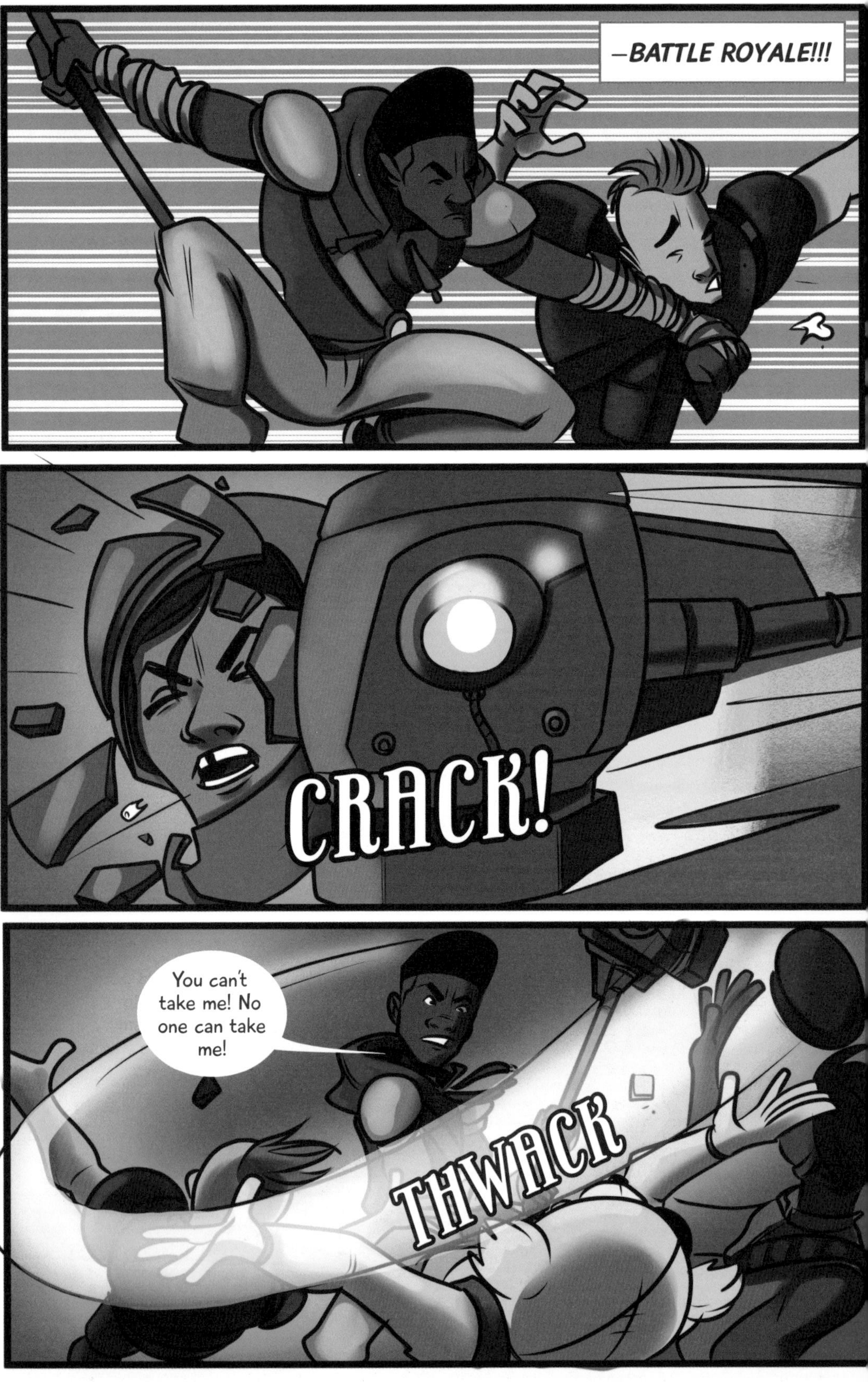
—BATTLE ROYALE!!!
CRACK!
You can't take me! No one can take me!
THWACK

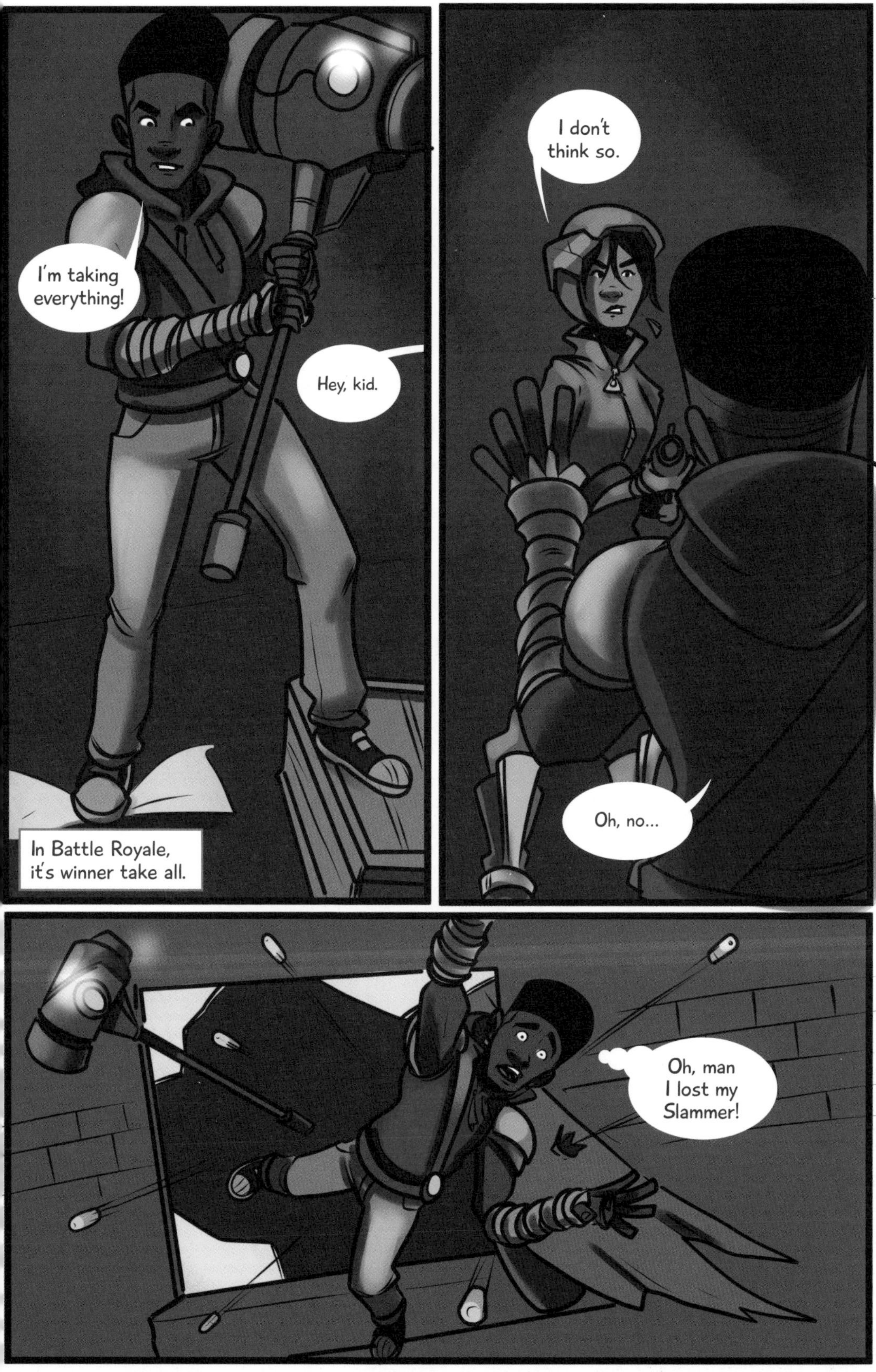
I'm taking everything!
Hey, kid.
In Battle Royale, it's winner take all.
I don't think so.
Oh, no...
Oh, man I lost my Slammer!

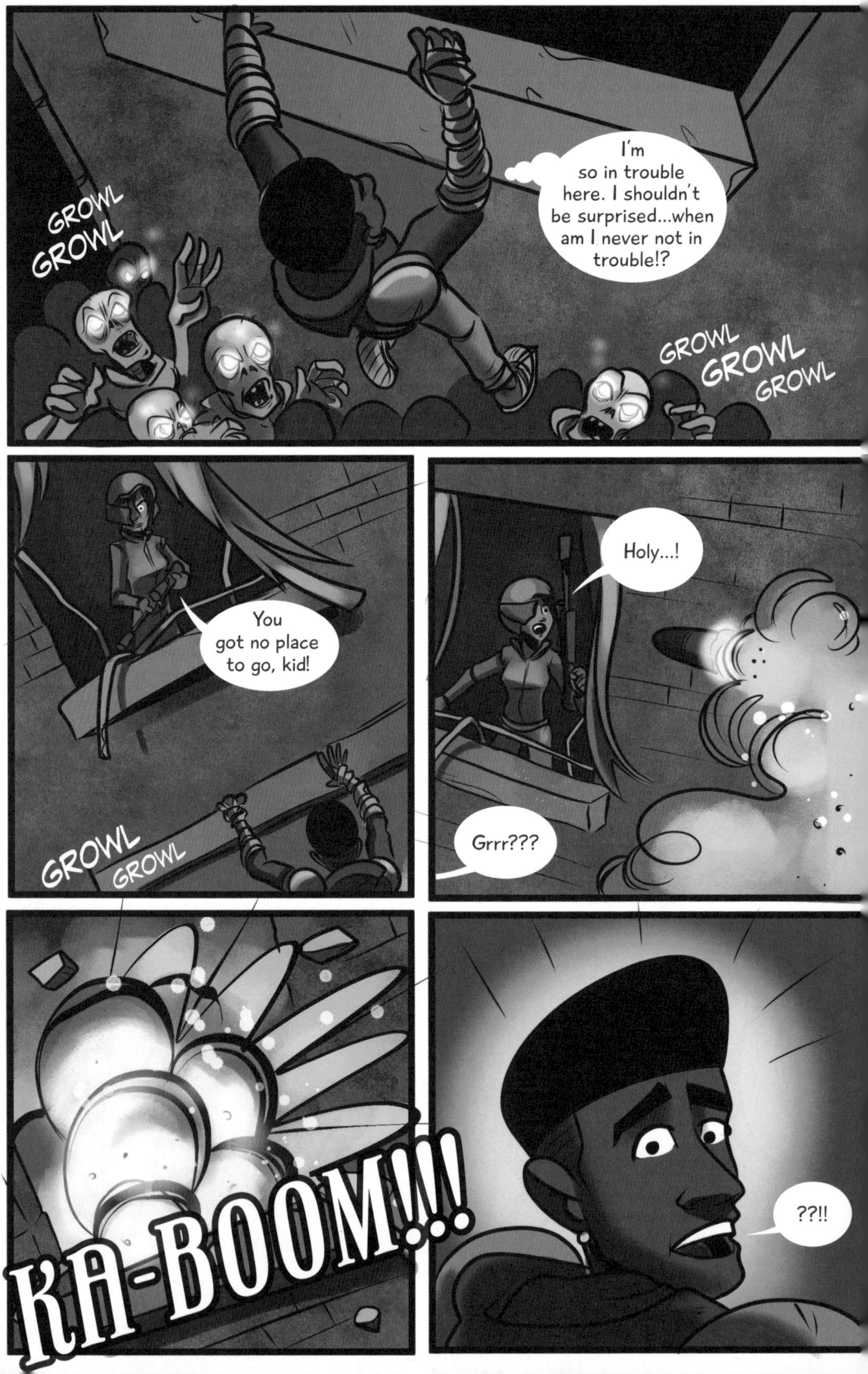
I'm so in trouble here. I shouldn't be surprised...when am I never not in trouble!?
GROWL GROWL
GROWL GROWL GROWL
You got no place to go, kid!
GROWL GROWL
Holy...!
Grrr???
KA-BOOM!!!
??!!

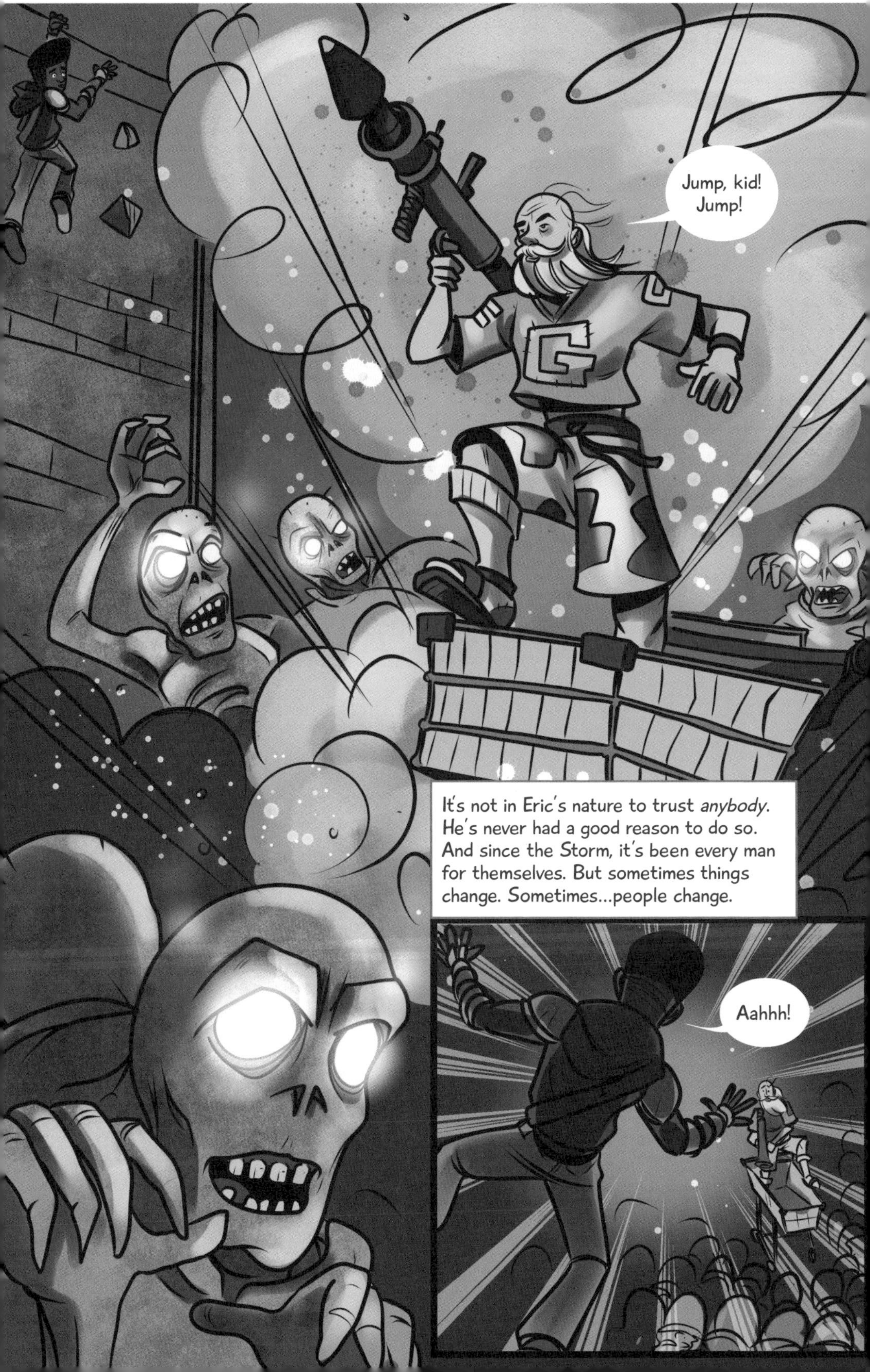
Jump, kid! Jump!
It's not in Eric's nature to trust *anybody*. He's never had a good reason to do so. And since the Storm, it's been every man for themselves. But sometimes things change. Sometimes...people change.
Aahhh!

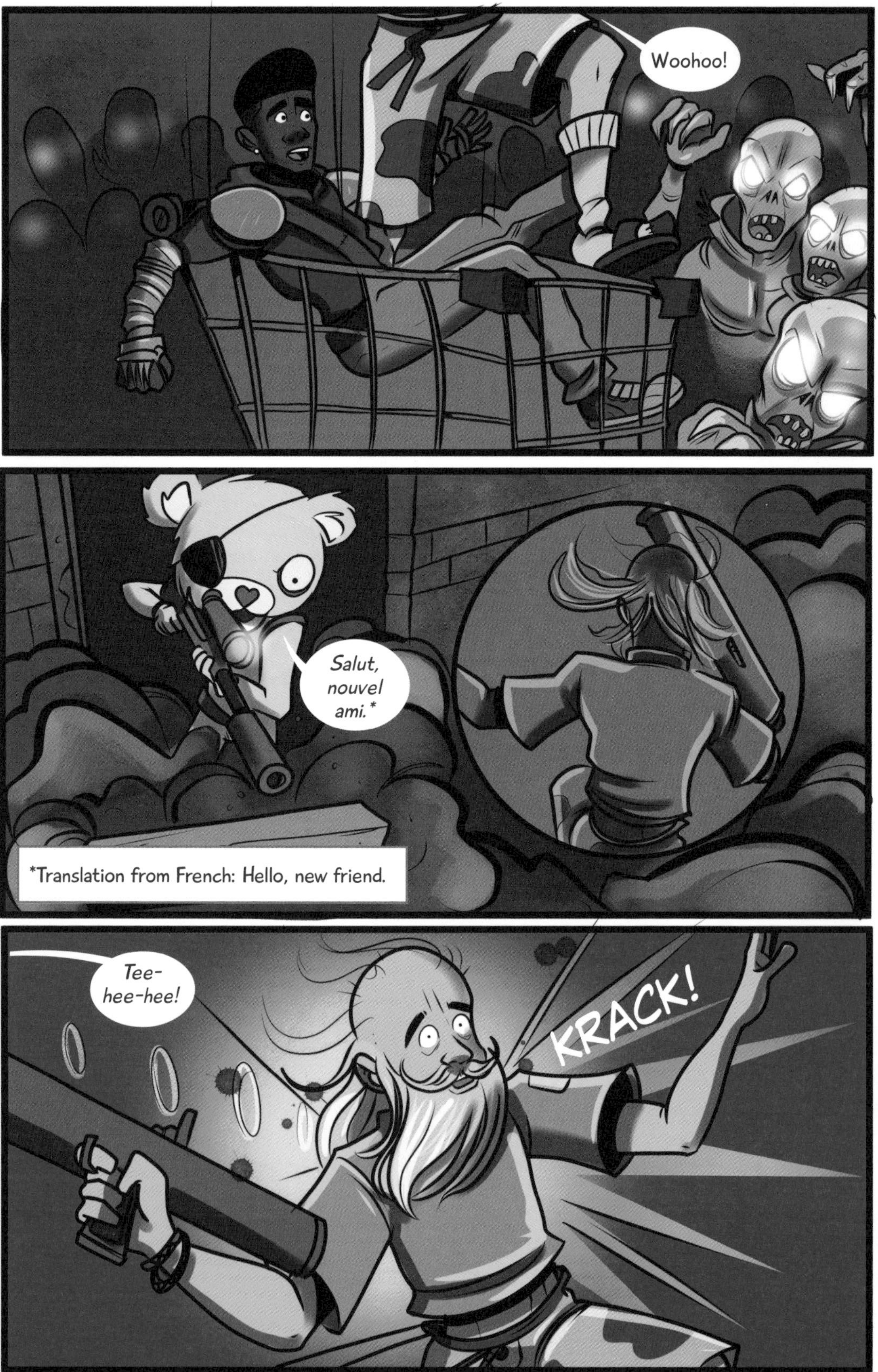
Woohoo!
Salut, nouvel ami.*
*Translation from French: Hello, new friend.
Tee-hee-hee!
KRACK!

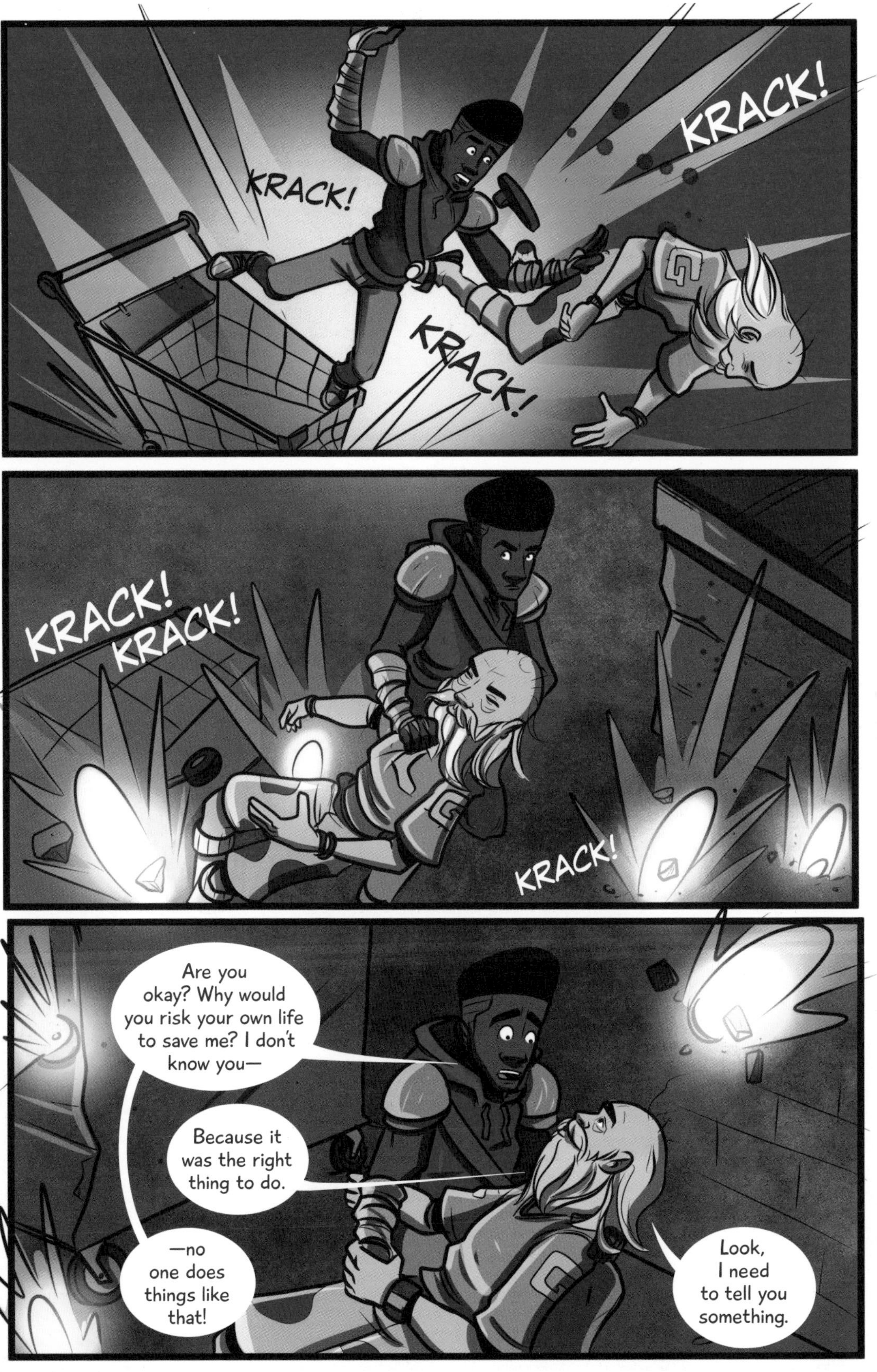
KRACK!
KRACK!
KRACK!
KRACK!
KRACK!
KRACK!
Are you okay? Why would you risk your own life to save me? I don't know you—
Because it was the right thing to do.
—no one does things like that!
Look, I need to tell you something.

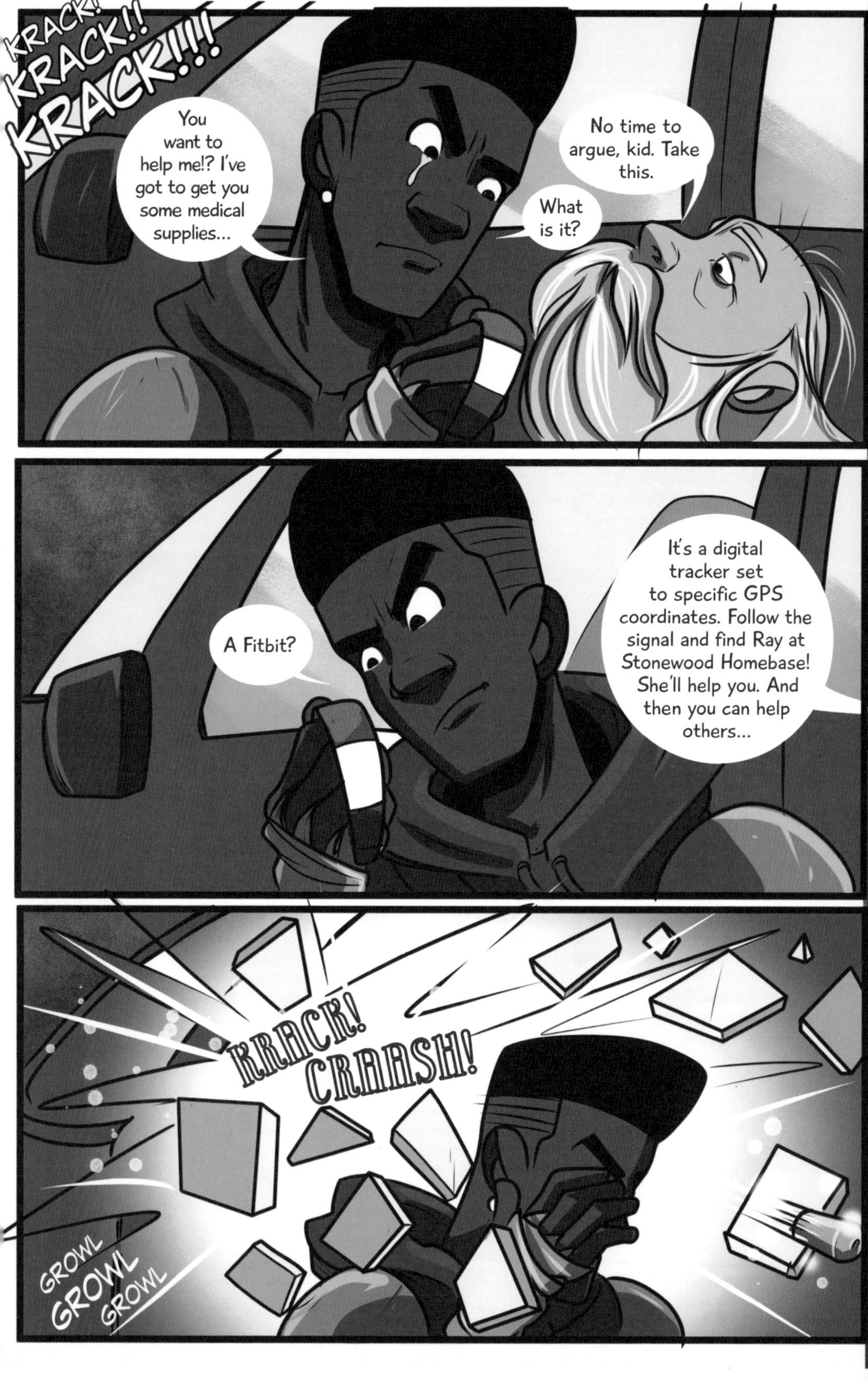
KRACK!
KRACK!!
KRACK!!!
You want to help me!? I've got to get you some medical supplies...
No time to argue, kid. Take this.
What is it?
It's a digital tracker set to specific GPS coordinates. Follow the signal and find Ray at Stonewood Homebase! She'll help you. And then you can help others...
A Fitbit?
KRACK!
CRAASH!
GROWL
GROWL
GROWL

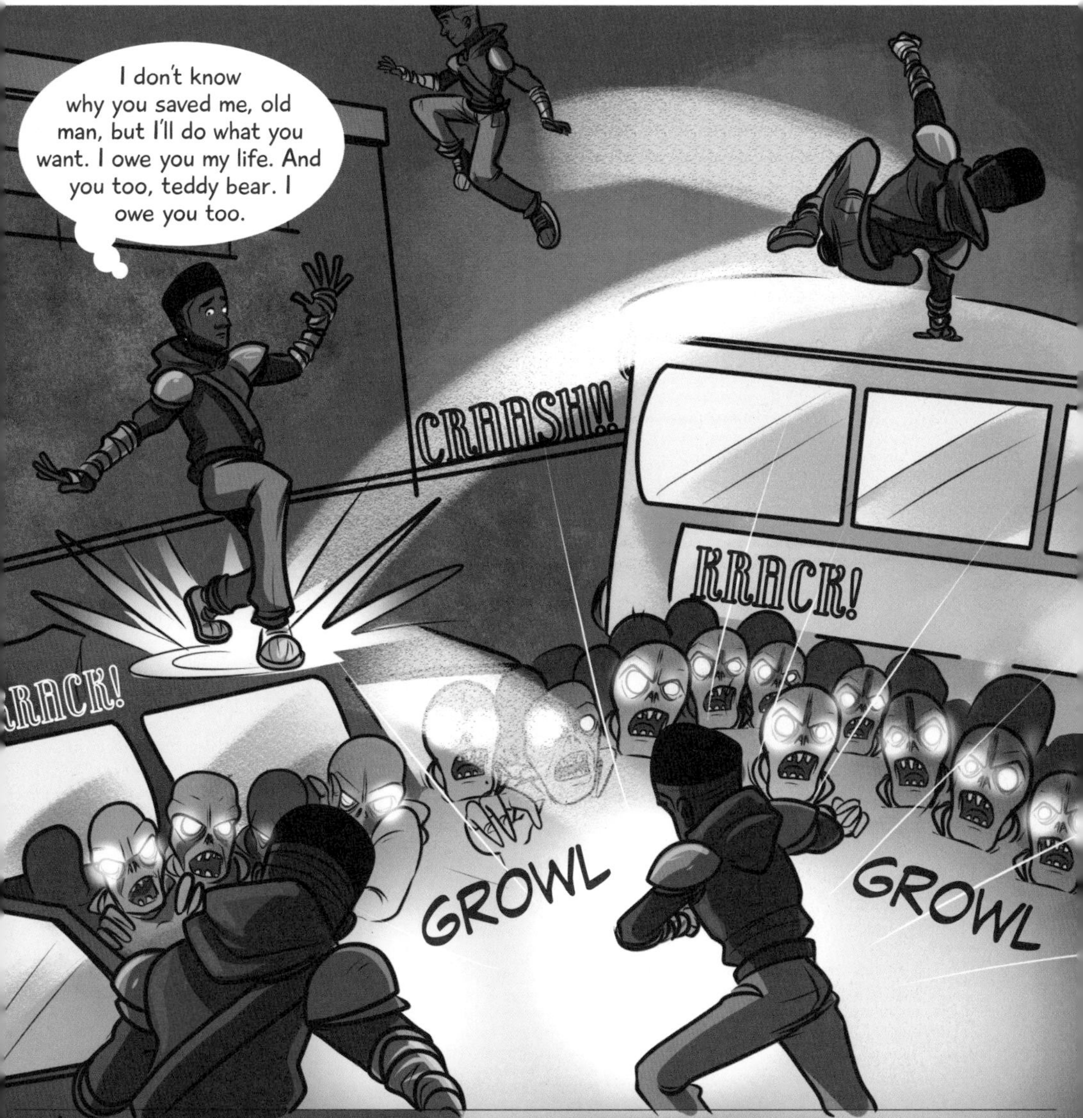
I don't know why you saved me, old man, but I'll do what you want. I owe you my life. And you too, teddy bear. I owe you too.
CRAASH!!
KRACK!
RACK!
GROWL
GROWL

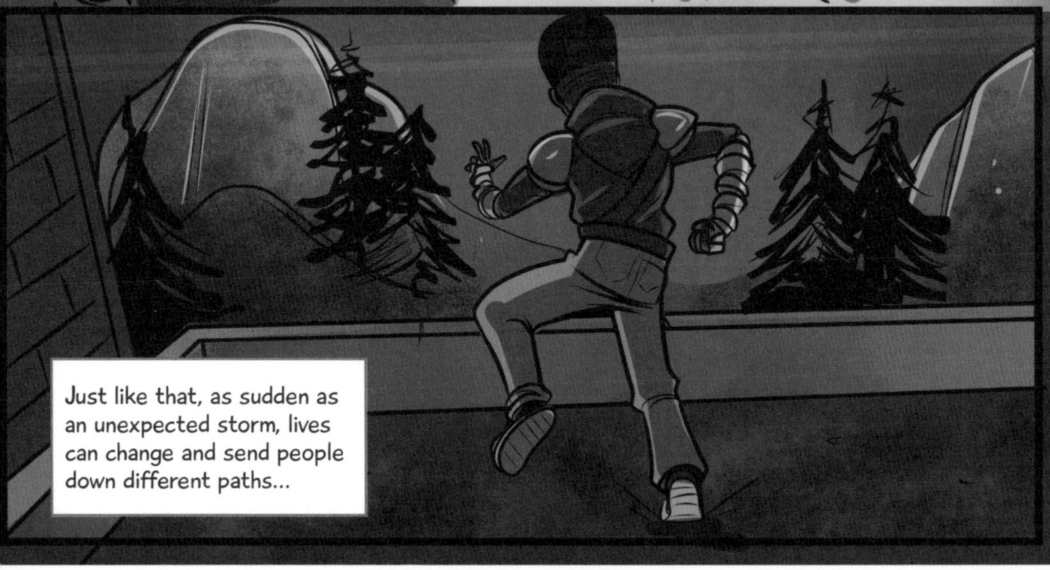
Just like that, as sudden as an unexpected storm, lives can change and send people down different paths...

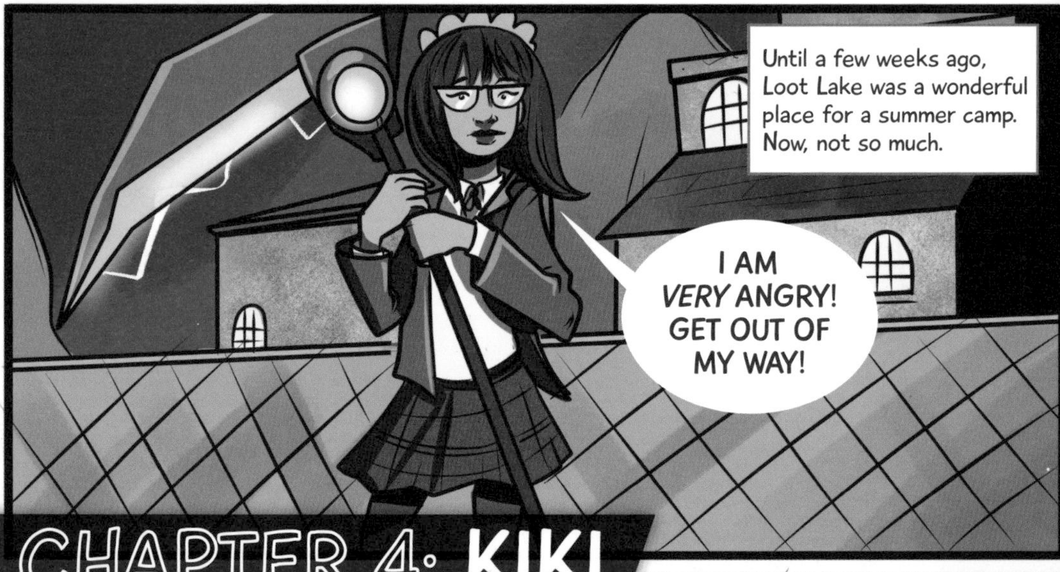
Until a few weeks ago, Loot Lake was a wonderful place for a summer camp. Now, not so much.
I AM *VERY* ANGRY! GET OUT OF MY WAY!

CHAPTER 4: KIKI

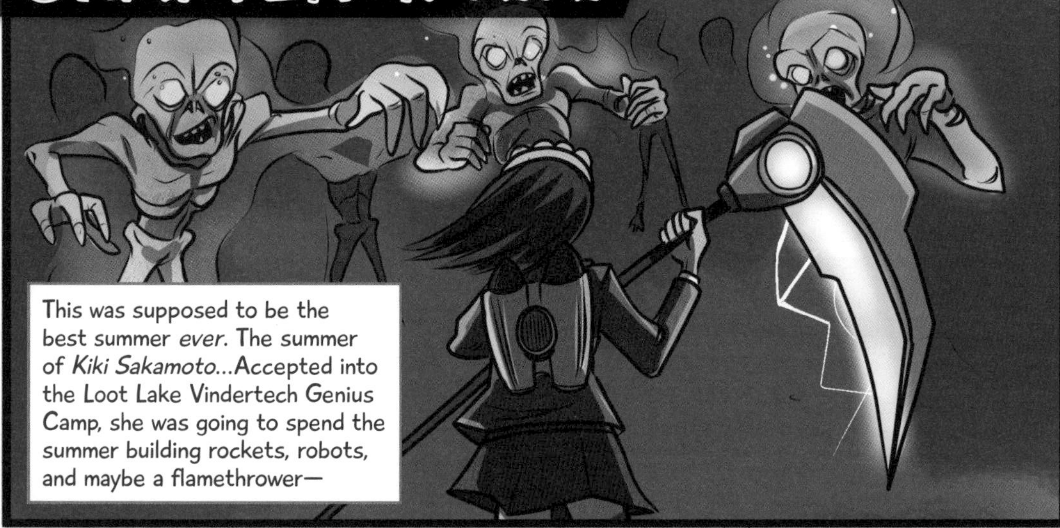
This was supposed to be the best summer *ever*. The summer of *Kiki Sakamoto*...Accepted into the Loot Lake Vindertech Genius Camp, she was going to spend the summer building rockets, robots, and maybe a flamethrower—

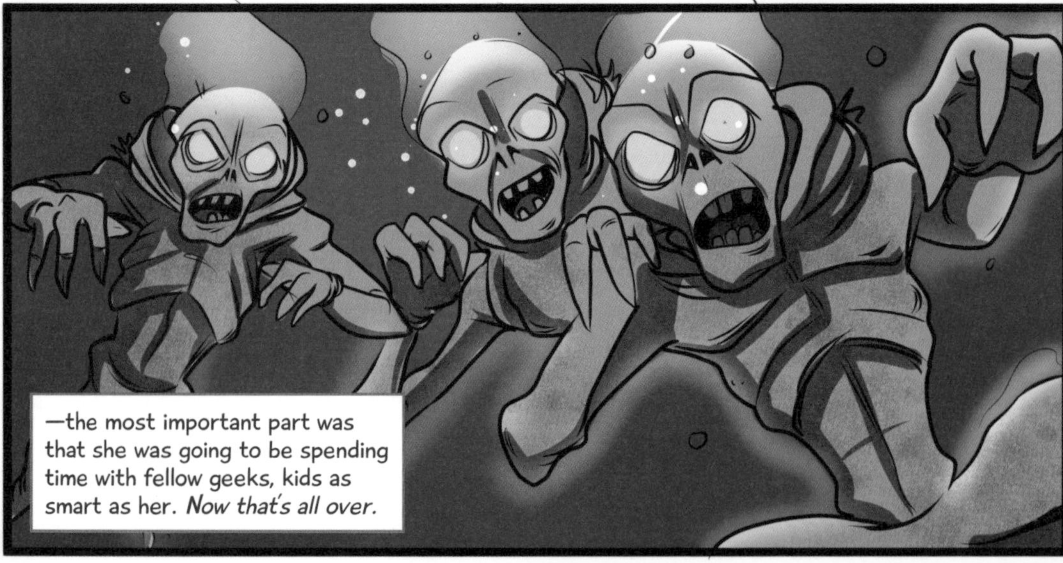
—the most important part was that she was going to be spending time with fellow geeks, kids as smart as her. *Now that's all over.*

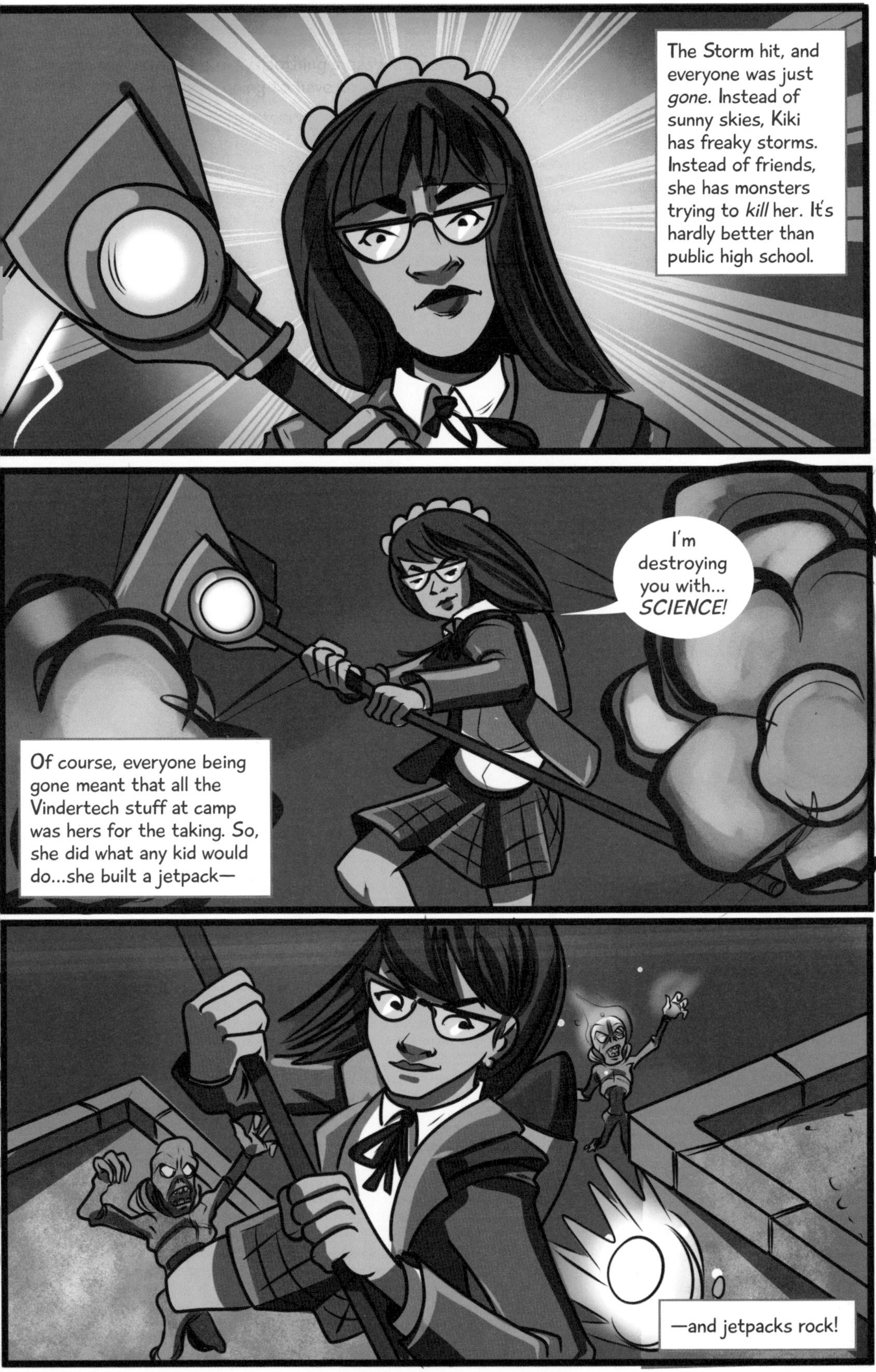
The Storm hit, and everyone was just *gone*. Instead of sunny skies, Kiki has freaky storms. Instead of friends, she has monsters trying to *kill* her. It's hardly better than public high school.
I'm destroying you with... *SCIENCE!*
Of course, everyone being gone meant that all the Vindertech stuff at camp was hers for the taking. So, she did what any kid would do...she built a jetpack—
—and jetpacks rock!

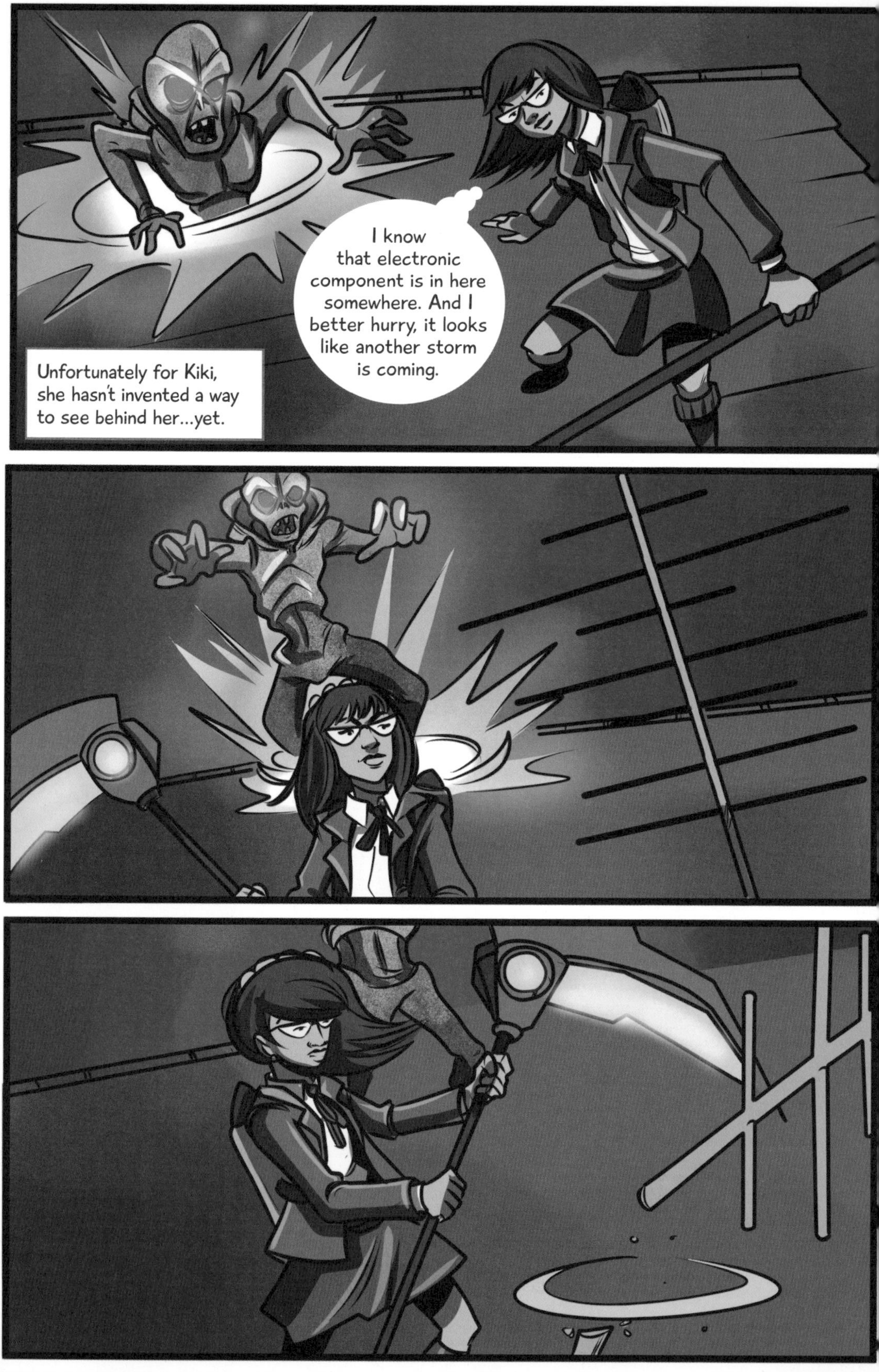
I know that electronic component is in here somewhere. And I better hurry, it looks like another storm is coming.
Unfortunately for Kiki, she hasn't invented a way to see behind her...yet.

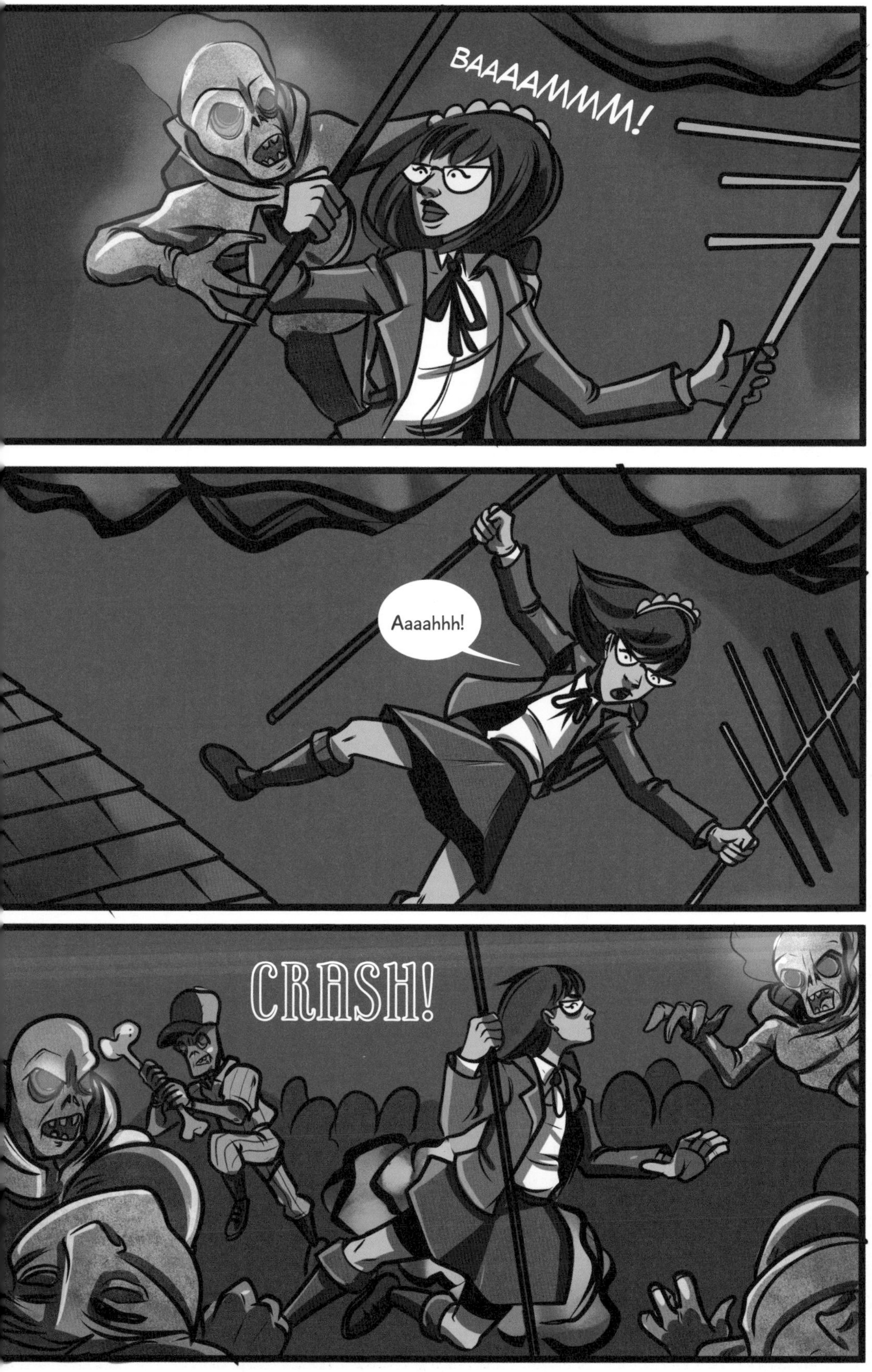
BAAAAMMMM!
Aaaahhh!
CRASH!

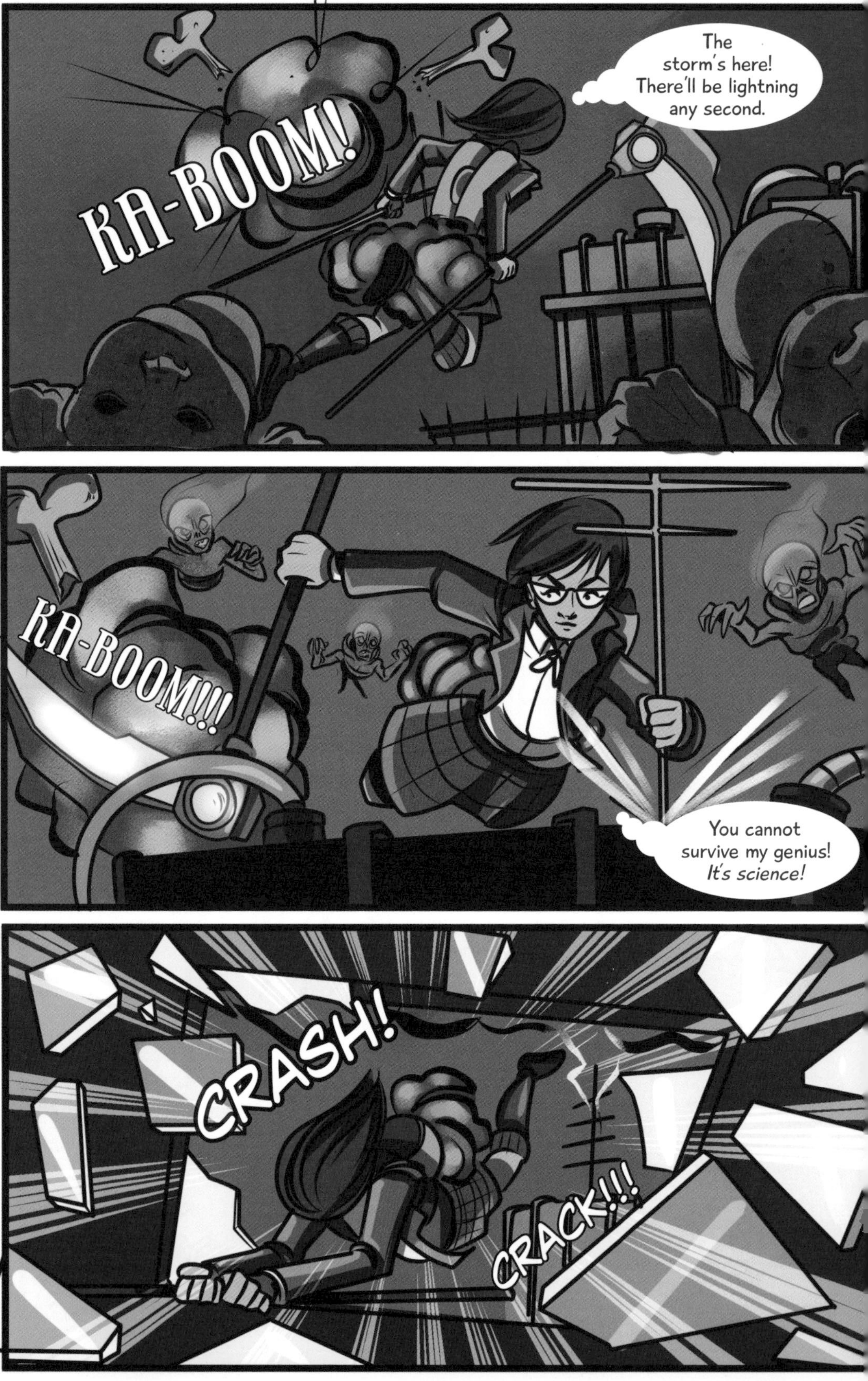
The storm's here! There'll be lightning any second.
KA-BOOM!
KA-BOOM!!!
You cannot survive my genius! *It's science!*
CRASH!
CRACK!!!

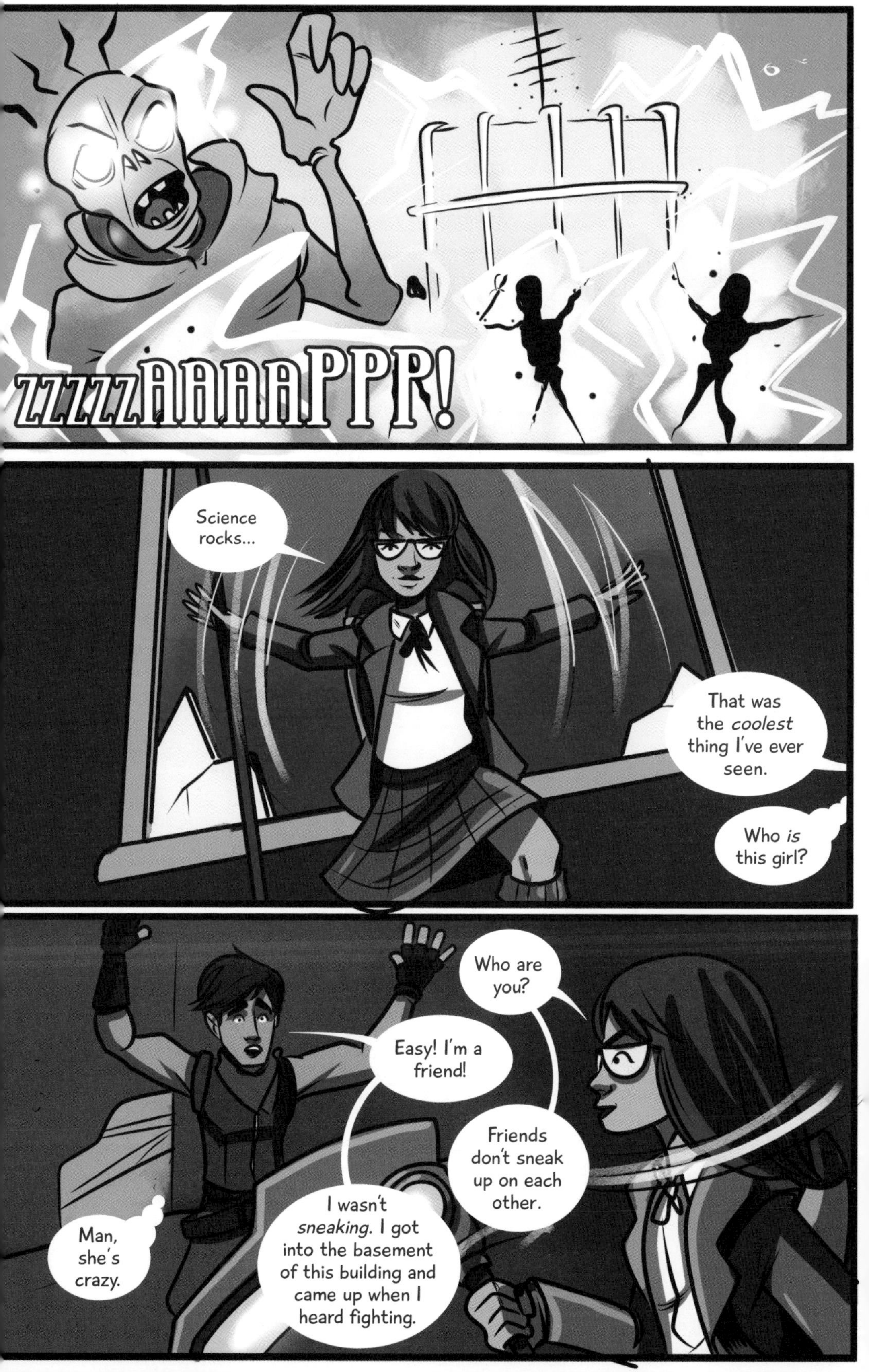
ZZZZZAAAAPPR!
Science rocks...
That was the *coolest* thing I've ever seen.
Who *is* this girl?
Who are you?
Easy! I'm a friend!
Friends don't sneak up on each other.
I wasn't *sneaking*. I got into the basement of this building and came up when I heard fighting.
Man, she's crazy.

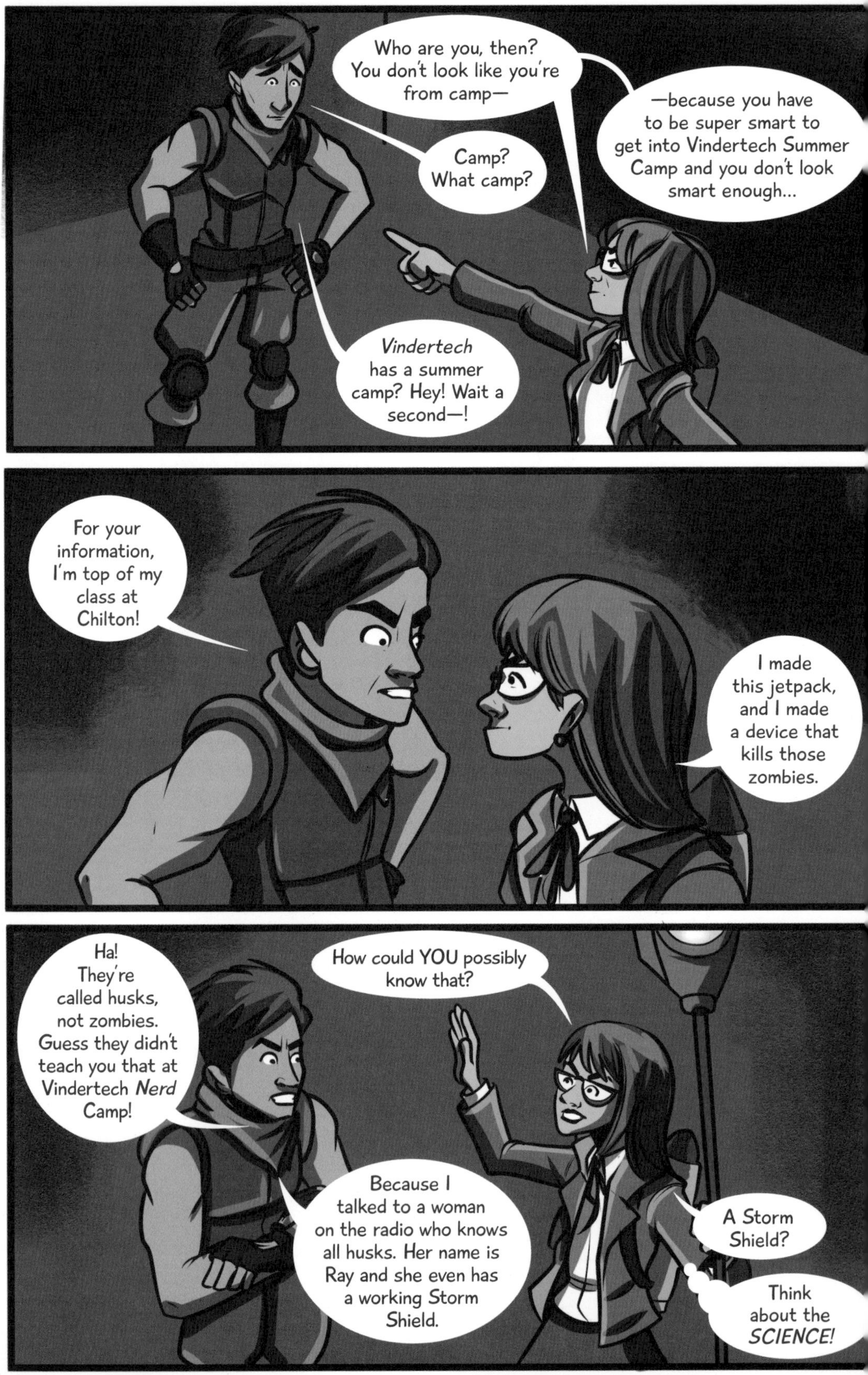
Who are you, then? You don't look like you're from camp—
Camp? What camp?
—because you have to be super smart to get into Vindertech Summer Camp and you don't look smart enough...
Vindertech has a summer camp? Hey! Wait a second—!
For your information, I'm top of my class at Chilton!
I made this jetpack, and I made a device that kills those zombies.
Ha! They're called husks, not zombies. Guess they didn't teach you that at Vindertech *Nerd* Camp!
How could YOU possibly know that?
Because I talked to a woman on the radio who knows all husks. Her name is Ray and she even has a working Storm Shield.
A Storm Shield?
Think about the *SCIENCE!*

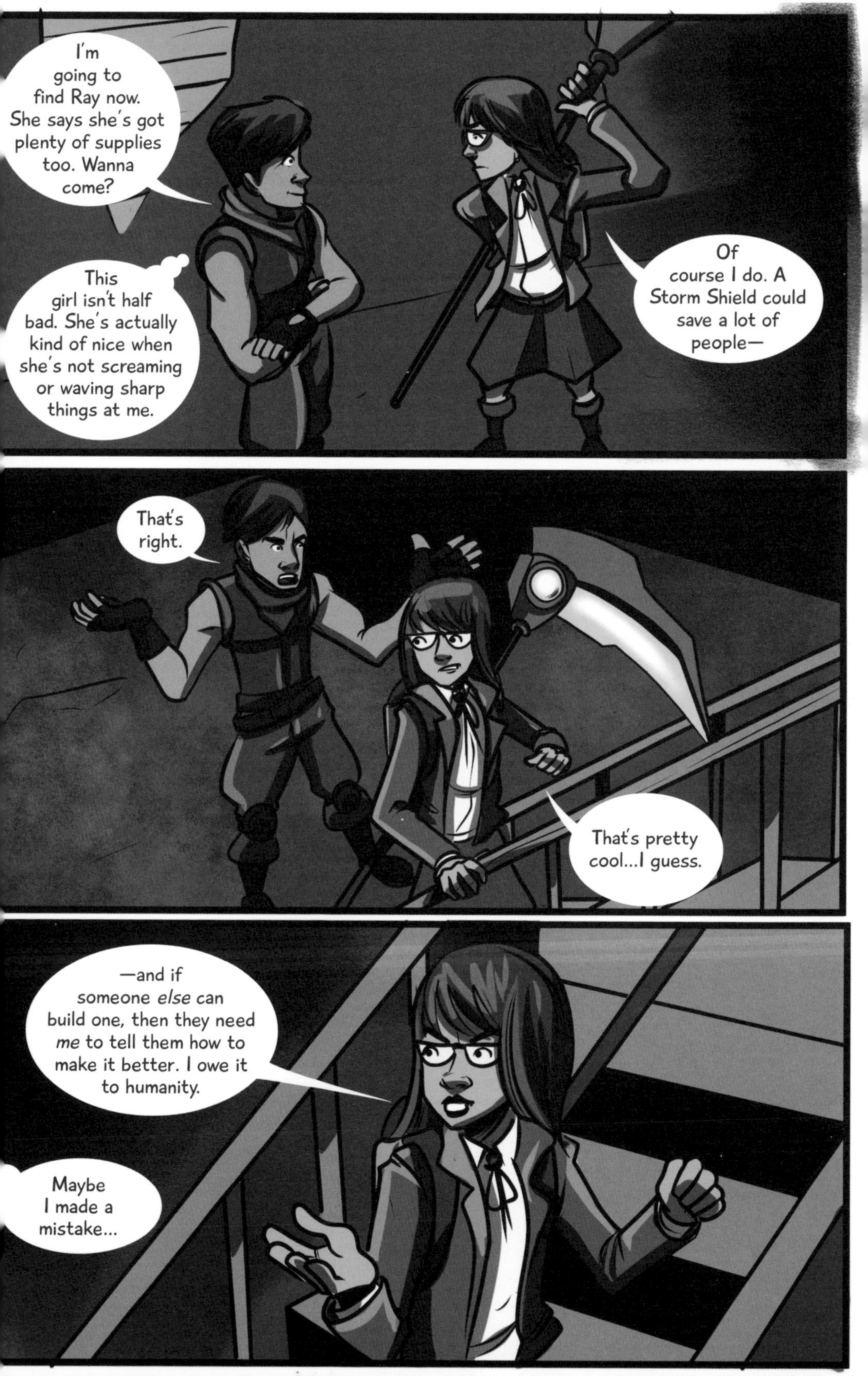
I'm going to find Ray now. She says she's got plenty of supplies too. Wanna come?
This girl isn't half bad. She's actually kind of nice when she's not screaming or waving sharp things at me.
Of course I do. A Storm Shield could save a lot of people—
That's right.
That's pretty cool...I guess.
—and if someone *else* can build one, then they need *me* to tell them how to make it better. I owe it to humanity.
Maybe I made a mistake...

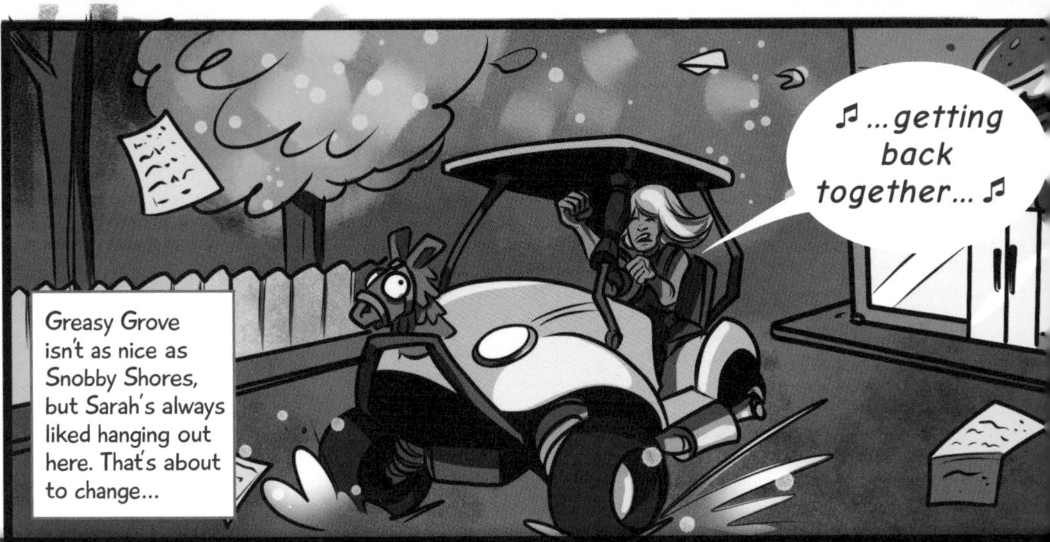
♫ ...getting back together... ♫
Greasy Grove isn't as nice as Snobby Shores, but Sarah's always liked hanging out here. That's about to change...

CHAPTER 5: BOYS MEET GIRLS

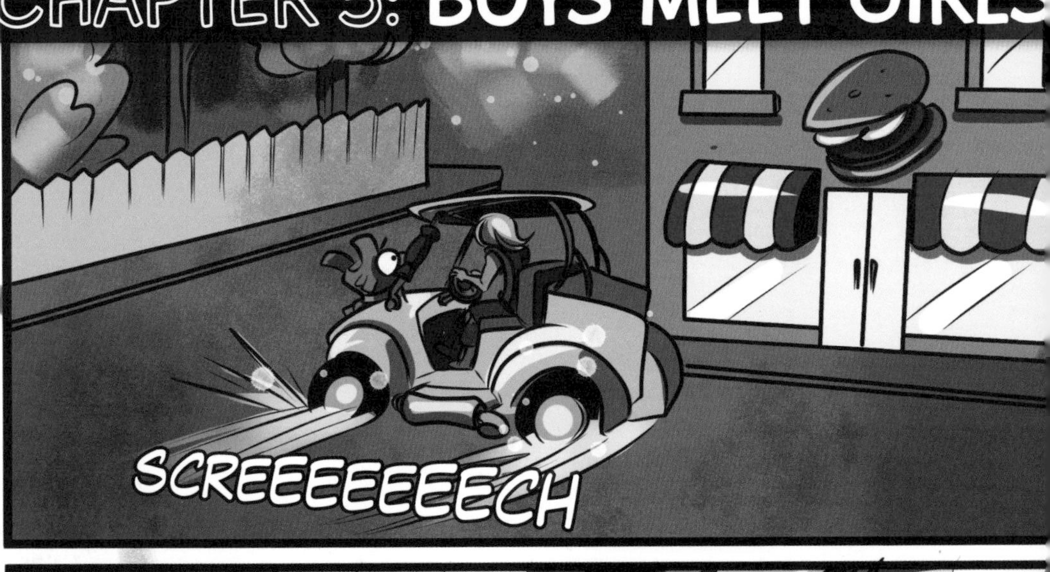
SCREEEEEEEEECH

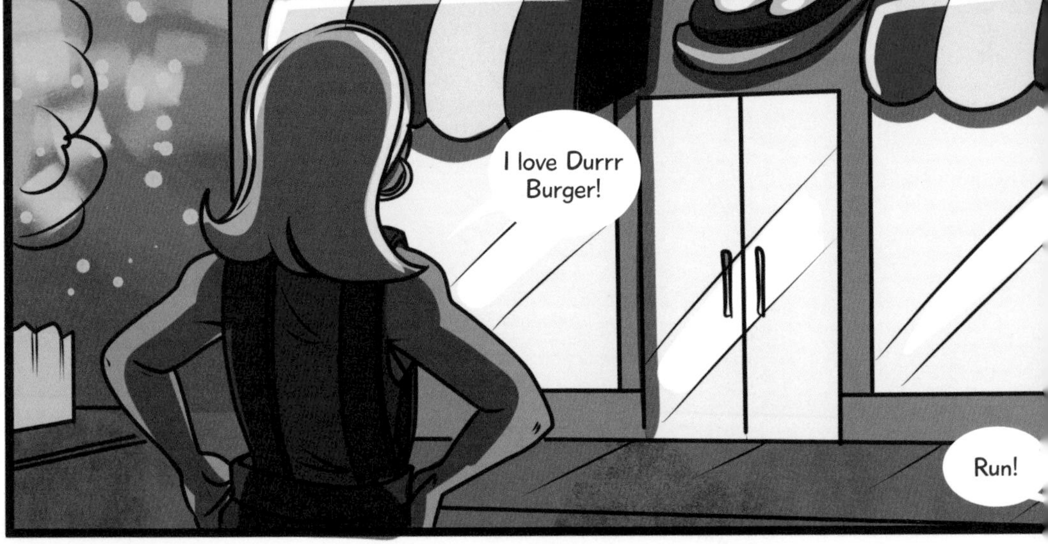
I love Durrr Burger!
Run!

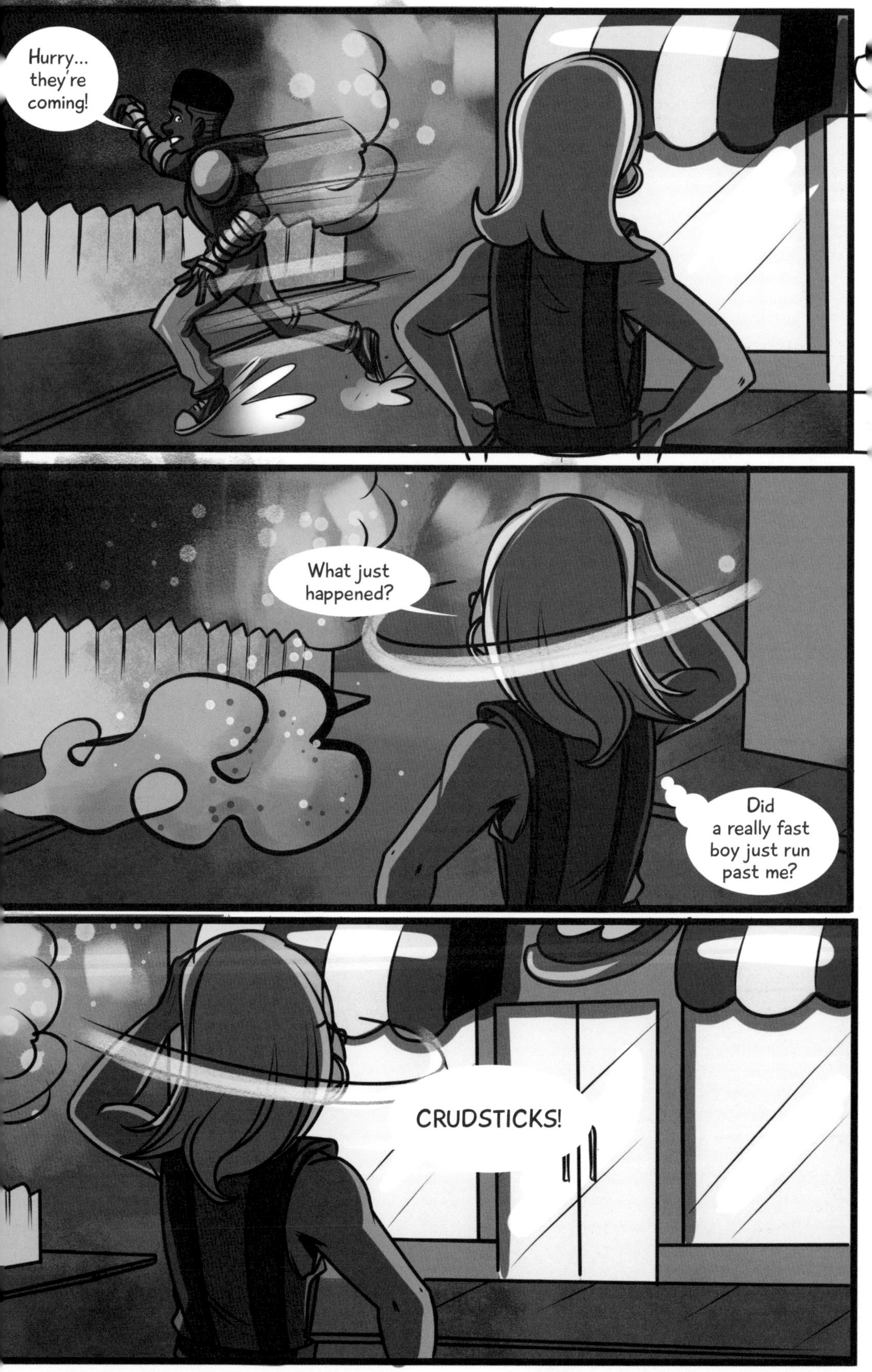
Hurry... they're coming!
What just happened?
Did a really fast boy just run past me?
CRUDSTICKS!

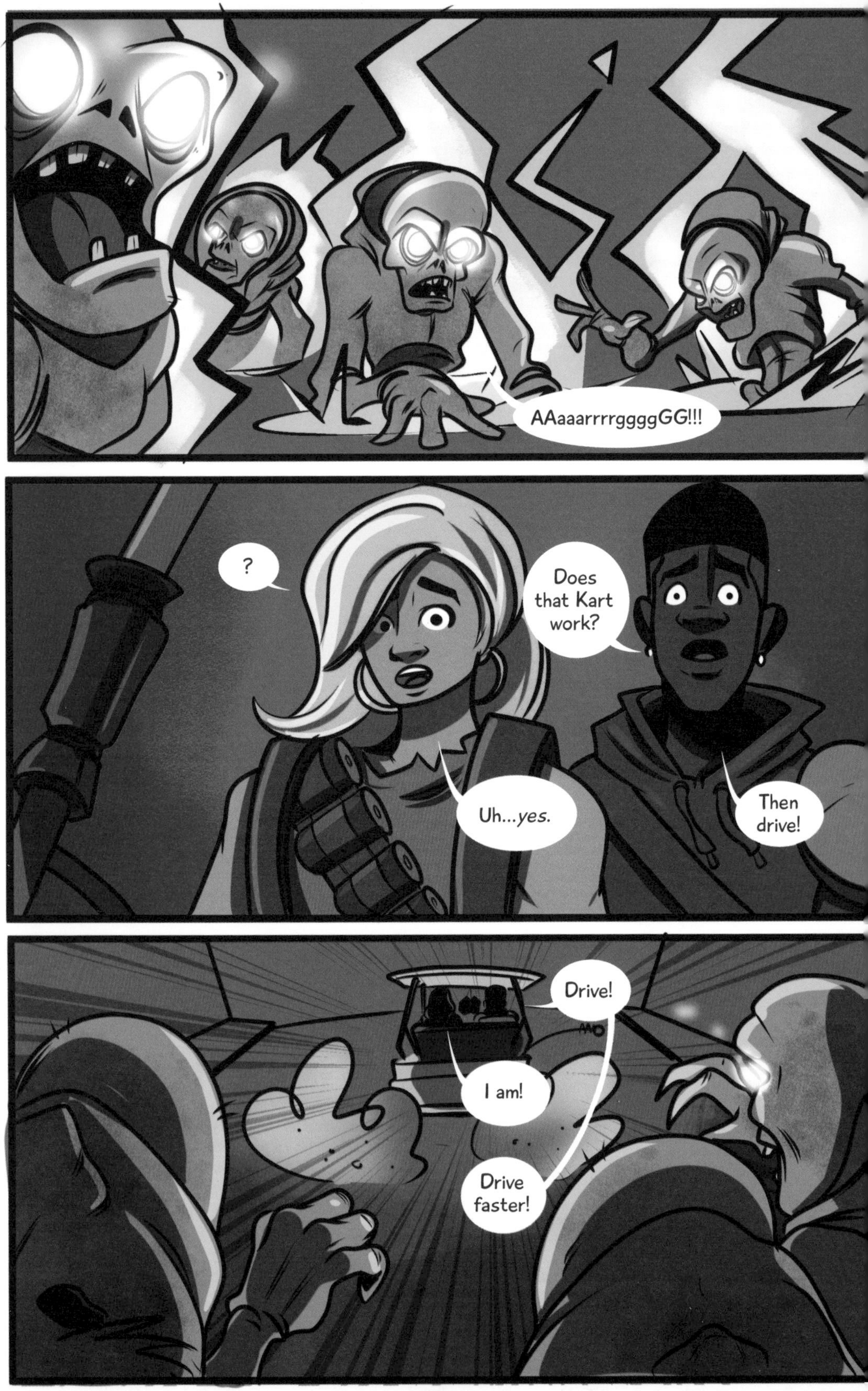
AAaaarrrrggggGG!!!
?
Does that Kart work?
Uh...*yes.*
Then drive!
Drive!
I am!
Drive faster!

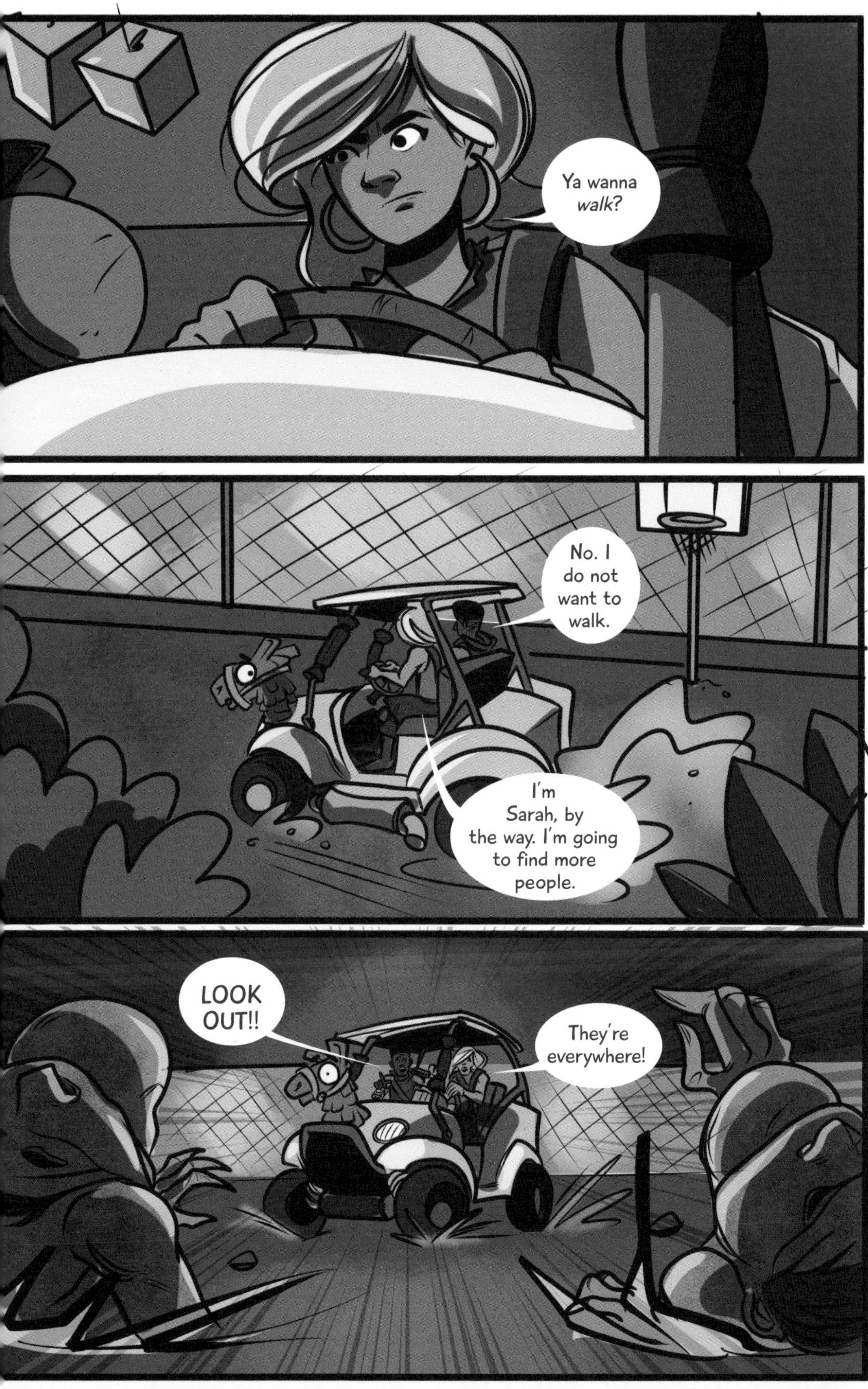
Ya wanna *walk*?
No. I do not want to walk.
I'm Sarah, by the way. I'm going to find more people.
LOOK OUT!!
They're everywhere!

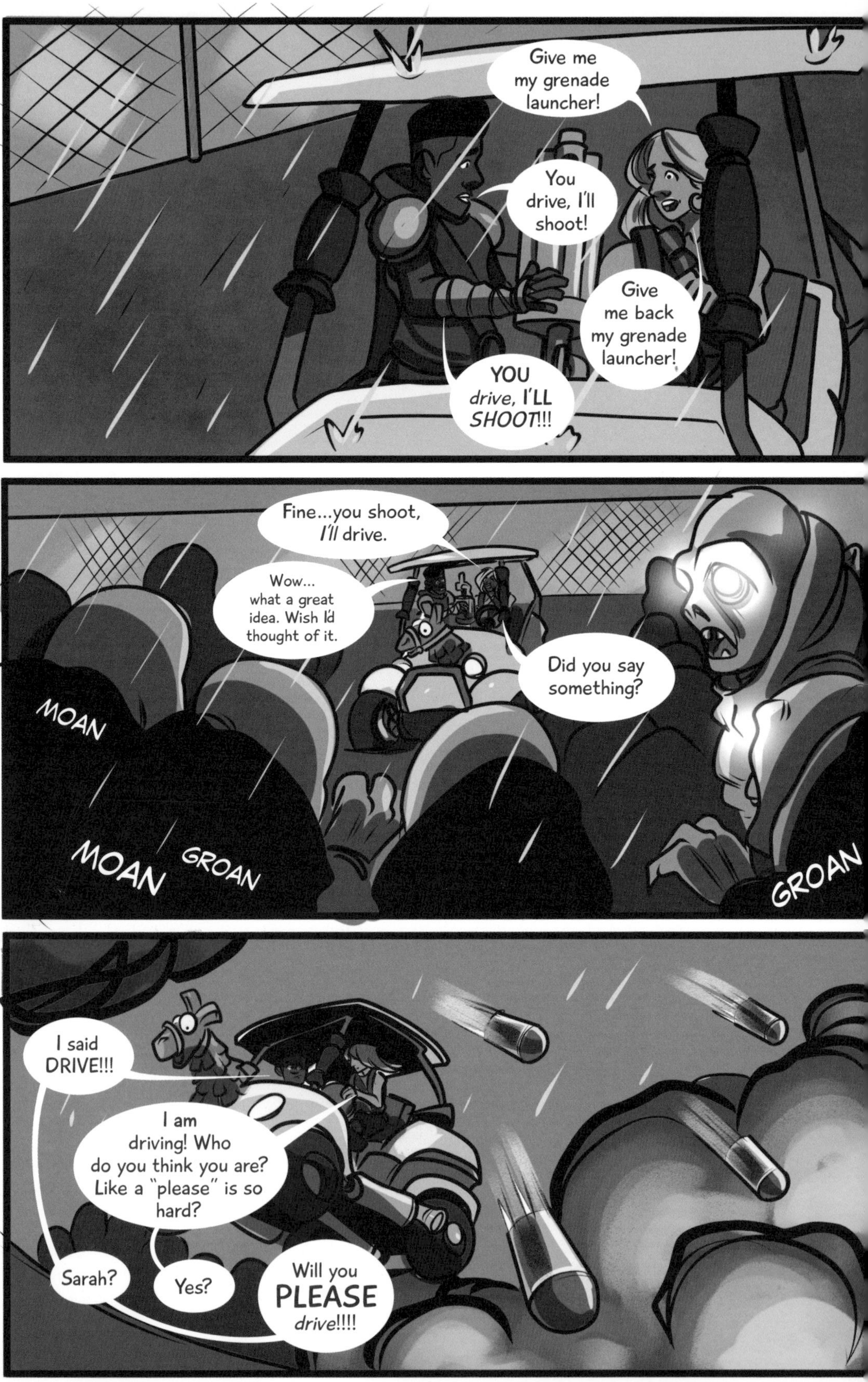
Give me my grenade launcher!
You drive, I'll shoot!
Give me back my grenade launcher!
YOU drive, I'LL SHOOT!!!
Fine...you shoot, I'll drive.
Wow... what a great idea. Wish I'd thought of it.
Did you say something?
MOAN
MOAN
GROAN
GROAN
I said DRIVE!!!
I am driving! Who do you think you are? Like a "please" is so hard?
Sarah?
Yes?
Will you PLEASE drive!!!!

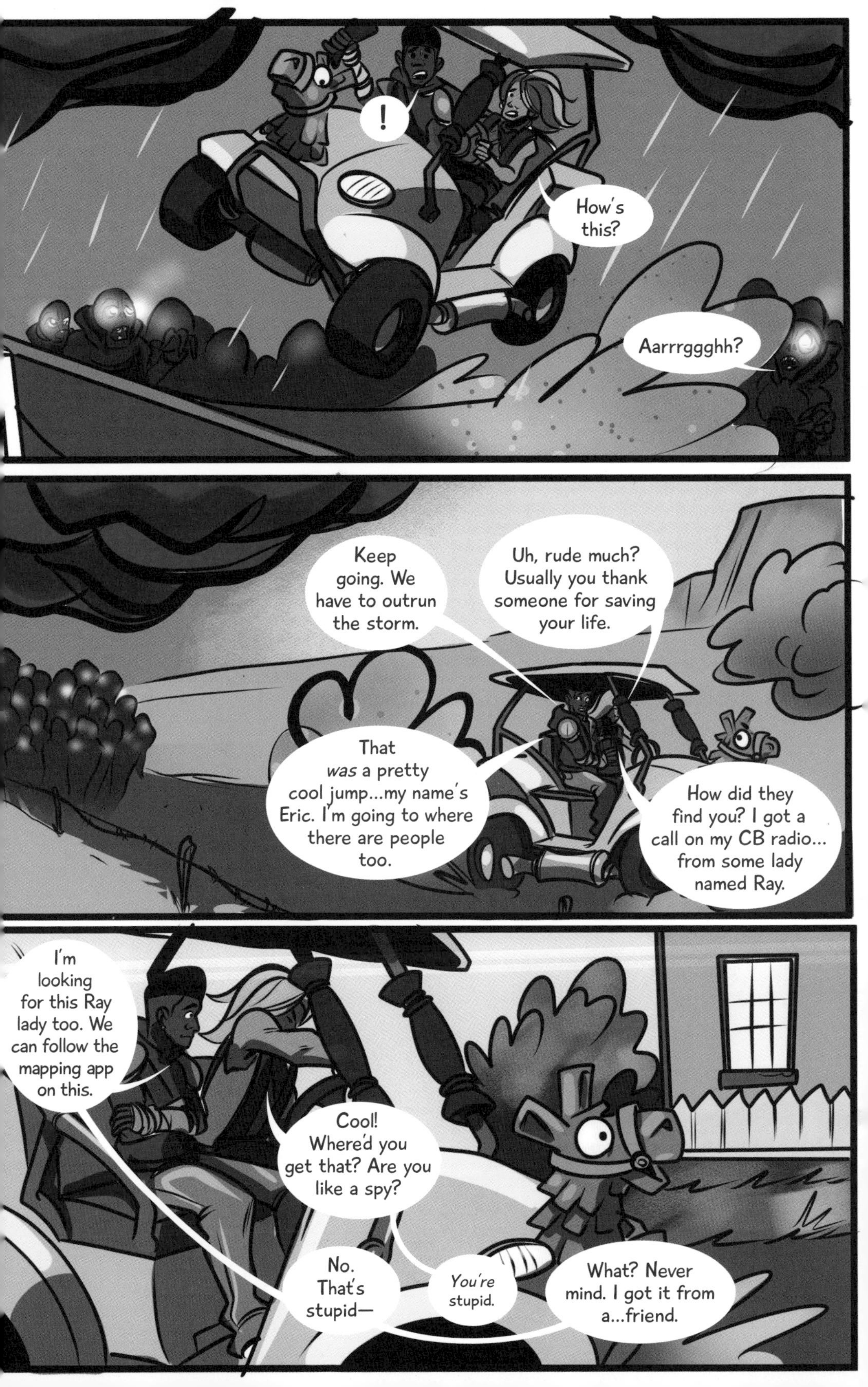
!
How's this?
Aarrrggghh?
Keep going. We have to outrun the storm.
Uh, rude much? Usually you thank someone for saving your life.
That *was* a pretty cool jump...my name's Eric. I'm going to where there are people too.
How did they find you? I got a call on my CB radio... from some lady named Ray.
I'm looking for this Ray lady too. We can follow the mapping app on this.
Cool! Where'd you get that? Are you like a spy?
No. That's stupid—
You're stupid.
What? Never mind. I got it from a...friend.

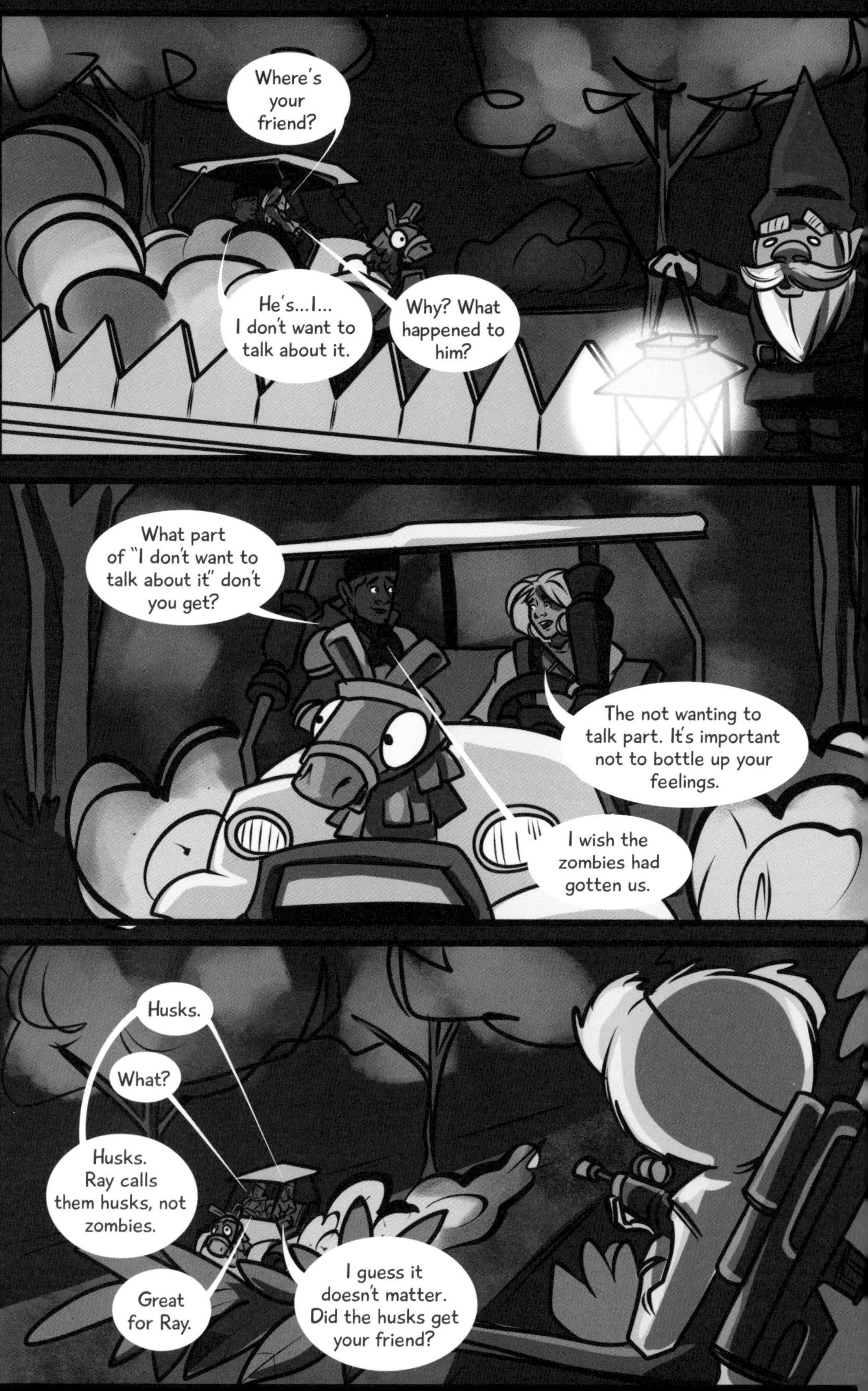
Where's your friend?
He's...I... I don't want to talk about it.
Why? What happened to him?
What part of "I don't want to talk about it" don't you get?
The not wanting to talk part. It's important not to bottle up your feelings.
I wish the zombies had gotten us.
Husks.
What?
Husks. Ray calls them husks, not zombies.
Great for Ray.
I guess it doesn't matter. Did the husks get your friend?

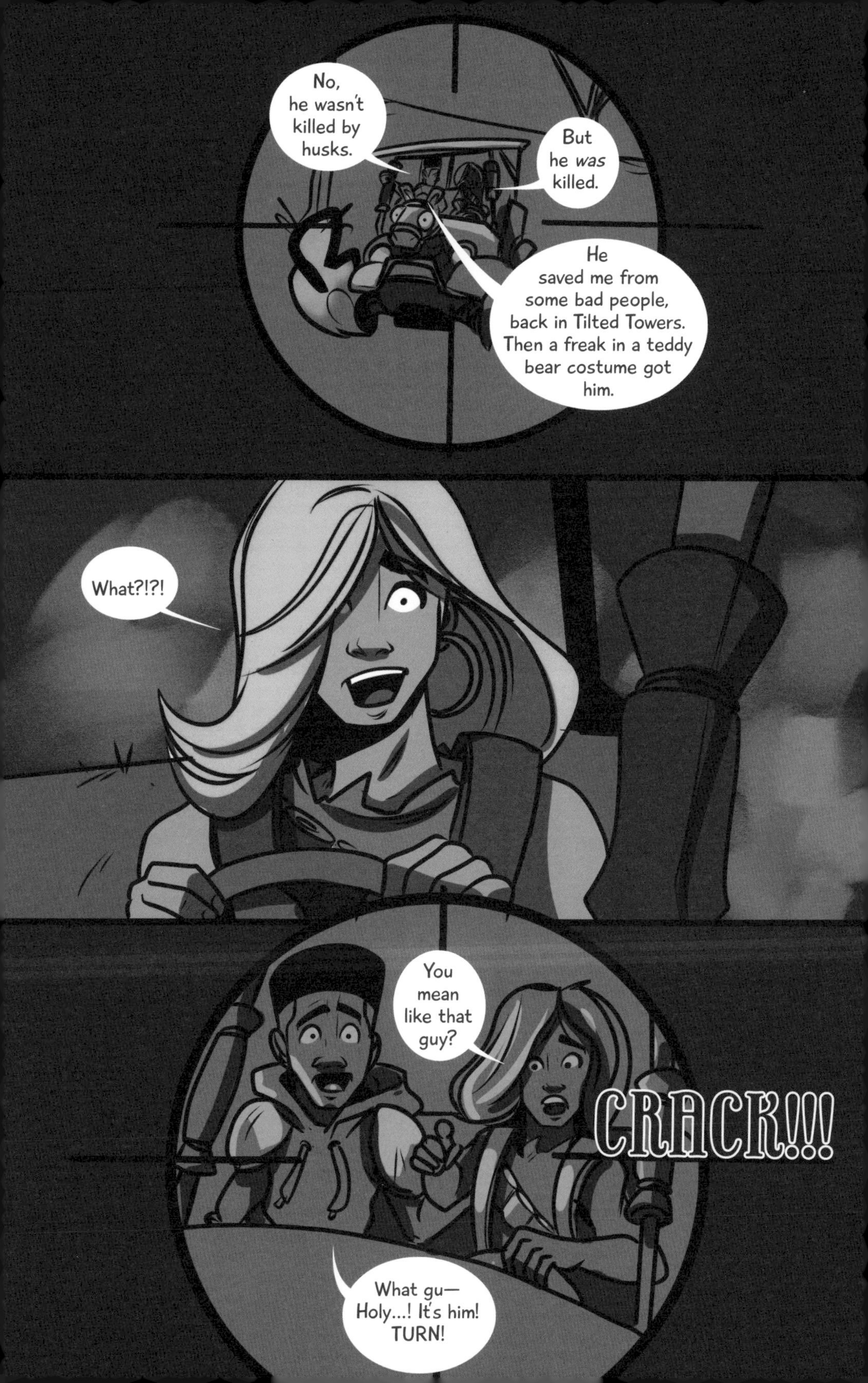
No, he wasn't killed by husks.
But he *was* killed.
He saved me from some bad people, back in Tilted Towers. Then a freak in a teddy bear costume got him.
What?!?!
You mean like that guy?
CRACK!!!
What gu— Holy...! It's him! TURN!

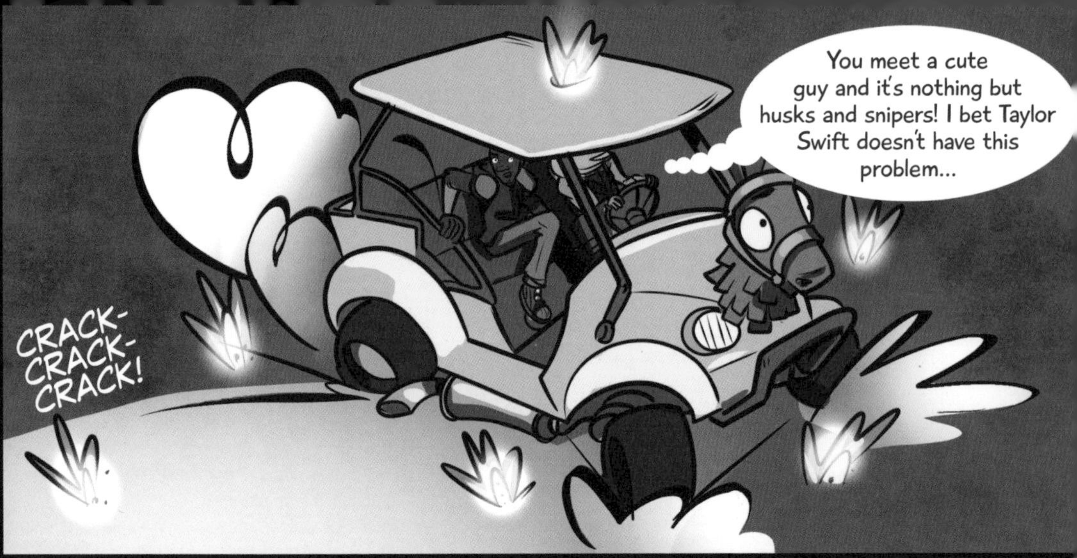
You meet a cute guy and it's nothing but husks and snipers! I bet Taylor Swift doesn't have this problem...
CRACK-CRACK-CRACK!

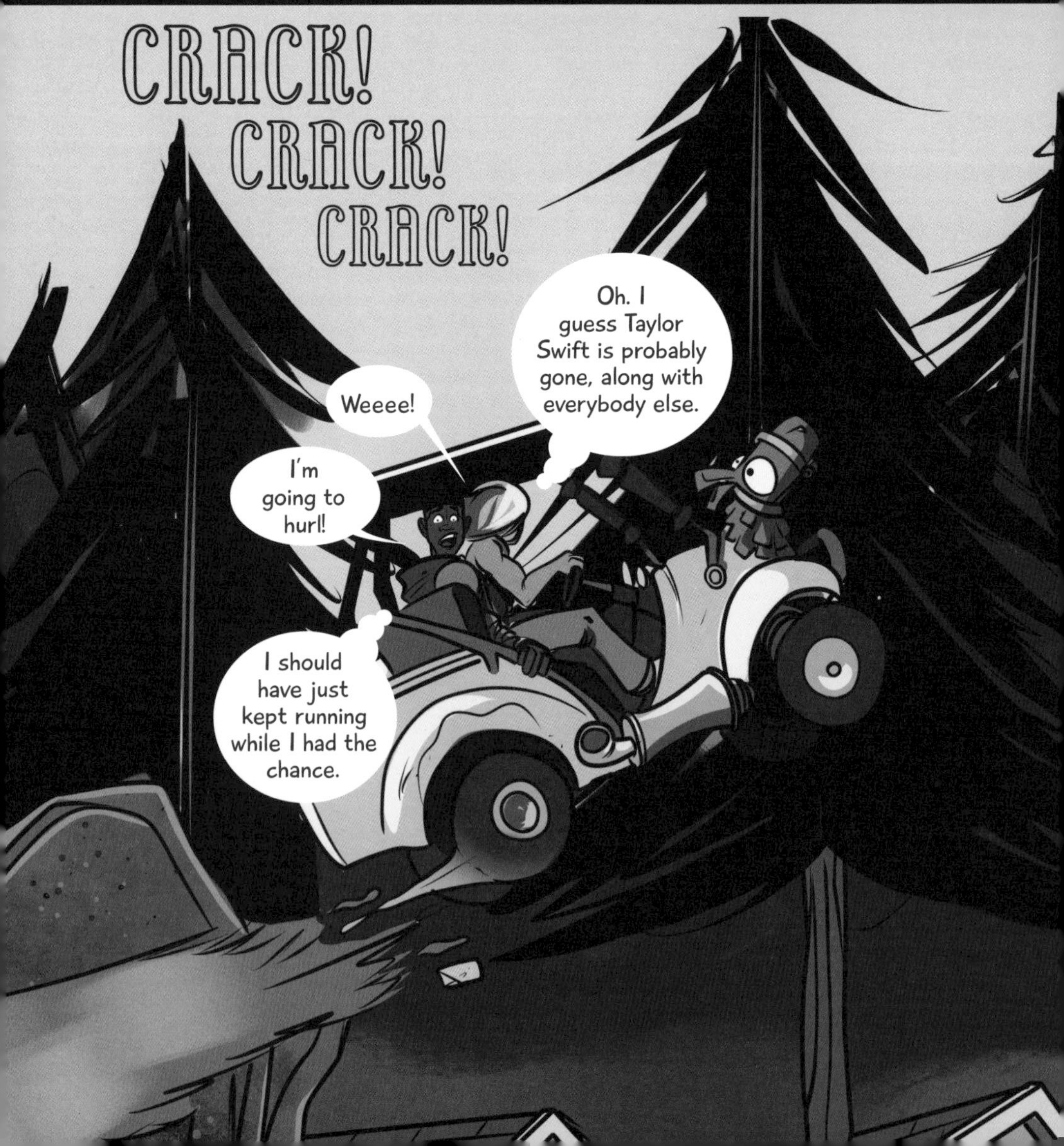
CRACK! CRACK! CRACK!
Weeee!
Oh. I guess Taylor Swift is probably gone, along with everybody else.
I'm going to hurl!
I should have just kept running while I had the chance.

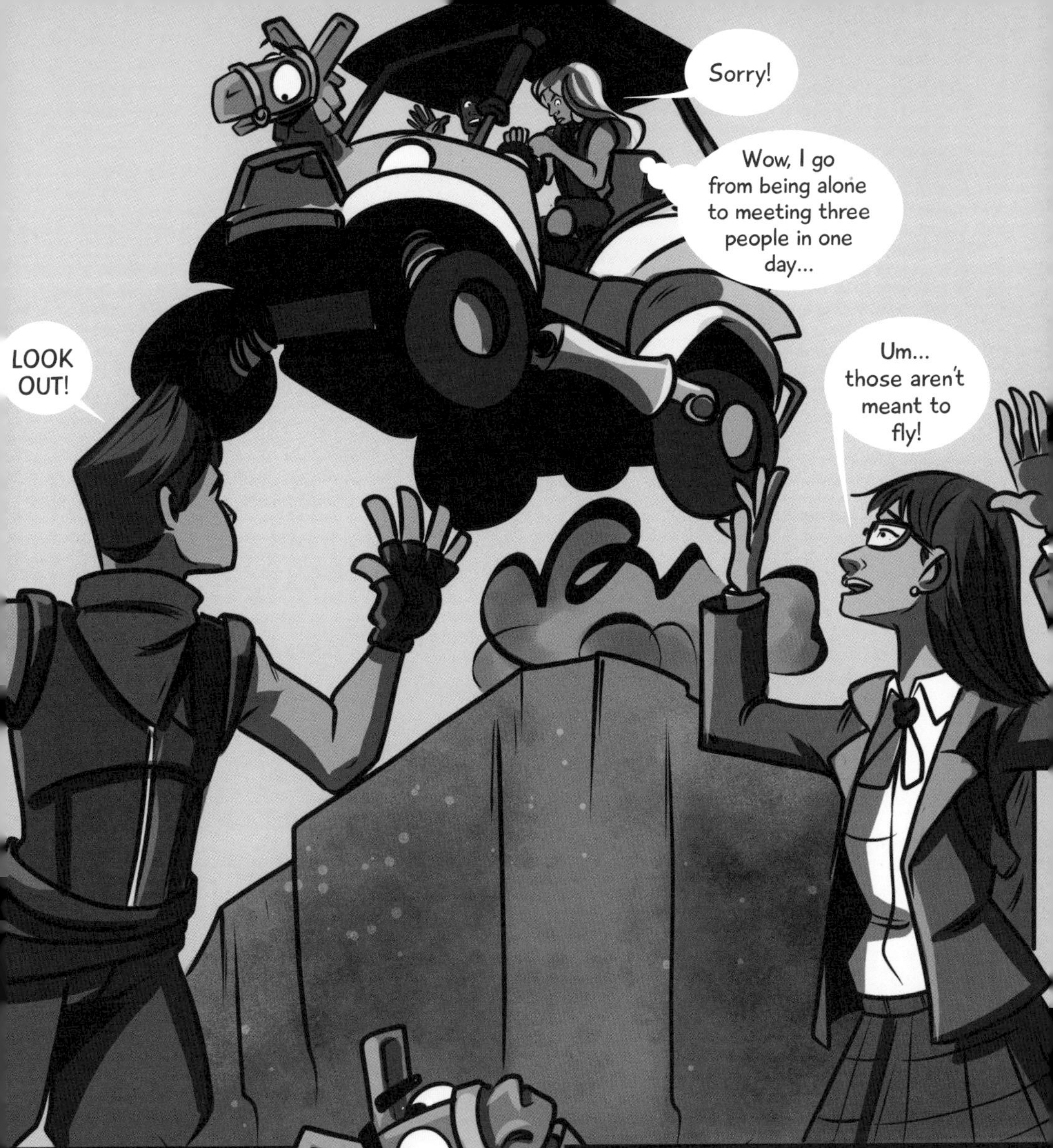
Sorry!
Wow, I go from being alone to meeting three people in one day...
LOOK OUT!
Um... those aren't meant to fly!

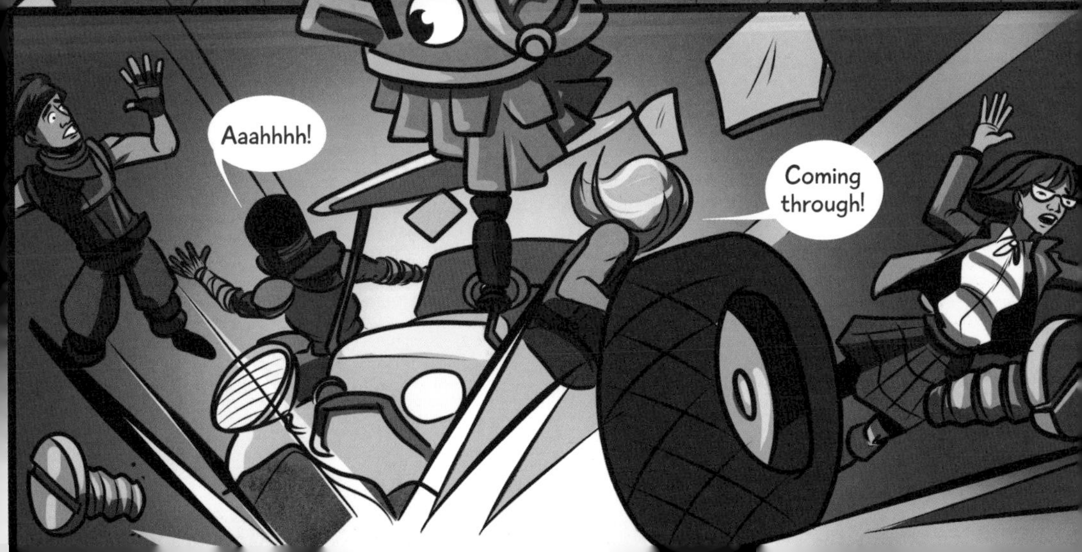
Aaahhhh!
Coming through!

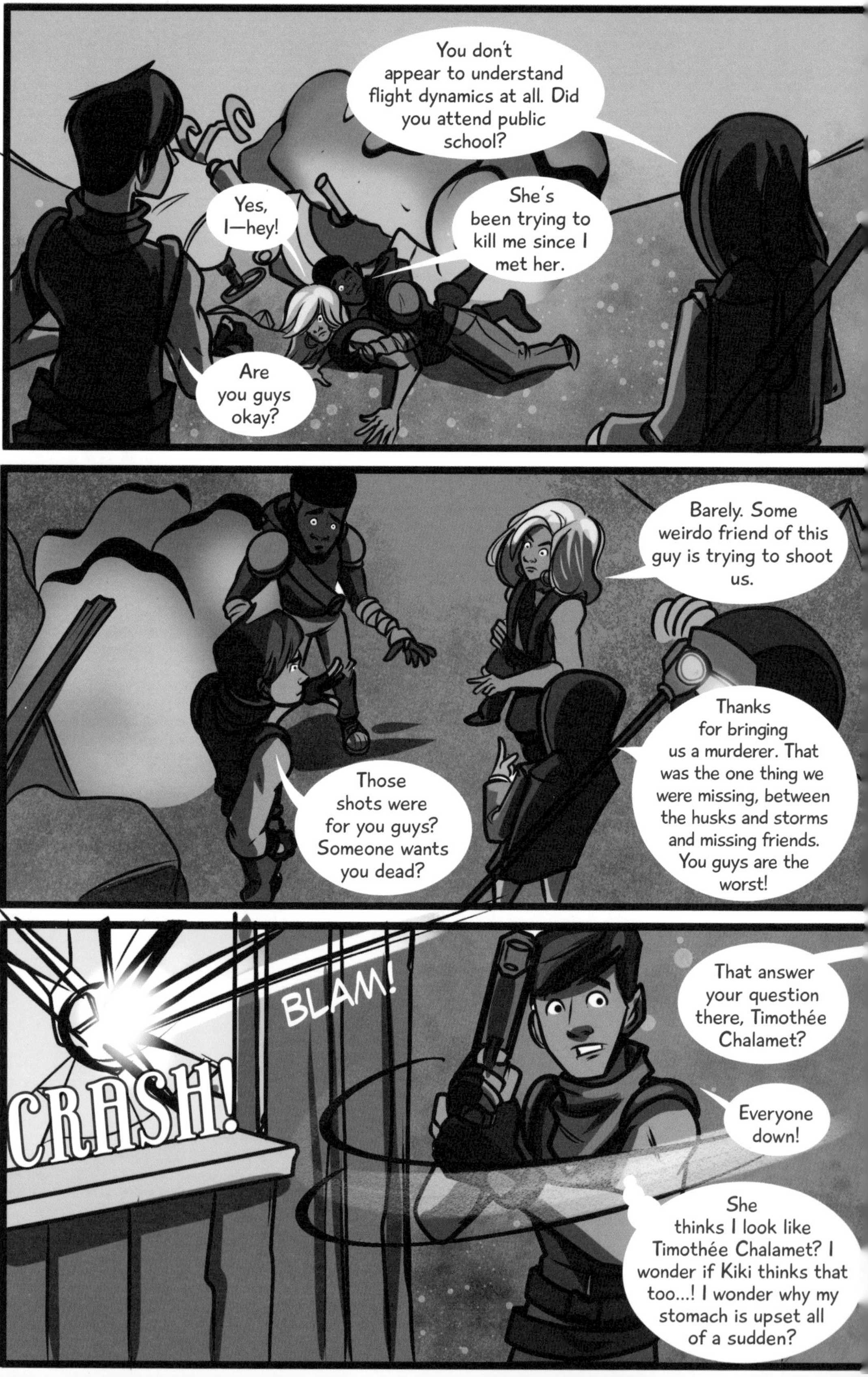
You don't appear to understand flight dynamics at all. Did you attend public school?
Yes, I—hey!
She's been trying to kill me since I met her.
Are you guys okay?
Barely. Some weirdo friend of this guy is trying to shoot us.
Those shots were for you guys? Someone wants you dead?
Thanks for bringing us a murderer. That was the one thing we were missing, between the husks and storms and missing friends. You guys are the worst!
CRASH!
BLAM!
That answer your question there, Timothée Chalamet?
Everyone down!
She thinks I look like Timothée Chalamet? I wonder if Kiki thinks that too...! I wonder why my stomach is upset all of a sudden?

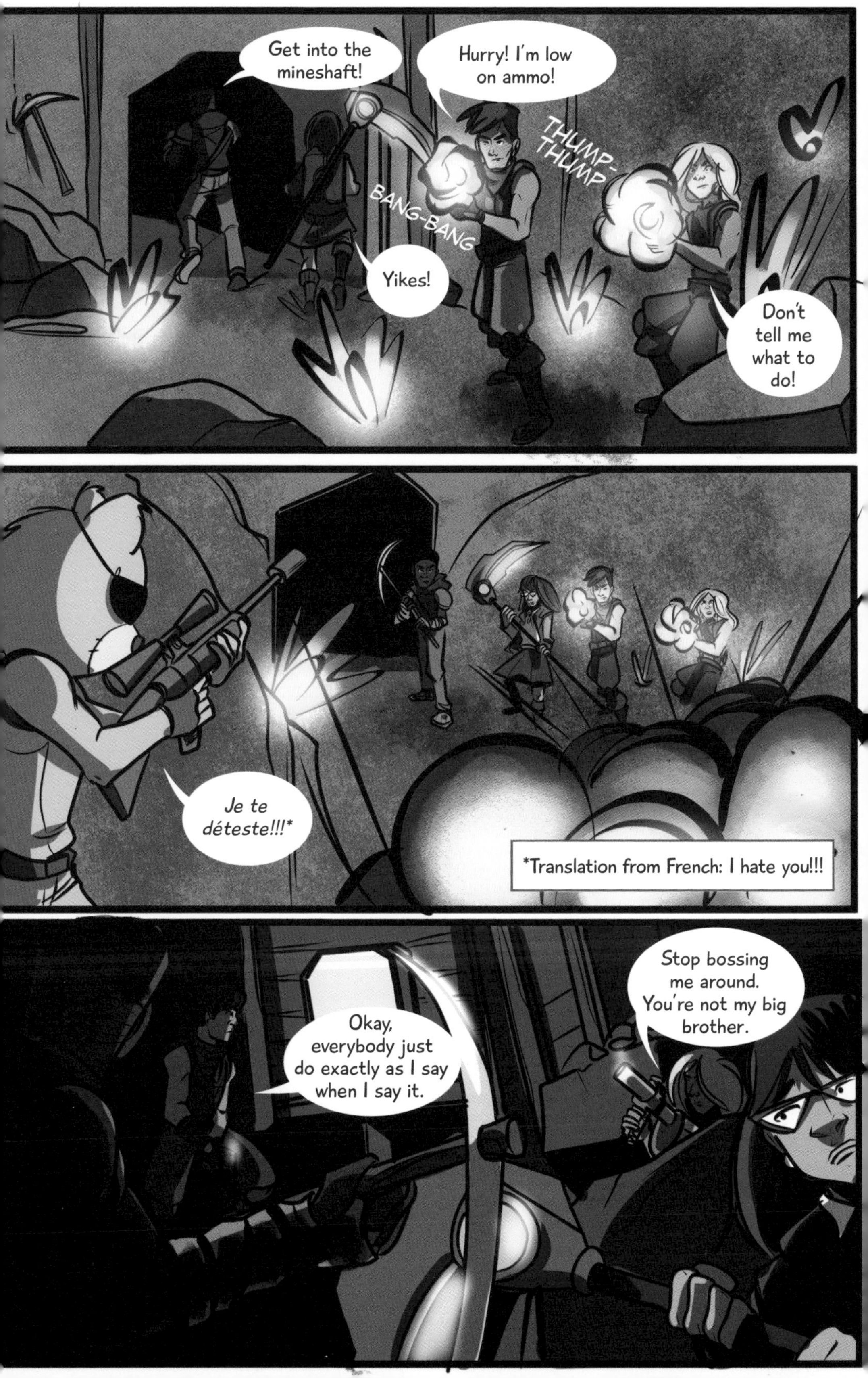
Get into the mineshaft!
Hurry! I'm low on ammo!
THUMP-THUMP
BANG-BANG
Yikes!
Don't tell me what to do!
Je te déteste!!!*
*Translation from French: I hate you!!!
Okay, everybody just do exactly as I say when I say it.
Stop bossing me around. You're not my big brother.

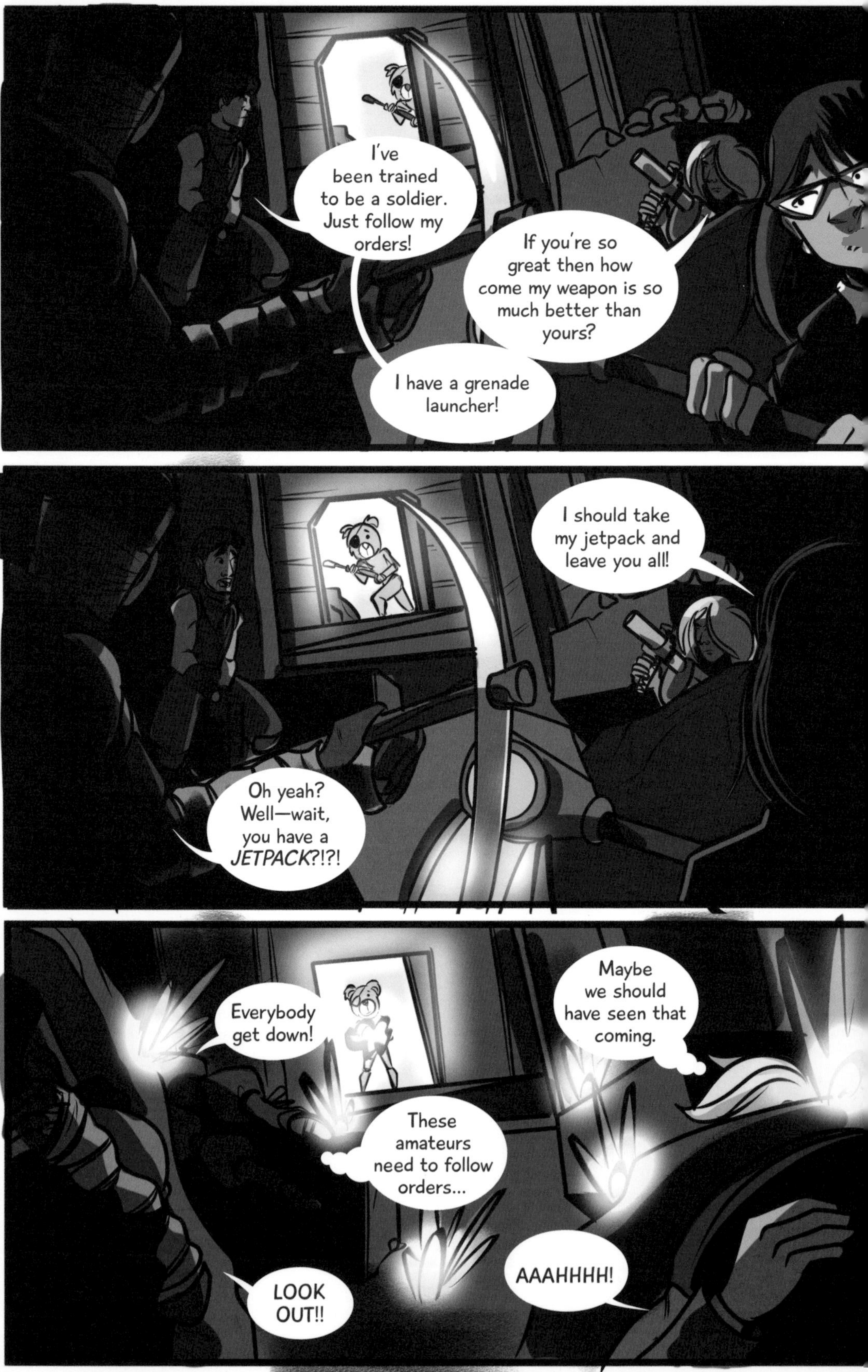
I've been trained to be a soldier. Just follow my orders!
If you're so great then how come my weapon is so much better than yours?
I have a grenade launcher!
I should take my jetpack and leave you all!
Oh yeah? Well—wait, you have a *JETPACK*?!?!
Everybody get down!
Maybe we should have seen that coming.
These amateurs need to follow orders...
LOOK OUT!!
AAAHHHH!

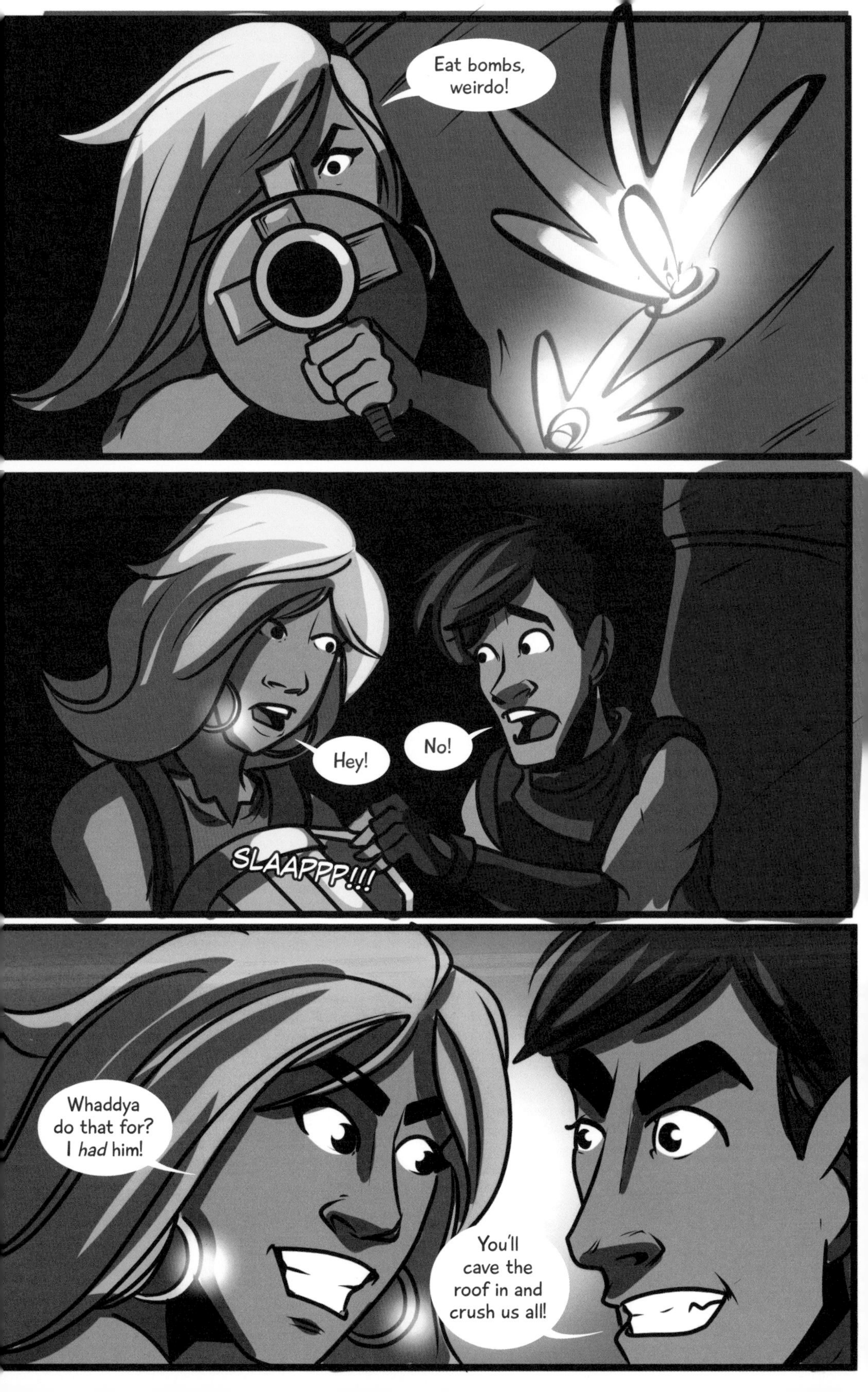
Eat bombs, weirdo!
Hey!
No!
SLAAPPP!!!
Whaddya do that for? I *had* him!
You'll cave the roof in and crush us all!

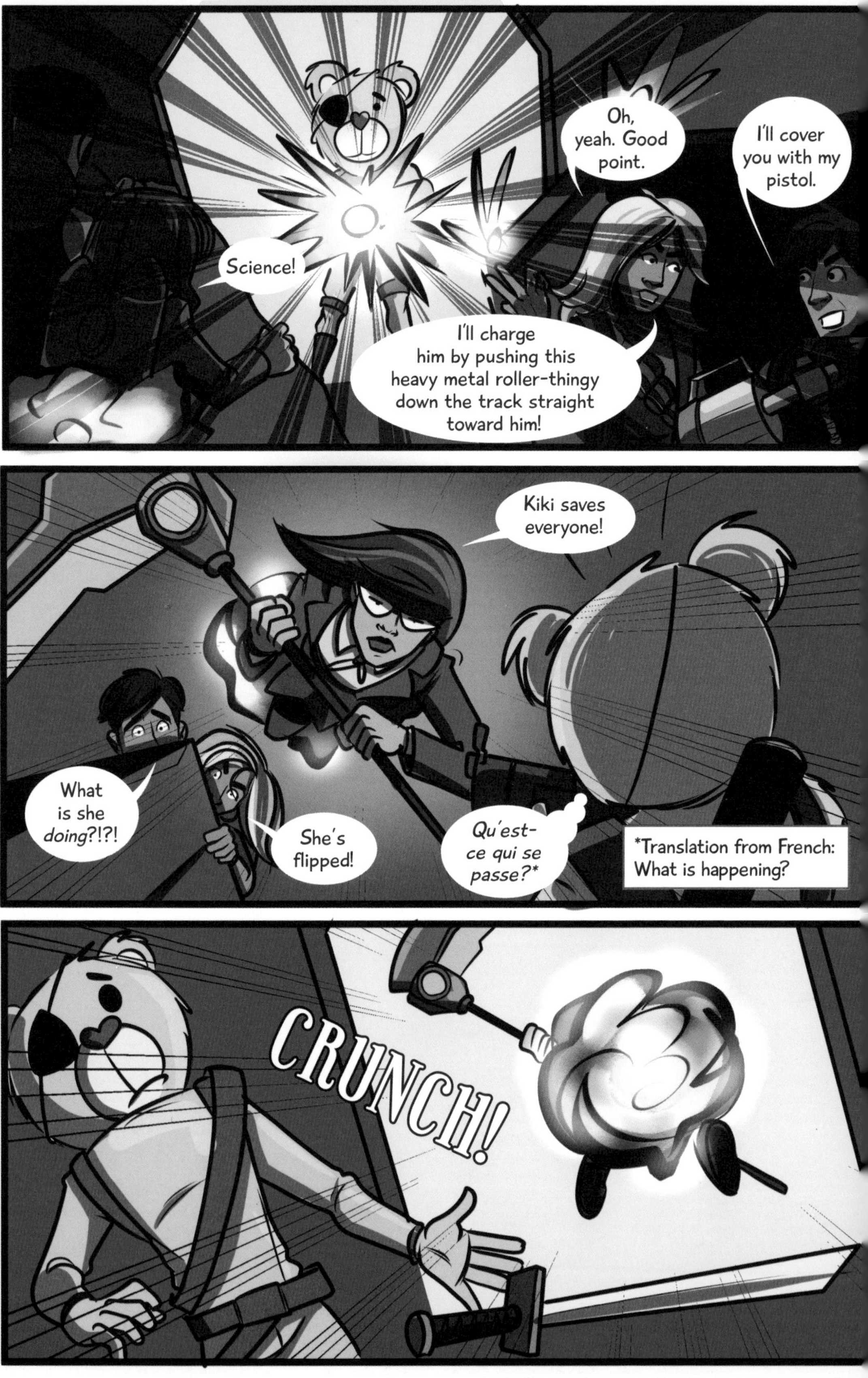
Science!
Oh, yeah. Good point.
I'll cover you with my pistol.
I'll charge him by pushing this heavy metal roller-thingy down the track straight toward him!
Kiki saves everyone!
What is she *doing?!?!*
She's flipped!
*Qu'est-ce qui se passe?**
*Translation from French: What is happening?
CRUNCH!

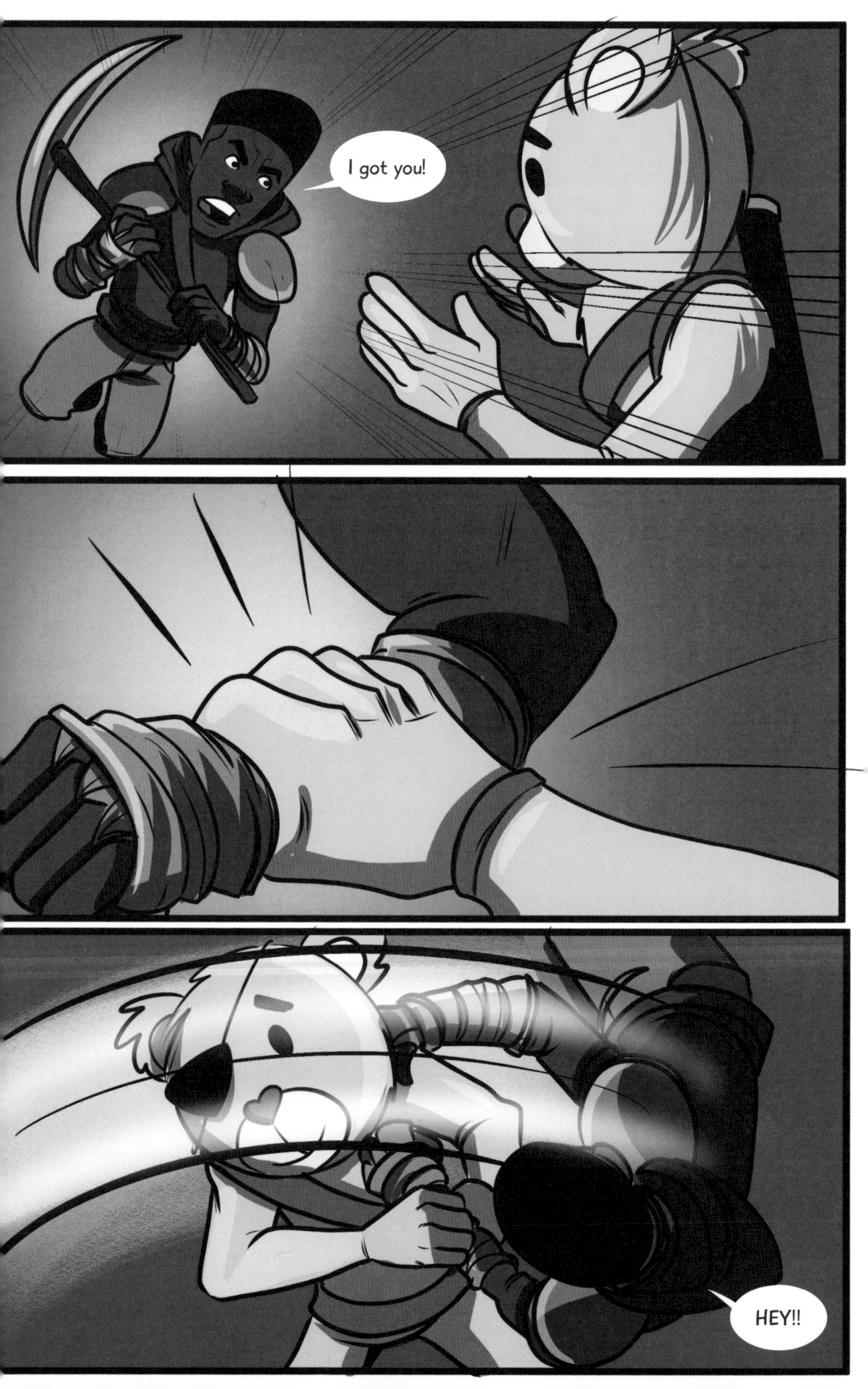
I got you!
HEY!!

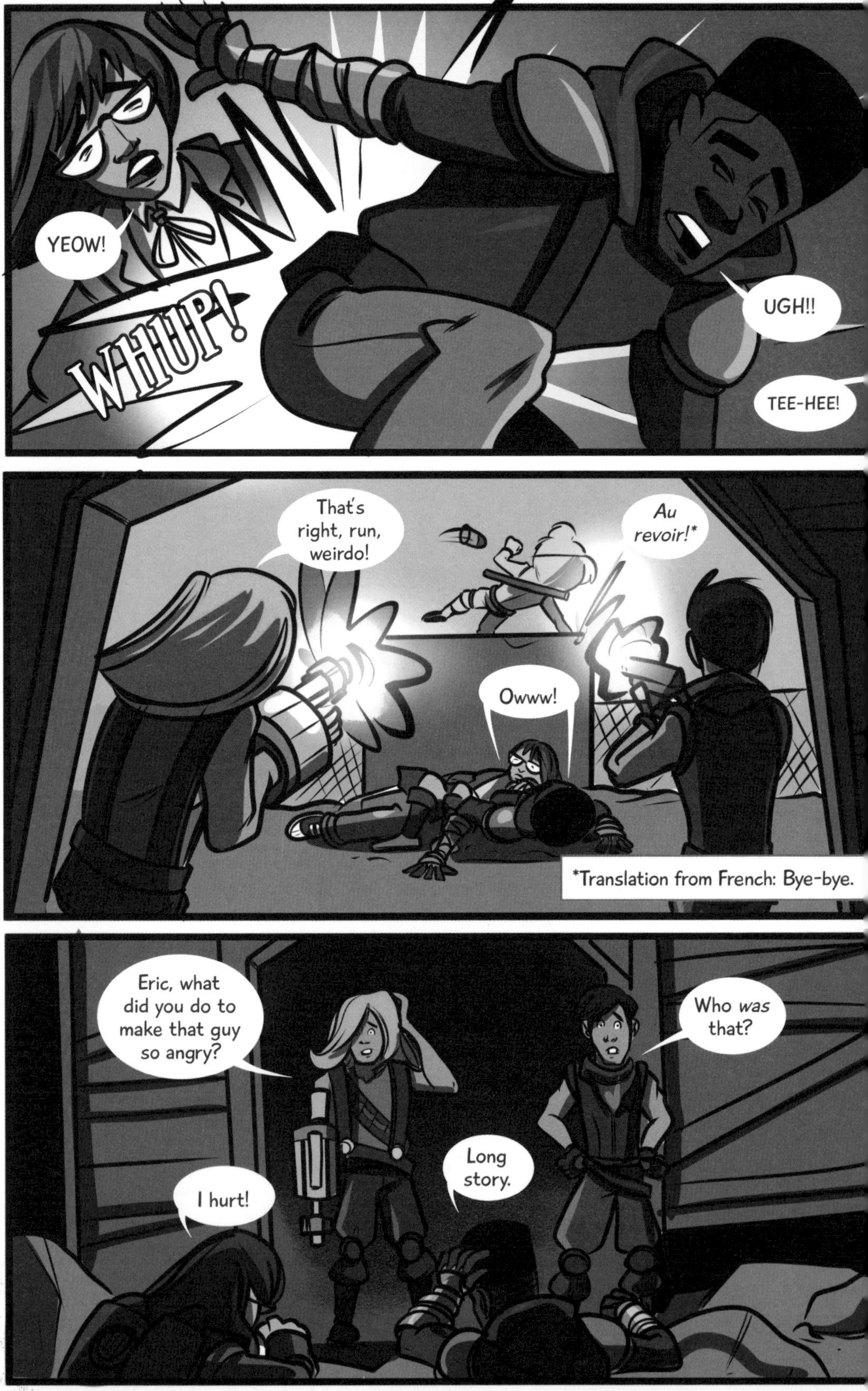
YEOW!
WHUP!
UGH!!
TEE-HEE!
That's right, run, weirdo!
Au revoir!*
Owww!
*Translation from French: Bye-bye.
Eric, what did you do to make that guy so angry?
Who was that?
Long story.
I hurt!

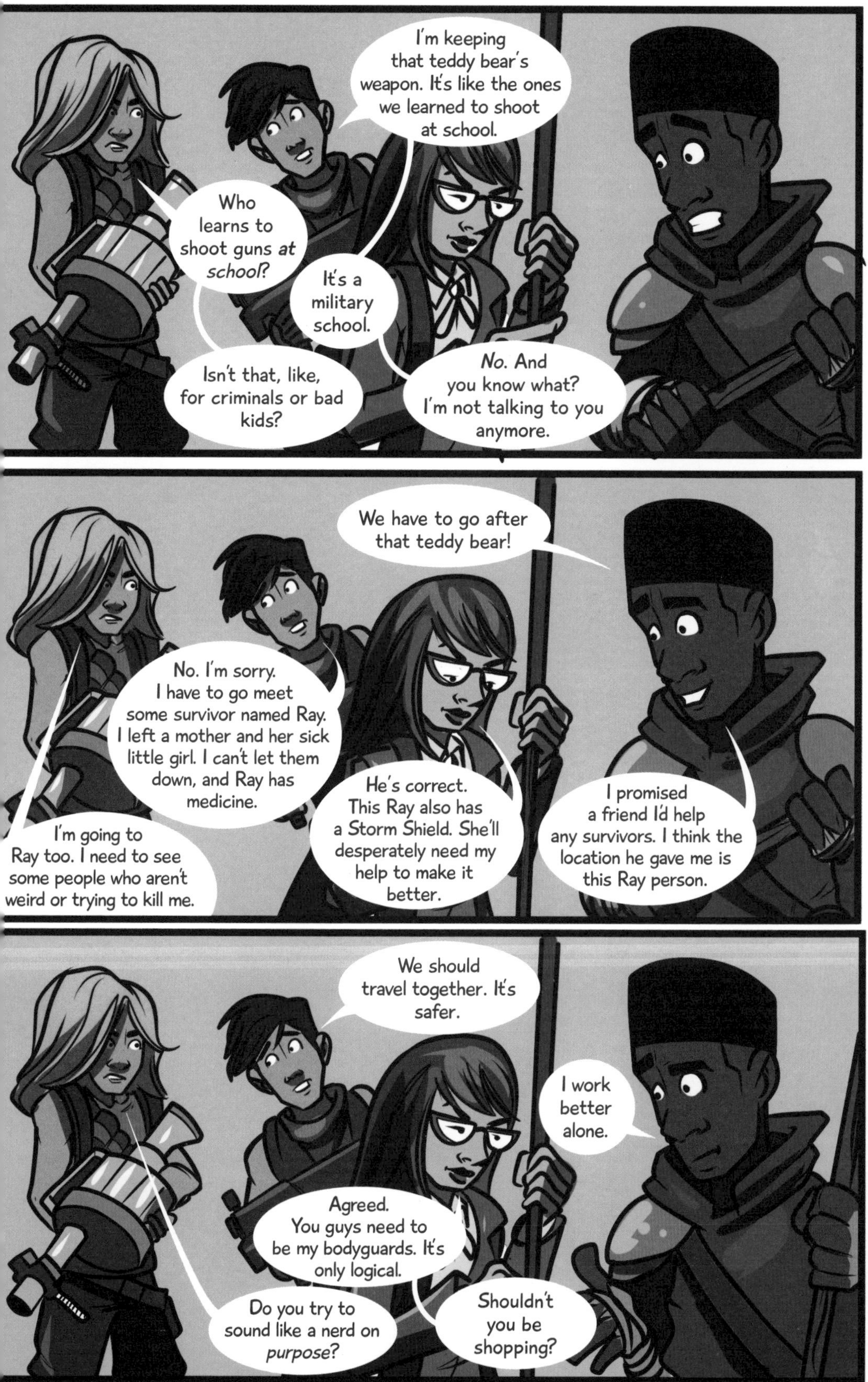
I'm keeping that teddy bear's weapon. It's like the ones we learned to shoot at school.
Who learns to shoot guns *at school*?
It's a military school.
Isn't that, like, for criminals or bad kids?
No. And you know what? I'm not talking to you anymore.
We have to go after that teddy bear!
No. I'm sorry. I have to go meet some survivor named Ray. I left a mother and her sick little girl. I can't let them down, and Ray has medicine.
I'm going to Ray too. I need to see some people who aren't weird or trying to kill me.
He's correct. This Ray also has a Storm Shield. She'll desperately need my help to make it better.
I promised a friend I'd help any survivors. I think the location he gave me is this Ray person.
We should travel together. It's safer.
I work better alone.
Agreed. You guys need to be my bodyguards. It's only logical.
Do you try to sound like a nerd on *purpose*?
Shouldn't you be shopping?

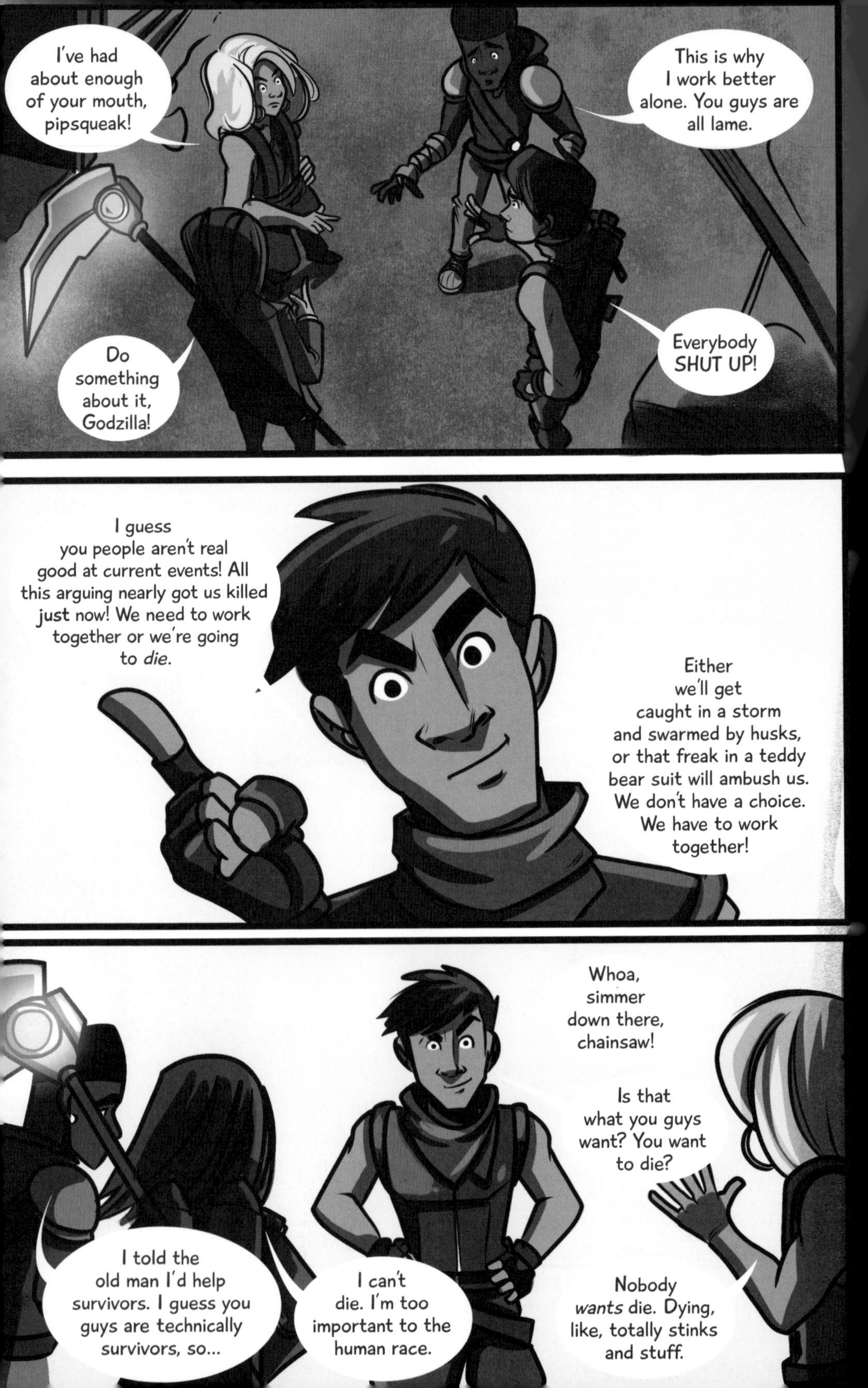
I've had about enough of your mouth, pipsqueak!
This is why I work better alone. You guys are all lame.
Do something about it, Godzilla!
Everybody SHUT UP!
I guess you people aren't real good at current events! All this arguing nearly got us killed just now! We need to work together or we're going to *die*.
Either we'll get caught in a storm and swarmed by husks, or that freak in a teddy bear suit will ambush us. We don't have a choice. We have to work together!
Whoa, simmer down there, chainsaw!
Is that what you guys want? You want to die?
I told the old man I'd help survivors. I guess you guys are technically survivors, so...
I can't die. I'm too important to the human race.
Nobody *wants* die. Dying, like, totally stinks and stuff.

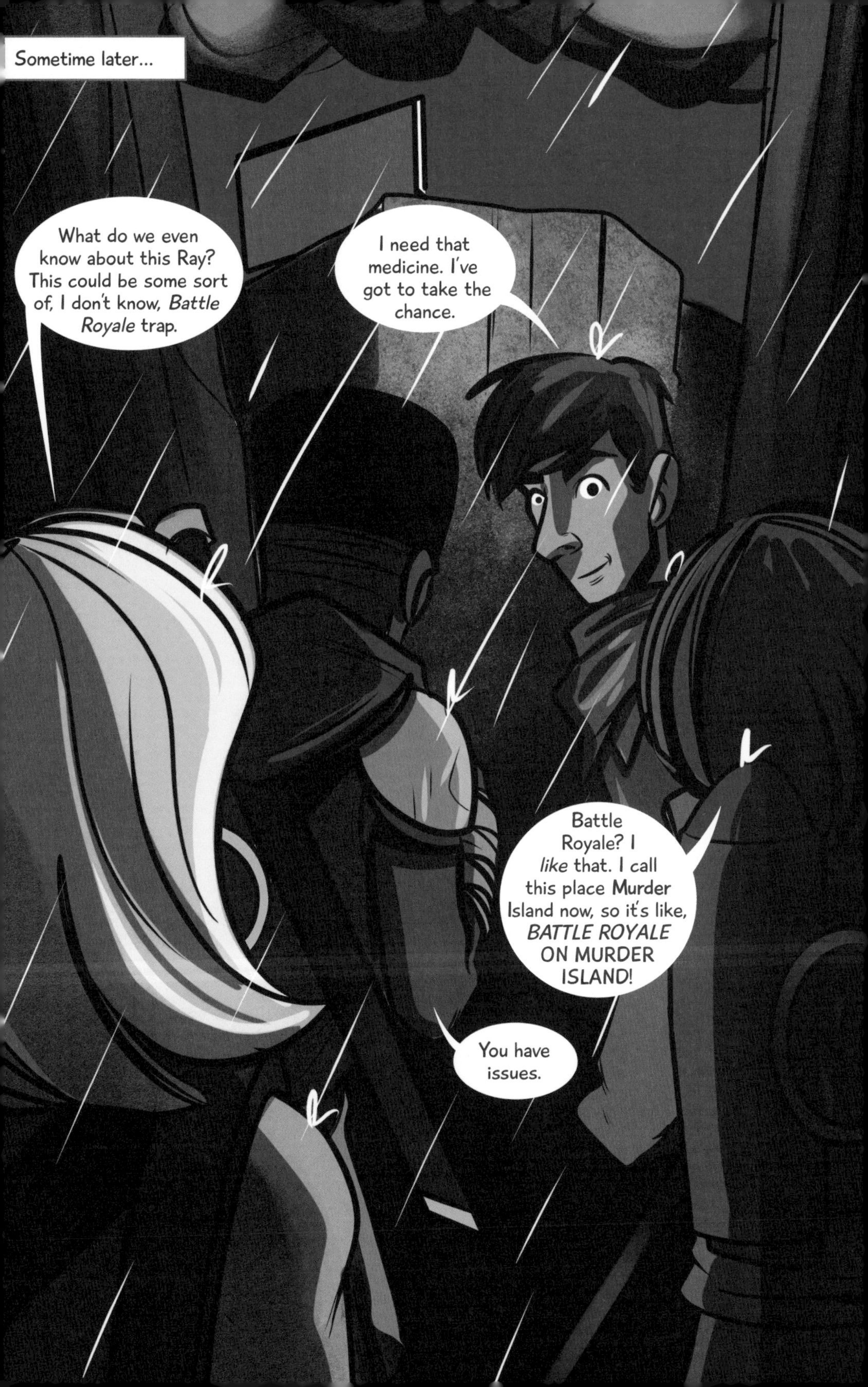
Sometime later...
What do we even know about this Ray? This could be some sort of, I don't know, *Battle Royale* trap.
I need that medicine. I've got to take the chance.
Battle Royale? I *like* that. I call this place **Murder** Island now, so it's like, *BATTLE ROYALE* ON MURDER ISLAND!
You have issues.

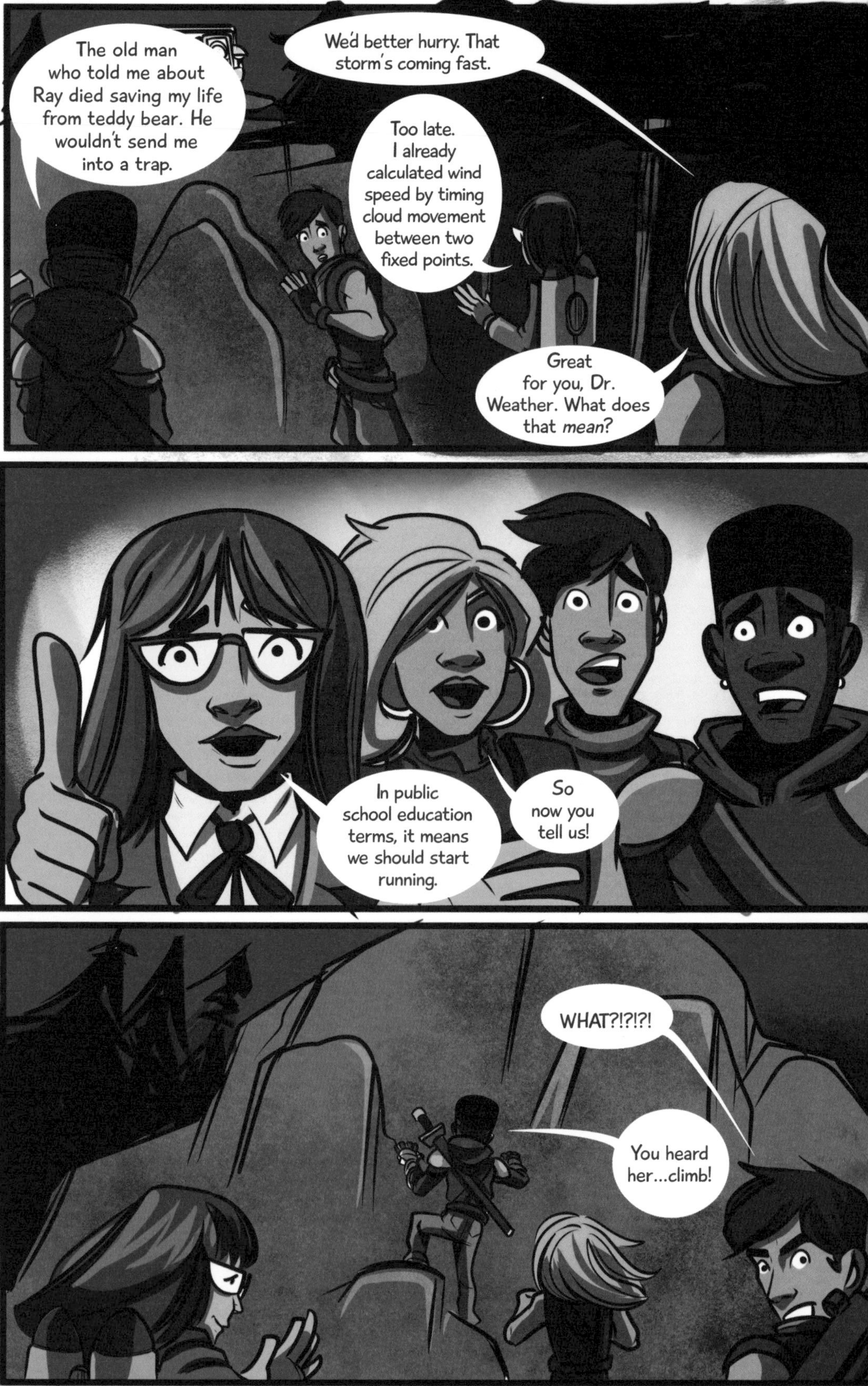
The old man who told me about Ray died saving my life from teddy bear. He wouldn't send me into a trap.
We'd better hurry. That storm's coming fast.
Too late. I already calculated wind speed by timing cloud movement between two fixed points.
Great for you, Dr. Weather. What does that *mean*?
In public school education terms, it means we should start running.
So now you tell us!
WHAT?!?!?!
You heard her...climb!

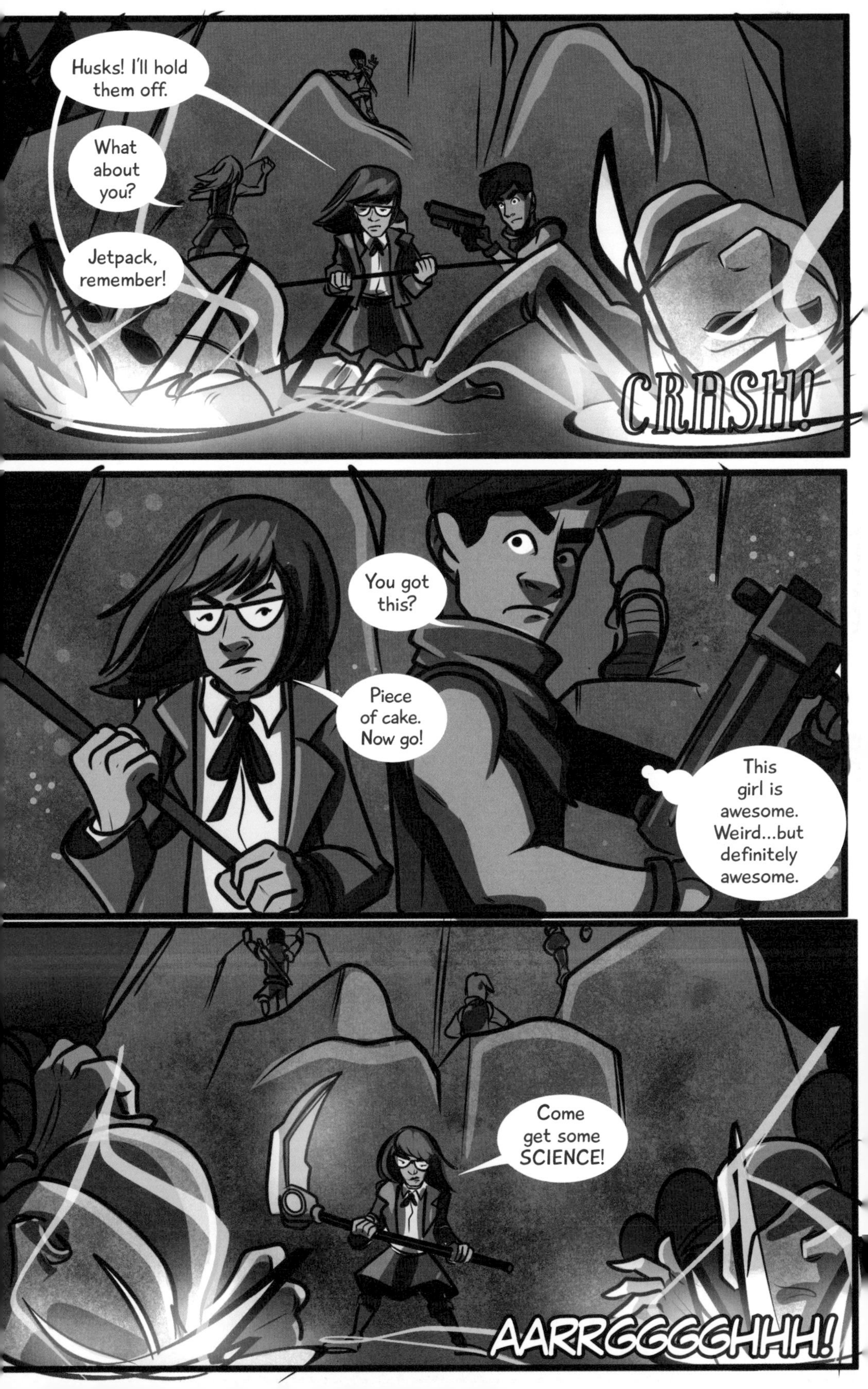
Husks! I'll hold them off.
What about you?
Jetpack, remember!
CRASH!
You got this?
Piece of cake. Now go!
This girl is awesome. Weird...but definitely awesome.
Come get some SCIENCE!
AARRGGGGHHH!

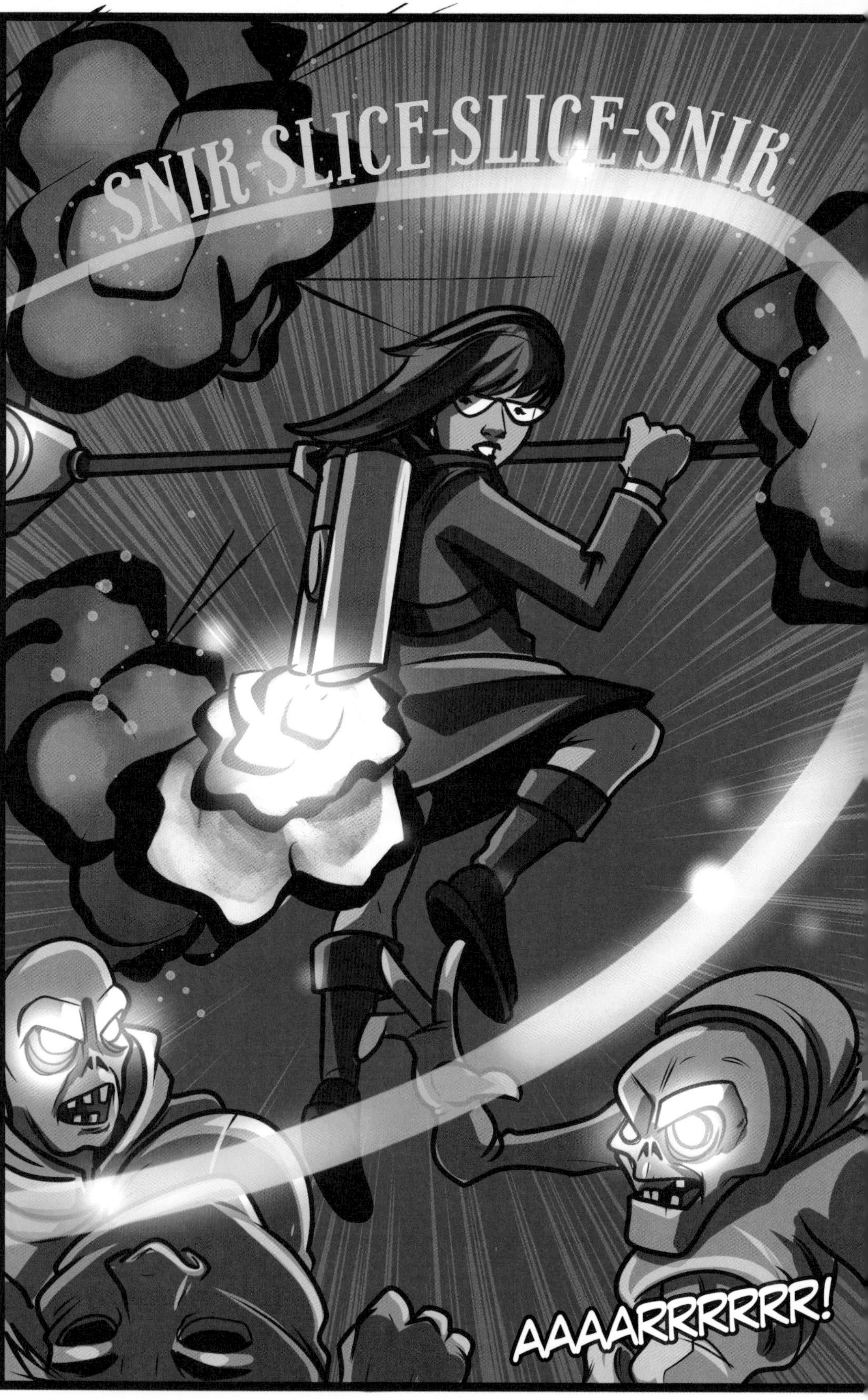
SNIK-SLICE-SLICE-SNIK
AAAARRRRRR!

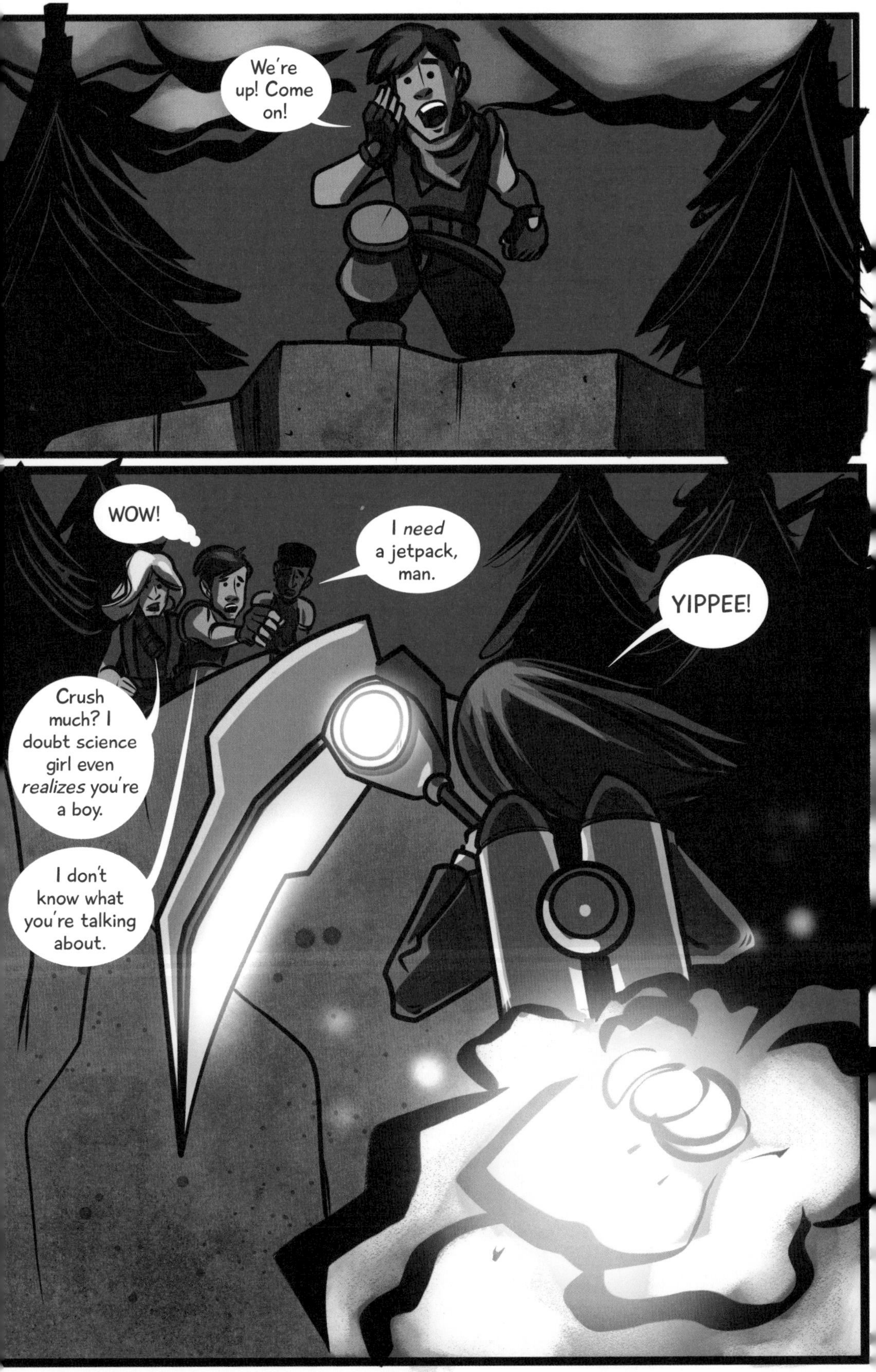
We're up! Come on!
WOW!
I *need* a jetpack, man.
YIPPEE!
Crush much? I doubt science girl even *realizes* you're a boy.
I don't know what you're talking about.

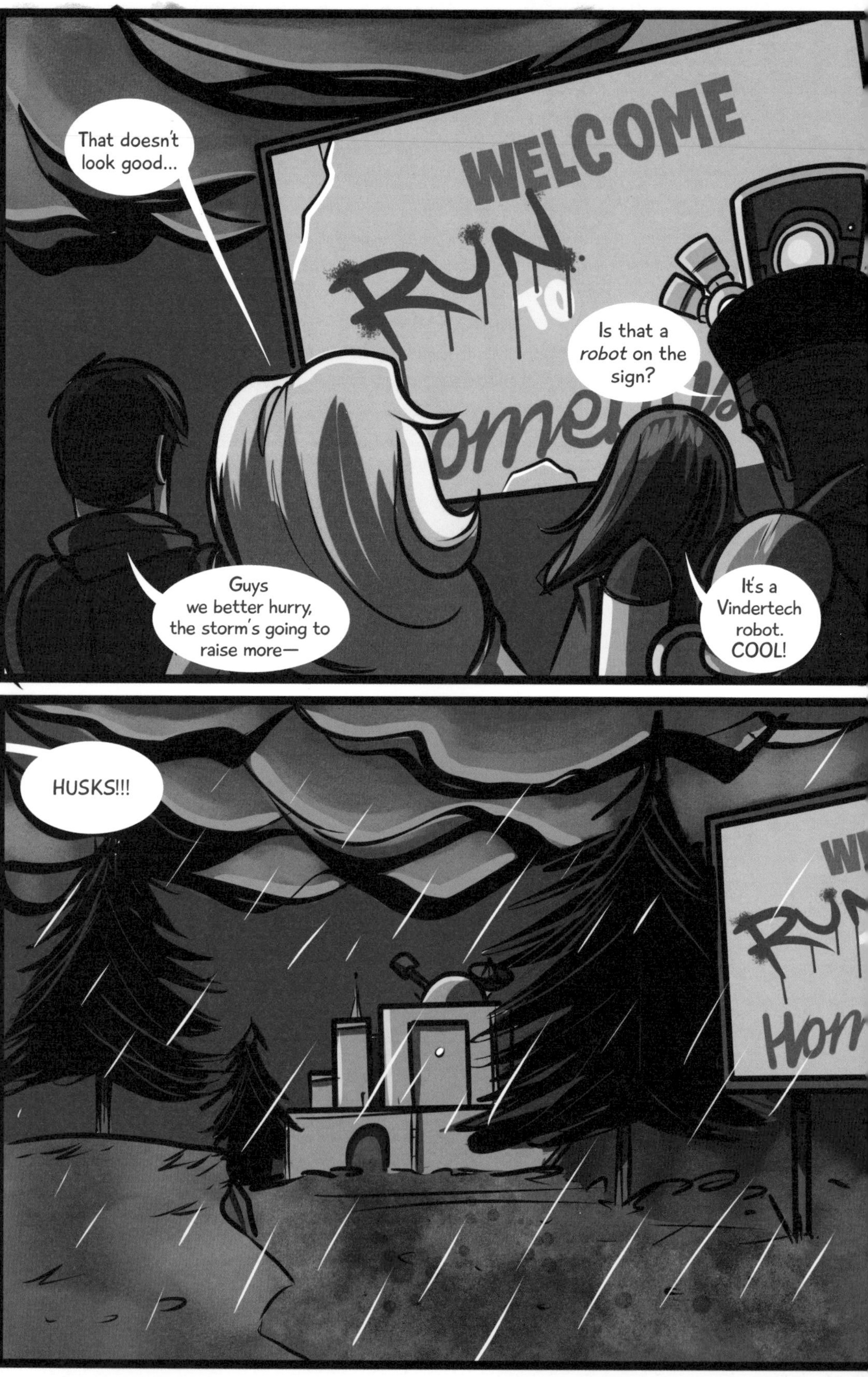

That doesn't look good...
WELCOME
RUN
Is that a *robot* on the sign?
Guys we better hurry, the storm's going to raise more—
It's a Vindertech robot. COOL!
HUSKS!!!

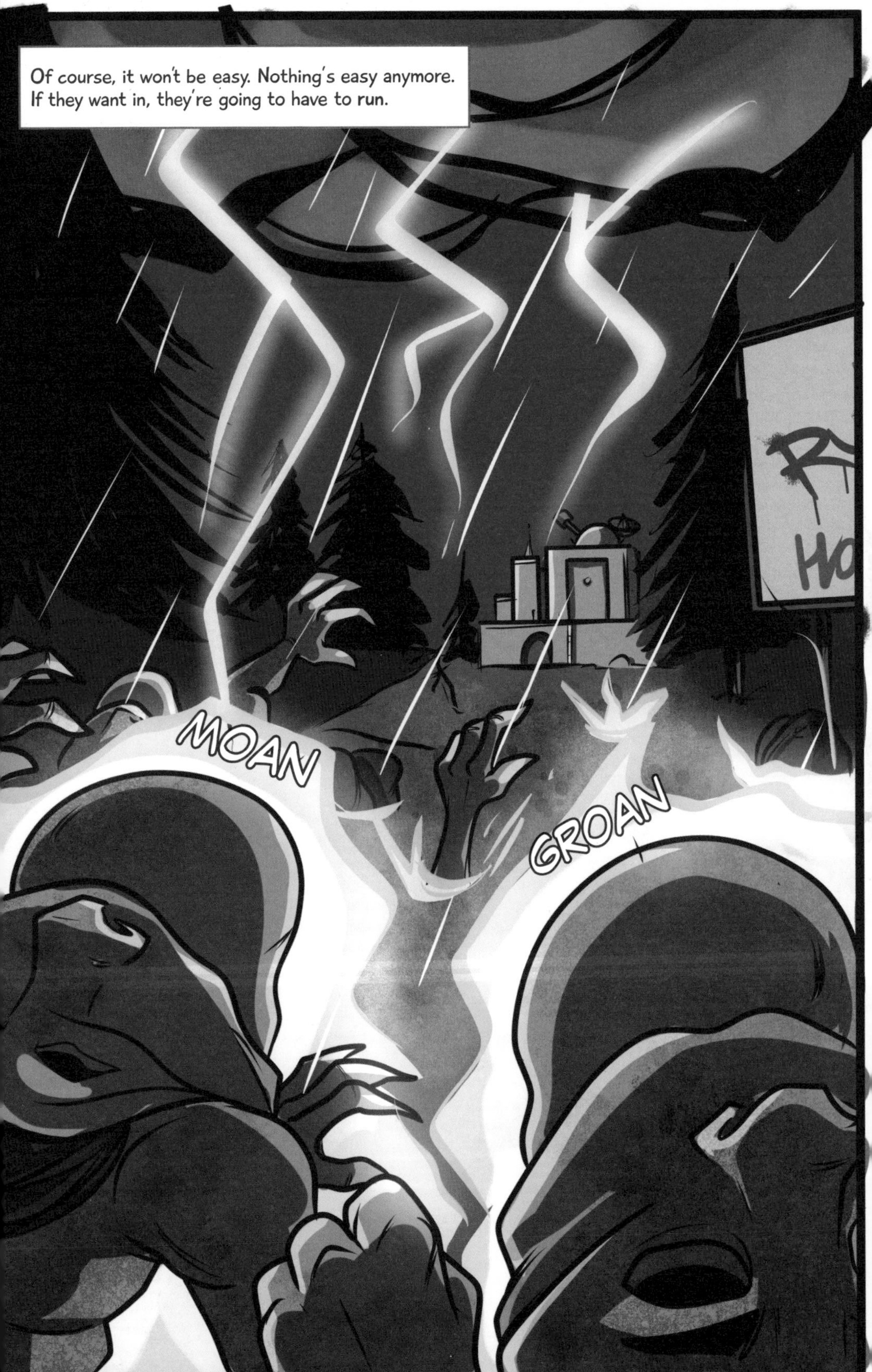
Of course, it won't be easy. Nothing's easy anymore. If they want in, they're going to have to **run**.
MOAN
GROAN

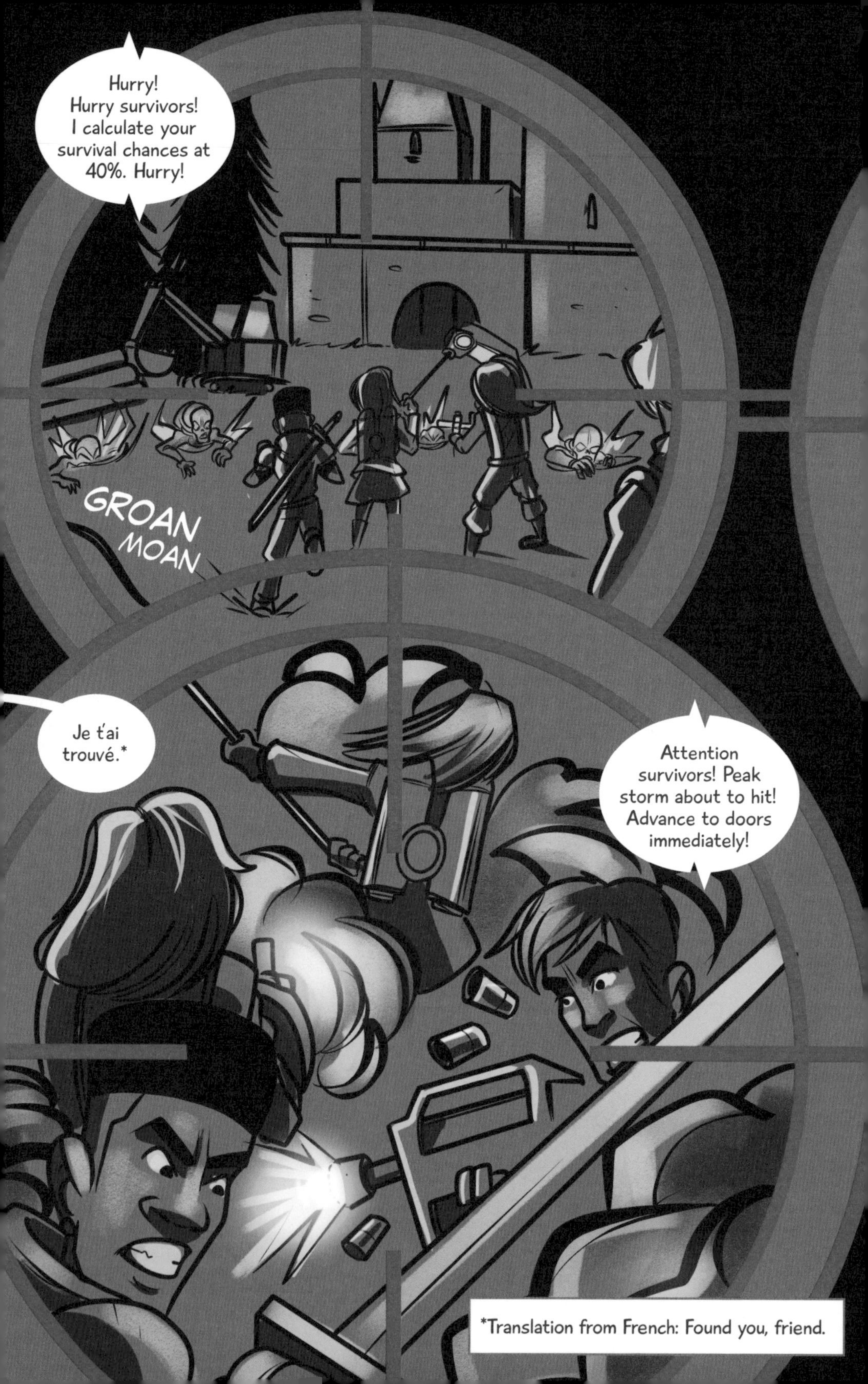
Hurry! Hurry survivors! I calculate your survival chances at 40%. Hurry!
GROAN
MOAN
Je t'ai trouvé.*
Attention survivors! Peak storm about to hit! Advance to doors immediately!
*Translation from French: Found you, friend.

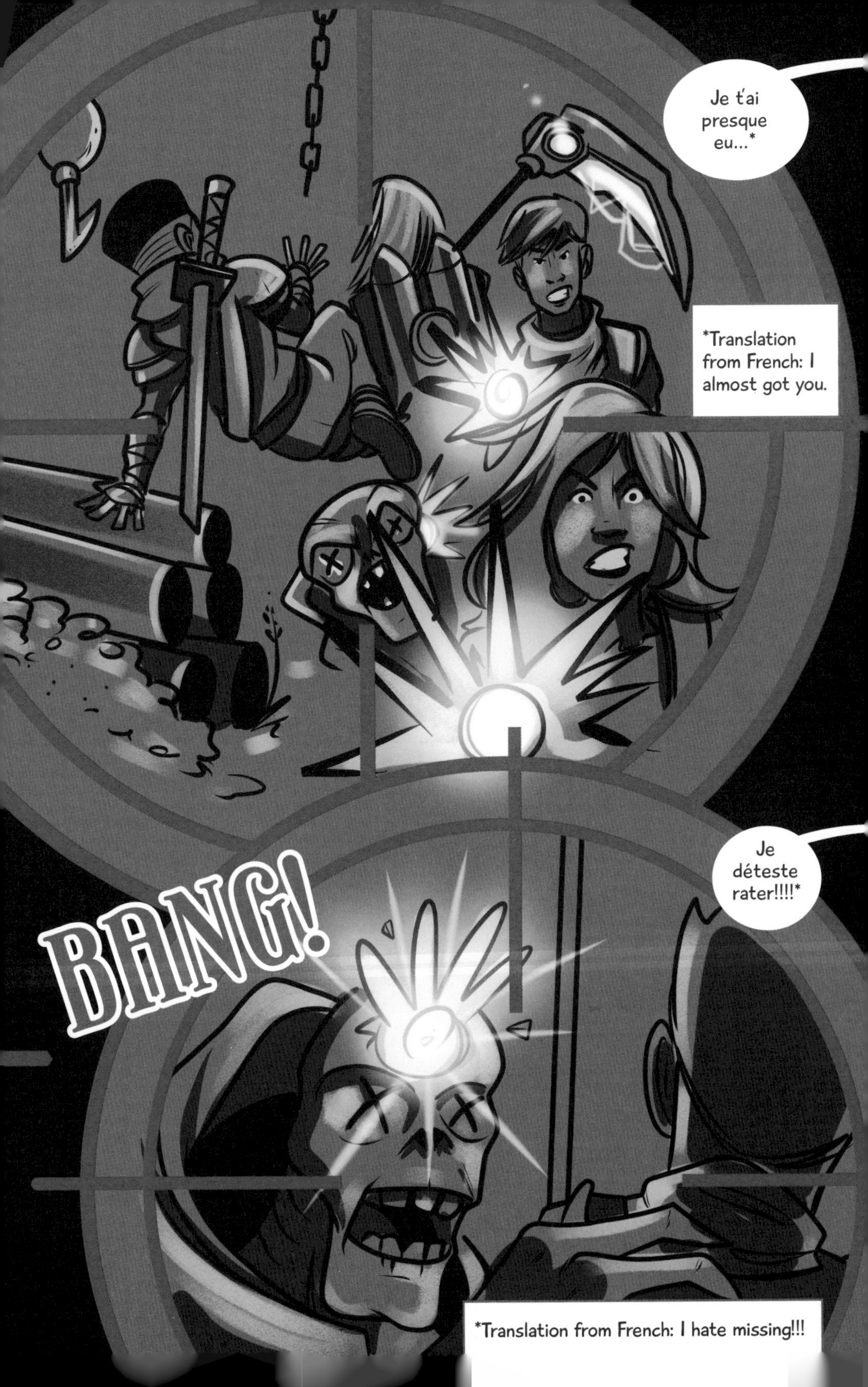
Je t'ai presque eu...*
*Translation from French: I almost got you.
BANG!
Je déteste rater!!!!*
*Translation from French: I hate missing!!!

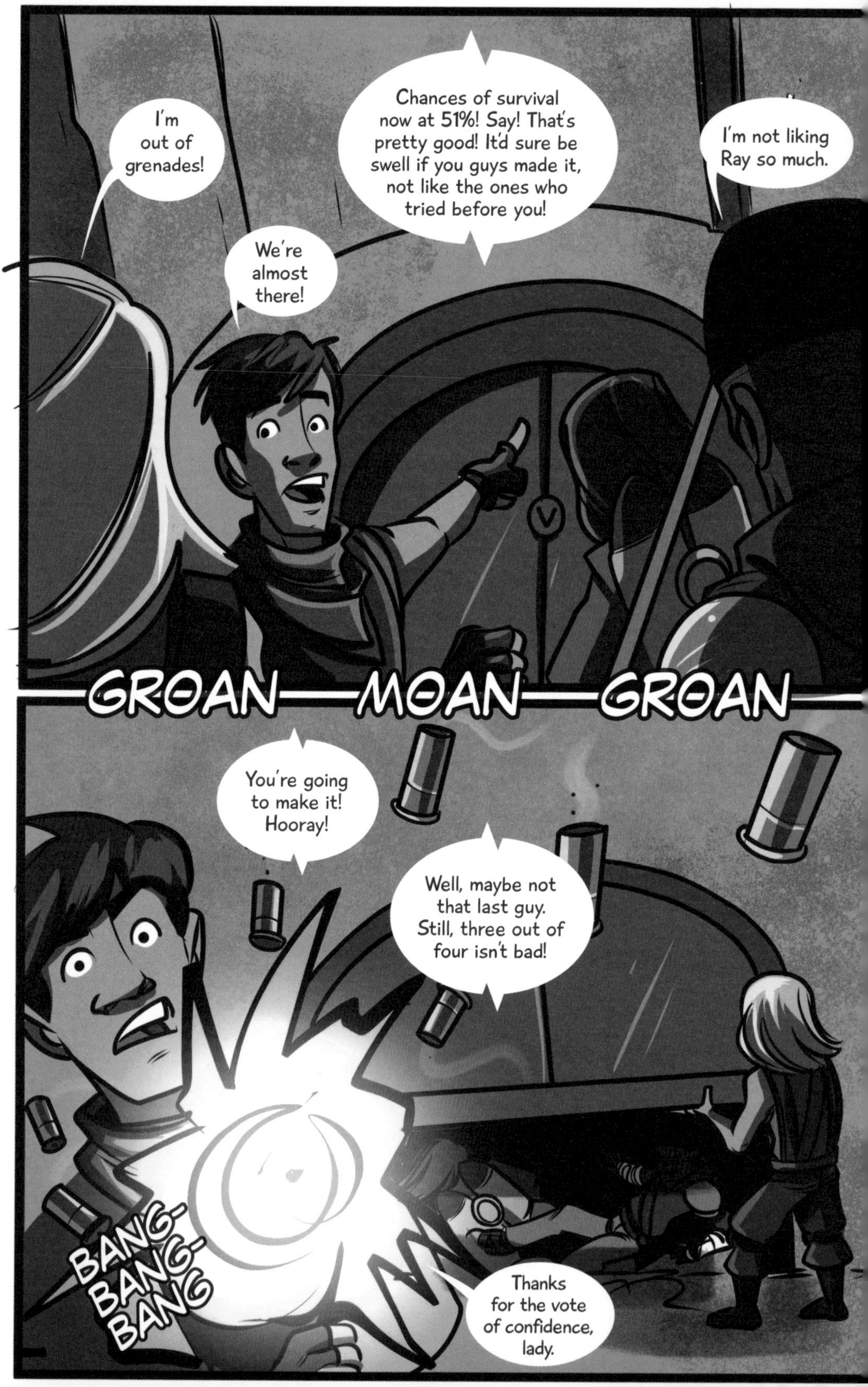
I'm out of grenades!
Chances of survival now at 51%! Say! That's pretty good! It'd sure be swell if you guys made it, not like the ones who tried before you!
I'm not liking Ray so much.
We're almost there!
GROAN
MOAN
GROAN
You're going to make it! Hooray!
Well, maybe not that last guy. Still, three out of four isn't bad!
BANG-BANG-BANG
Thanks for the vote of confidence, lady.

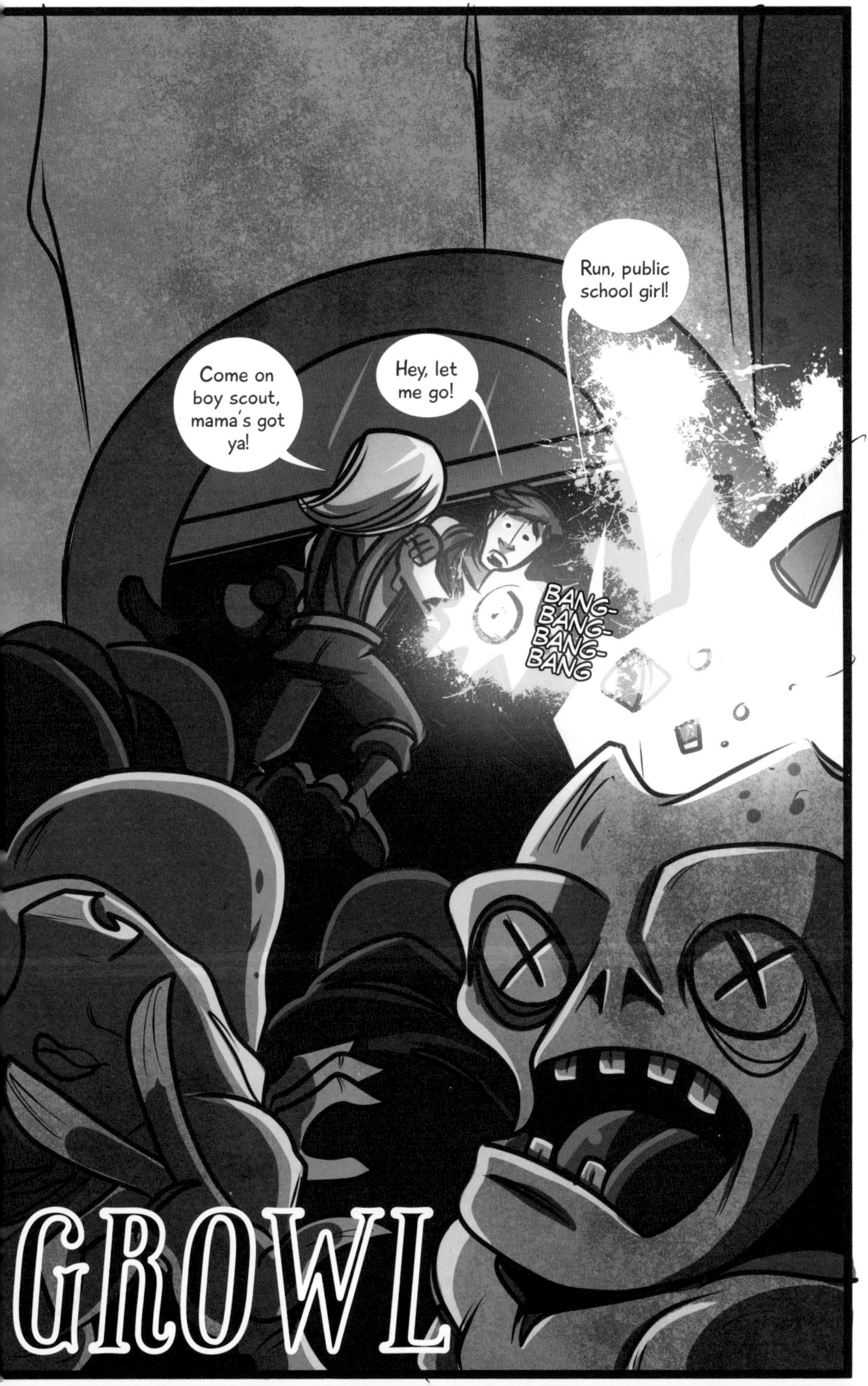
Come on boy scout, mama's got ya!
Hey, let me go!
Run, public school girl!
BANG-BANG-BANG-BANG
GROWL

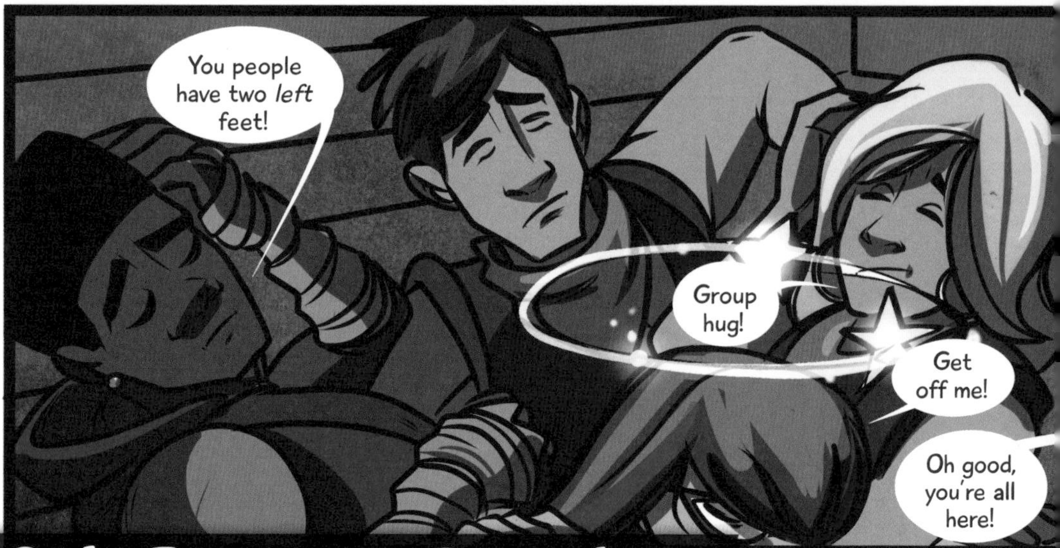
You people have two *left* feet!
Group hug!
Get off me!
Oh good, you're all here!

CHAPTER 7: PLAN B

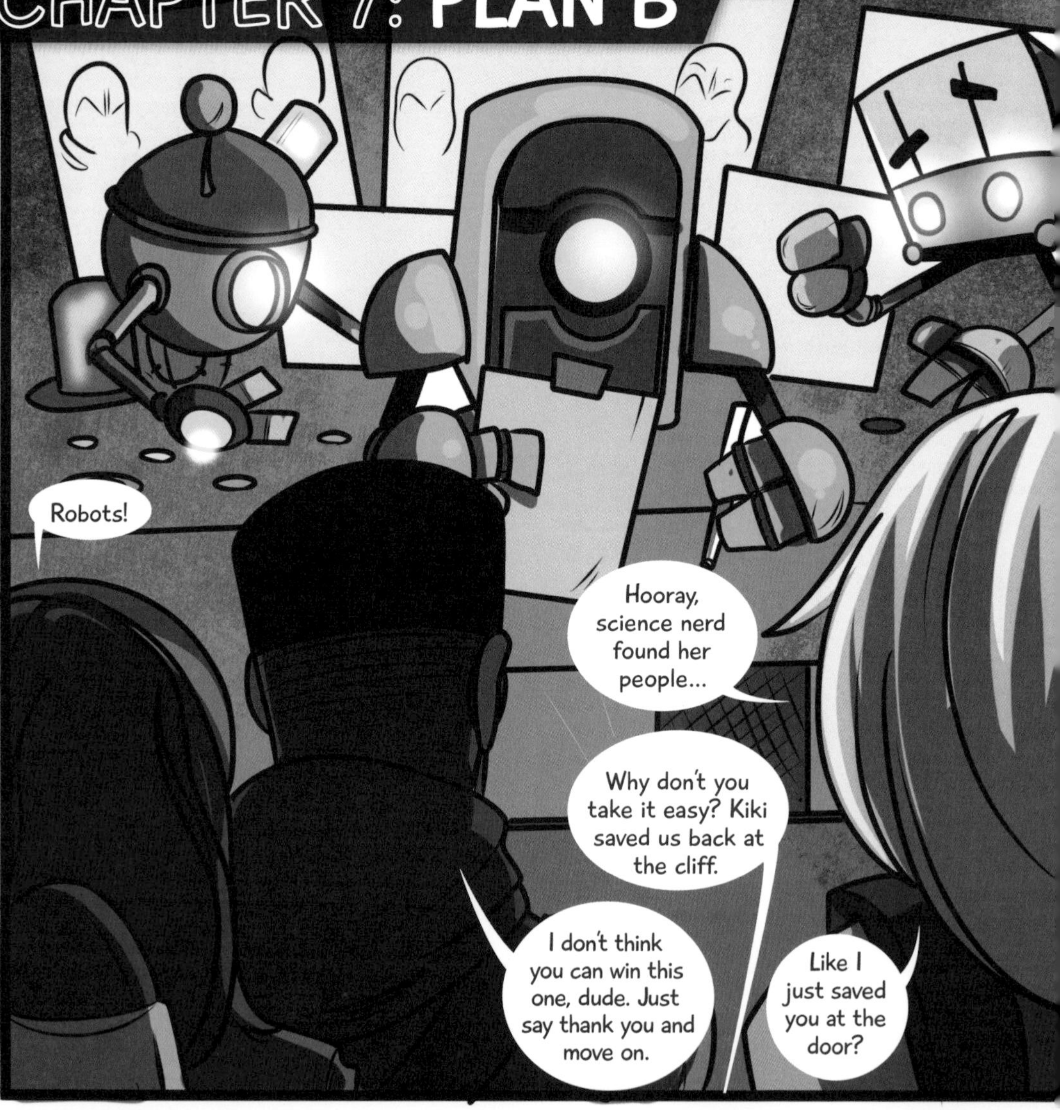
Robots!
Hooray, science nerd found her people...
Why don't you take it easy? Kiki saved us back at the cliff.
I don't think you can win this one, dude. Just say thank you and move on.
Like I just saved you at the door?

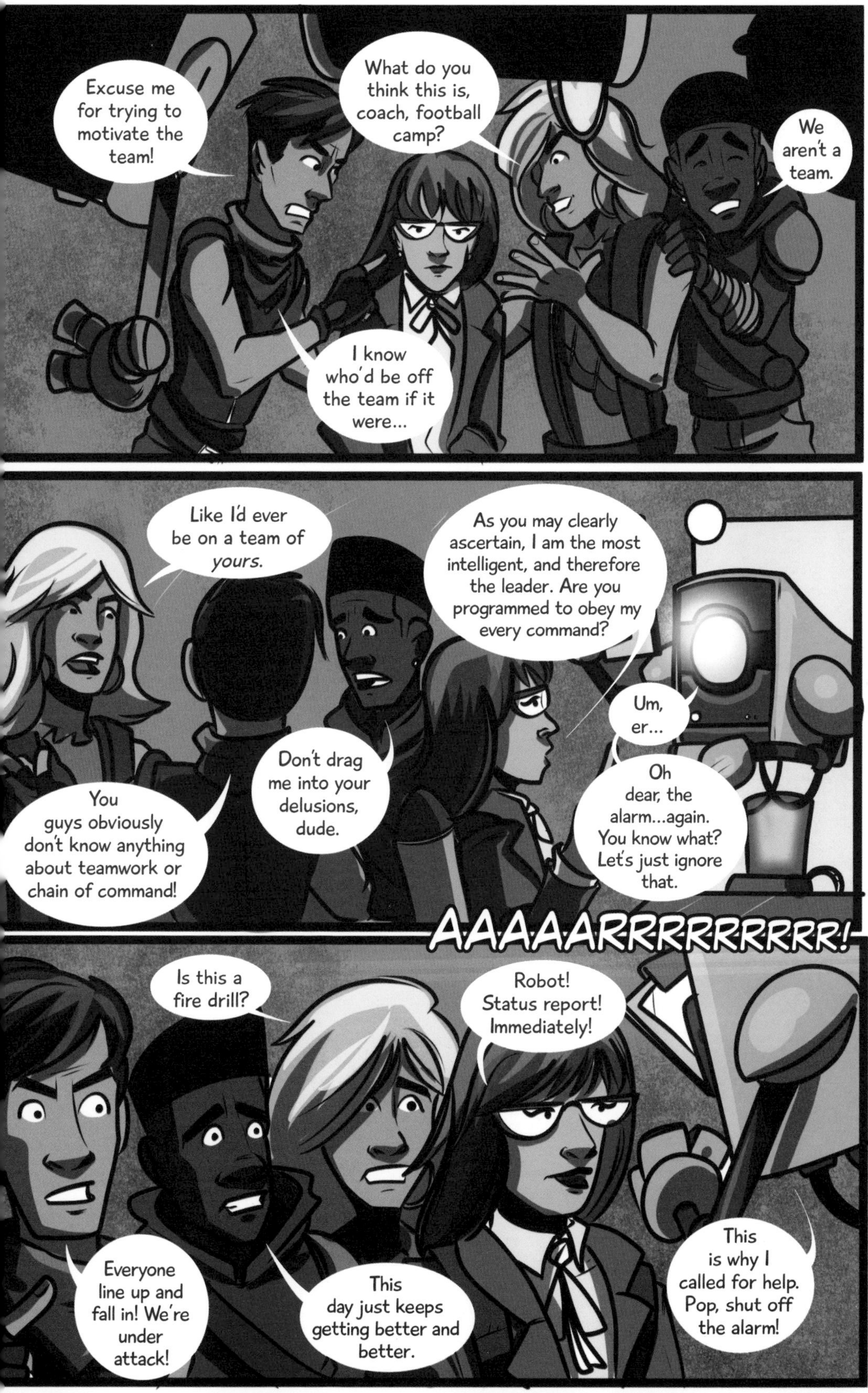
Excuse me for trying to motivate the team!
What do you think this is, coach, football camp?
We aren't a team.
I know who'd be off the team if it were...
Like I'd ever be on a team of *yours.*
As you may clearly ascertain, I am the most intelligent, and therefore the leader. Are you programmed to obey my every command?
You guys obviously don't know anything about teamwork or chain of command!
Don't drag me into your delusions, dude.
Um, er...
Oh dear, the alarm...again. You know what? Let's just ignore that.
AAAAARRRRRRRR!
Is this a fire drill?
Robot! Status report! Immediately!
Everyone line up and fall in! We're under attack!
This day just keeps getting better and better.
This is why I called for help. Pop, shut off the alarm!

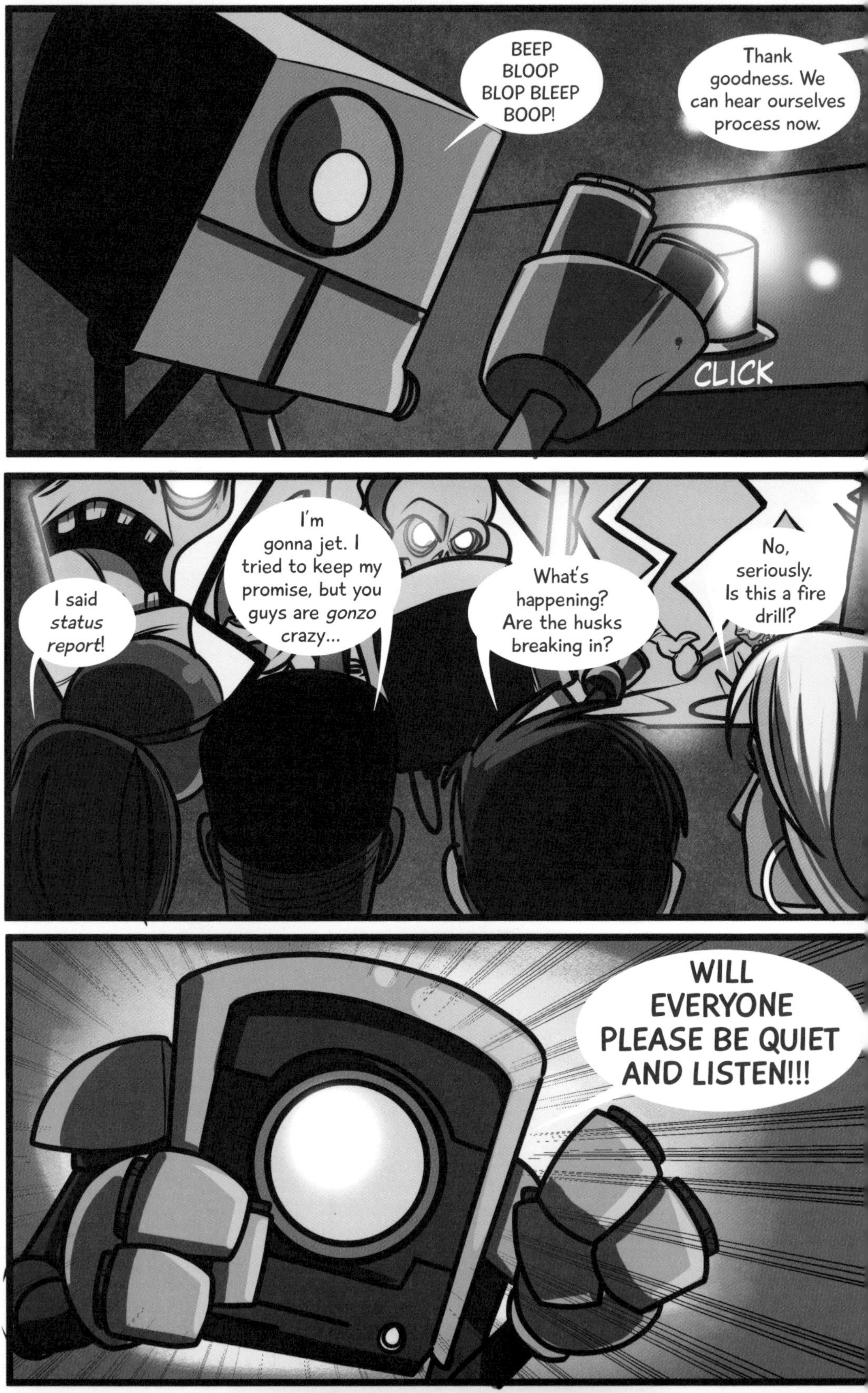
BEEP BLOOP BLOP BLEEP BOOP!
Thank goodness. We can hear ourselves process now.
CLICK
I said *status report*!
I'm gonna jet. I tried to keep my promise, but you guys are *gonzo* crazy...
What's happening? Are the husks breaking in?
No, seriously. Is this a fire drill?
WILL EVERYONE PLEASE BE QUIET AND LISTEN!!!

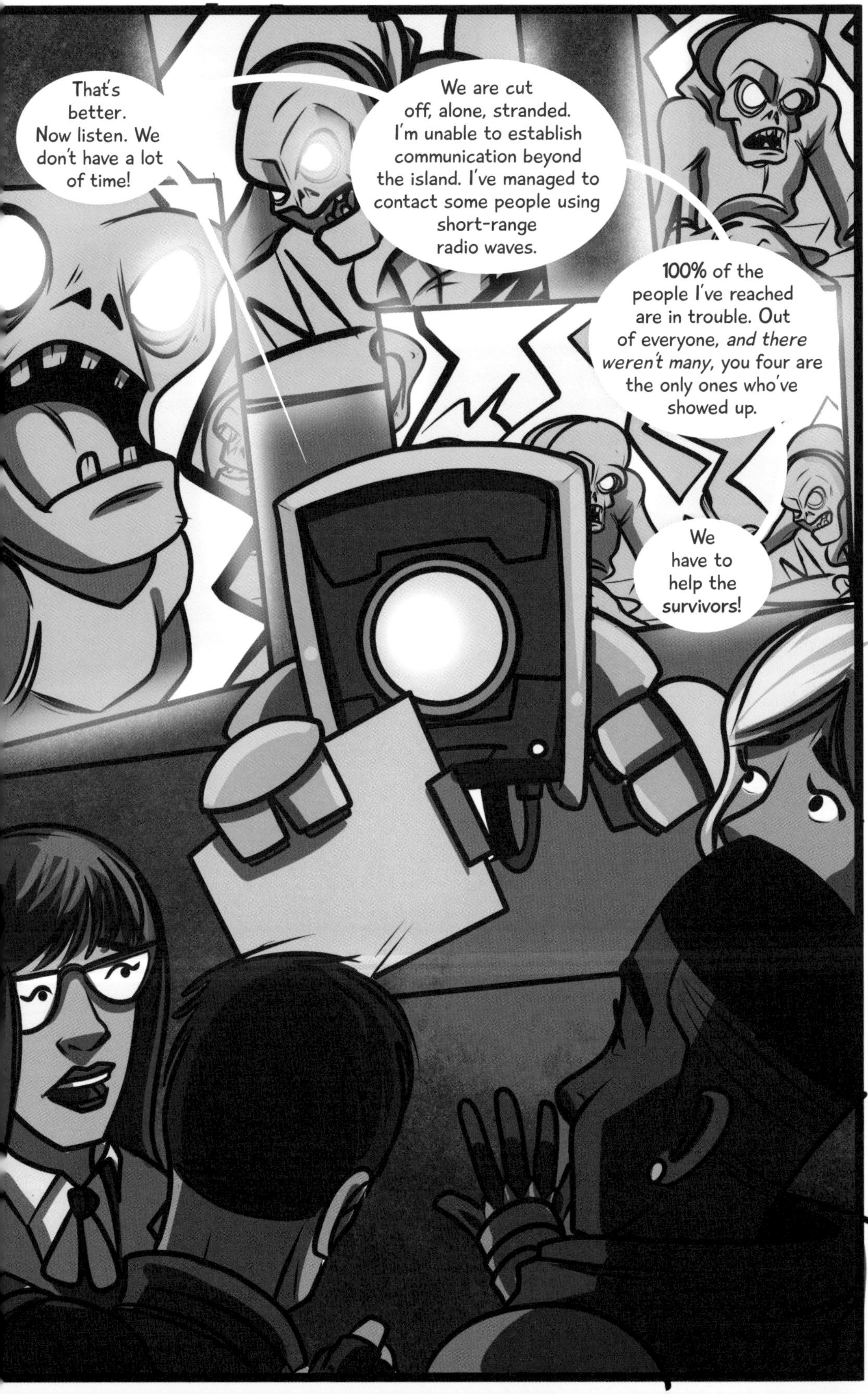
That's better. Now listen. We don't have a lot of time!
We are cut off, alone, stranded. I'm unable to establish communication beyond the island. I've managed to contact some people using short-range radio waves.
100% of the people I've reached are in trouble. Out of everyone, *and there weren't many*, you four are the only ones who've showed up.
We have to help the **survivors!**

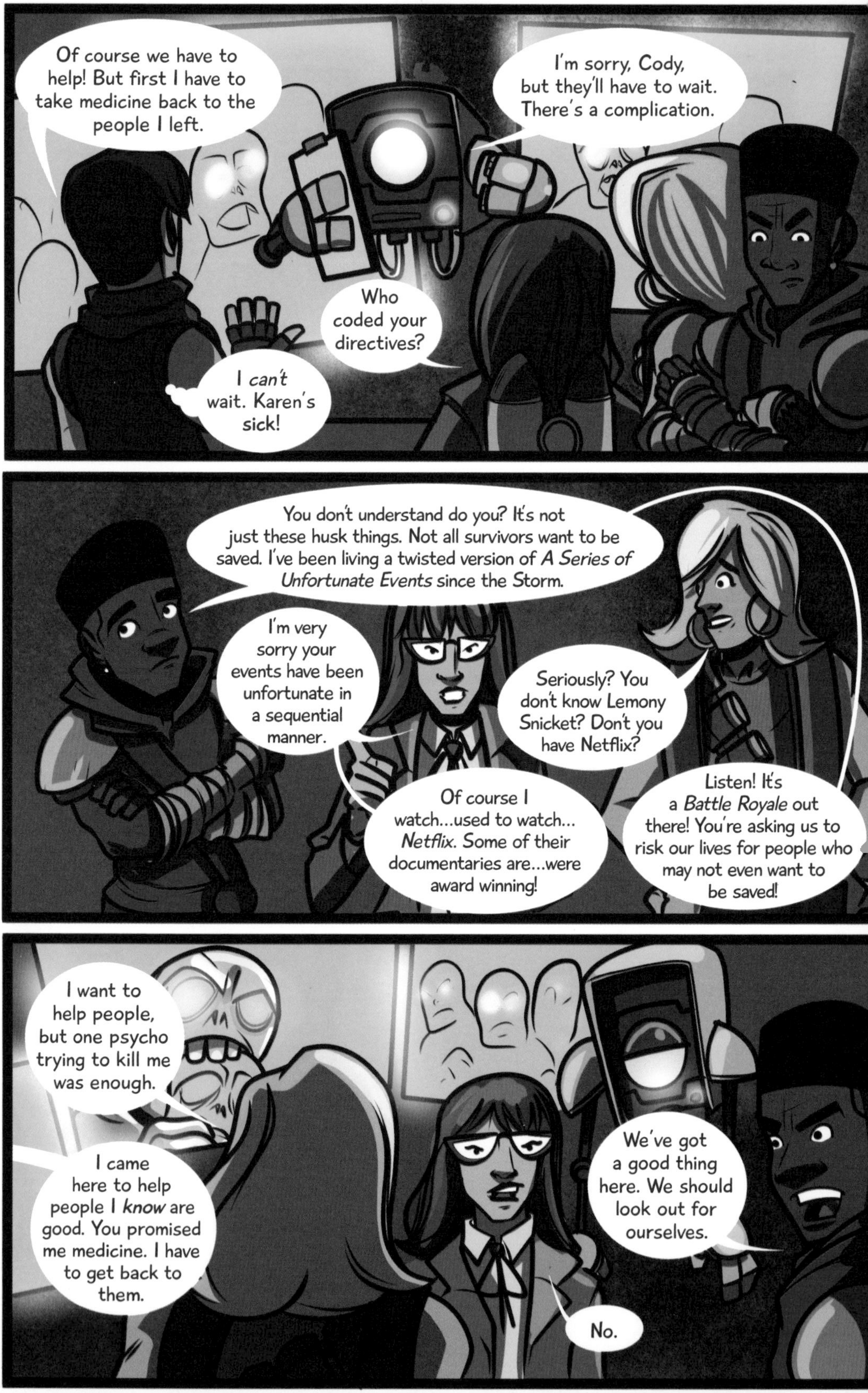

Of course we have to help! But first I have to take medicine back to the people I left.
I'm sorry, Cody, but they'll have to wait. There's a complication.
Who coded your directives?
I *can't* wait. Karen's sick!
You don't understand do you? It's not just these husk things. Not all survivors want to be saved. I've been living a twisted version of *A Series of Unfortunate Events* since the Storm.
I'm very sorry your events have been unfortunate in a sequential manner.
Seriously? You don't know Lemony Snicket? Don't you have Netflix?
Of course I watch...used to watch... *Netflix*. Some of their documentaries are...were award winning!
Listen! It's a *Battle Royale* out there! You're asking us to risk our lives for people who may not even want to be saved!
I want to help people, but one psycho trying to kill me was enough.
I came here to help people I *know* are good. You promised me medicine. I have to get back to them.
We've got a good thing here. We should look out for ourselves.
No.

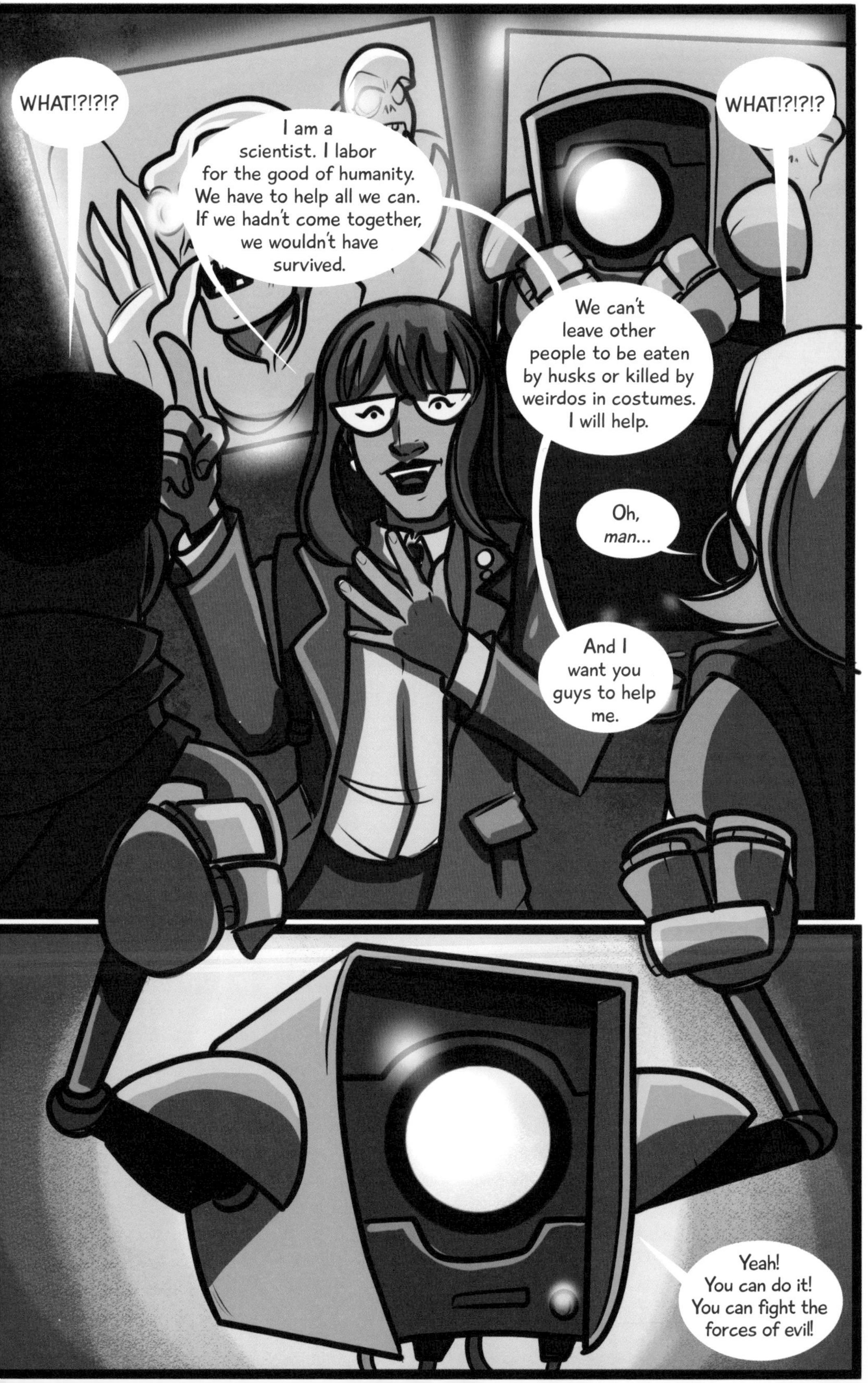
WHAT!?!?!?
I am a scientist. I labor for the good of humanity. We have to help all we can. If we hadn't come together, we wouldn't have survived.
WHAT!?!?!?
We can't leave other people to be eaten by husks or killed by weirdos in costumes. I will help.
Oh, *man*...
And I want you guys to help me.
Yeah! You can do it! You can fight the forces of evil!

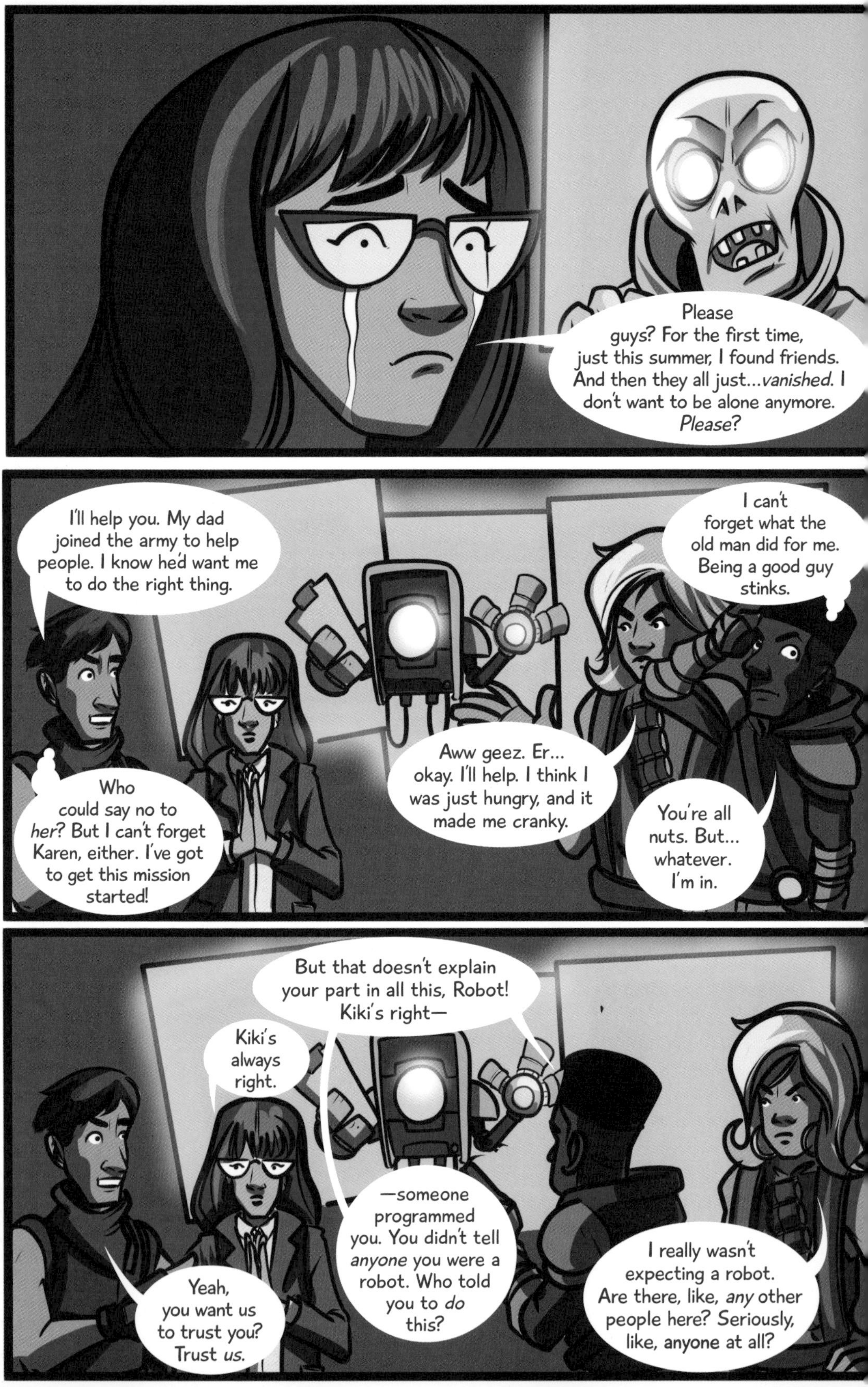
Please guys? For the first time, just this summer, I found friends. And then they all just...*vanished*. I don't want to be alone anymore. *Please*?
I'll help you. My dad joined the army to help people. I know he'd want me to do the right thing.
Who could say no to *her*? But I can't forget Karen, either. I've got to get this mission started!
Aww geez. Er... okay. I'll help. I think I was just hungry, and it made me cranky.
I can't forget what the old man did for me. Being a good guy stinks.
You're all nuts. But... whatever. I'm in.
But that doesn't explain your part in all this, Robot! Kiki's right—
Kiki's always right.
—someone programmed you. You didn't tell *anyone* you were a robot. Who told you to *do* this?
Yeah, you want us to trust you? Trust *us*.
I really wasn't expecting a robot. Are there, like, *any* other people here? Seriously, like, anyone at all?

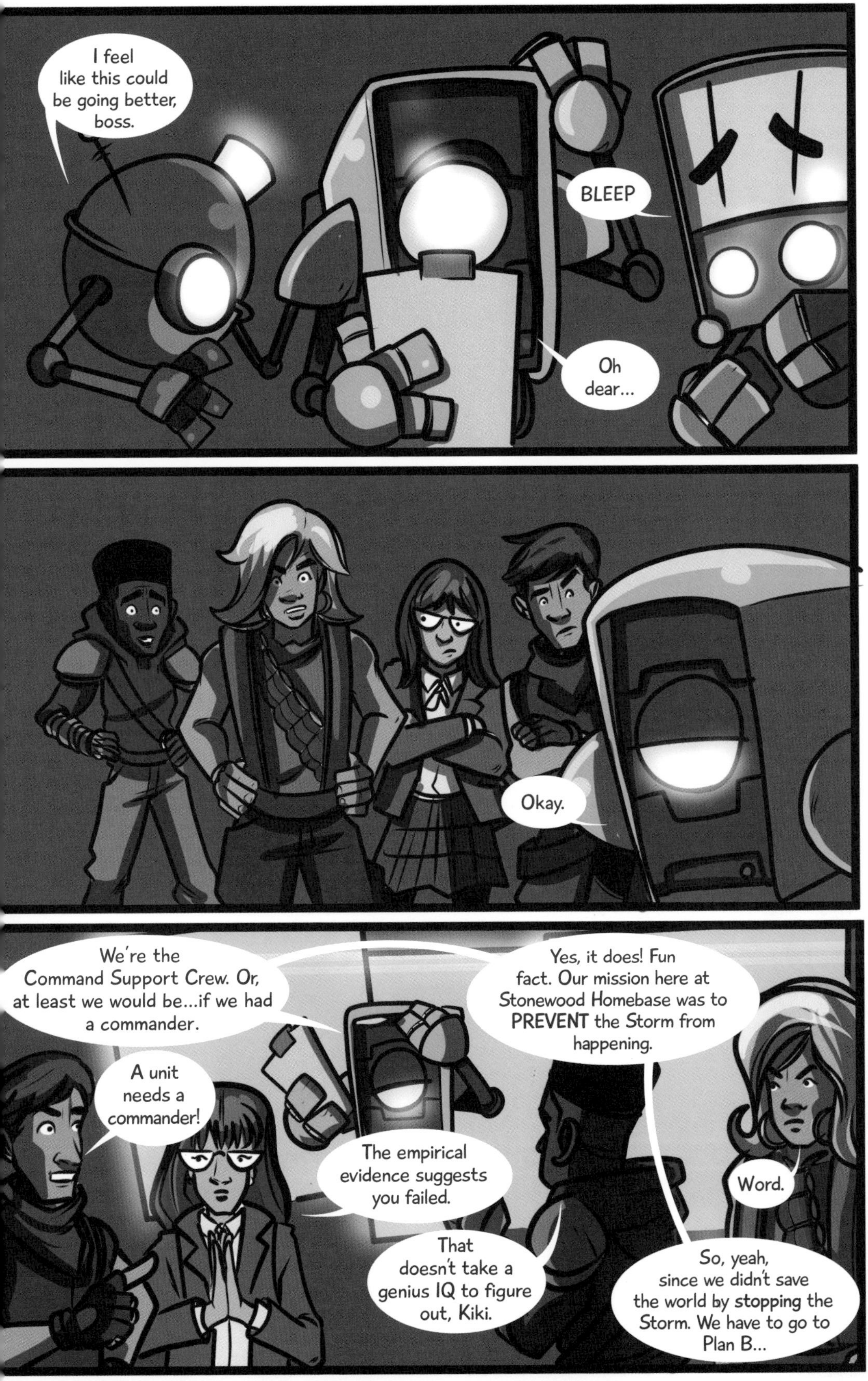
I feel like this could be going better, boss.
BLEEP
Oh dear...
Okay.
We're the Command Support Crew. Or, at least we would be...if we had a commander.
A unit needs a commander!
Yes, it does! Fun fact. Our mission here at Stonewood Homebase was to **PREVENT** the Storm from happening.
The empirical evidence suggests you failed.
Word.
That doesn't take a genius IQ to figure out, Kiki.
So, yeah, since we didn't save the world by **stopping** the Storm. We have to go to Plan B...

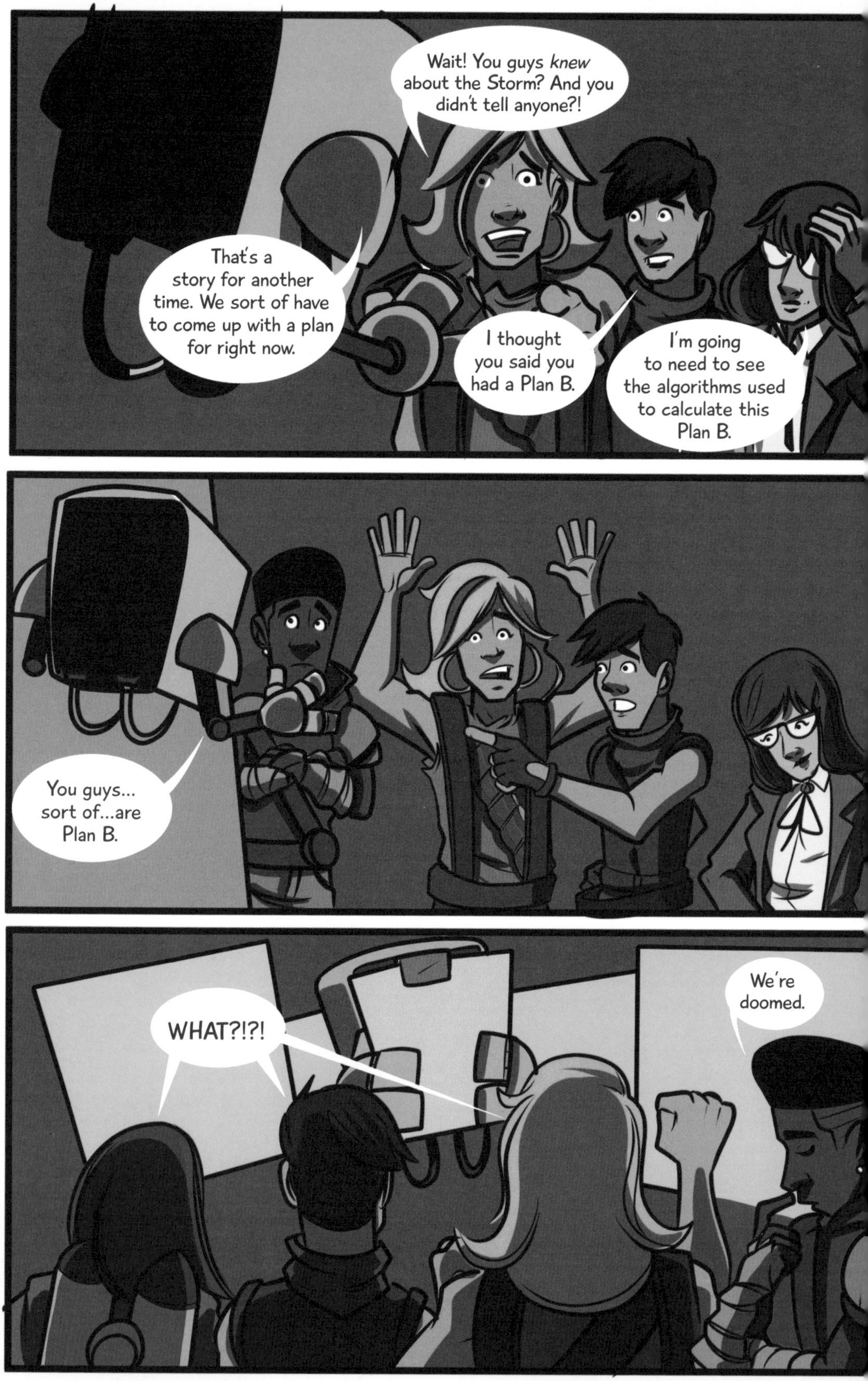

Wait! You guys *knew* about the Storm? And you didn't tell anyone?!
That's a story for another time. We sort of have to come up with a plan for right now.
I thought you said you had a Plan B.
I'm going to need to see the algorithms used to calculate this Plan B.
You guys... sort of...are Plan B.
WHAT?!?!
We're doomed.

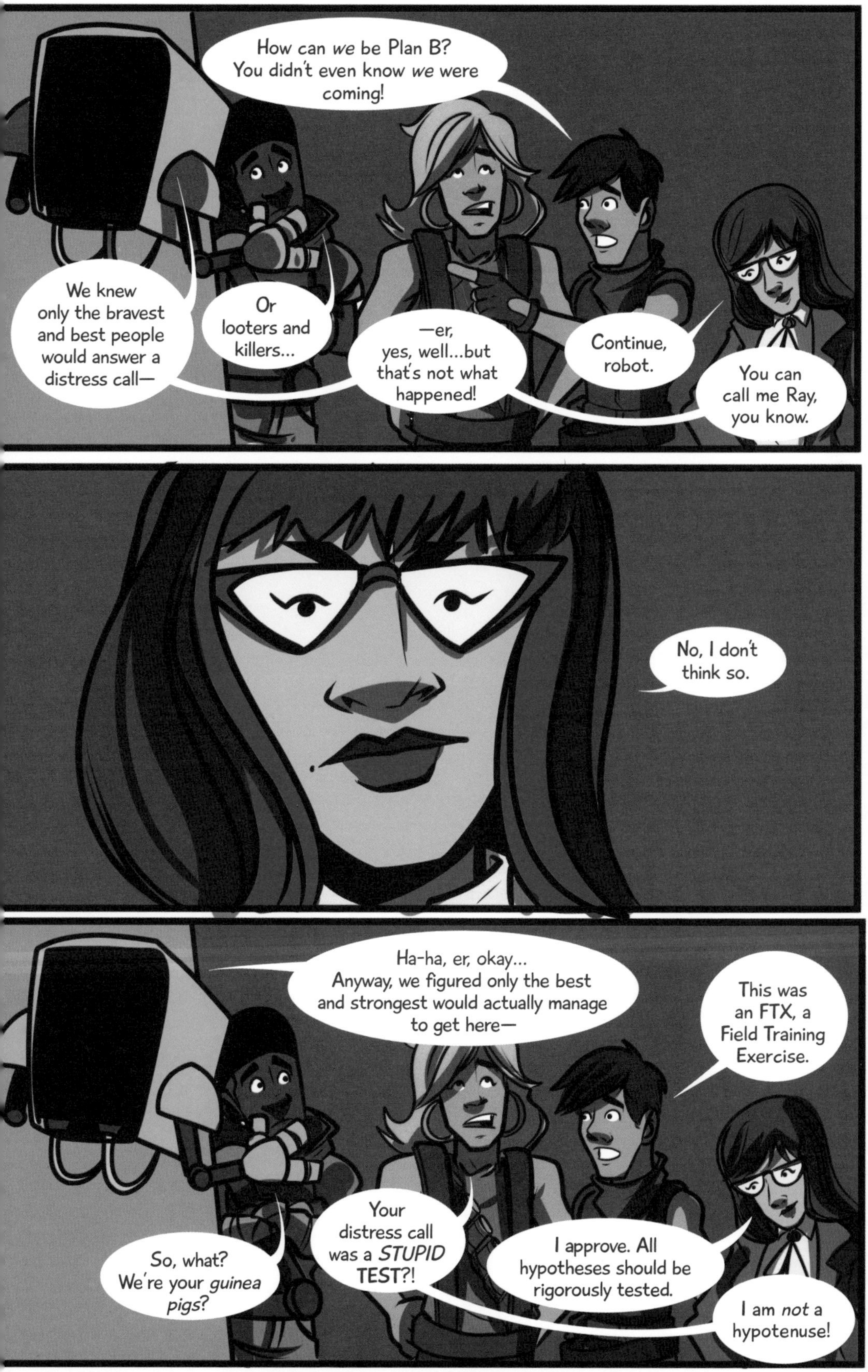
How can *we* be Plan B? You didn't even know *we* were coming!
We knew only the bravest and best people would answer a distress call—
Or looters and killers...
—er, yes, well...but that's not what happened!
Continue, robot.
You can call me Ray, you know.
No, I don't think so.
Ha-ha, er, okay... Anyway, we figured only the best and strongest would actually manage to get here—
This was an FTX, a Field Training Exercise.
So, what? We're your *guinea pigs*?
Your distress call was a *STUPID* TEST?!
I approve. All hypotheses should be rigorously tested.
I am *not* a hypotenuse!

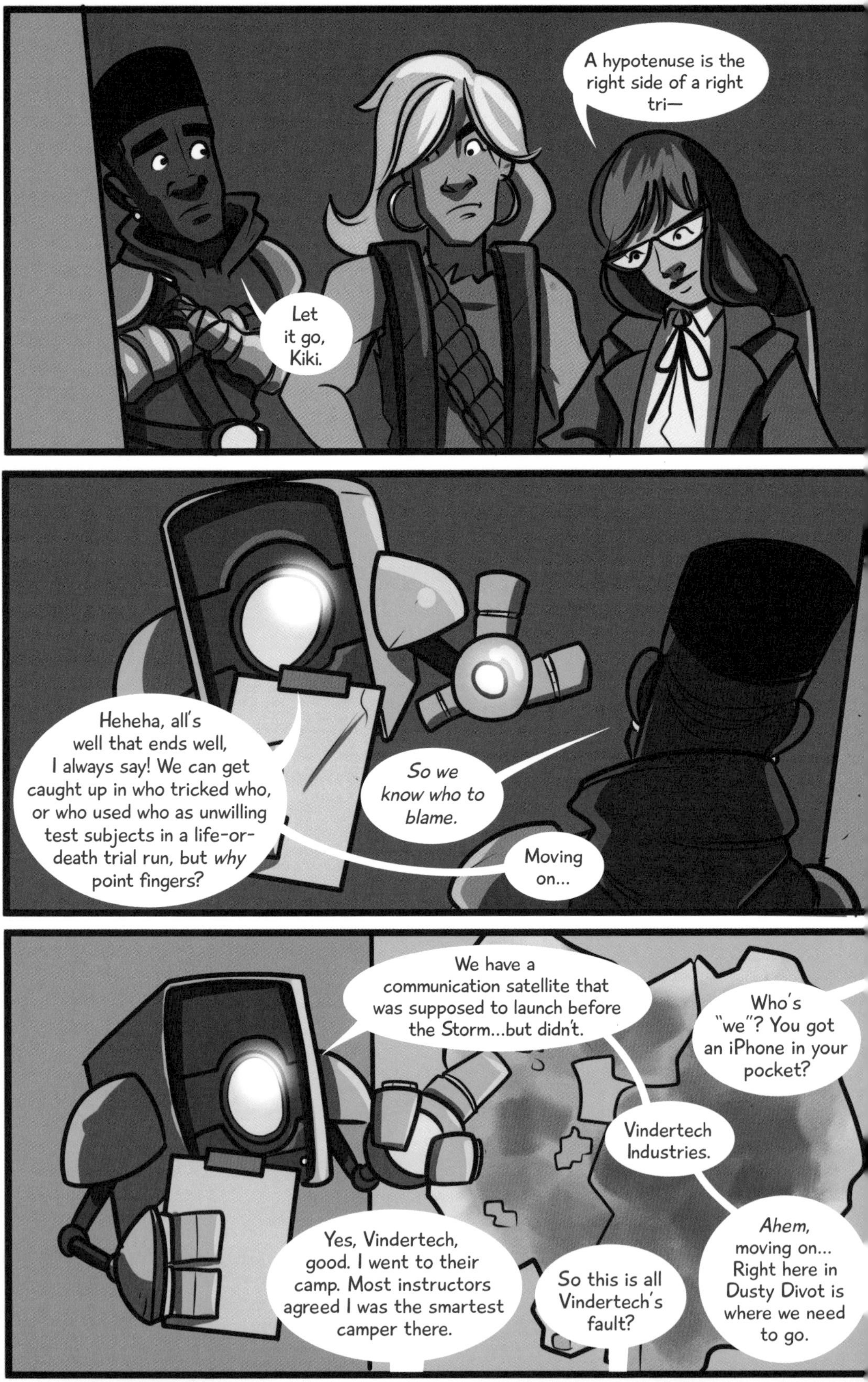
A hypotenuse is the right side of a right tri—
Let it go, Kiki.
Heheha, all's well that ends well, I always say! We can get caught up in who tricked who, or who used who as unwilling test subjects in a life-or-death trial run, but *why* point fingers?
So we know who to blame.
Moving on...
We have a communication satellite that was supposed to launch before the Storm...but didn't.
Who's "we"? You got an iPhone in your pocket?
Vindertech Industries.
Yes, Vindertech, good. I went to their camp. Most instructors agreed I was the smartest camper there.
So this is all Vindertech's fault?
Ahem, moving on... Right here in Dusty Divot is where we need to go.

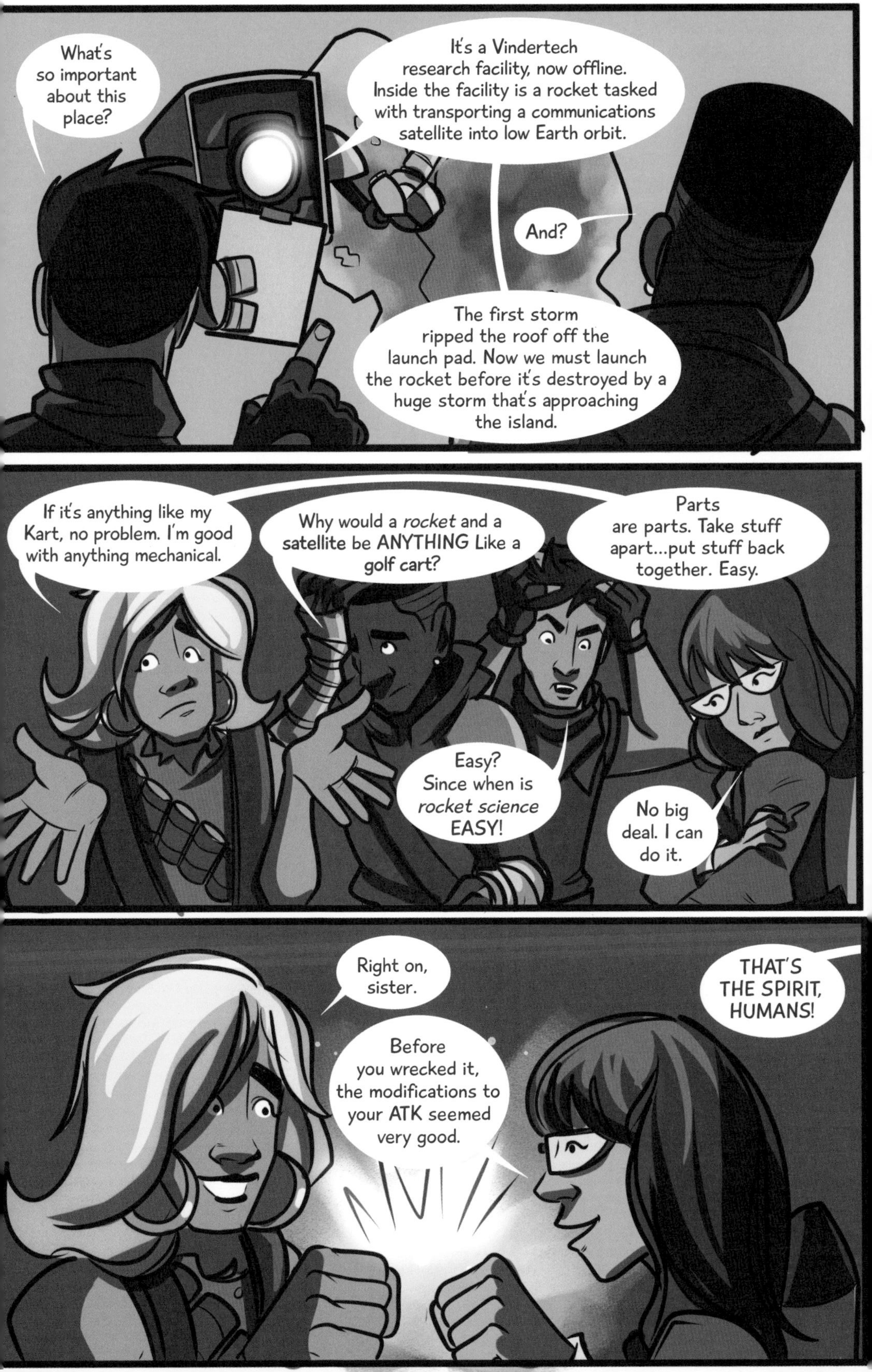
What's so important about this place?
It's a Vindertech research facility, now offline. Inside the facility is a rocket tasked with transporting a communications satellite into low Earth orbit.
And?
The first storm ripped the roof off the launch pad. Now we must launch the rocket before it's destroyed by a huge storm that's approaching the island.
If it's anything like my Kart, no problem. I'm good with anything mechanical.
Why would a *rocket* and a satellite be ANYTHING Like a golf cart?
Parts are parts. Take stuff apart...put stuff back together. Easy.
Easy? Since when is *rocket science* EASY!
No big deal. I can do it.
Right on, sister.
Before you wrecked it, the modifications to your ATK seemed very good.
THAT'S THE SPIRIT, HUMANS!

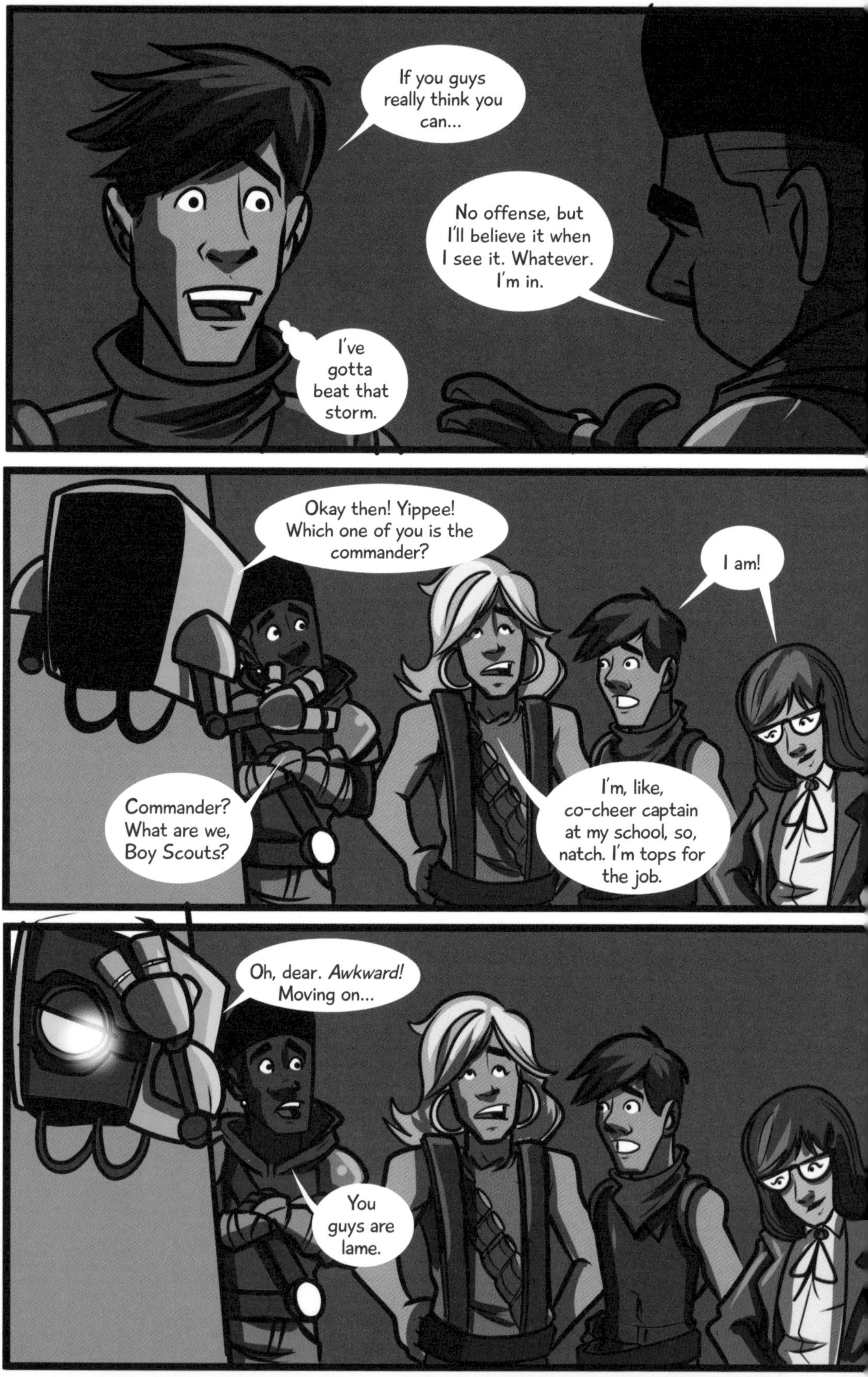
If you guys really think you can...
No offense, but I'll believe it when I see it. Whatever. I'm in.
I've gotta beat that storm.
Okay then! Yippee! Which one of you is the commander?
I am!
Commander? What are we, Boy Scouts?
I'm, like, co-cheer captain at my school, so, natch. I'm tops for the job.
Oh, dear. *Awkward!* Moving on...
You guys are lame.

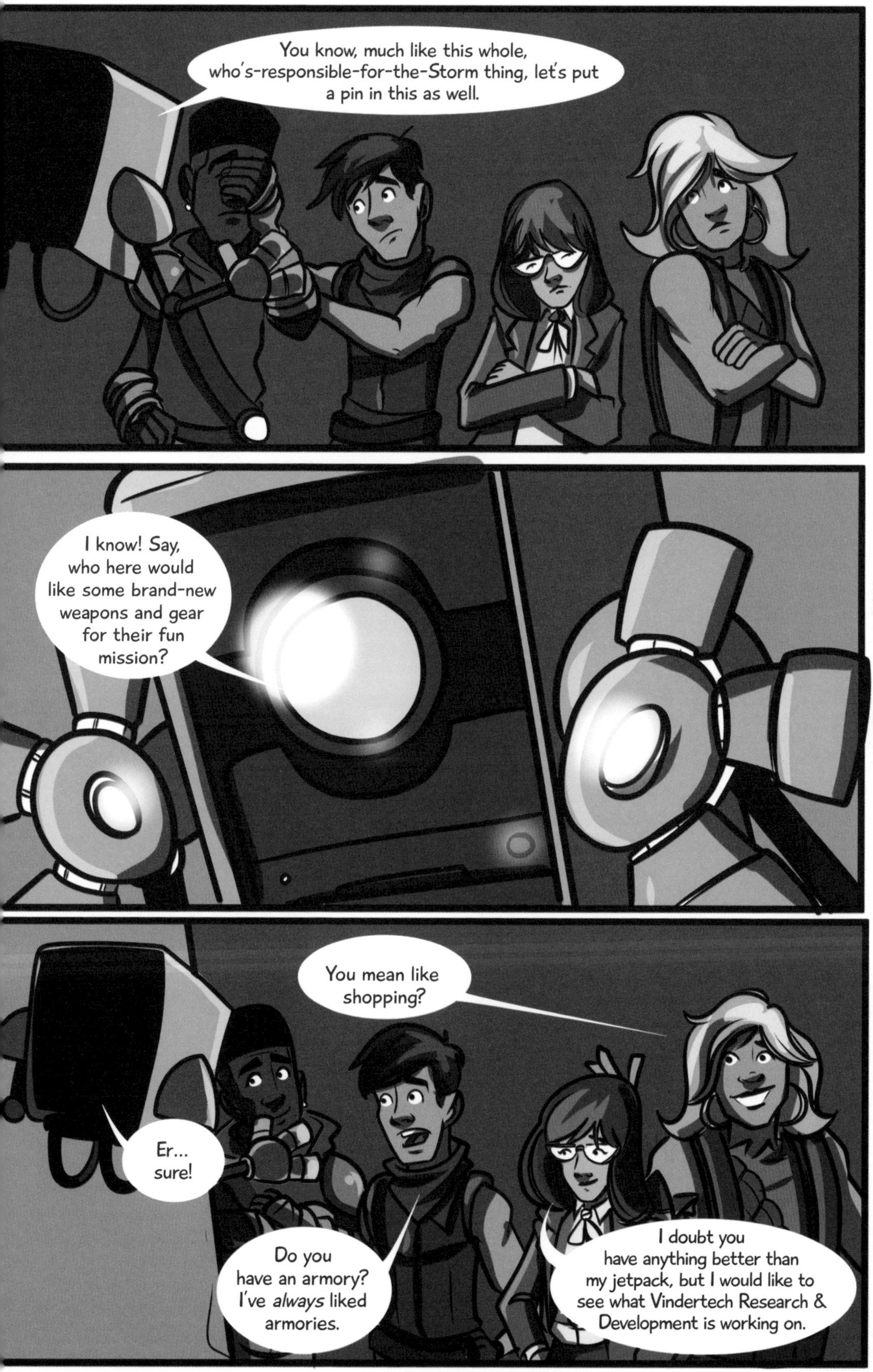
You know, much like this whole, who's-responsible-for-the-Storm thing, let's put a pin in this as well.
I know! Say, who here would like some brand-new weapons and gear for their fun mission?
You mean like shopping?
Er... sure!
Do you have an armory? I've *always* liked armories.
I doubt you have anything better than my jetpack, but I would like to see what Vindertech Research & Development is working on.

CHAPTER 8: NEW LOOKS

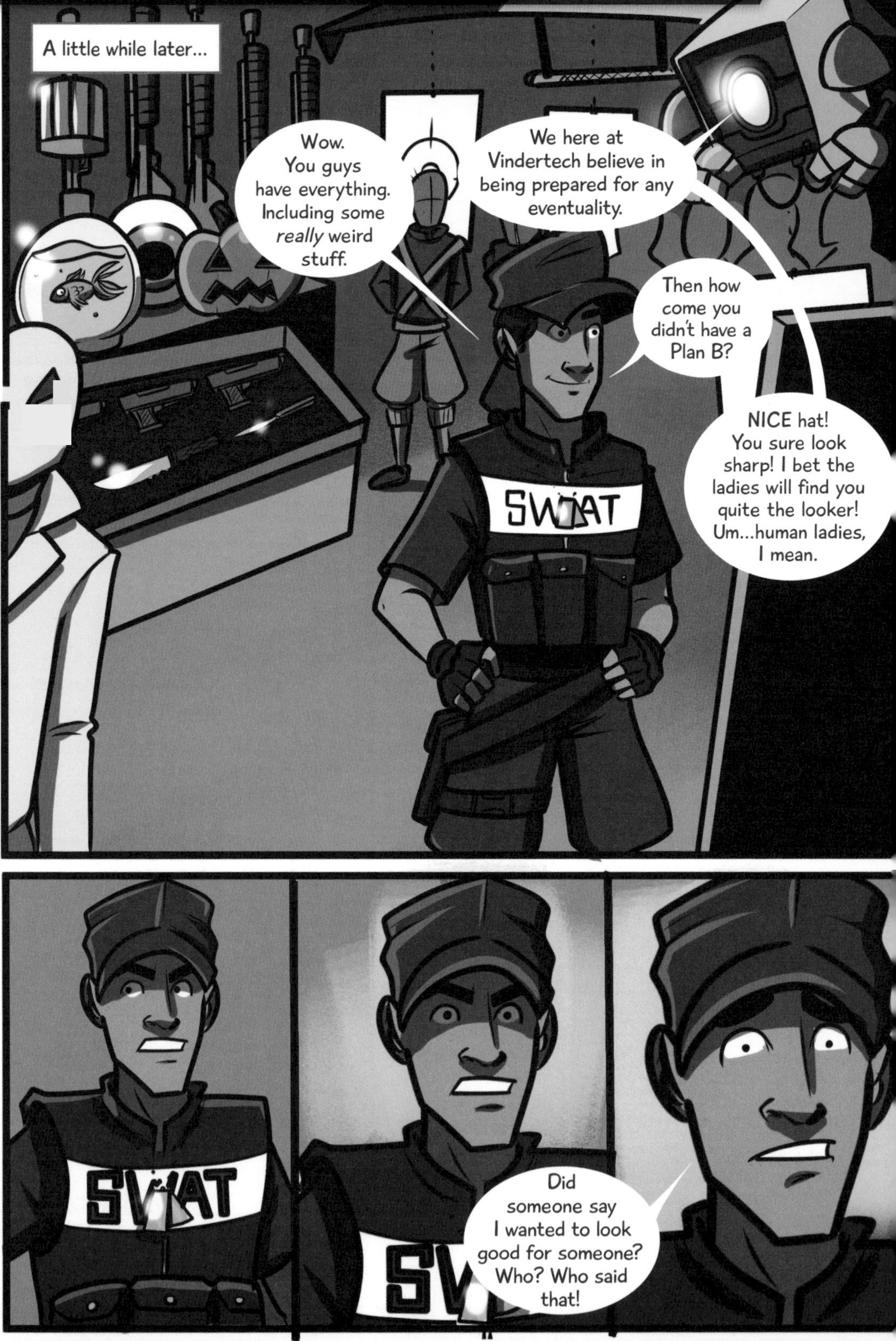

A little while later...
Wow. You guys have everything. Including some *really* weird stuff.
We here at Vindertech believe in being prepared for any eventuality.
Then how come you didn't have a Plan B?
NICE hat! You sure look sharp! I bet the ladies will find you quite the looker! Um...human ladies, I mean.
SWAT
Did someone say I wanted to look good for someone? Who? Who said that!

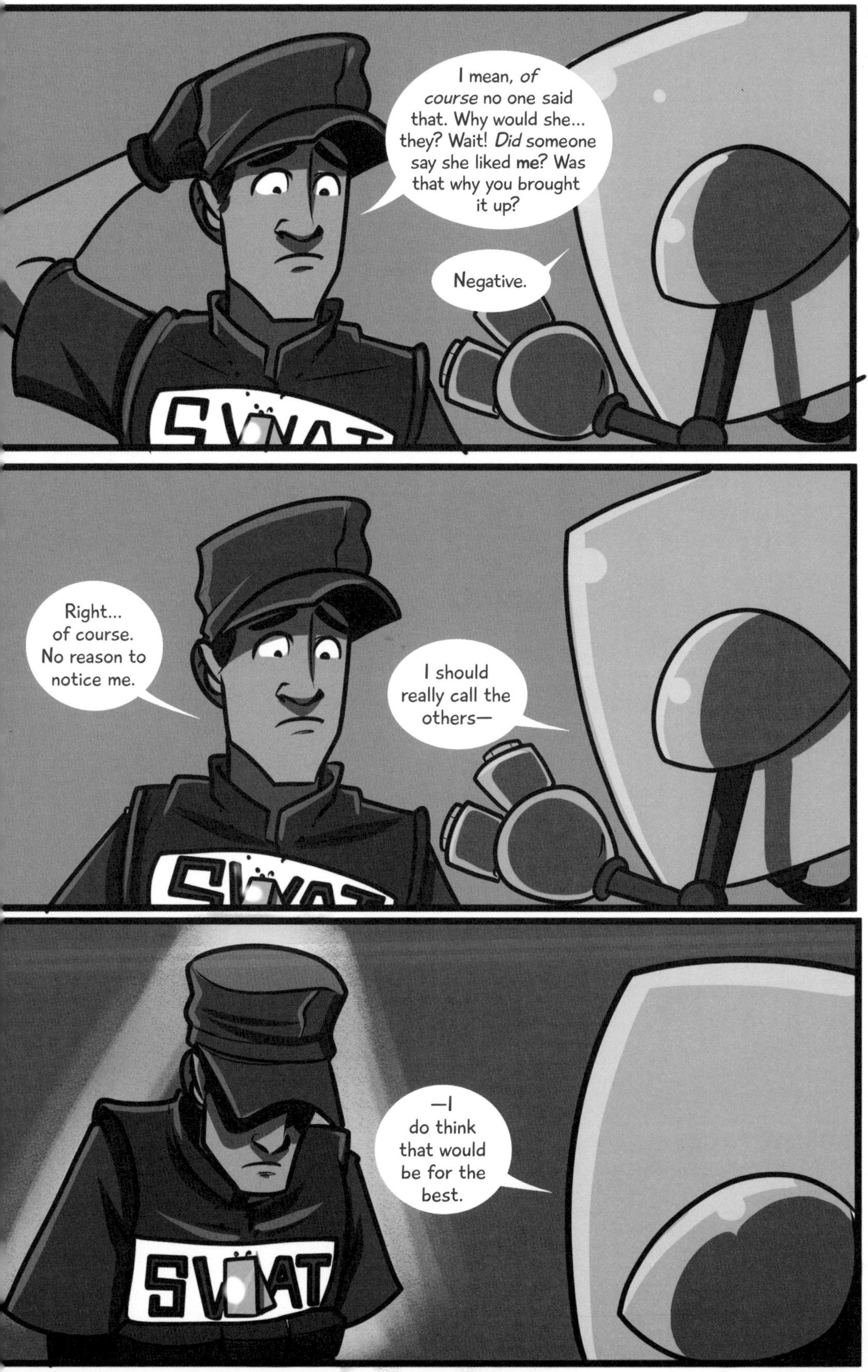
I mean, *of course* no one said that. Why would she... they? Wait! *Did* someone say she liked **me**? Was that why you brought it up?
Negative.
Right... of course. No reason to notice me.
I should really call the others—
SWAT
—I do think that would be for the best.
SWAT

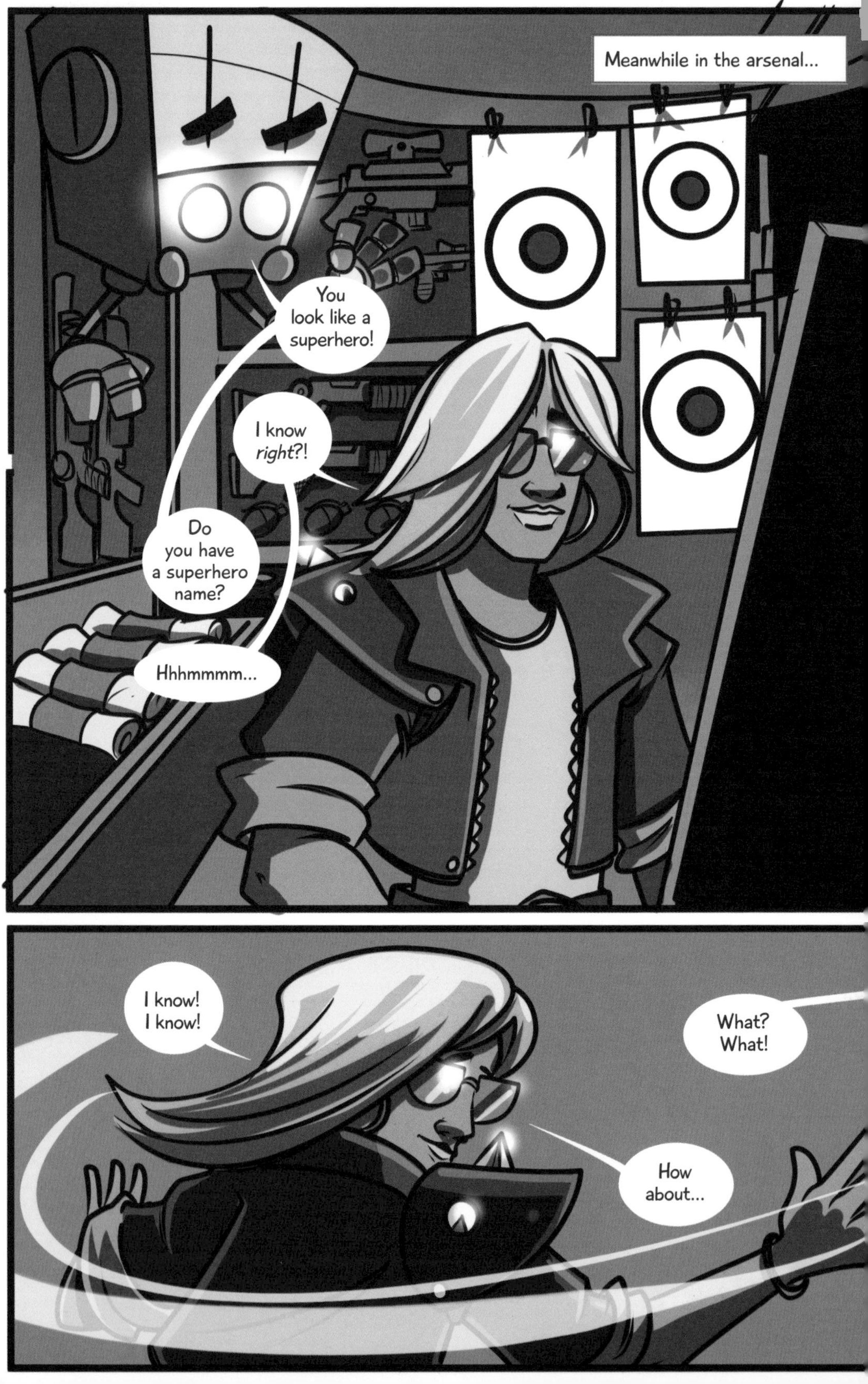
Meanwhile in the arsenal...
You look like a superhero!
I know *right*?!
Do you have a superhero name?
Hhhmmmm...
I know! I know!
What? What!
How about...

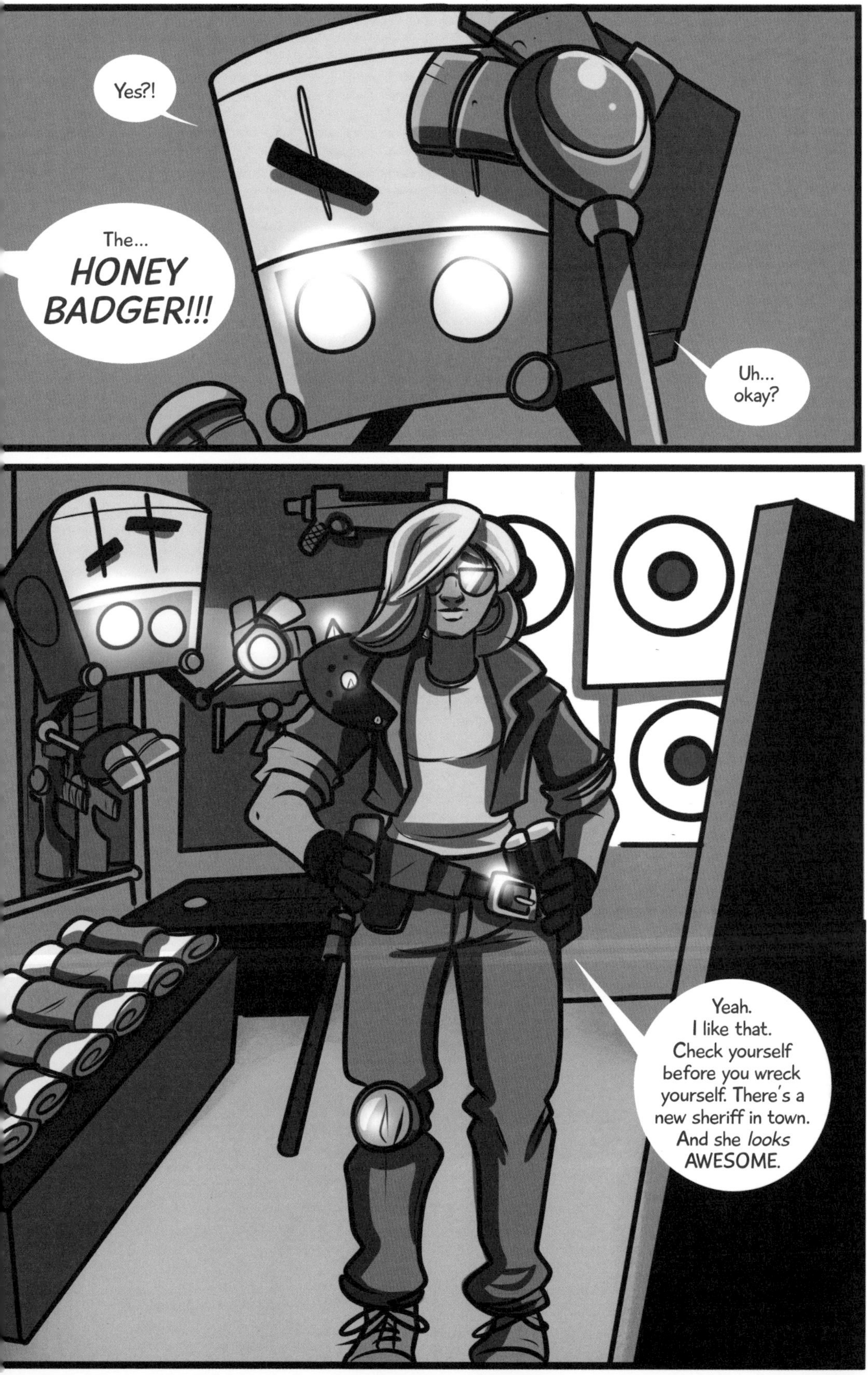

Yes?!
The... HONEY BADGER!!!
Uh... okay?
Yeah. I like that. Check yourself before you wreck yourself. There's a new sheriff in town. And she *looks* AWESOME.

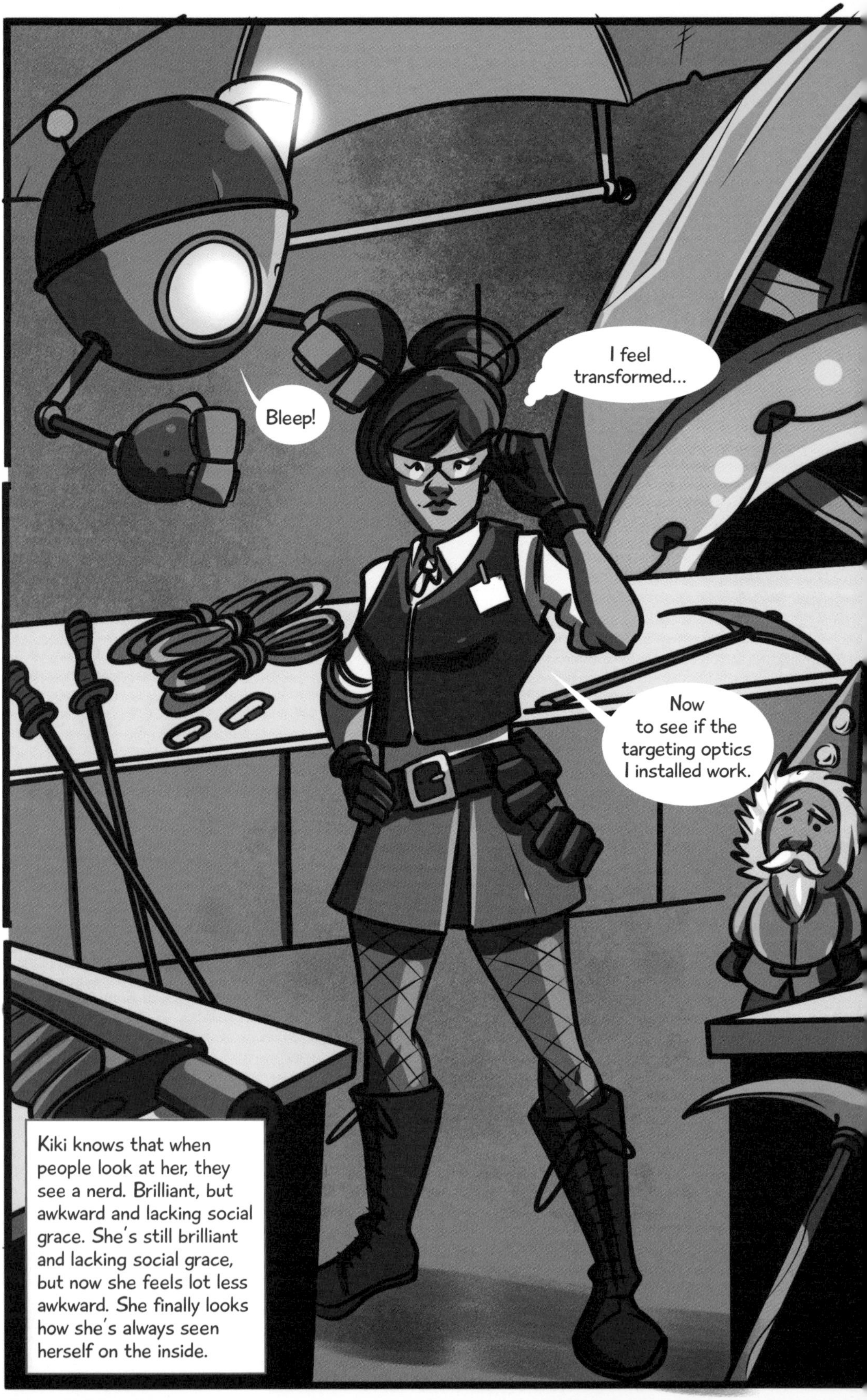
Bleep!
I feel transformed...
Now to see if the targeting optics I installed work.
Kiki knows that when people look at her, they see a nerd. Brilliant, but awkward and lacking social grace. She's still brilliant and lacking social grace, but now she feels lot less awkward. She finally looks how she's always seen herself on the inside.

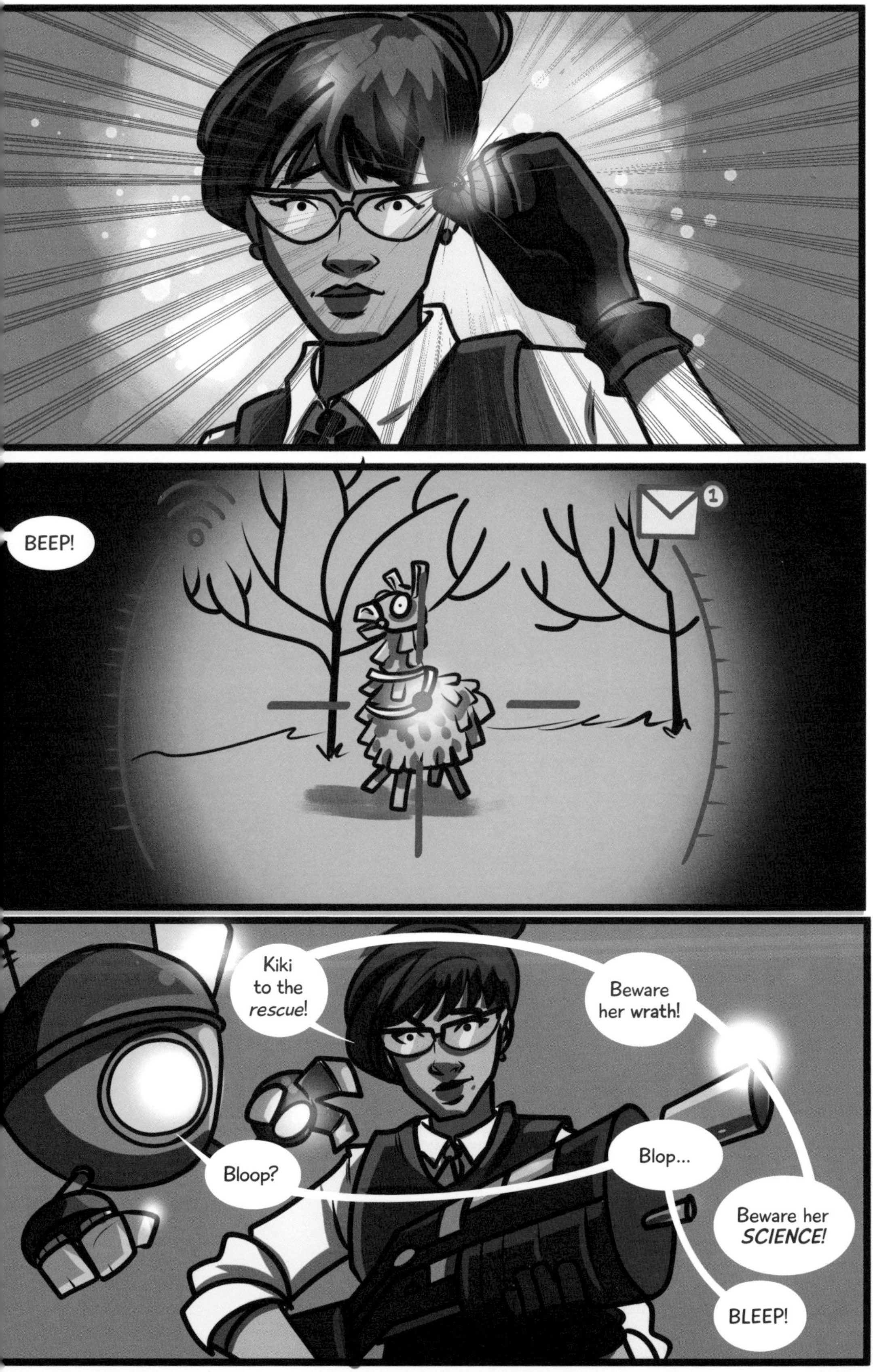
BEEP!
Kiki to the *rescue*!
Beware her wrath!
Bloop?
Blop...
Beware her *SCIENCE!*
BLEEP!

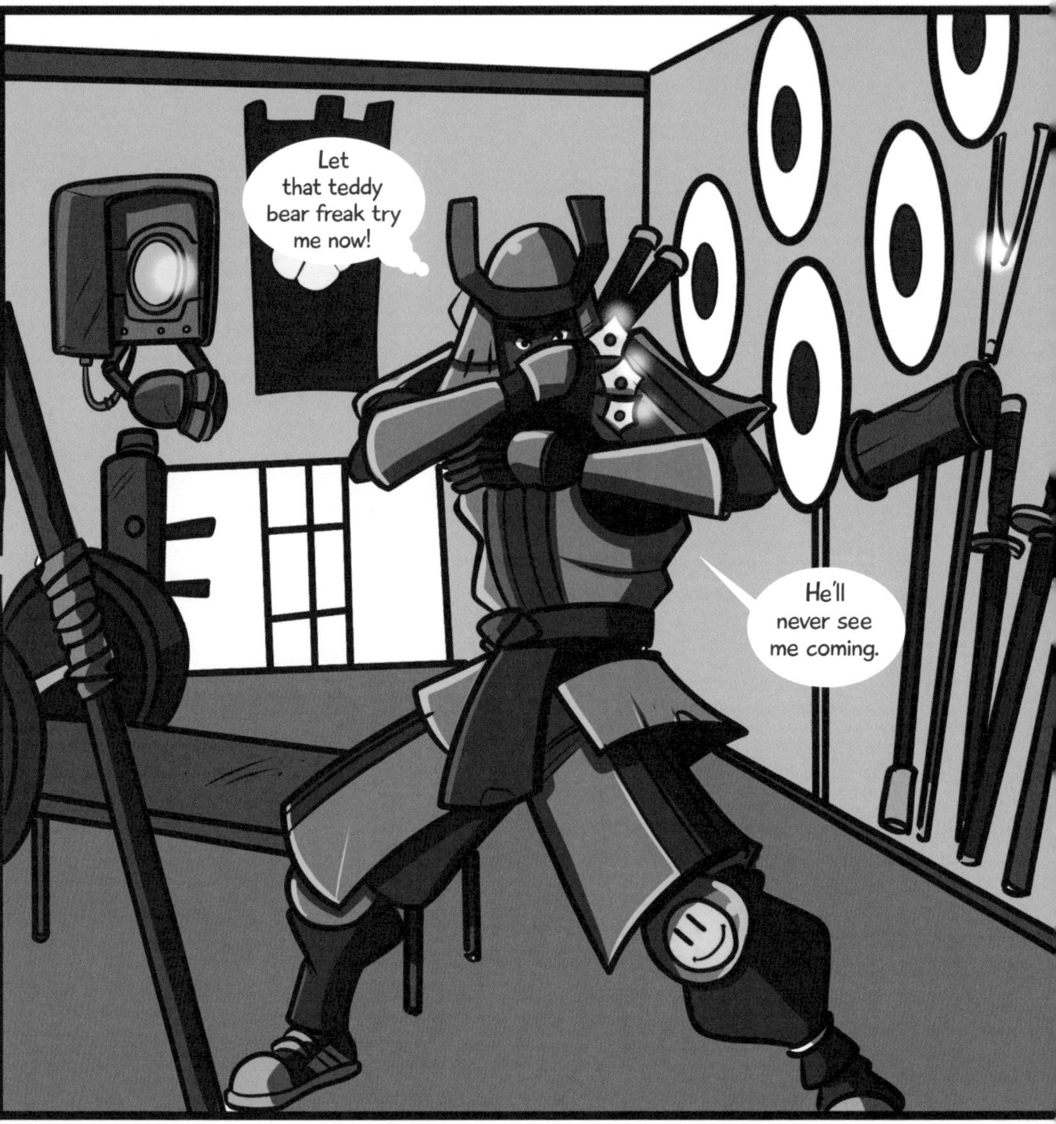
Let that teddy bear freak try me now!
He'll never see me coming.

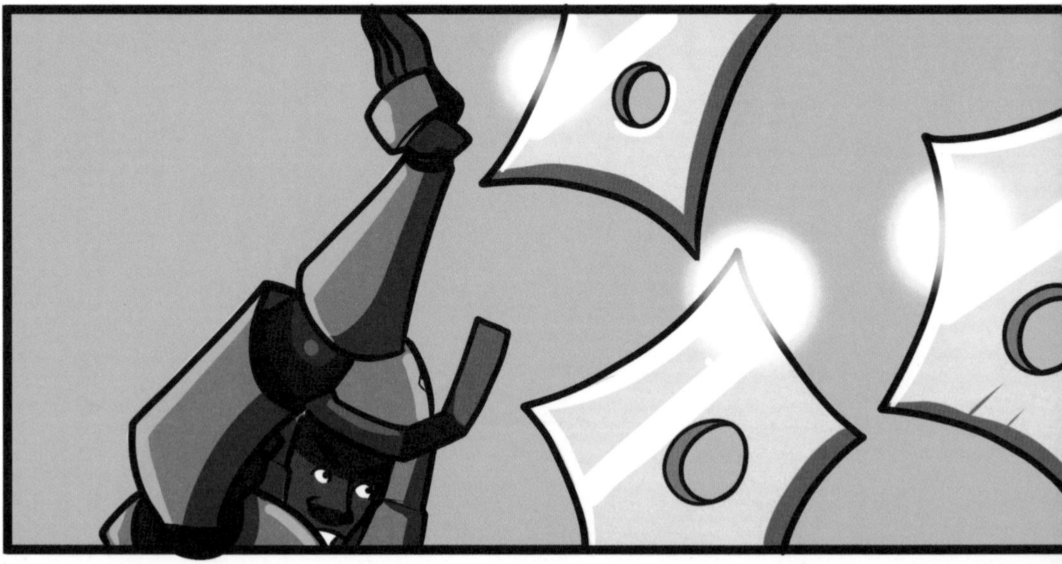

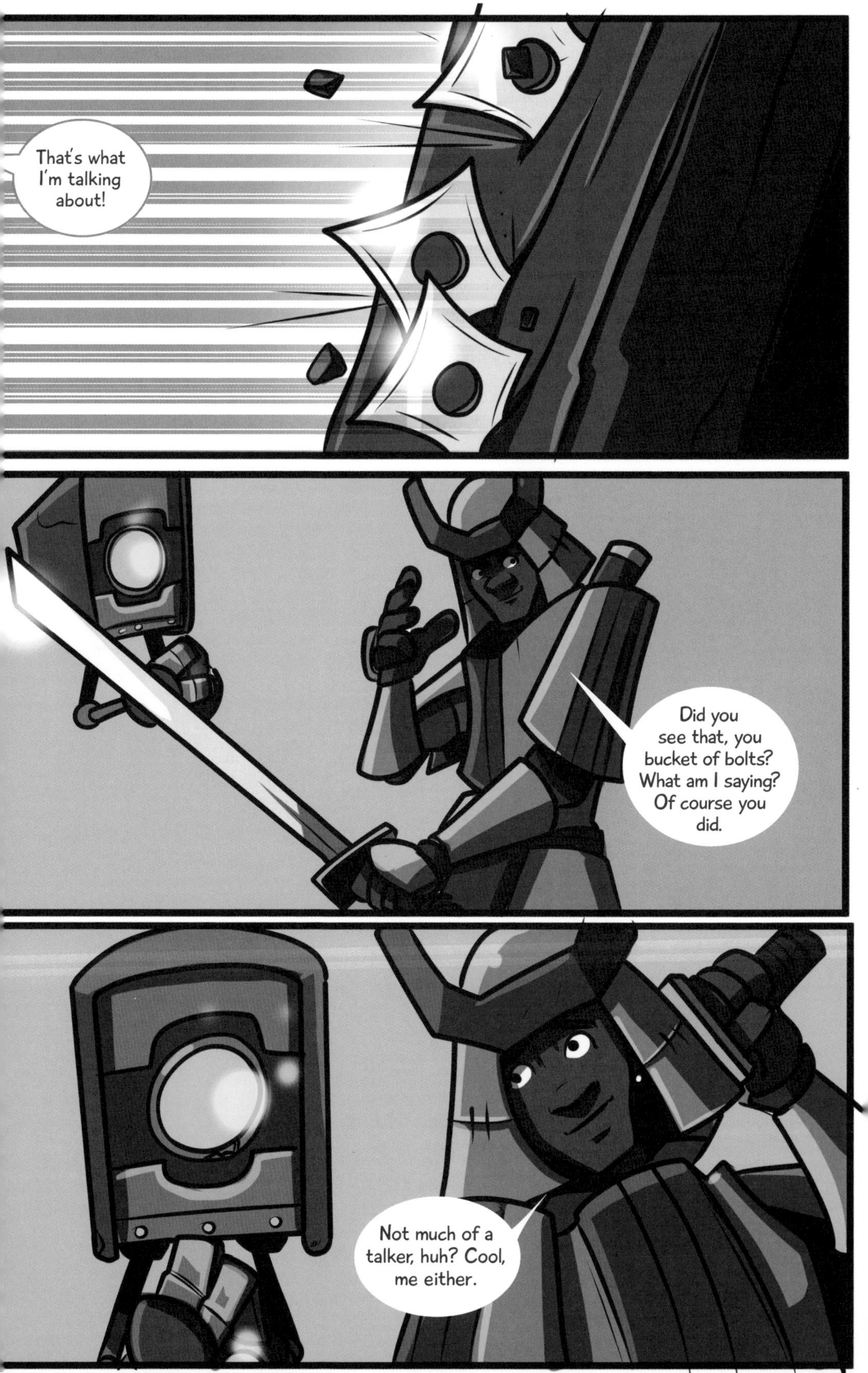
That's what I'm talking about!
Did you see that, you bucket of bolts? What am I saying? Of course you did.
Not much of a talker, huh? Cool, me either.

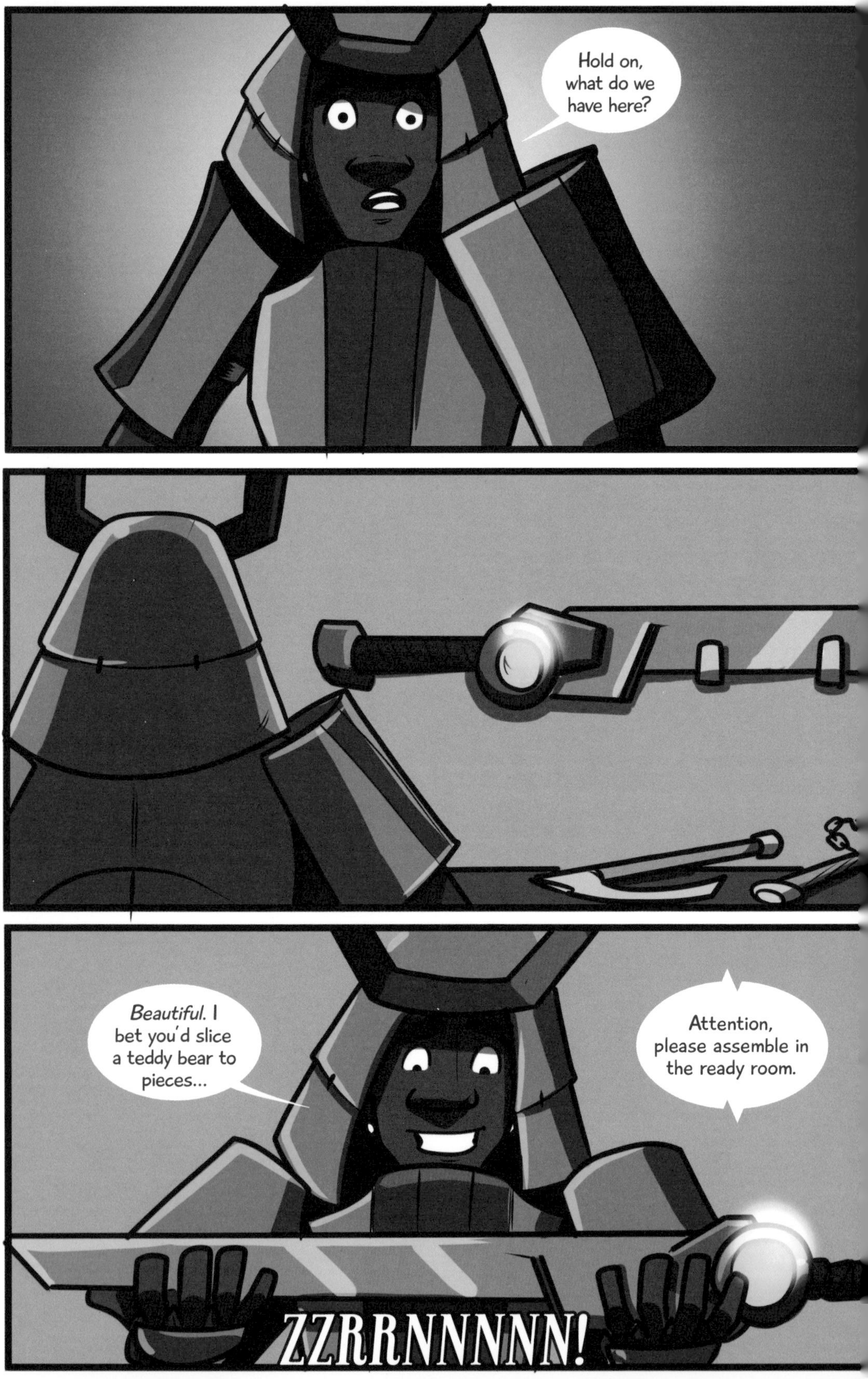
Hold on, what do we have here?
Beautiful. I bet you'd slice a teddy bear to pieces...
Attention, please assemble in the ready room.
ZZRRNNNNN!

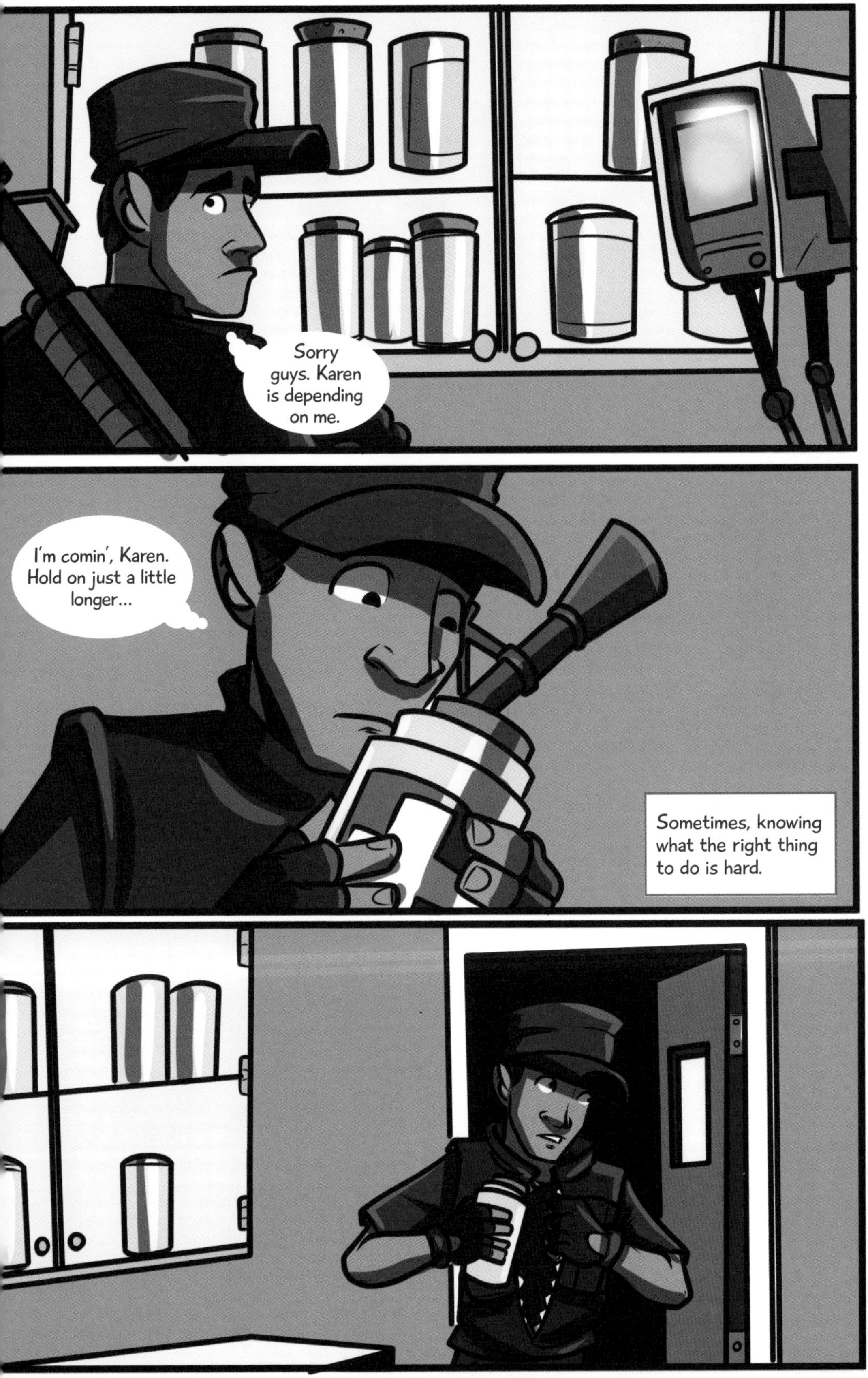
Sorry guys. Karen is depending on me.
I'm comin', Karen. Hold on just a little longer...
Sometimes, knowing what the right thing to do is hard.

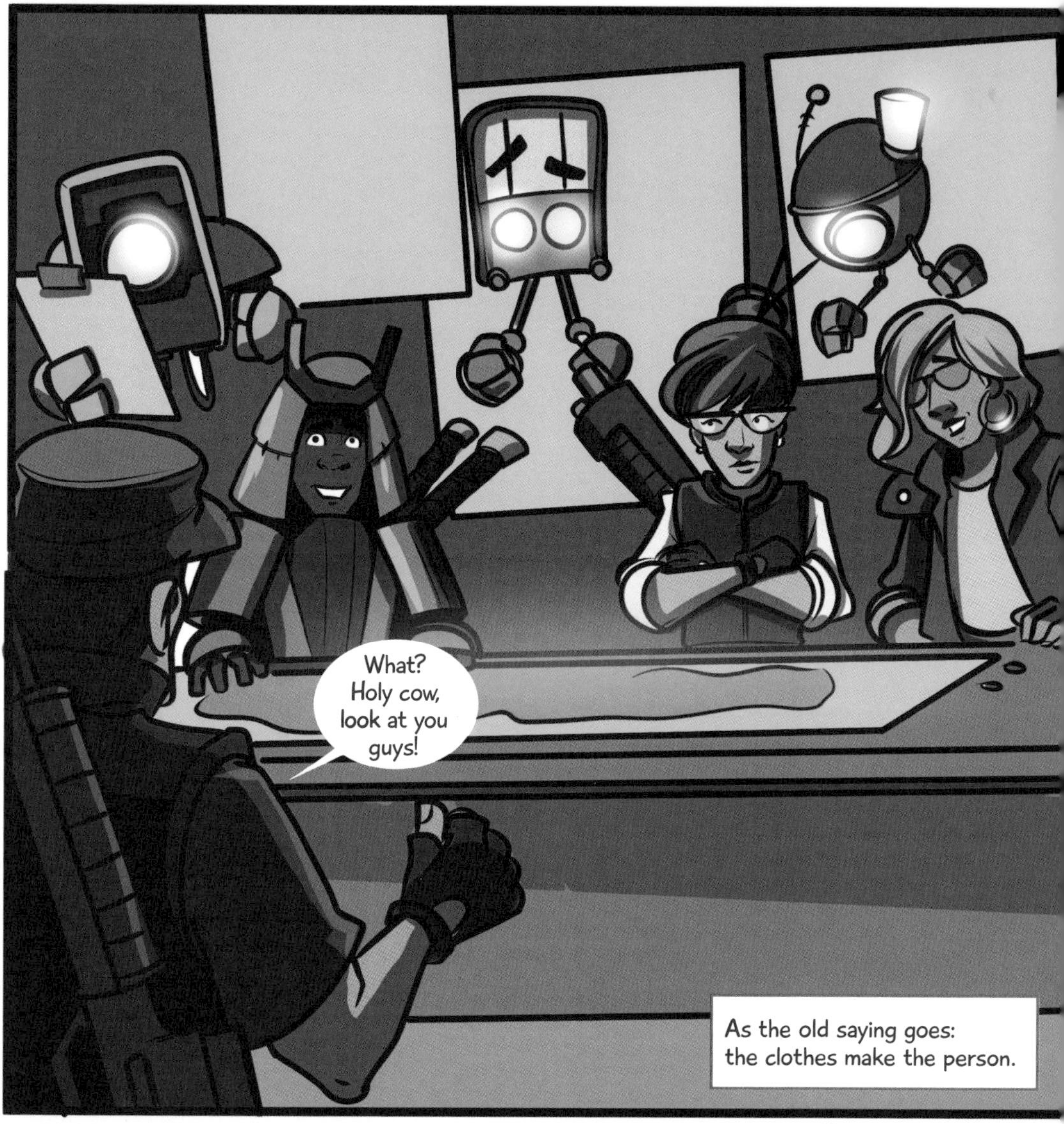
What? Holy cow, look at you guys!
As the old saying goes: the clothes make the person.

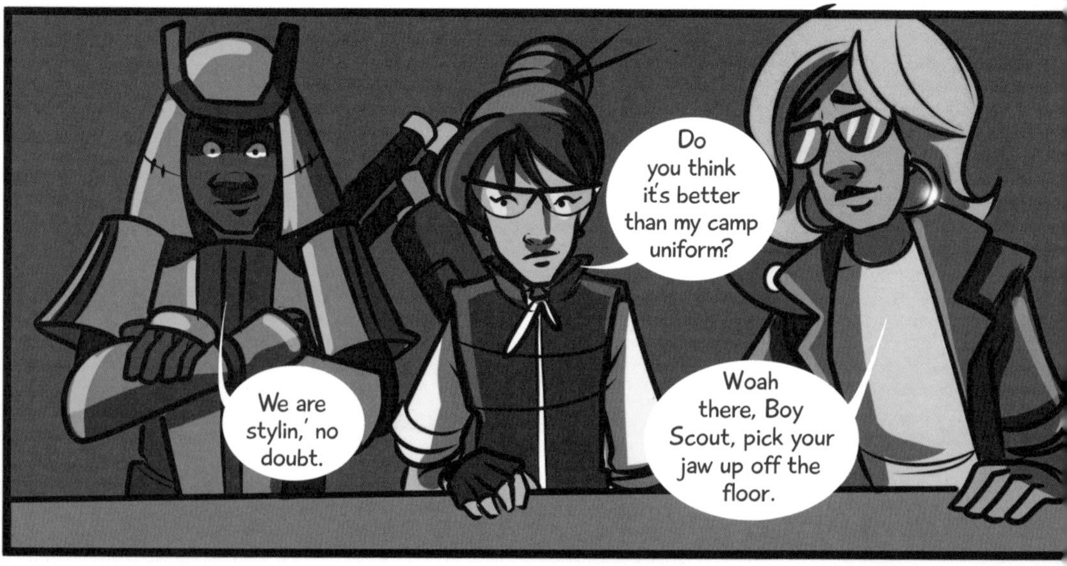
We are stylin,' no doubt.
Do you think it's better than my camp uniform?
Woah there, Boy Scout, pick your jaw up off the floor.

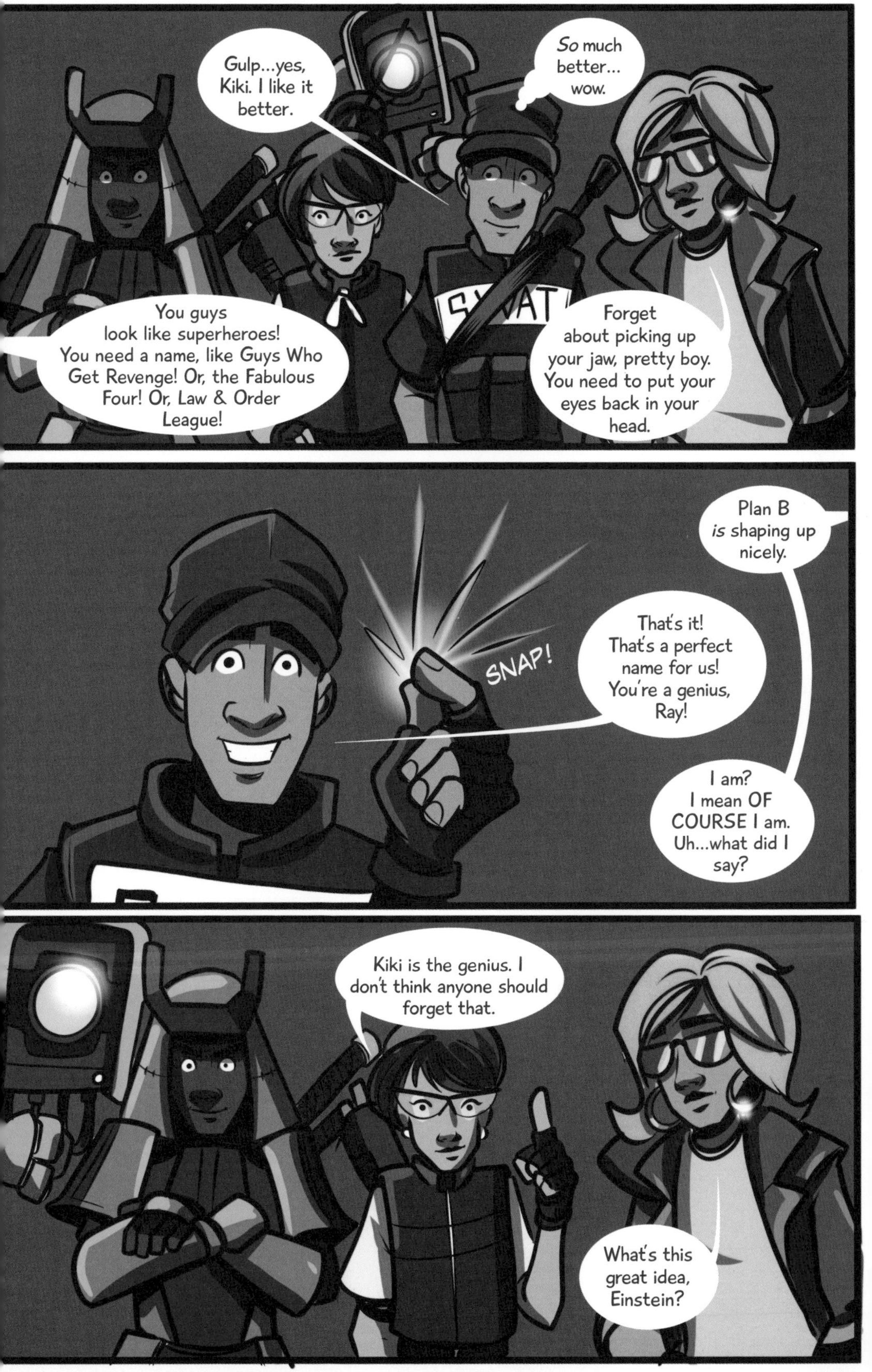
Gulp...yes, Kiki. I like it better.
So much better... wow.
You guys look like superheroes! You need a name, like Guys Who Get Revenge! Or, the Fabulous Four! Or, Law & Order League!
Forget about picking up your jaw, pretty boy. You need to put your eyes back in your head.
SWAT
Plan B is shaping up nicely.
SNAP!
That's it! That's a perfect name for us! You're a genius, Ray!
I am? I mean OF COURSE I am. Uh...what did I say?
Kiki is the genius. I don't think anyone should forget that.
What's this great idea, Einstein?

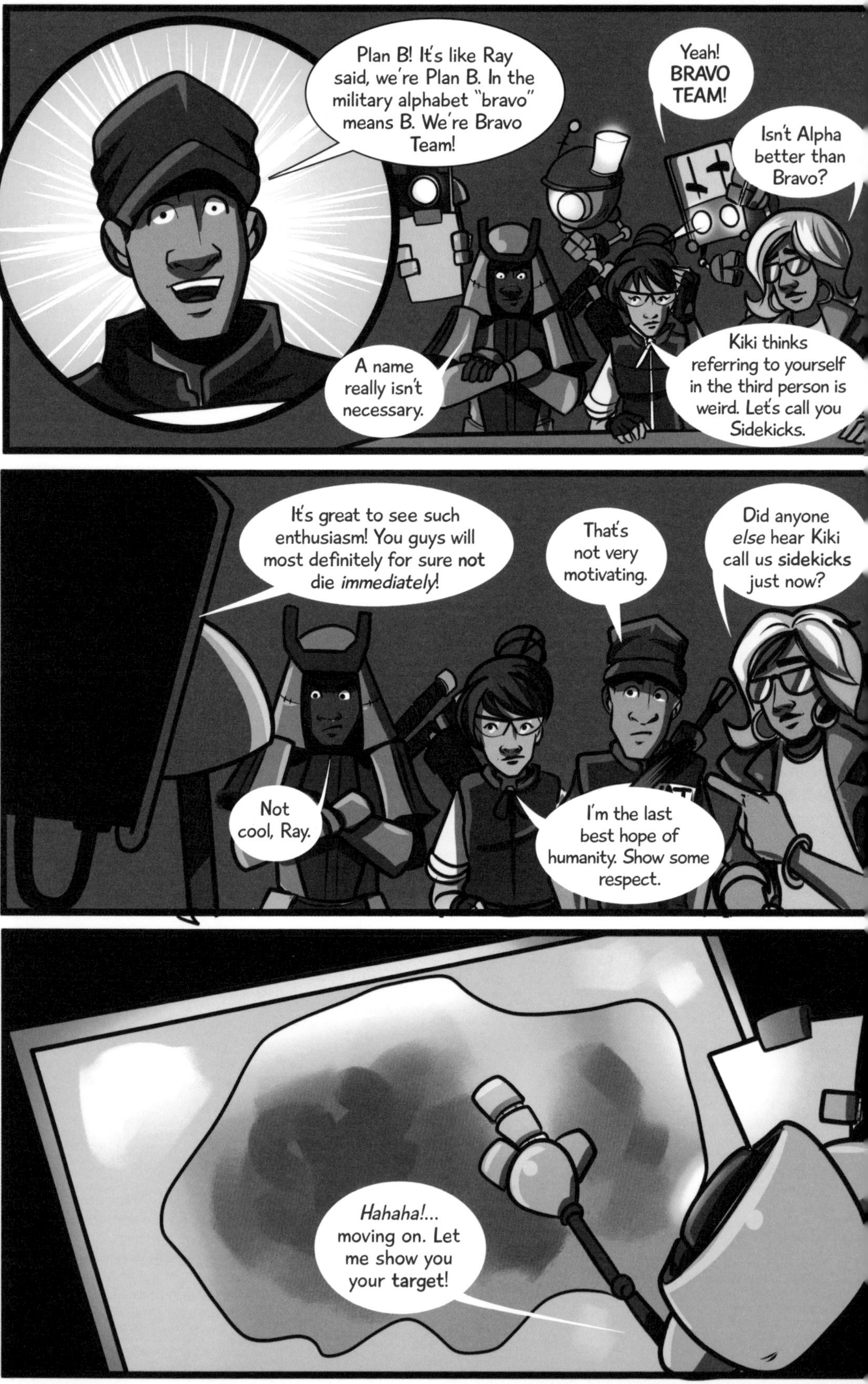
Plan B! It's like Ray said, we're Plan B. In the military alphabet "bravo" means B. We're Bravo Team!
Yeah! BRAVO TEAM!
Isn't Alpha better than Bravo?
A name really isn't necessary.
Kiki thinks referring to yourself in the third person is weird. Let's call you Sidekicks.
It's great to see such enthusiasm! You guys will most definitely for sure not die *immediately*!
That's not very motivating.
Did anyone *else* hear Kiki call us sidekicks just now?
Not cool, Ray.
I'm the last best hope of humanity. Show some respect.
Hahaha!... moving on. Let me show you your target!

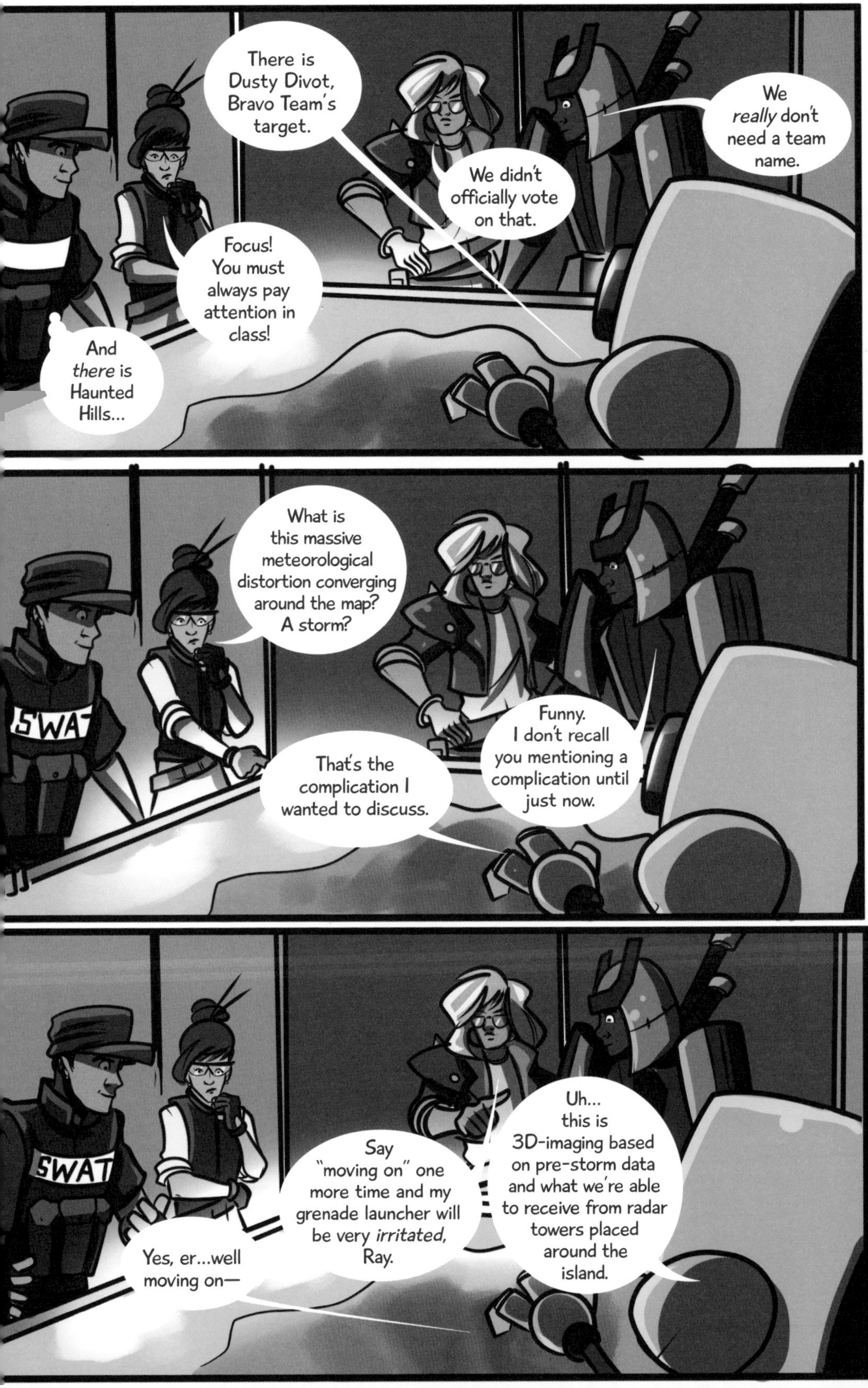
There is Dusty Divot, Bravo Team's target.
We didn't officially vote on that.
We *really* don't need a team name.
Focus! You must always pay attention in class!
And *there* is Haunted Hills...
What is this massive meteorological distortion converging around the map? A storm?
SWAT
That's the complication I wanted to discuss.
Funny. I don't recall you mentioning a complication until just now.
SWAT
Uh... this is 3D-imaging based on pre-storm data and what we're able to receive from radar towers placed around the island.
Yes, er...well moving on—
Say "moving on" one more time and my grenade launcher will be very *irritated,* Ray.

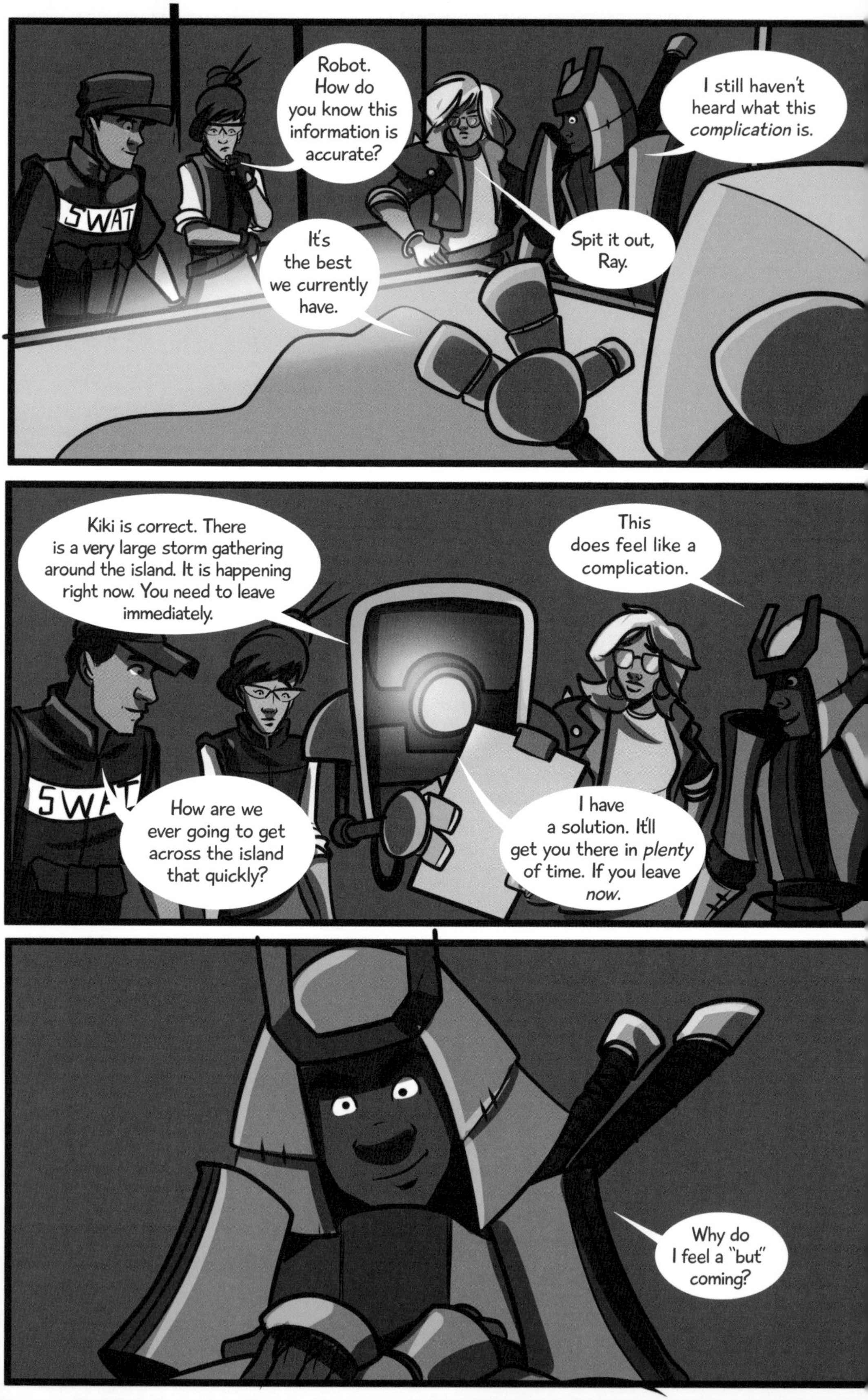
SWAT
Robot. How do you know this information is accurate?
I still haven't heard what this *complication* is.
It's the best we currently have.
Spit it out, Ray.
Kiki is correct. There is a very large storm gathering around the island. It is happening right now. You need to leave immediately.
This does feel like a complication.
SWAT
How are we ever going to get across the island that quickly?
I have a solution. It'll get you there in *plenty* of time. If you leave *now*.
Why do I feel a "but" coming?

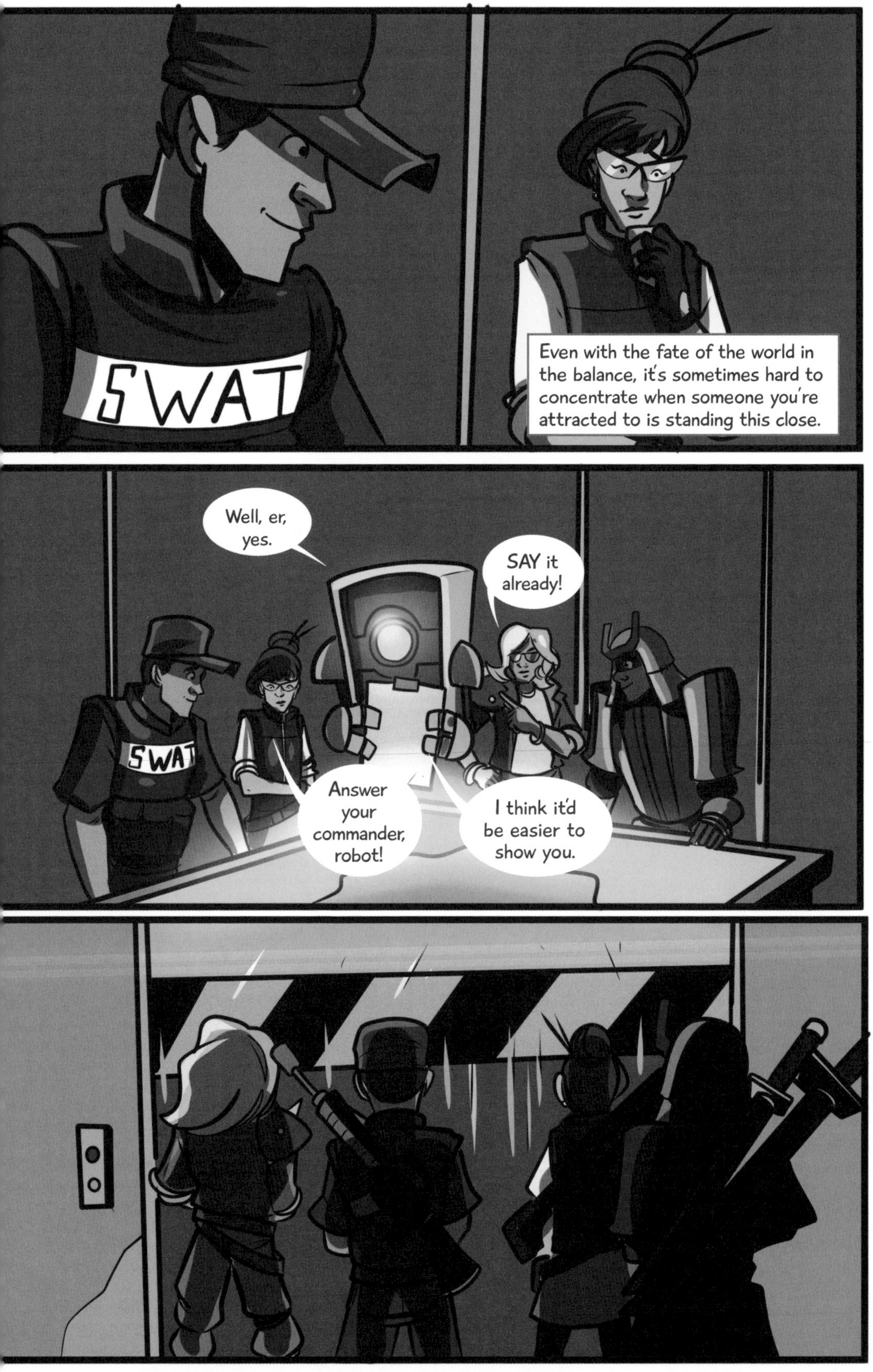
Even with the fate of the world in the balance, it's sometimes hard to concentrate when someone you're attracted to is standing this close.
SWAT
Well, er, yes.
SAY it already!
SWAT
Answer your commander, robot!
I think it'd be easier to show you.

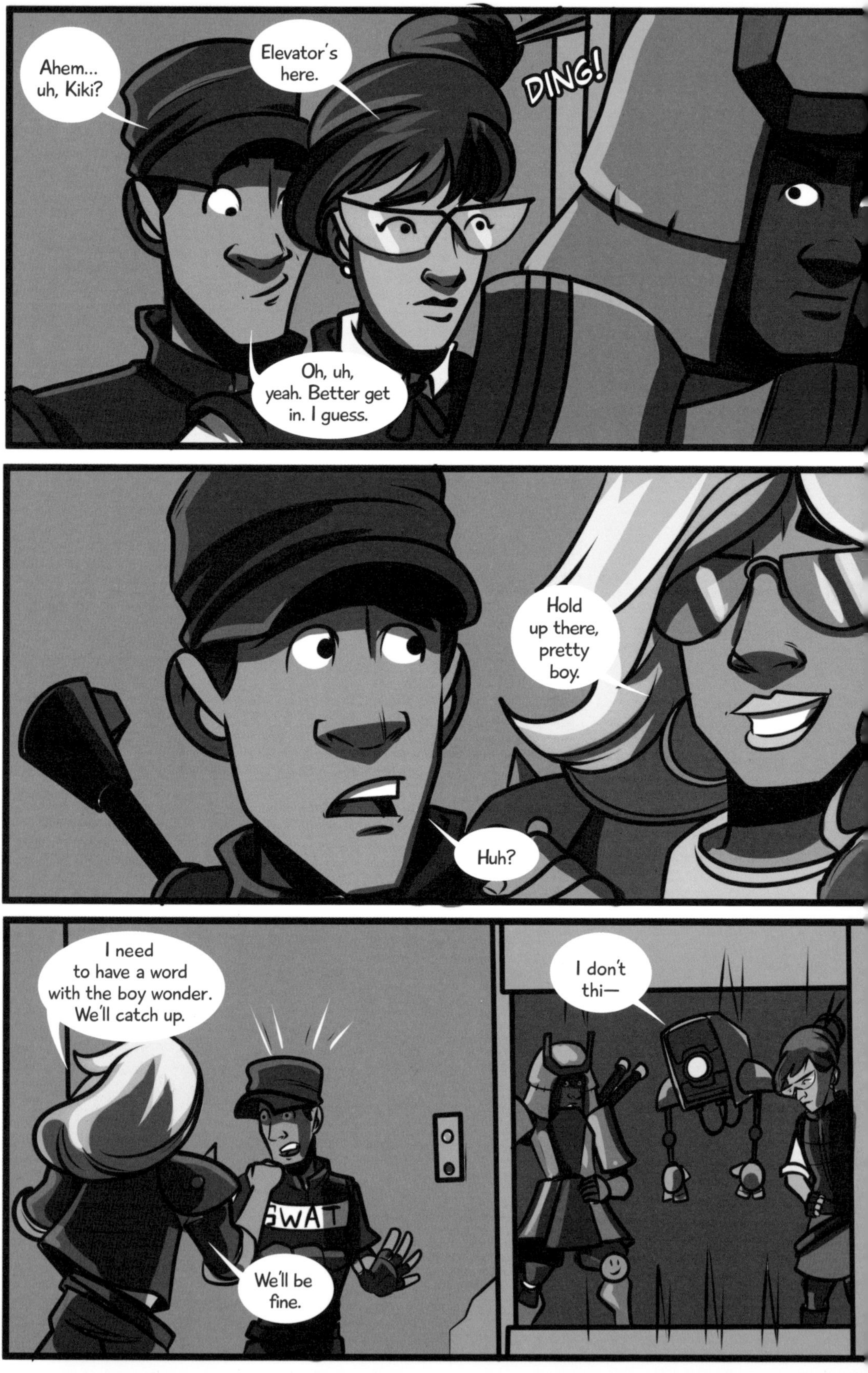
Ahem... uh, Kiki?
Elevator's here.
DING!
Oh, uh, yeah. Better get in. I guess.
Hold up there, pretty boy.
Huh?
I need to have a word with the boy wonder. We'll catch up.
SWAT
We'll be fine.
I don't thi—

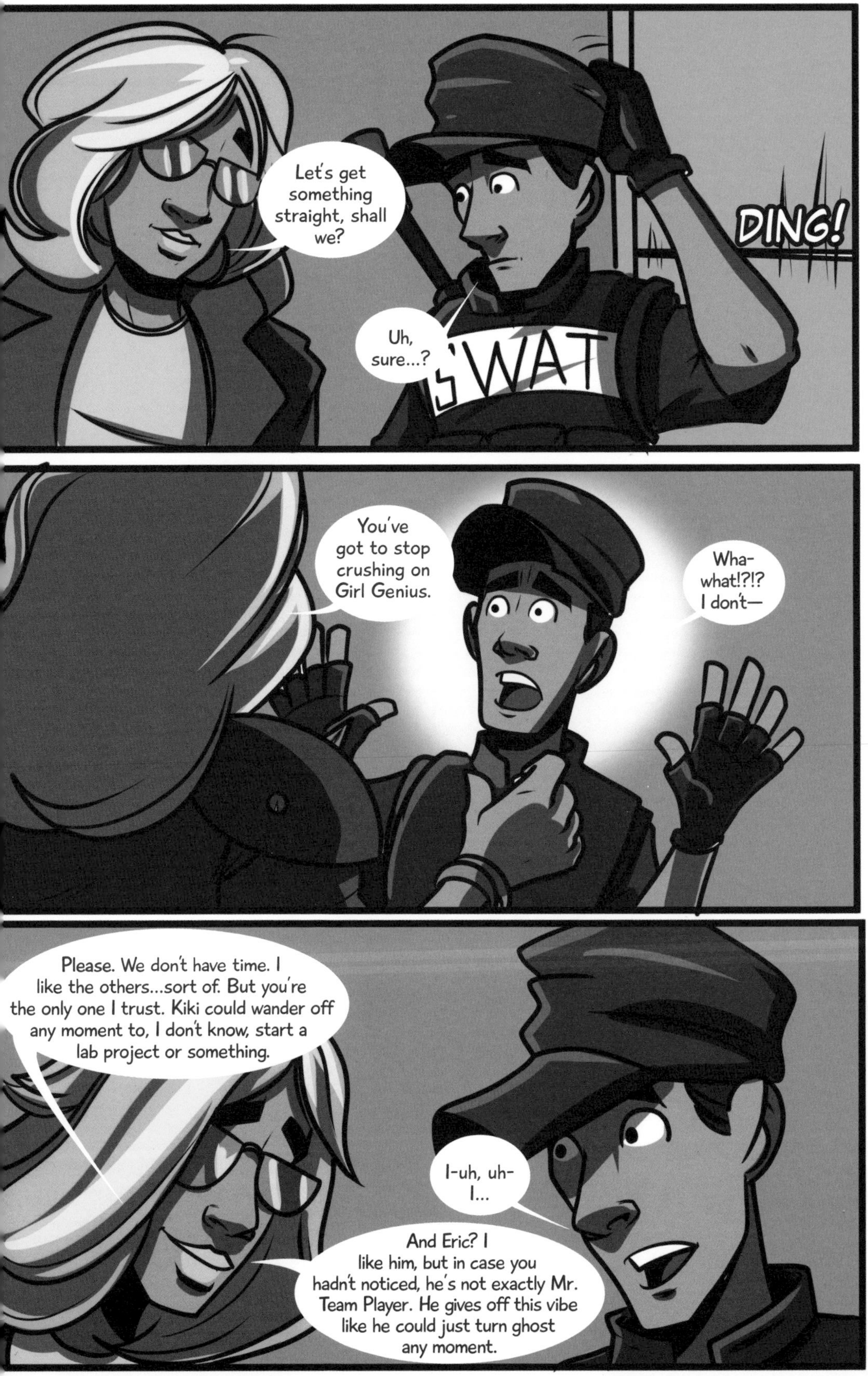
Let's get something straight, shall we?
Uh, sure...?
DING!
SWAT
You've got to stop crushing on Girl Genius.
Wha-what!?!? I don't—
Please. We don't have time. I like the others...sort of. But you're the only one I trust. Kiki could wander off any moment to, I don't know, start a lab project or something.
I-uh, uh-I...
And Eric? I like him, but in case you hadn't noticed, he's not exactly Mr. Team Player. He gives off this vibe like he could just turn ghost any moment.

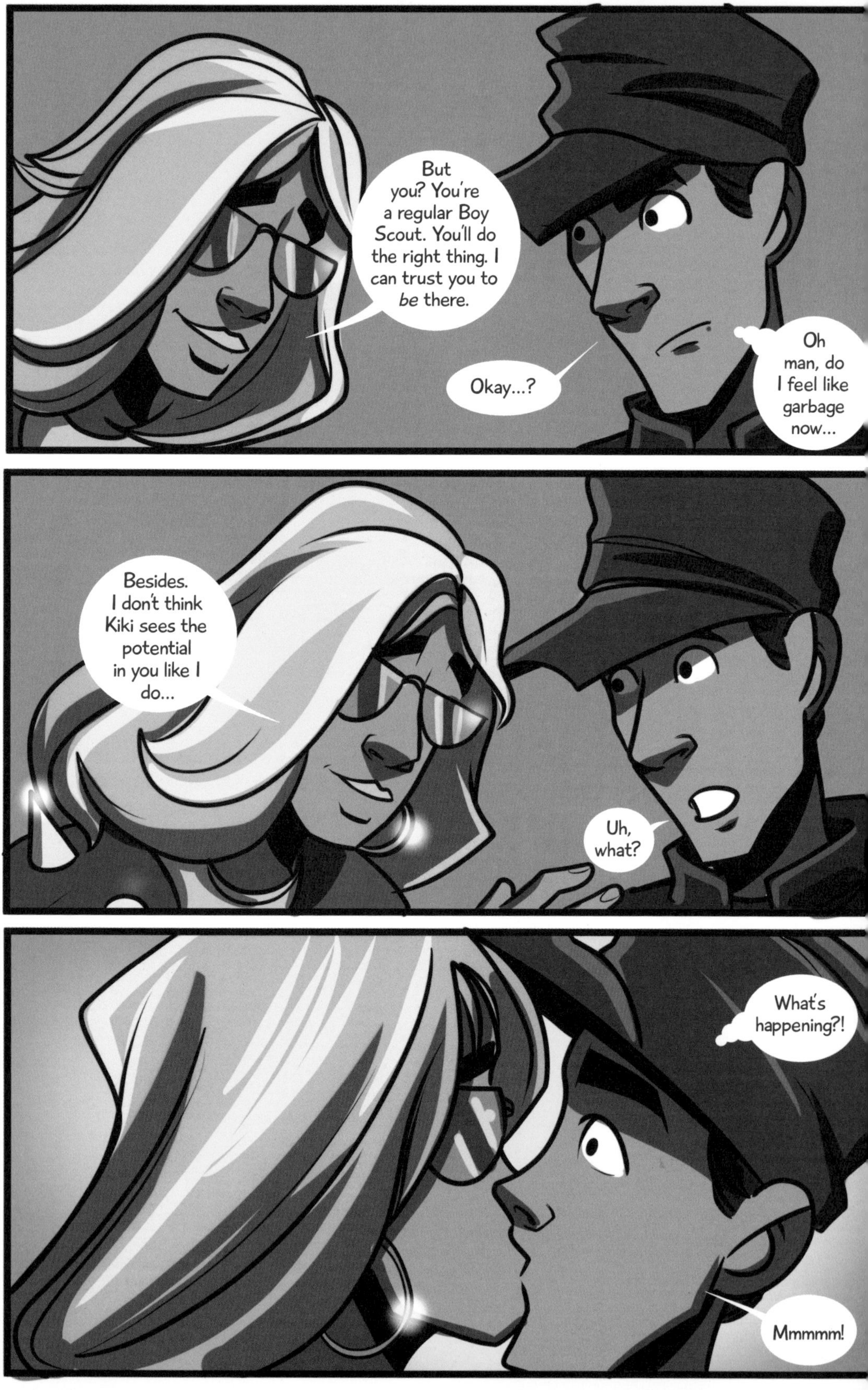
But you? You're a regular Boy Scout. You'll do the right thing. I can trust you to *be* there.
Okay...?
Oh man, do I feel like garbage now...
Besides. I don't think Kiki sees the potential in you like I do...
Uh, what?
What's happening?!
Mmmmm!

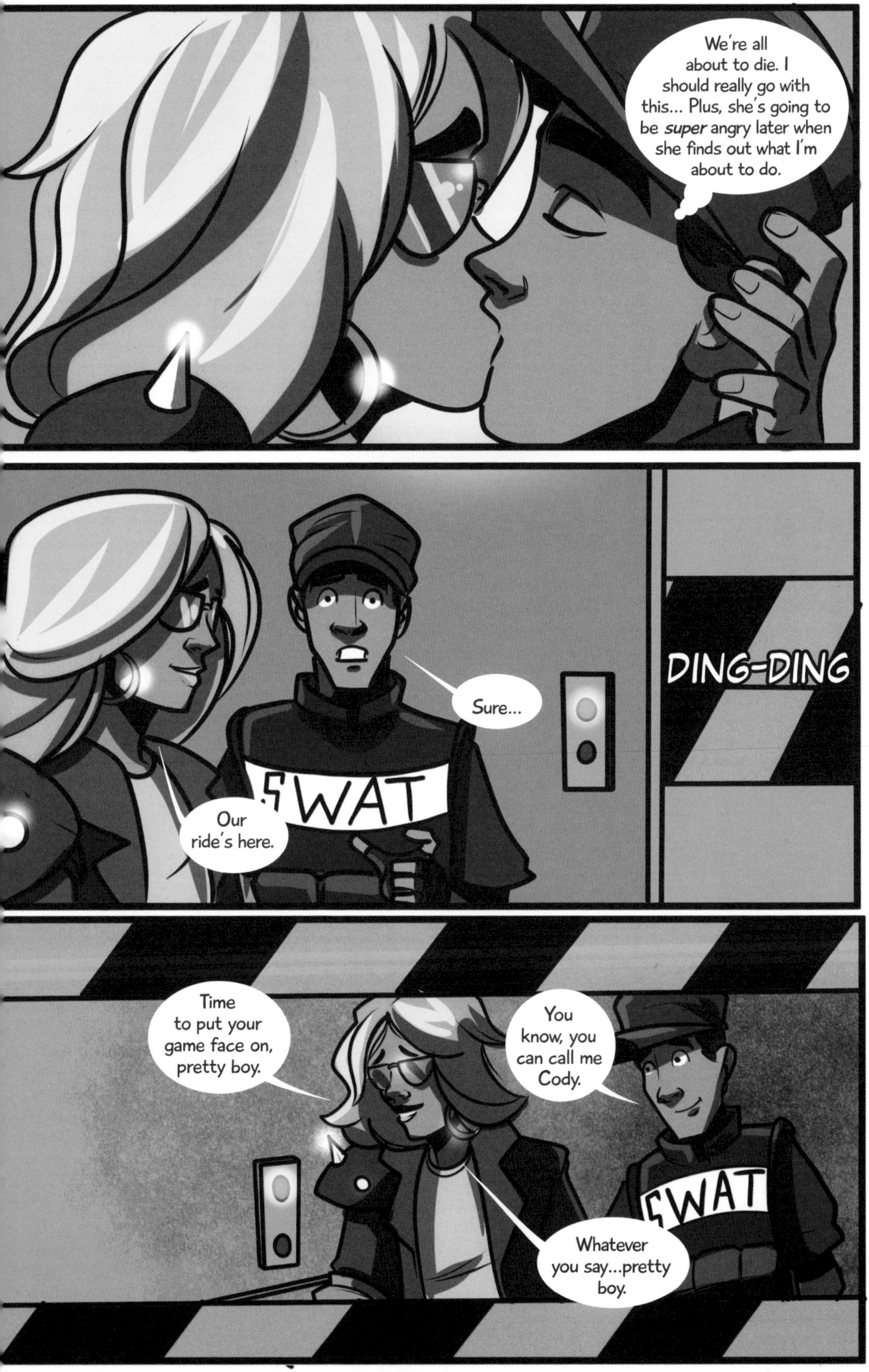
We're all about to die. I should really go with this... Plus, she's going to be *super* angry later when she finds out what I'm about to do.
DING-DING
Sure...
Our ride's here.
Time to put your game face on, pretty boy.
You know, you can call me Cody.
Whatever you say...pretty boy.
SWAT

CHAPTER 9: BETRAYAL

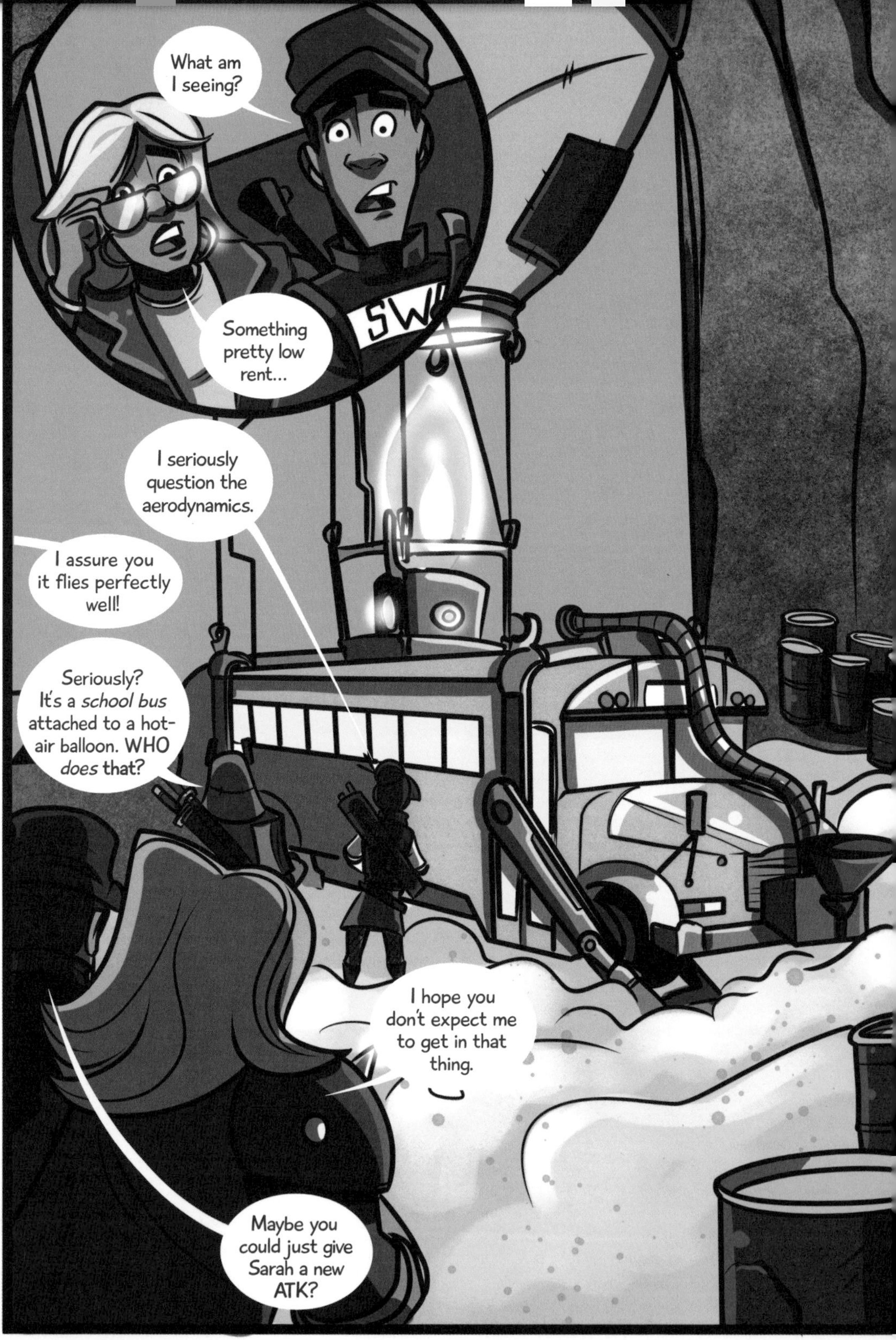

SW
What am I seeing?
Something pretty low rent...
I seriously question the aerodynamics.
I assure you it flies perfectly well!
Seriously? It's a *school bus* attached to a hot-air balloon. WHO *does* that?
I hope you don't expect me to get in that thing.
Maybe you could just give Sarah a new ATK?

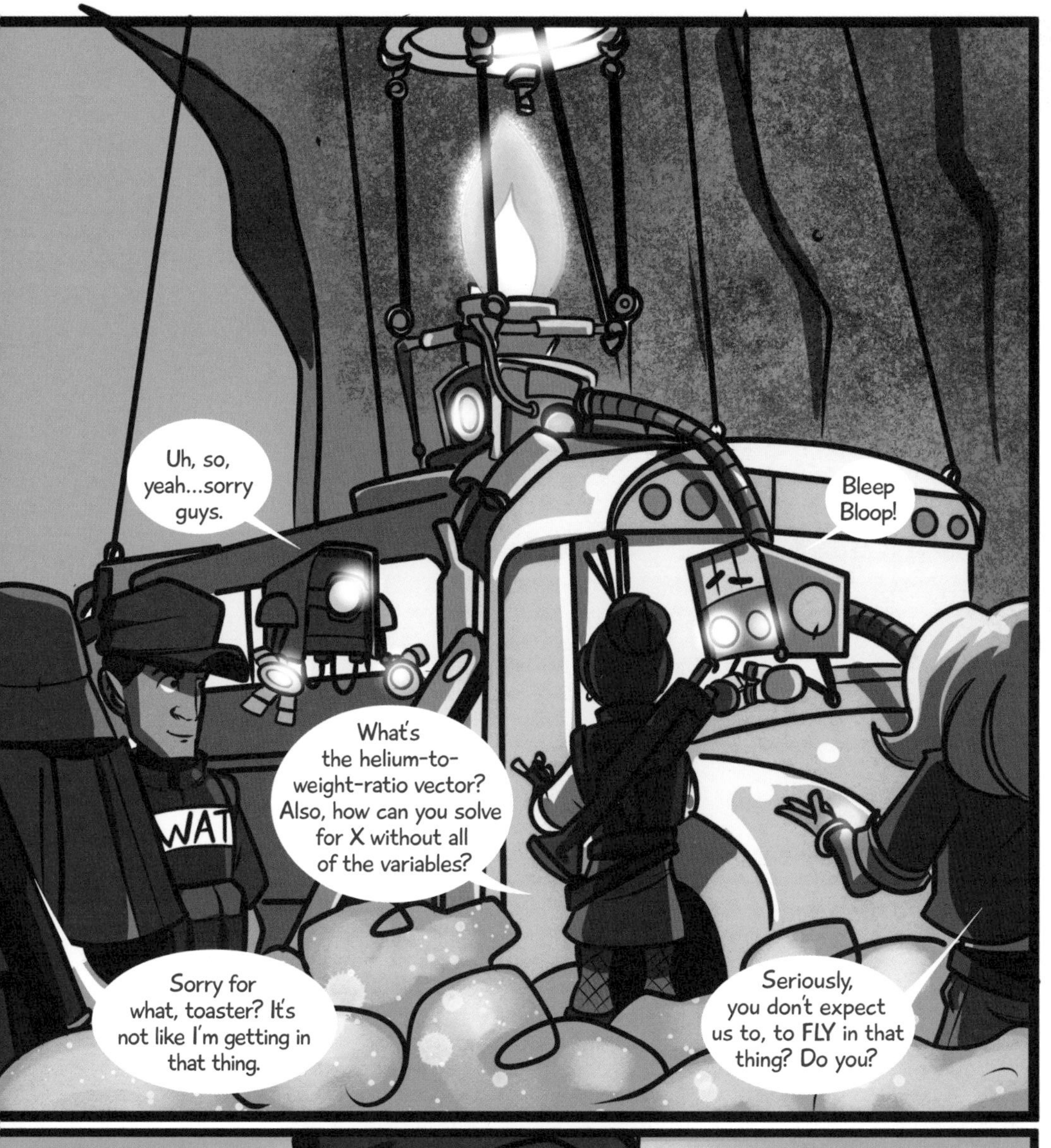
Uh, so, yeah...sorry guys.
Bleep Bloop!
What's the helium-to-weight-ratio vector? Also, how can you solve for X without all of the variables?
Sorry for what, toaster? It's not like I'm getting in that thing.
Seriously, you don't expect us to, to FLY in that thing? Do you?
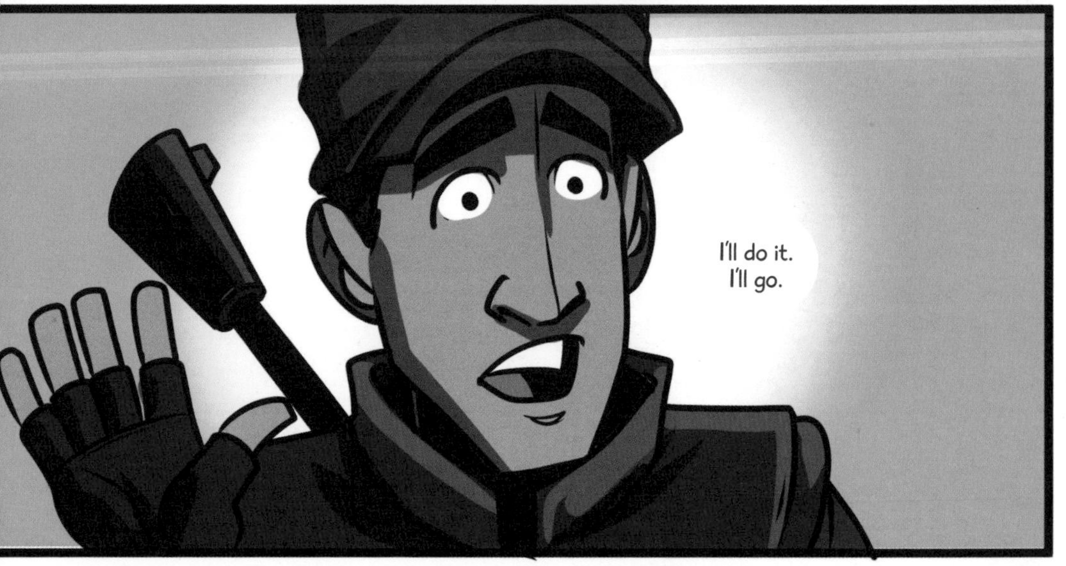
I'll do it. I'll go.

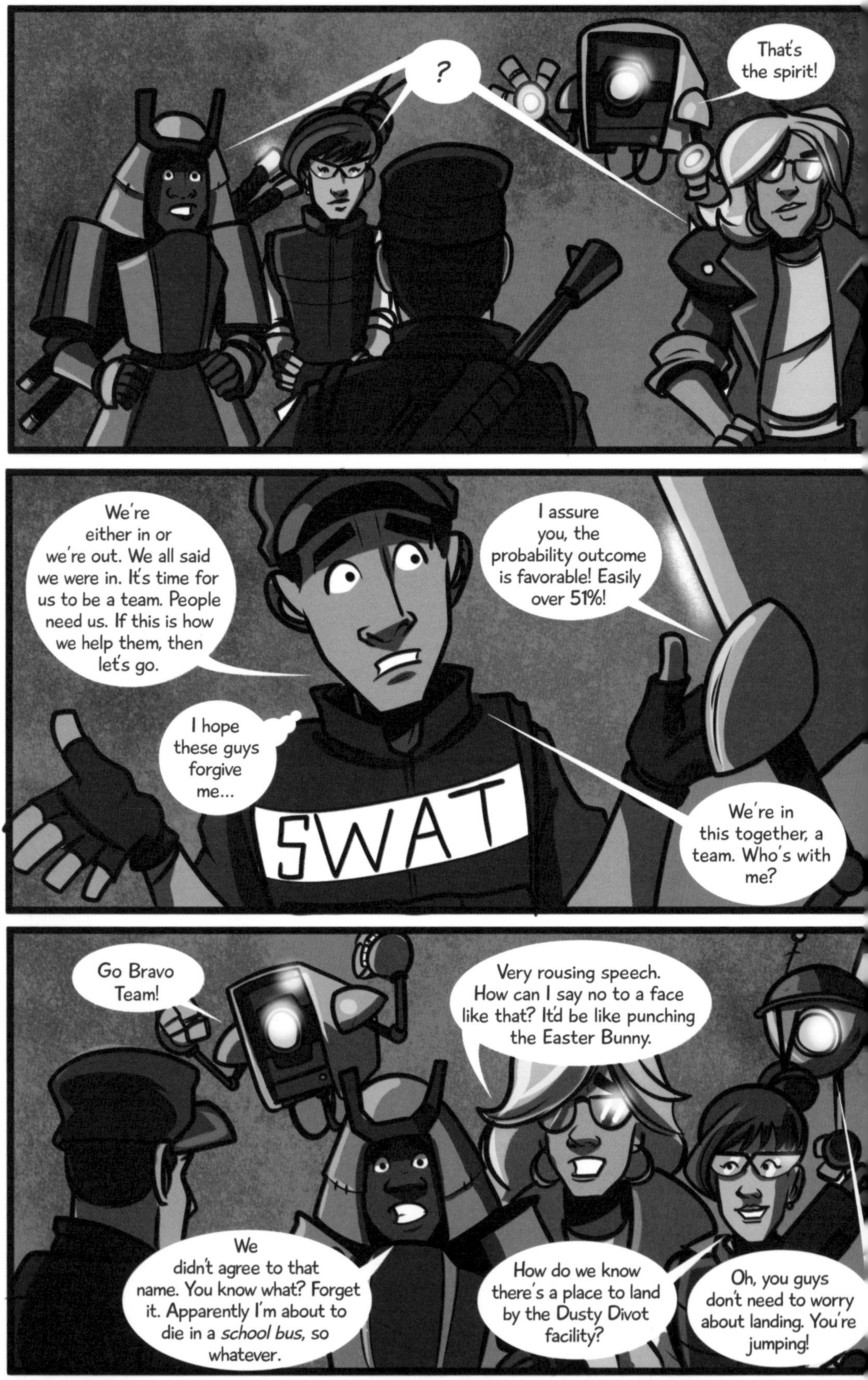
?
That's the spirit!
We're either in or we're out. We all said we were in. It's time for us to be a team. People need us. If this is how we help them, then let's go.
I assure you, the probability outcome is favorable! Easily over 51%!
I hope these guys forgive me...
SWAT
We're in this together, a team. Who's with me?
Go Bravo Team!
Very rousing speech. How can I say no to a face like that? It'd be like punching the Easter Bunny.
We didn't agree to that name. You know what? Forget it. Apparently I'm about to die in a *school bus*, so whatever.
How do we know there's a place to land by the Dusty Divot facility?
Oh, you guys don't need to worry about landing. You're jumping!

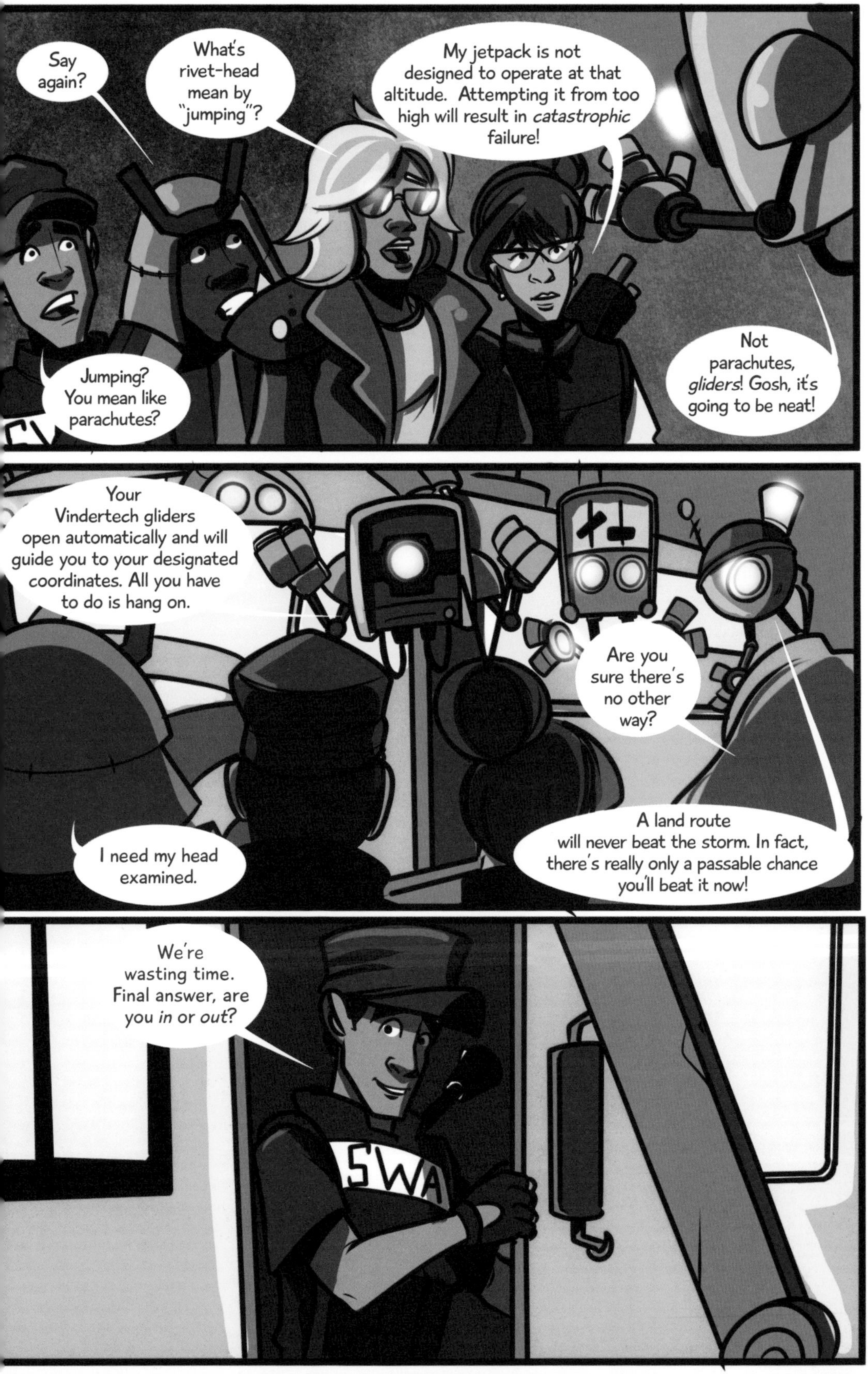
Say again?
What's rivet-head mean by "jumping"?
My jetpack is not designed to operate at that altitude. Attempting it from too high will result in *catastrophic* failure!
Jumping? You mean like parachutes?
Not parachutes, *gliders*! Gosh, it's going to be neat!
Your Vindertech gliders open automatically and will guide you to your designated coordinates. All you have to do is hang on.
Are you sure there's no other way?
I need my head examined.
A land route will never beat the storm. In fact, there's really only a passable chance you'll beat it now!
We're wasting time. Final answer, are you *in* or *out*?
SWA

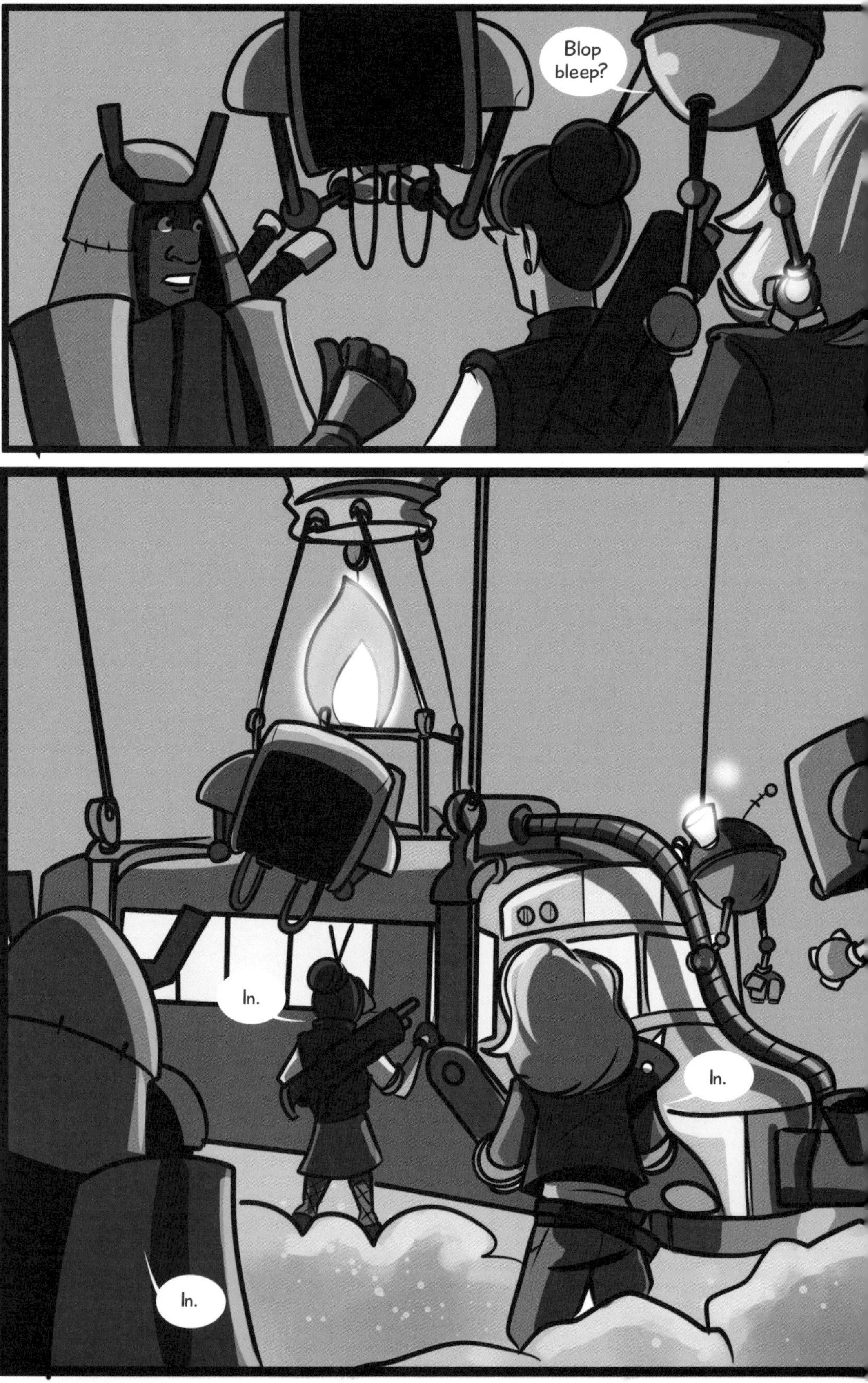
Blop bleep?
In.
In.
In.

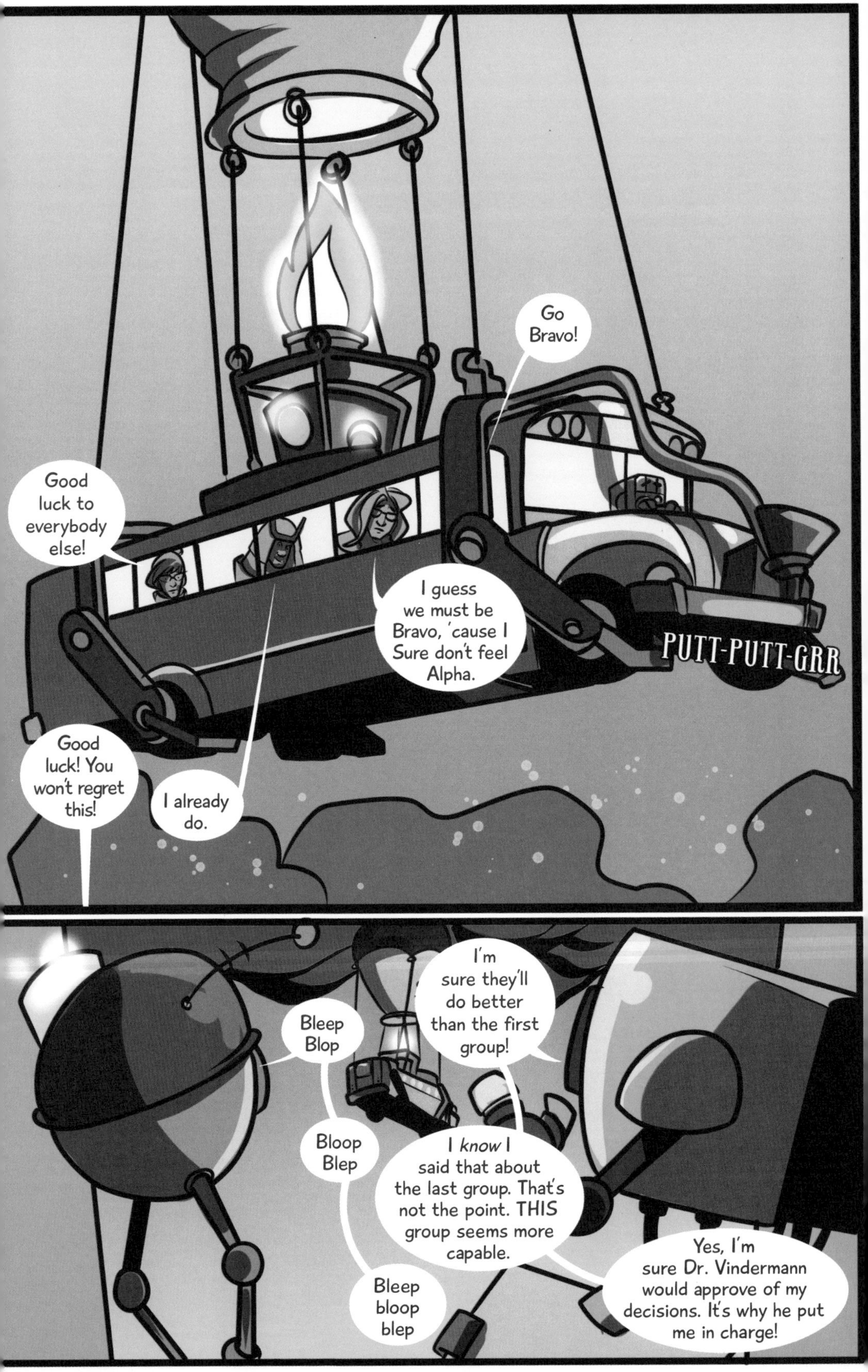
Go Bravo!
Good luck to everybody else!
I guess we must be Bravo, 'cause I Sure don't feel Alpha.
PUTT-PUTT-GRR
Good luck! You won't regret this!
I already do.
Bleep Blop
I'm sure they'll do better than the first group!
Bloop Blep
I *know* I said that about the last group. That's not the point. THIS group seems more capable.
Bleep bloop blep
Yes, I'm sure Dr. Vindermann would approve of my decisions. It's why he put me in charge!

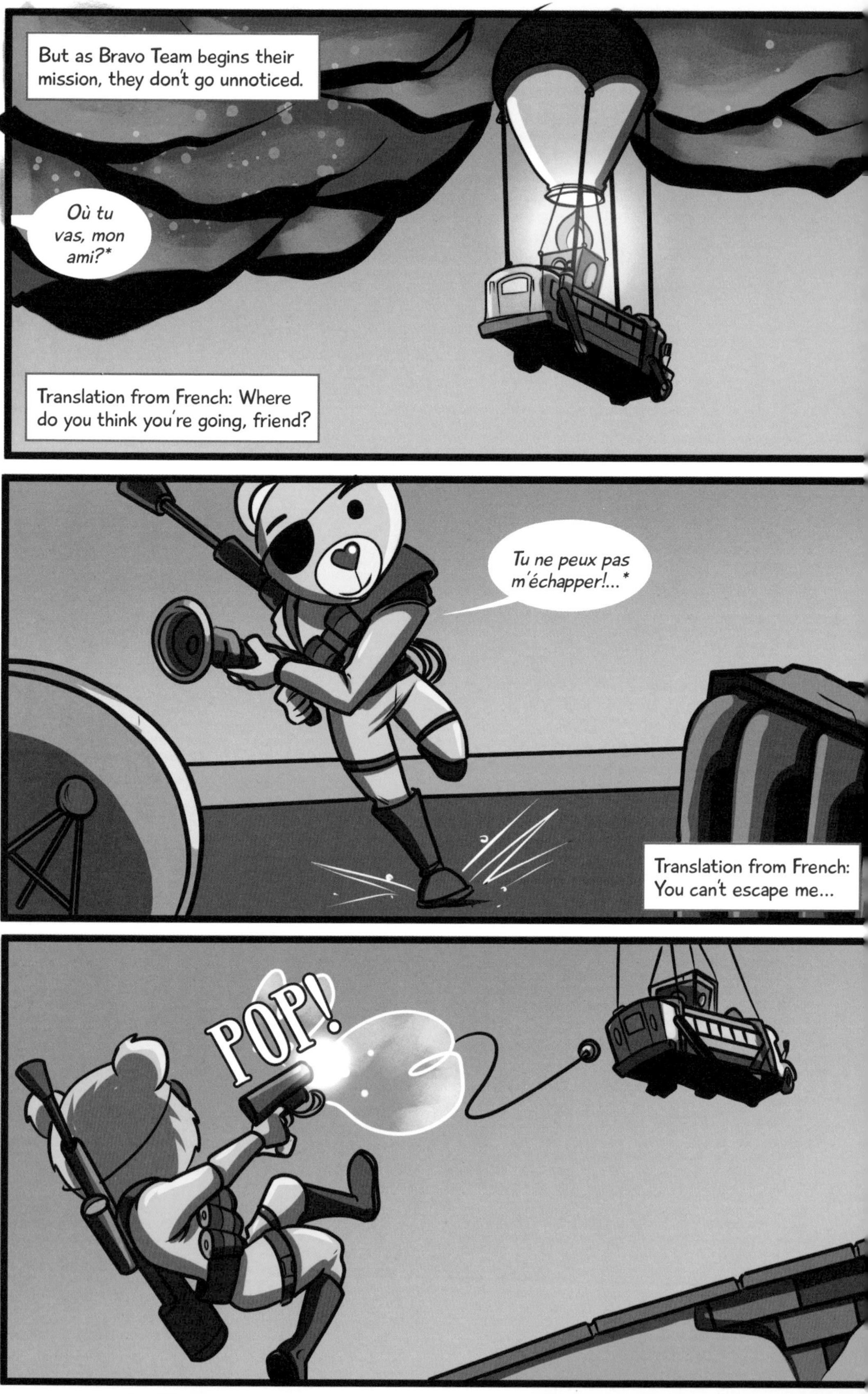

But as Bravo Team begins their mission, they don't go unnoticed.
Où tu vas, mon ami?*
Translation from French: Where do you think you're going, friend?
Tu ne peux pas m'échapper!...*
Translation from French: You can't escape me...
POP!

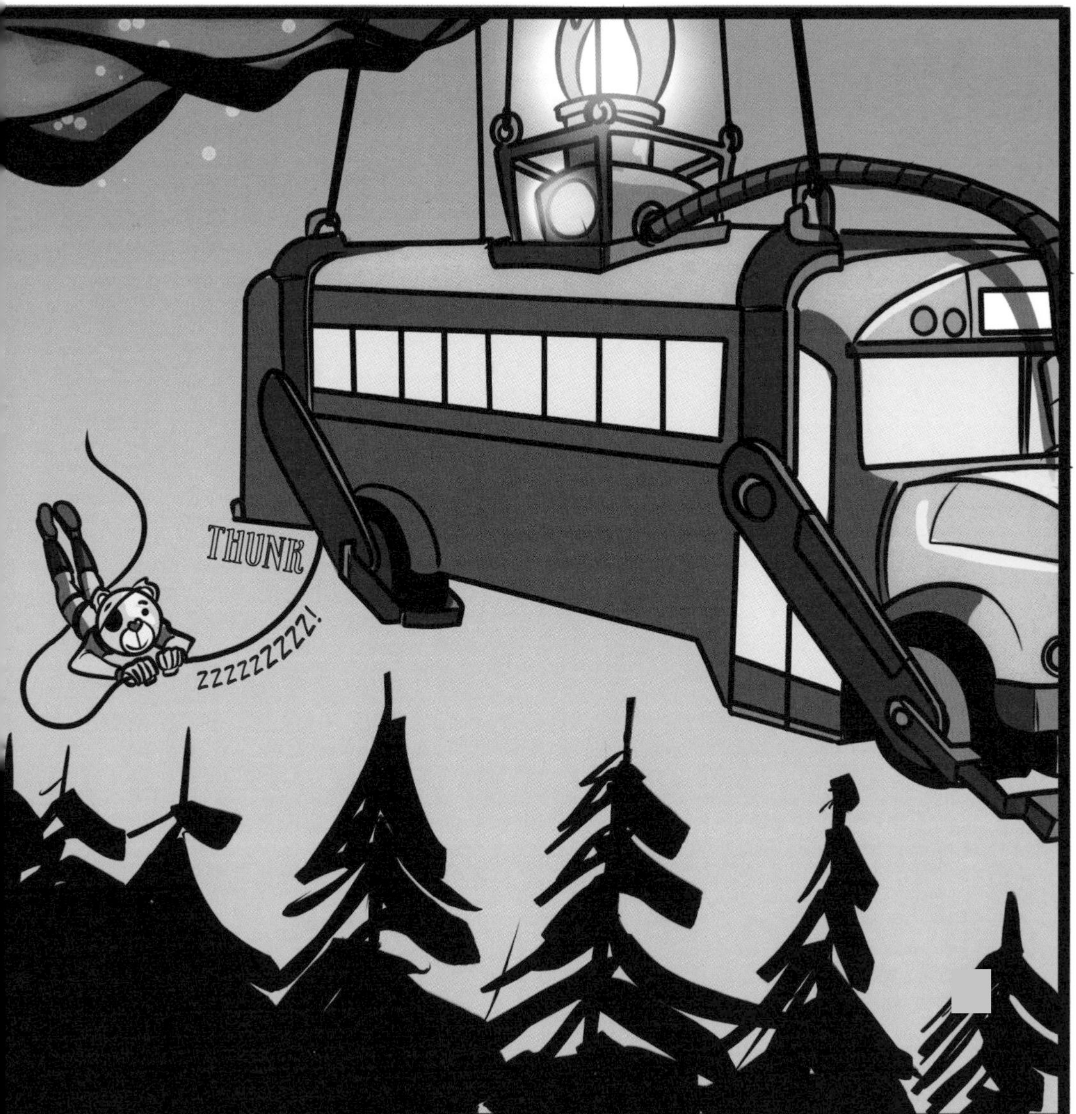
THUNK
ZZZZZZZZZ!

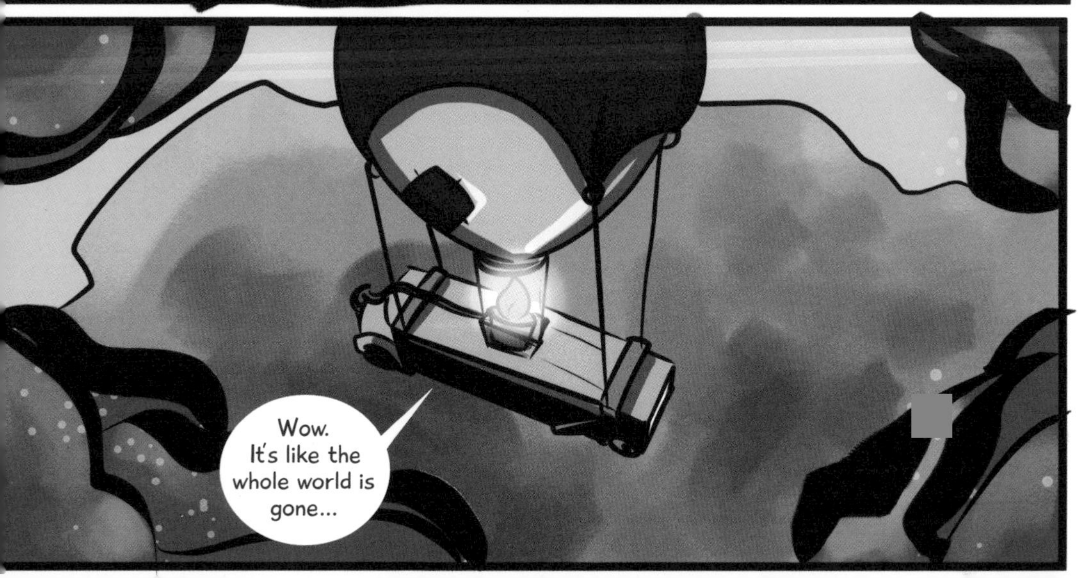
Wow.
It's like the whole world is gone...

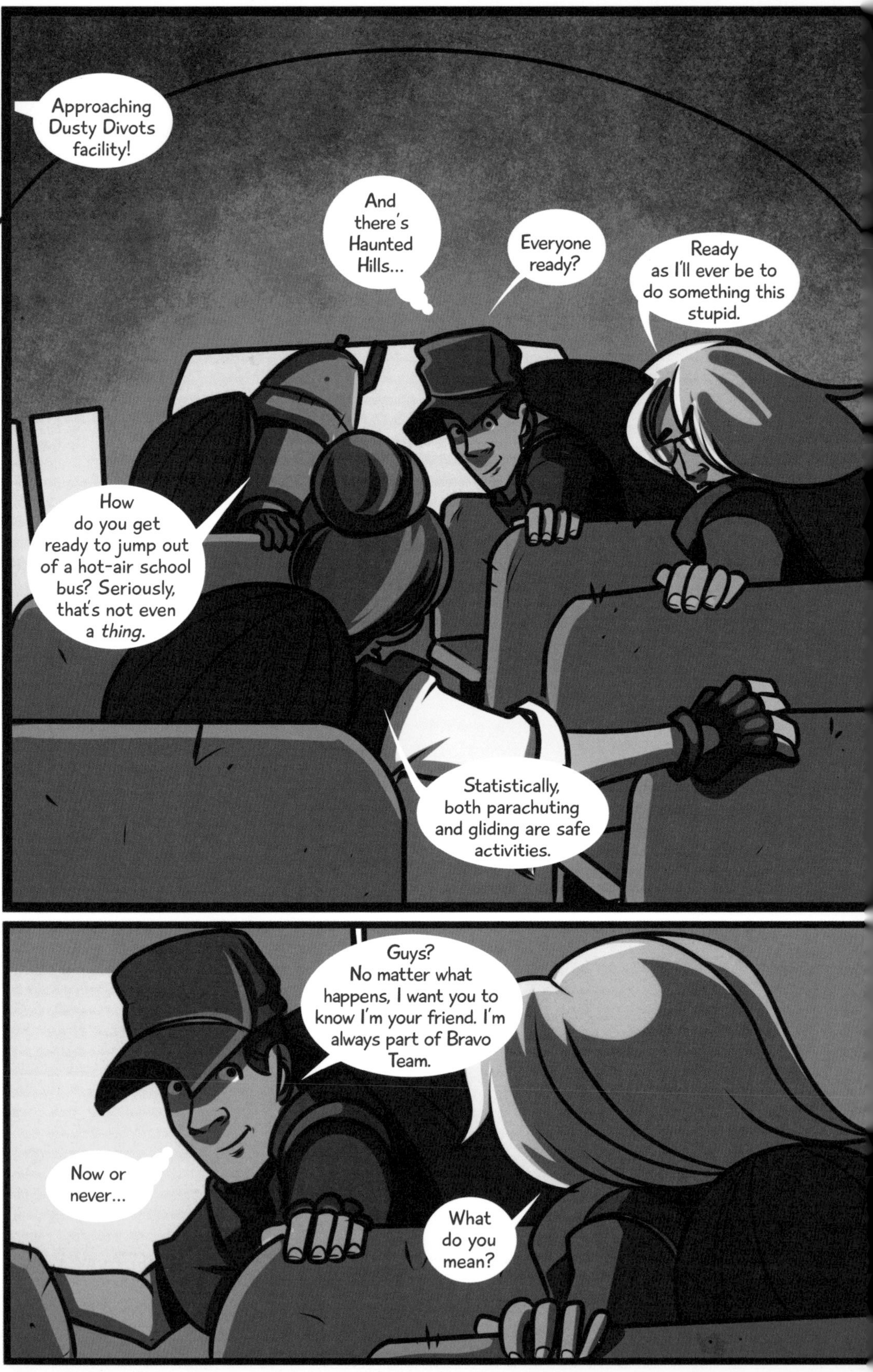

Approaching Dusty Divots facility!
And there's Haunted Hills...
Everyone ready?
Ready as I'll ever be to do something this stupid.
How do you get ready to jump out of a hot-air school bus? Seriously, that's not even a *thing*.
Statistically, both parachuting and gliding are safe activities.
Guys? No matter what happens, I want you to know I'm your friend. I'm always part of Bravo Team.
Now or never...
What do you mean?

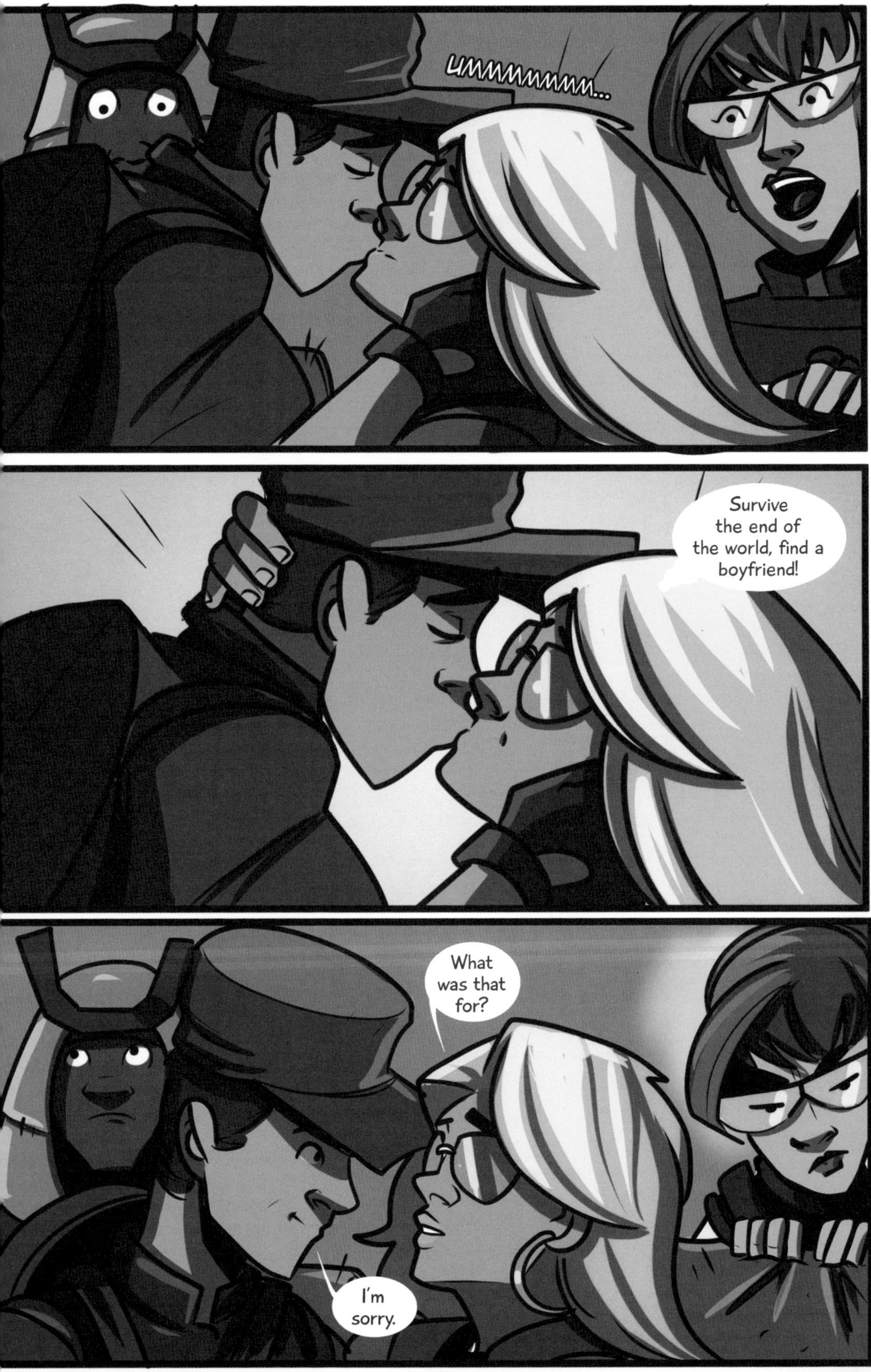
UMMMMMMM...
Survive the end of the world, find a boyfriend!
What was that for?
I'm sorry.

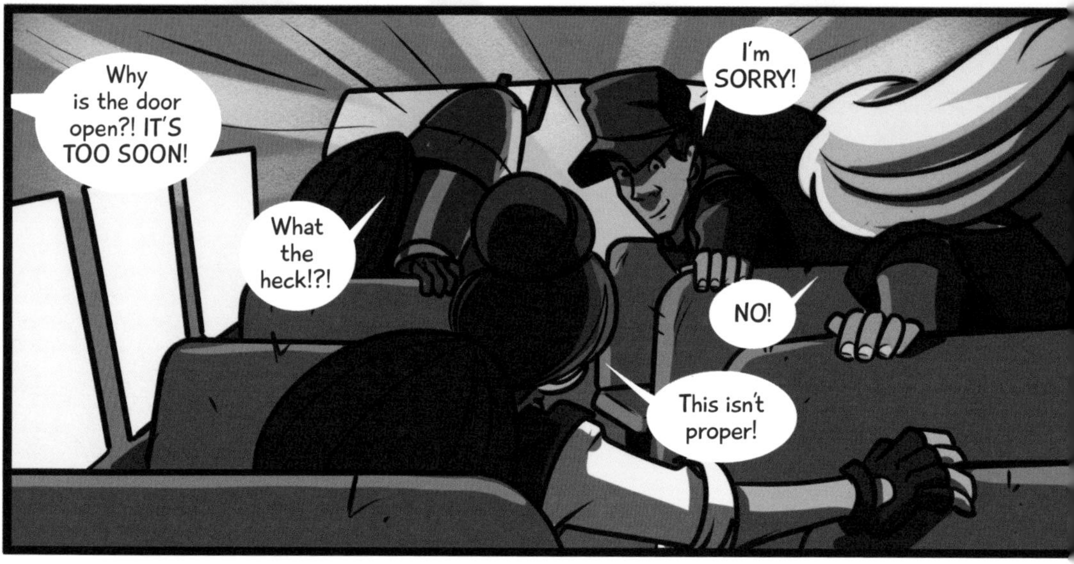
Why is the door open?! IT'S TOO SOON!
I'm SORRY!
What the heck!?!
NO!
This isn't proper!

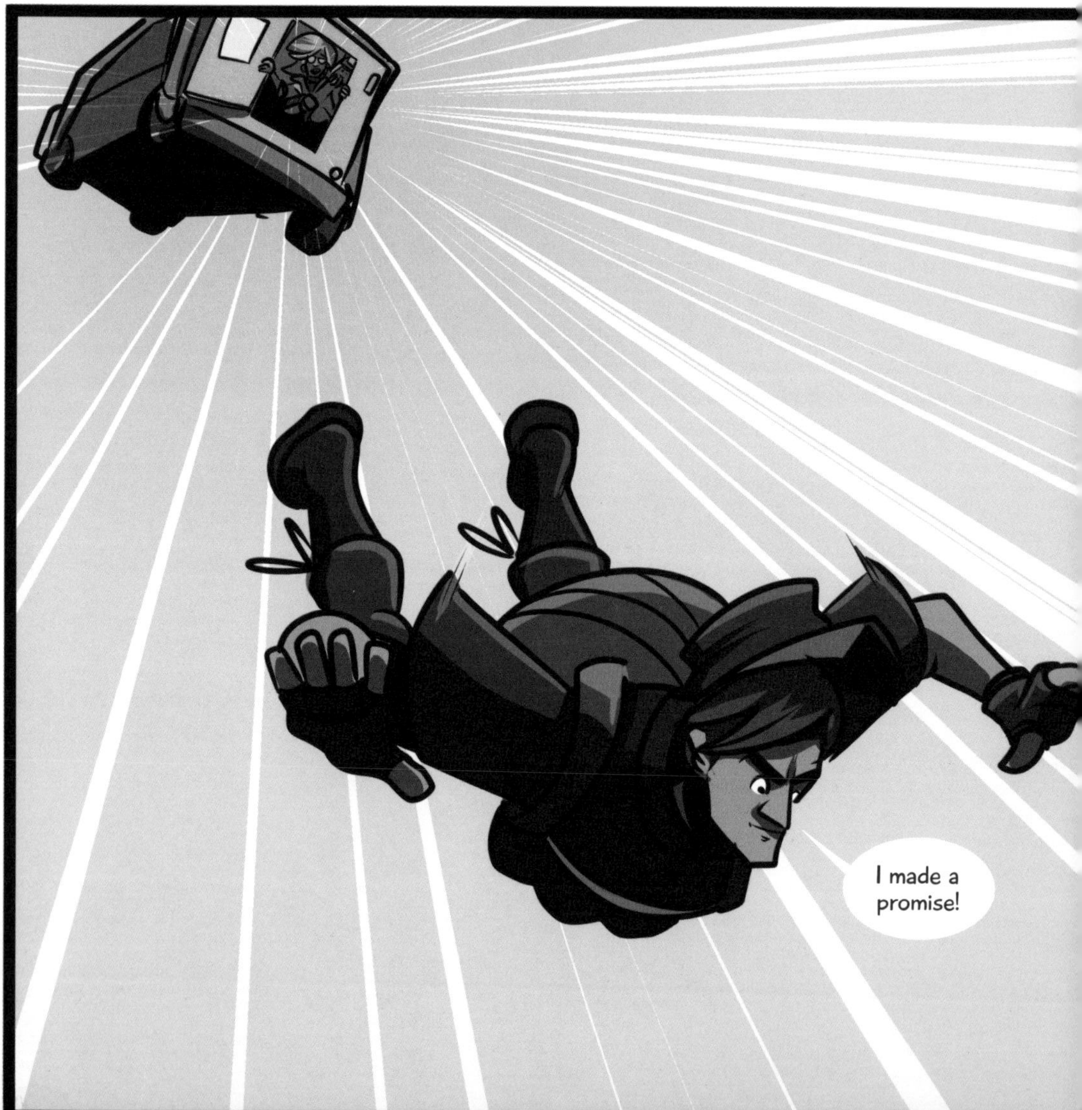
I made a promise!

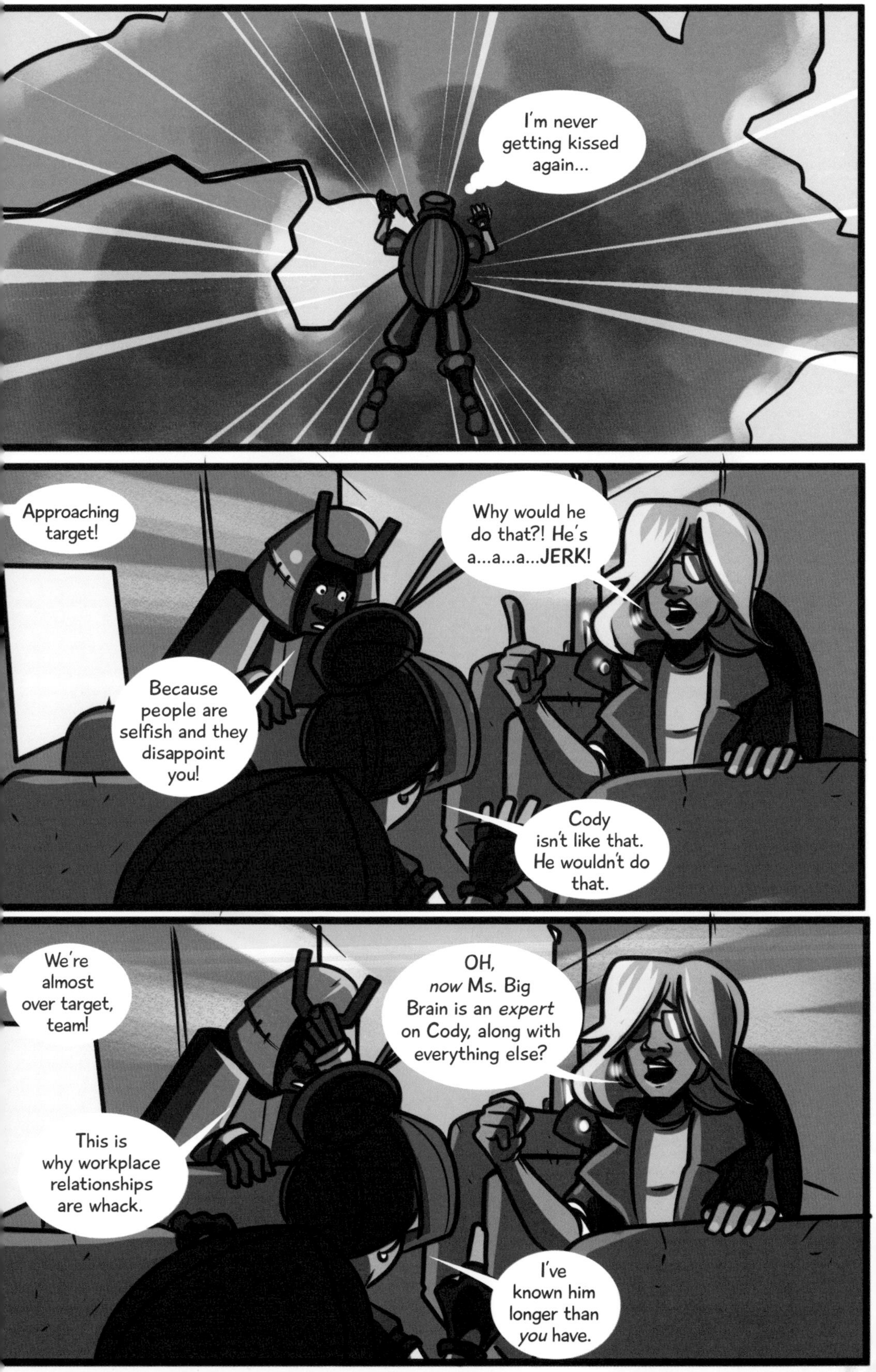
I'm never getting kissed again...
Approaching target!
Why would he do that?! He's a...a...a...**JERK!**
Because people are selfish and they disappoint you!
Cody isn't like that. He wouldn't do that.
We're almost over target, team!
OH, *now* Ms. Big Brain is an *expert* on Cody, along with everything else?
This is why workplace relationships are whack.
I've known him longer than *you* have.

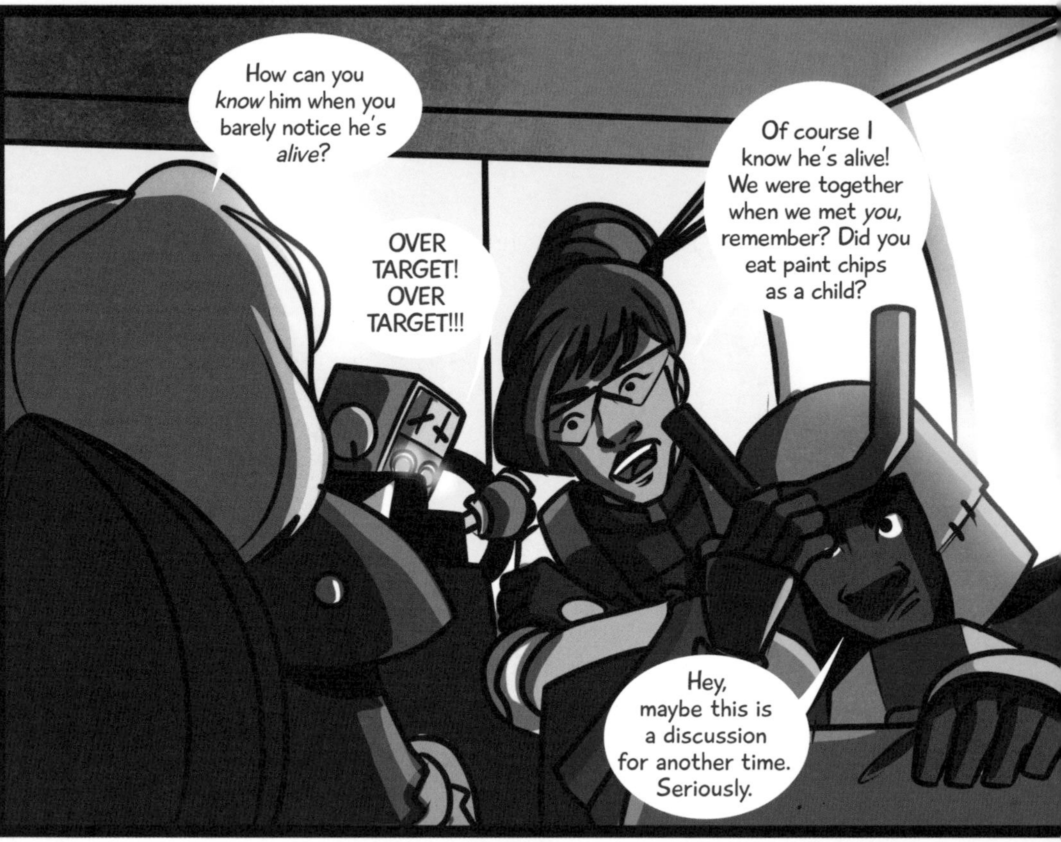
How can you *know* him when you barely notice he's *alive*?
OVER TARGET! OVER TARGET!!!
Of course I know he's alive! We were together when we met *you*, remember? Did you eat paint chips as a child?
Hey, maybe this is a discussion for another time. Seriously.

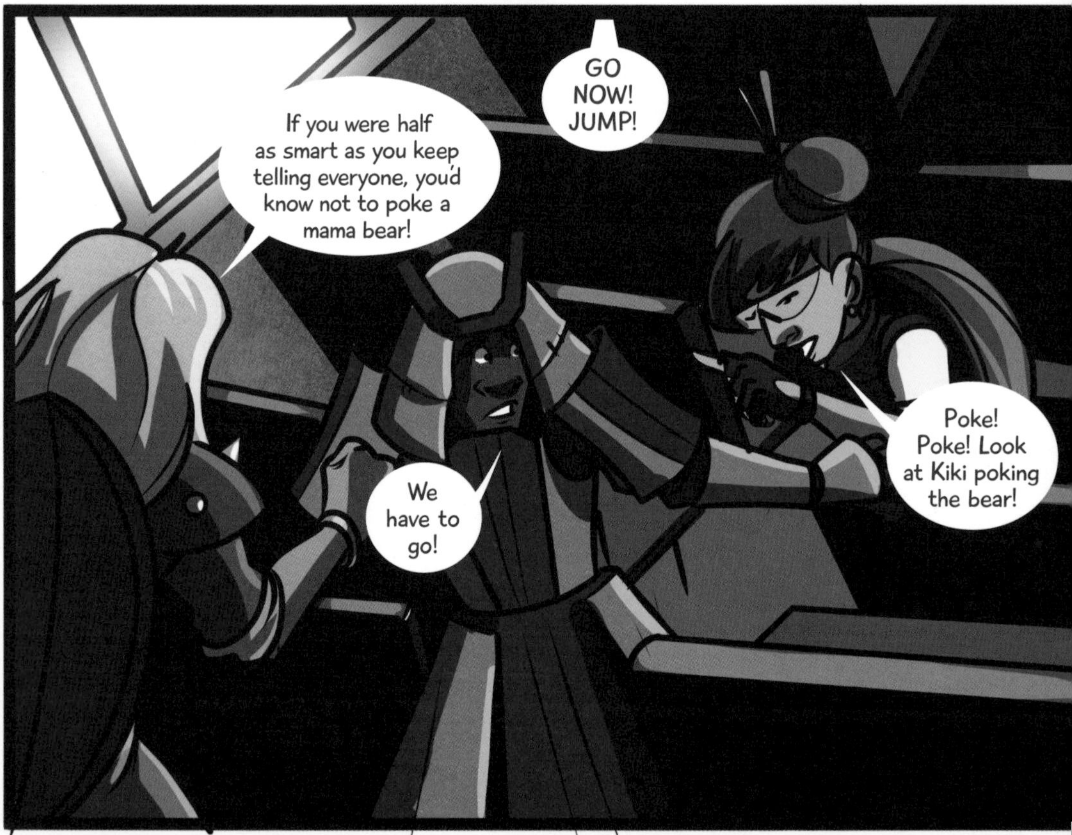
If you were half as smart as you keep telling everyone, you'd know not to poke a mama bear!
GO NOW! JUMP!
Poke! Poke! Look at Kiki poking the bear!
We have to go!

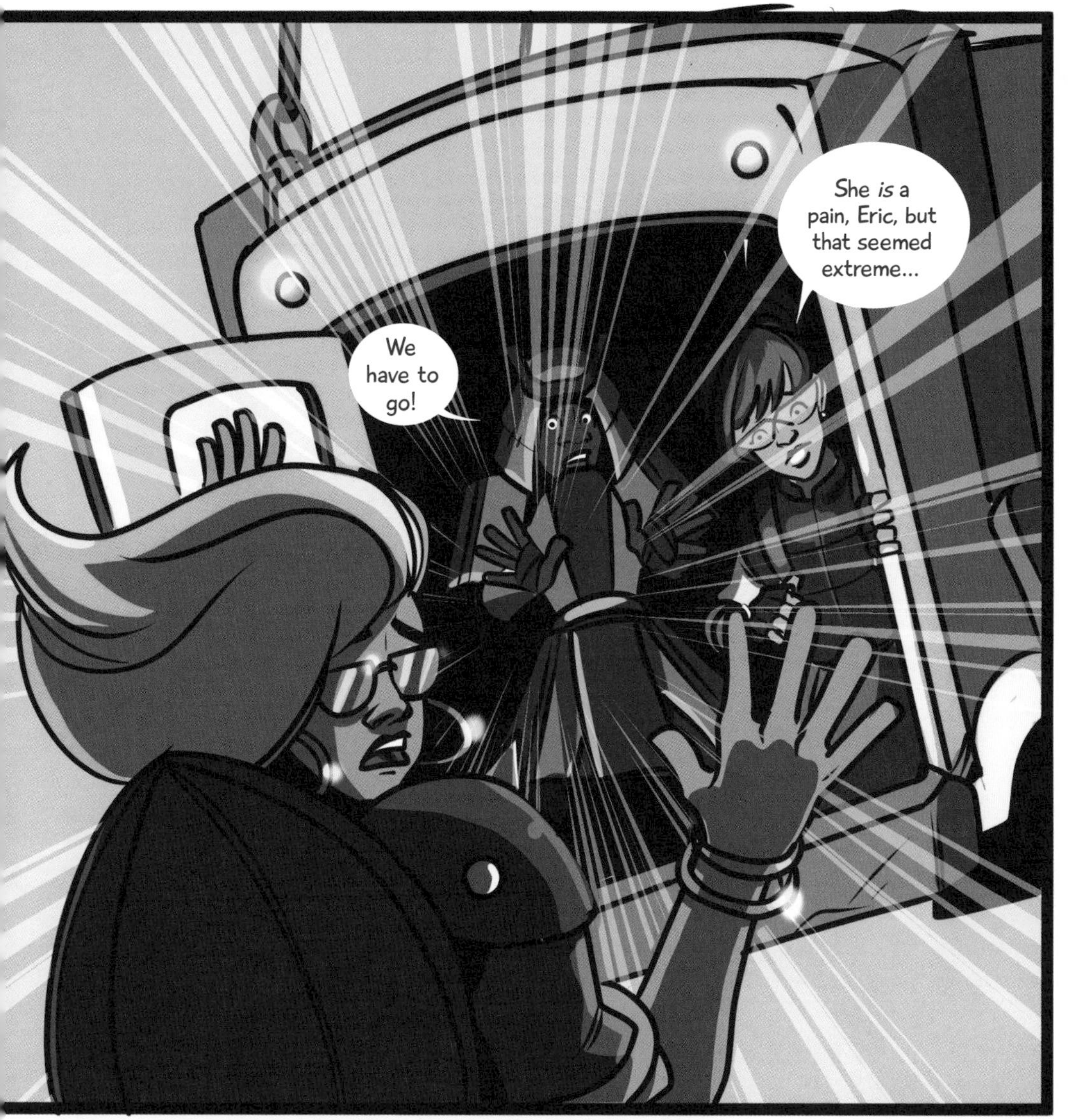
She *is* a pain, Eric, but that seemed extreme...
We have to go!
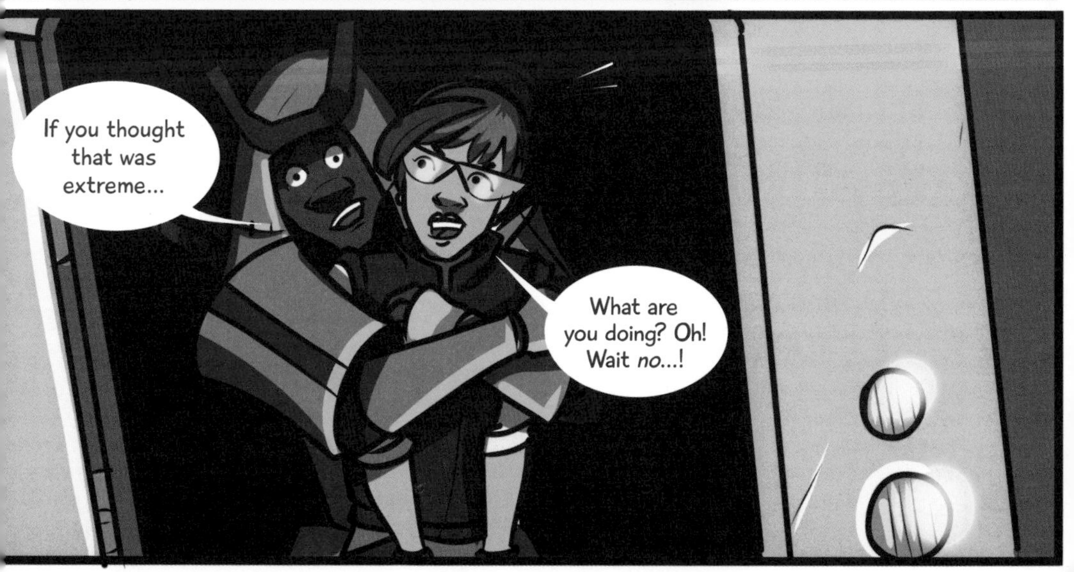
If you thought that was extreme...
What are you doing? Oh! Wait *no*...!

CHAPTER 10: AND THEN THERE WERE TWO

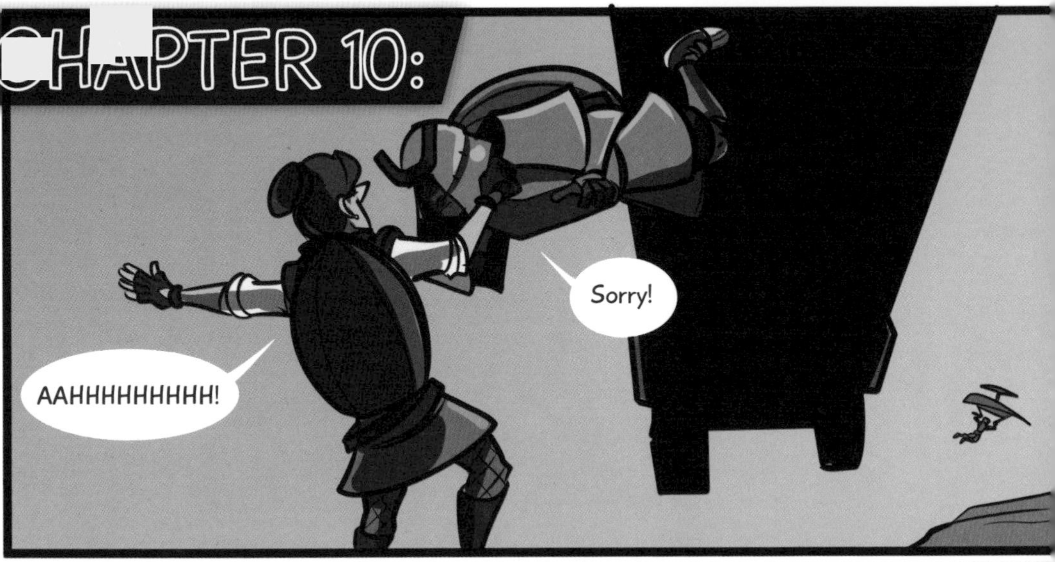
Sorry!
AAHHHHHHHHH!

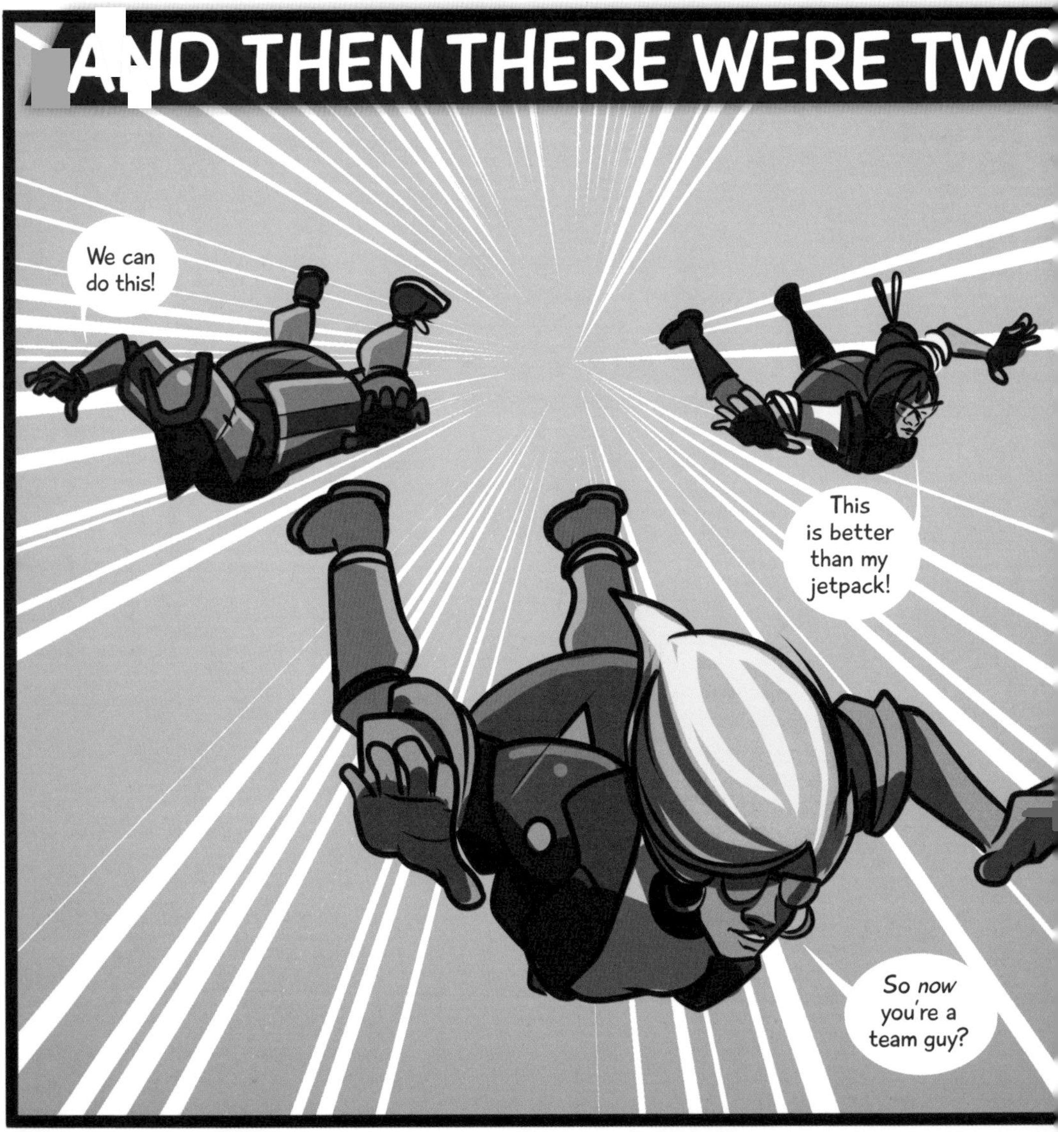
We can do this!
This is better than my jetpack!
So *now* you're a team guy?

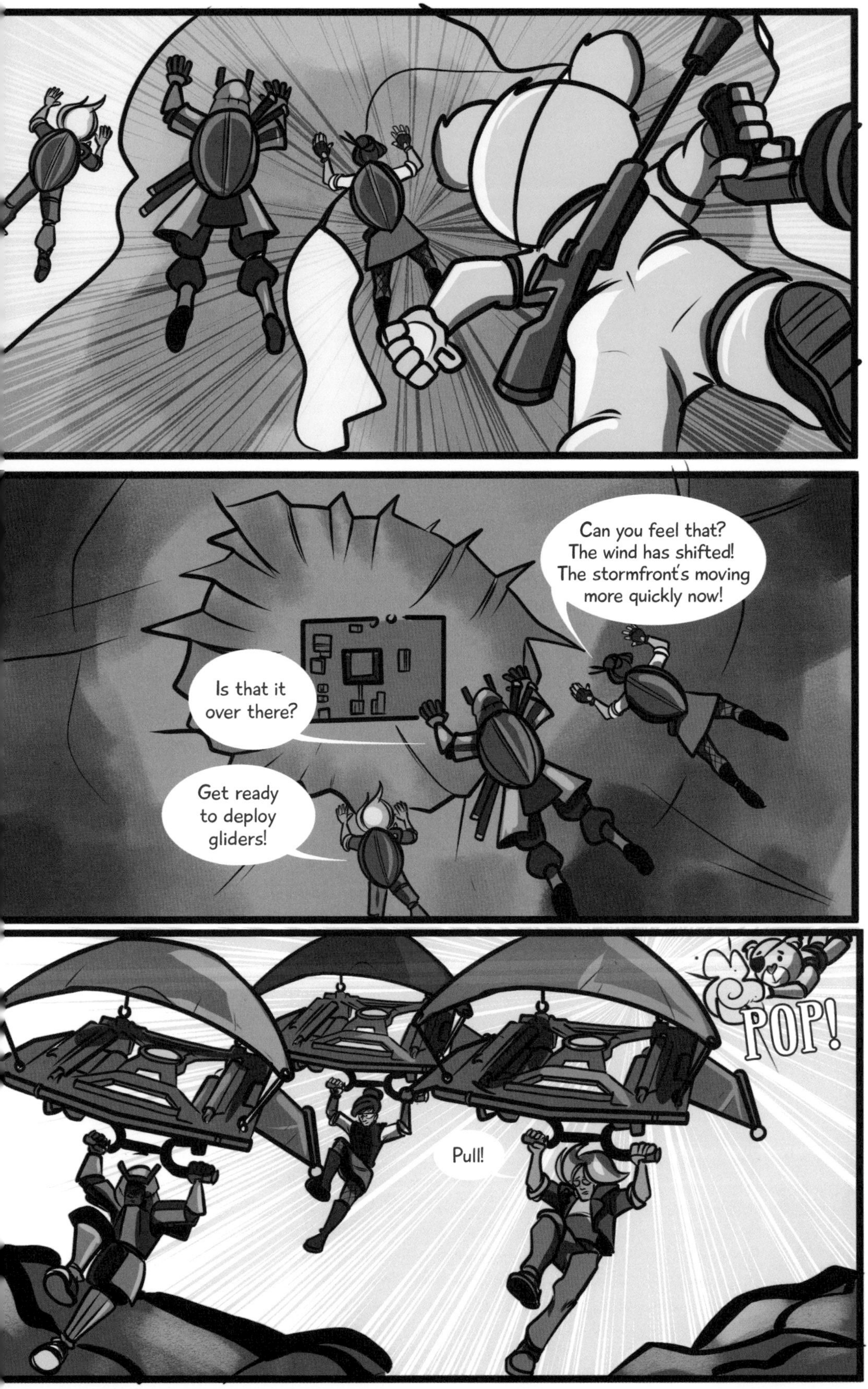
Can you feel that? The wind has shifted! The stormfront's moving more quickly now!
Is that it over there?
Get ready to deploy gliders!
POP!
Pull!

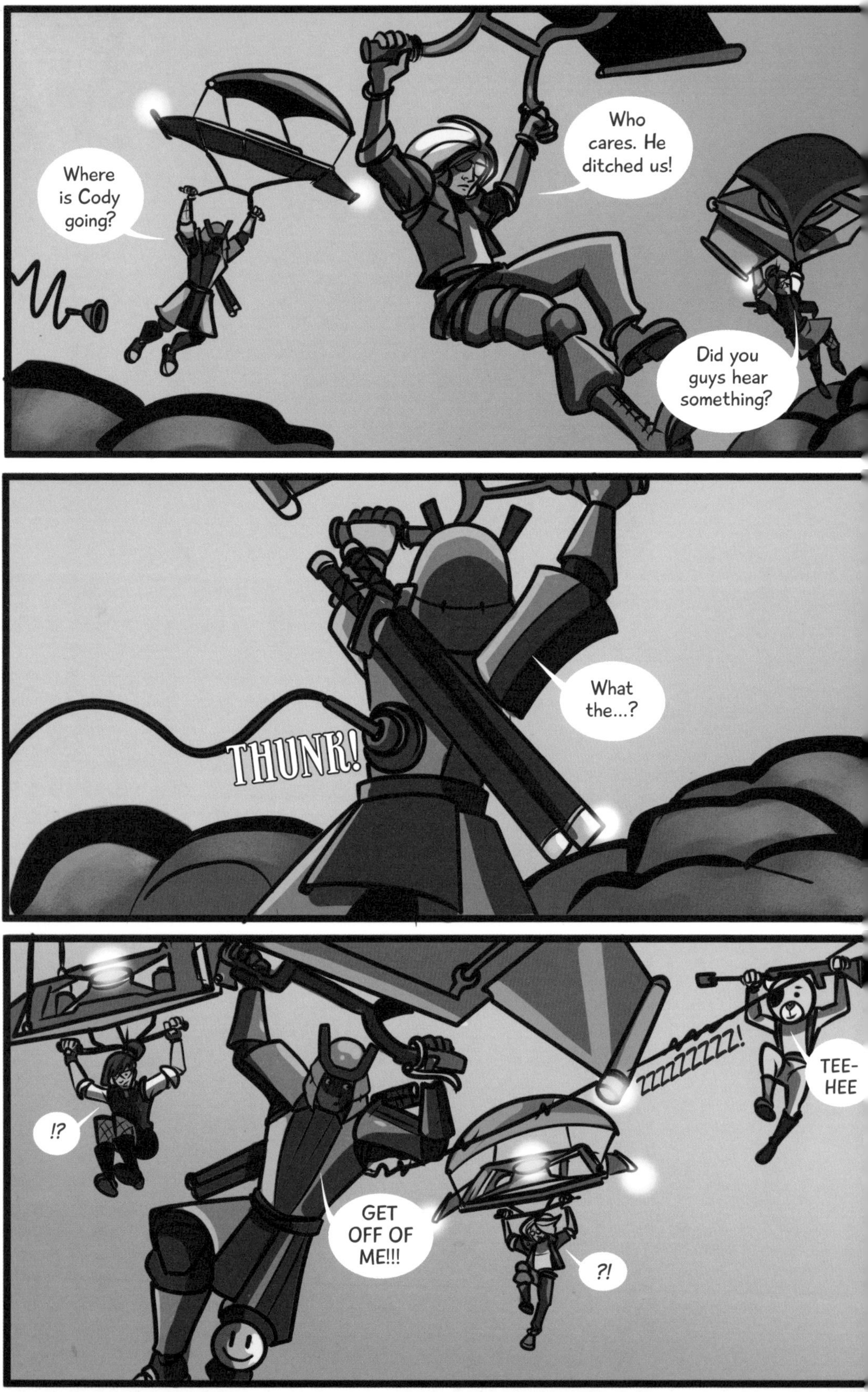
Where is Cody going?
Who cares. He ditched us!
Did you guys hear something?
THUNK!
What the...?
ZZZZZZZZZ!
TEE-HEE
!?
GET OFF OF ME!!!
?!

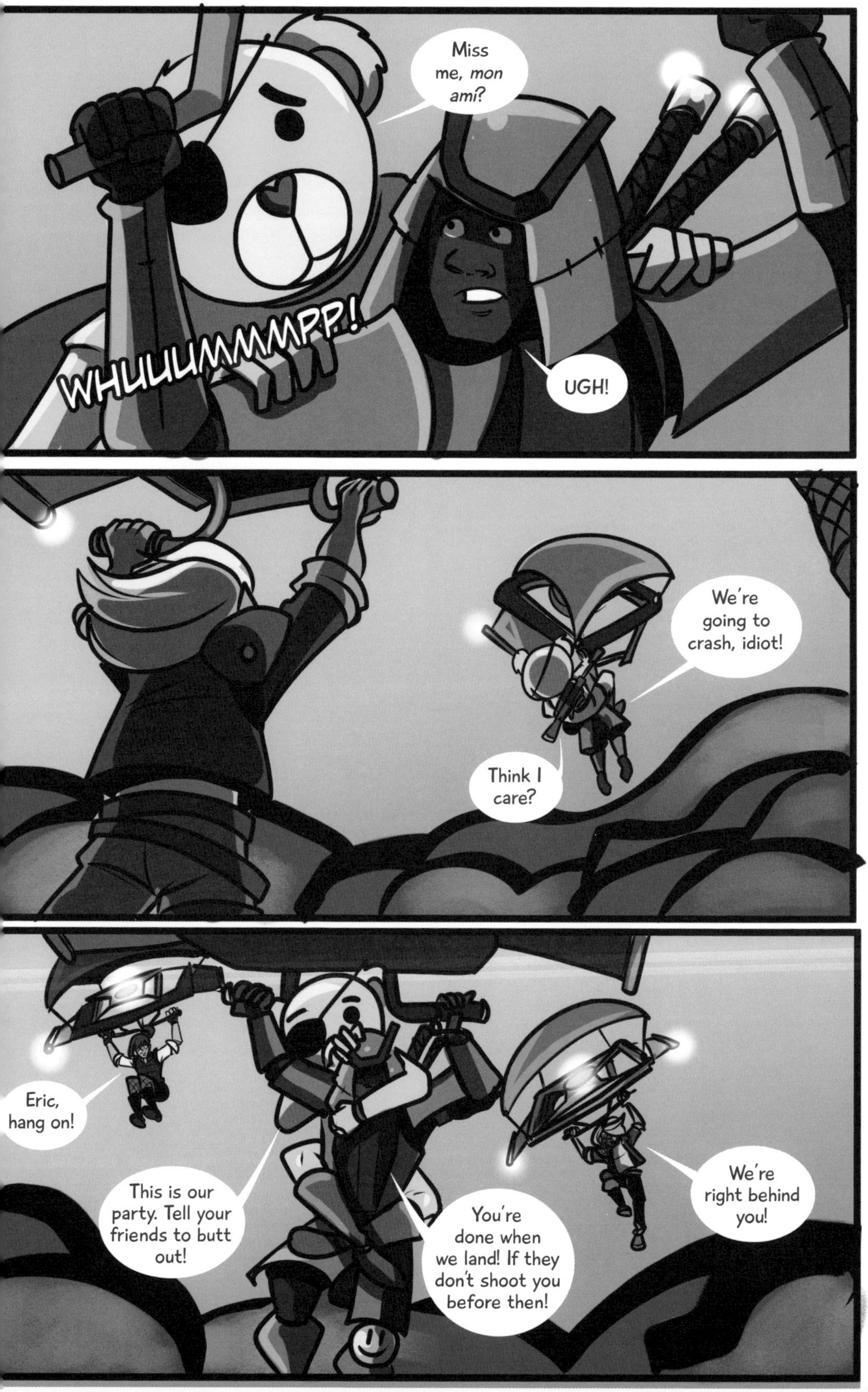
Miss me, *mon ami*?
WHUUUMMMMPP!
UGH!
We're going to crash, idiot!
Think I care?
Eric, hang on!
This is our party. Tell your friends to butt out!
You're done when we land! If they don't shoot you before then!
We're right behind you!

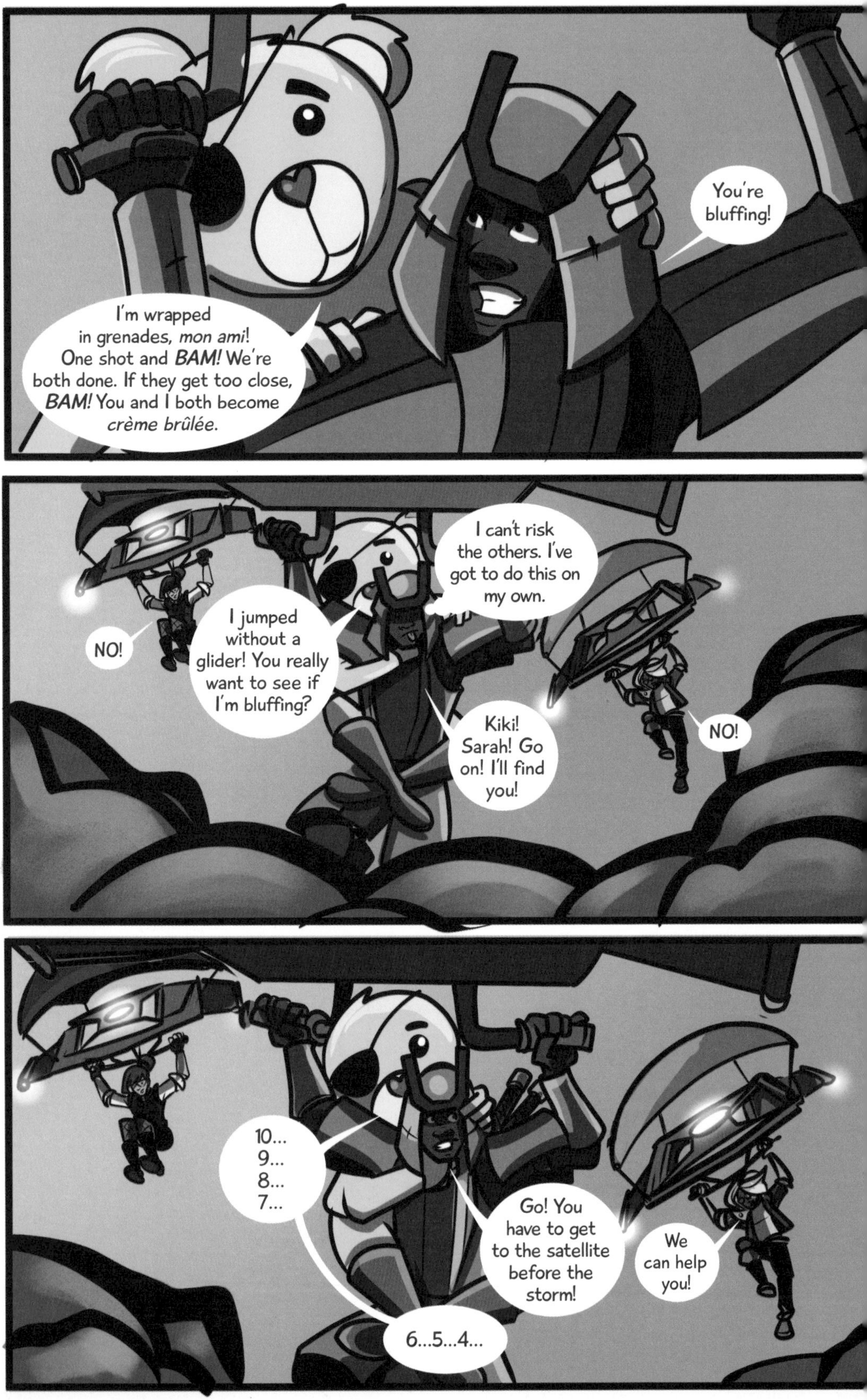
I'm wrapped in grenades, *mon ami*! One shot and ***BAM!*** We're both done. If they get too close, ***BAM!*** You and I both become *crème brûlée*.
You're bluffing!
NO!
I jumped without a glider! You really want to see if I'm bluffing?
I can't risk the others. I've got to do this on my own.
Kiki! Sarah! Go on! I'll find you!
NO!
10... 9... 8... 7...
Go! You have to get to the satellite before the storm!
We can help you!
6...5...4...

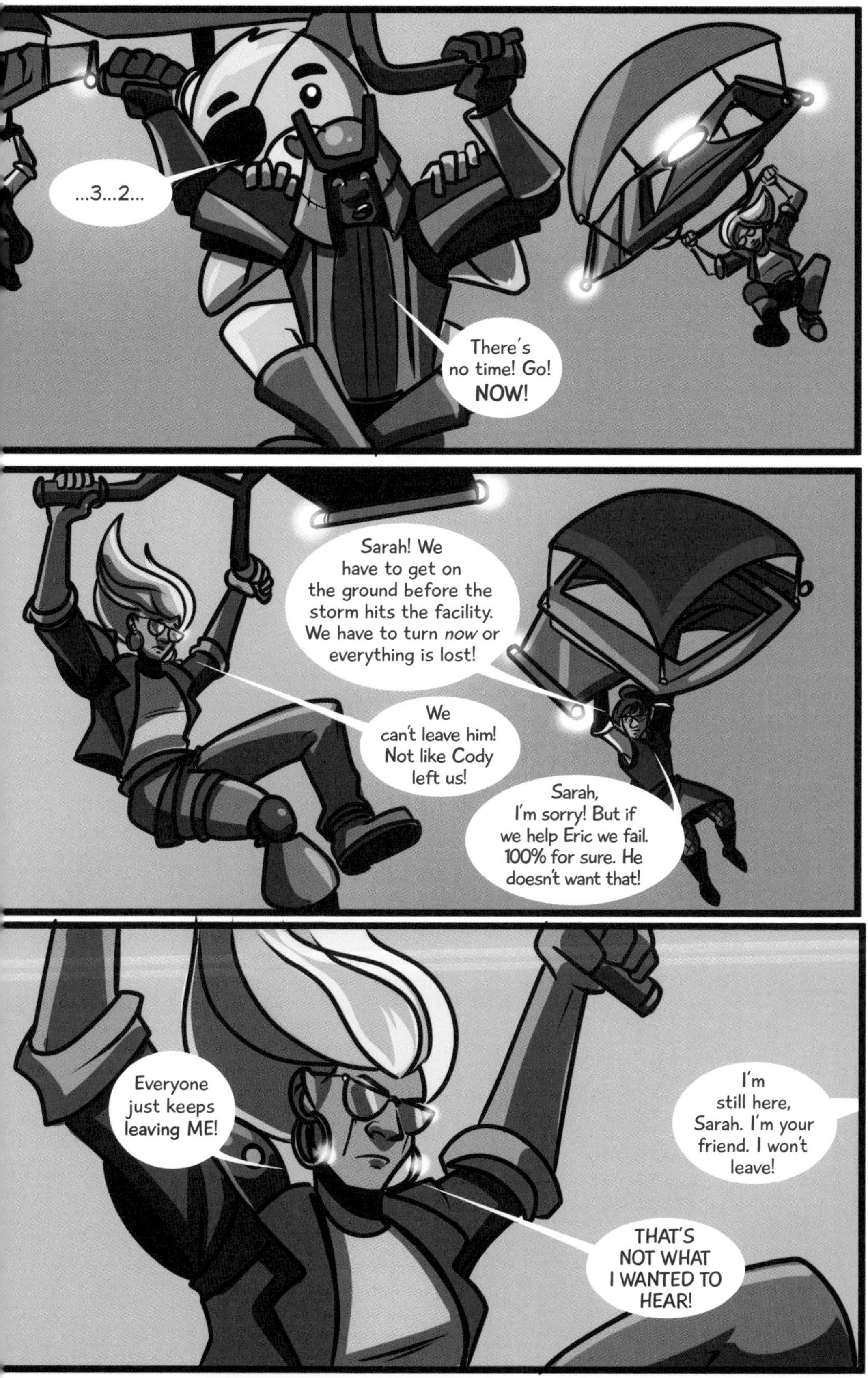
...3...2...
There's no time! Go! **NOW!**
Sarah! We have to get on the ground before the storm hits the facility. We have to turn *now* or everything is lost!
We can't leave him! Not like Cody left us!
Sarah, I'm sorry! But if we help Eric we fail. 100% for sure. He doesn't want that!
Everyone just keeps leaving ME!
I'm still here, Sarah. I'm your friend. I won't leave!
THAT'S NOT WHAT I WANTED TO HEAR!

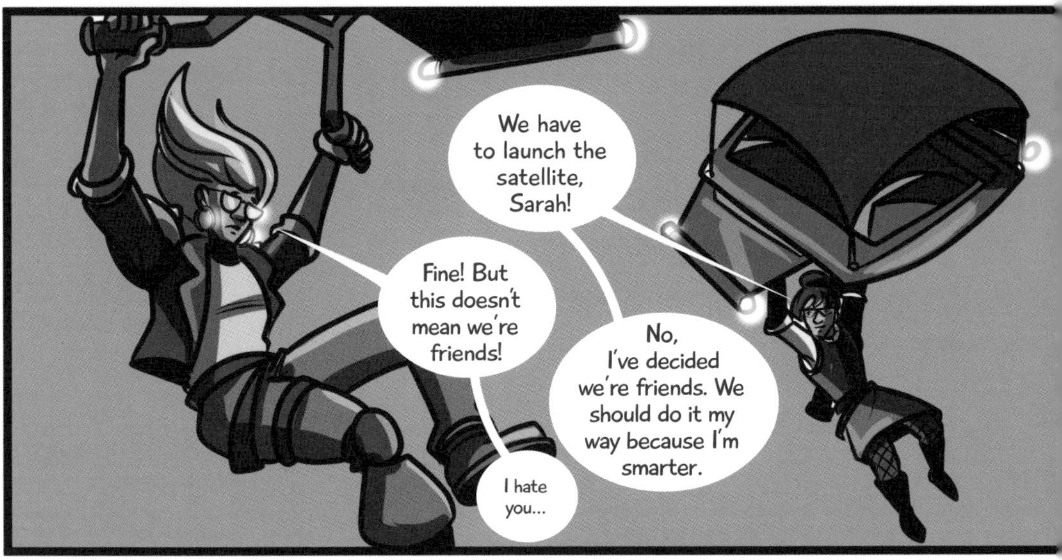
We have to launch the satellite, Sarah!
Fine! But this doesn't mean we're friends!
No, I've decided we're friends. We should do it my way because I'm smarter.
I hate you...

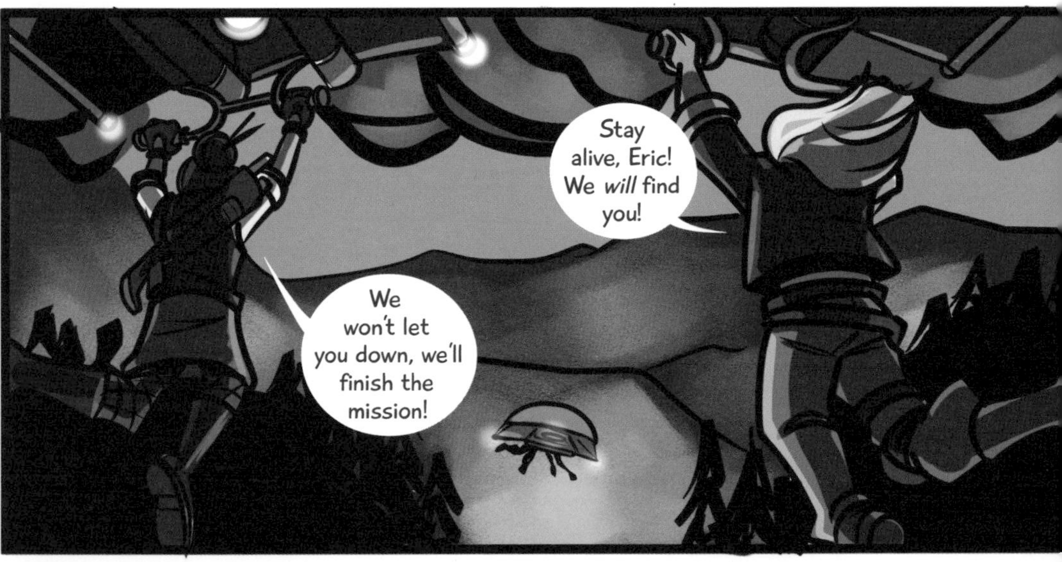
Stay alive, Eric! We *will* find you!
We won't let you down, we'll finish the mission!

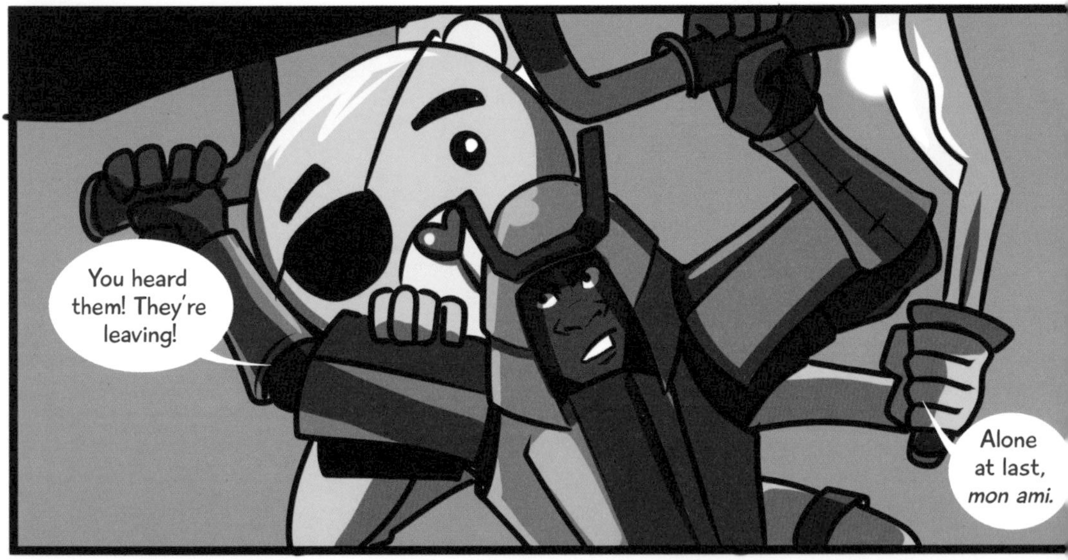
You heard them! They're leaving!
Alone at last, *mon ami.*

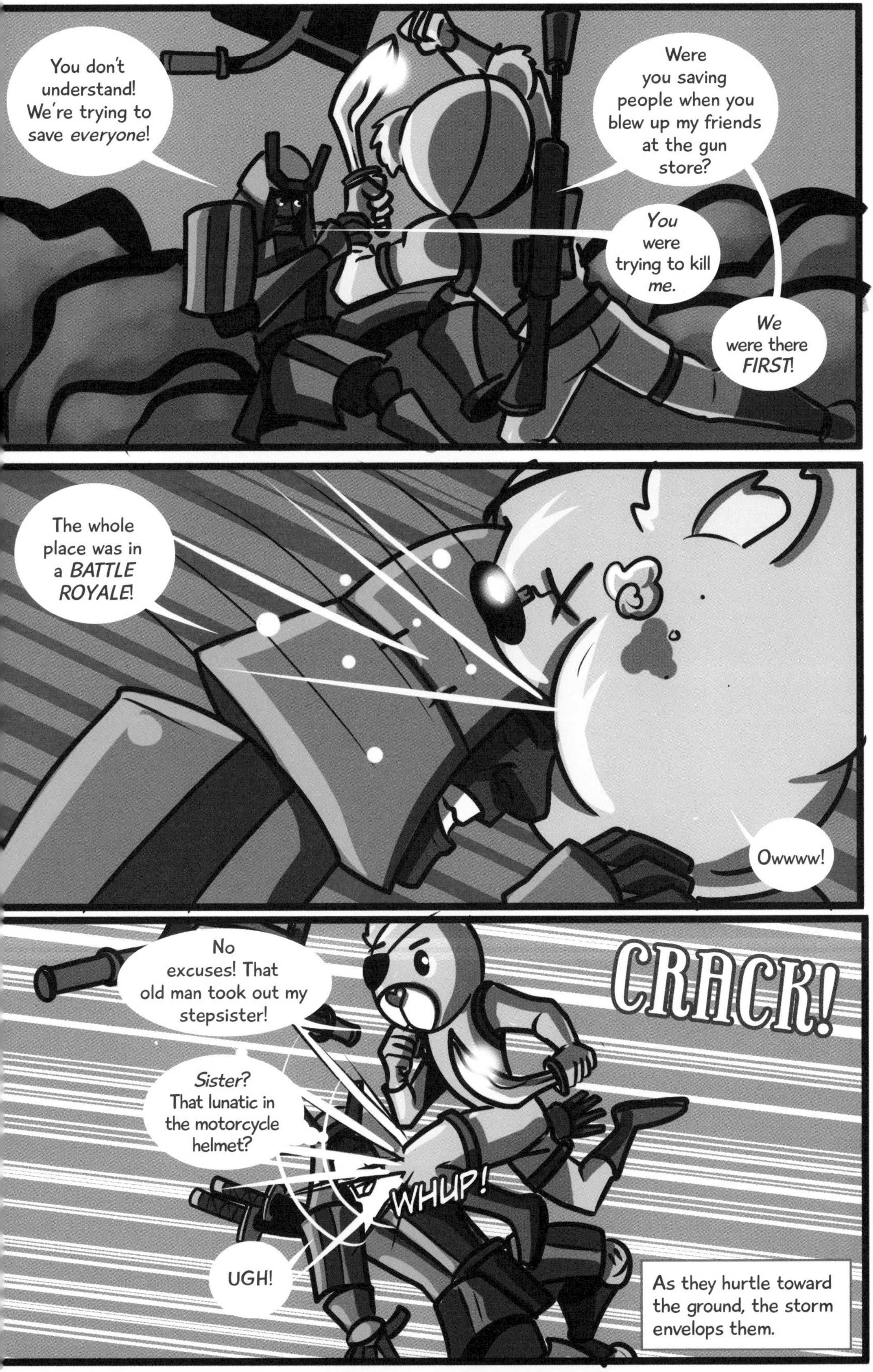
You don't understand! We're trying to save *everyone*!
Were you saving people when you blew up my friends at the gun store?
You were trying to kill *me*.
We were there *FIRST*!
The whole place was in a *BATTLE ROYALE*!
Owwww!
No excuses! That old man took out my stepsister!
CRACK!
Sister? That lunatic in the motorcycle helmet?
WHUP!
UGH!
As they hurtle toward the ground, the storm envelops them.

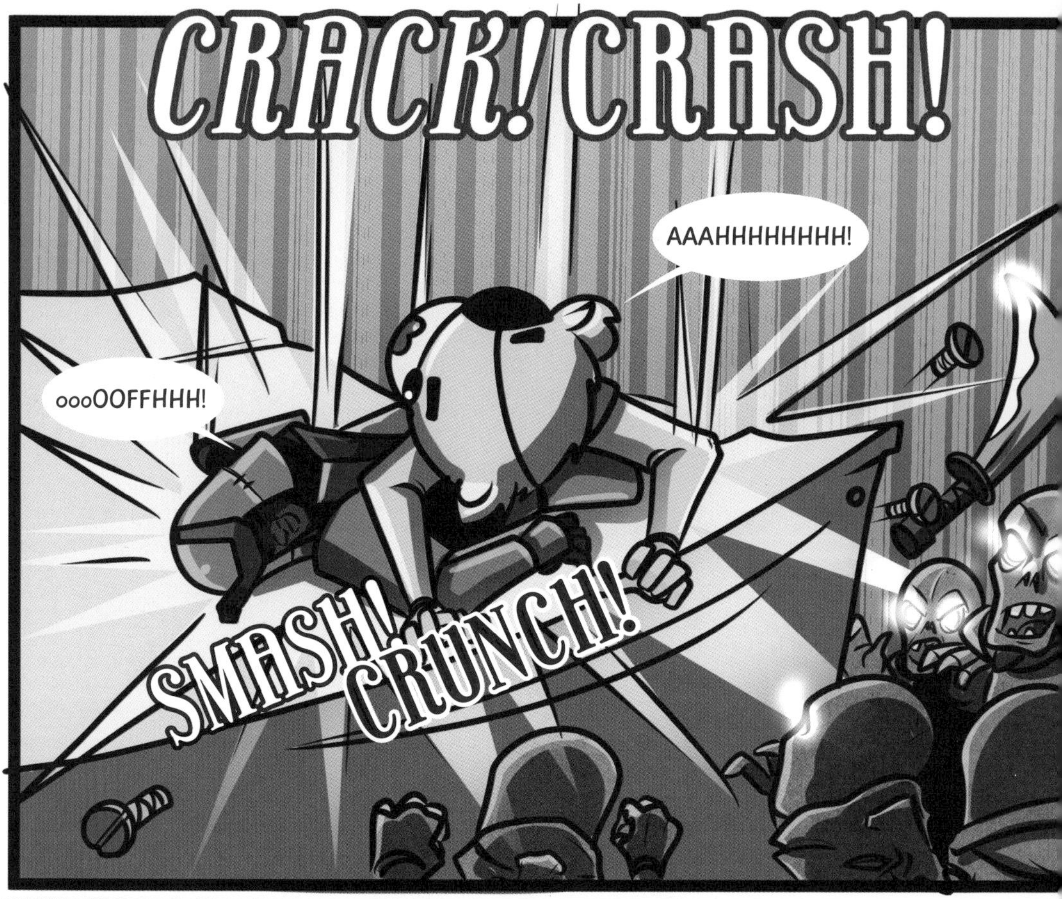
CRACK! CRASH!
AAAHHHHHHHH!
oooOOFFHHH!
SMASH! CRUNCH!

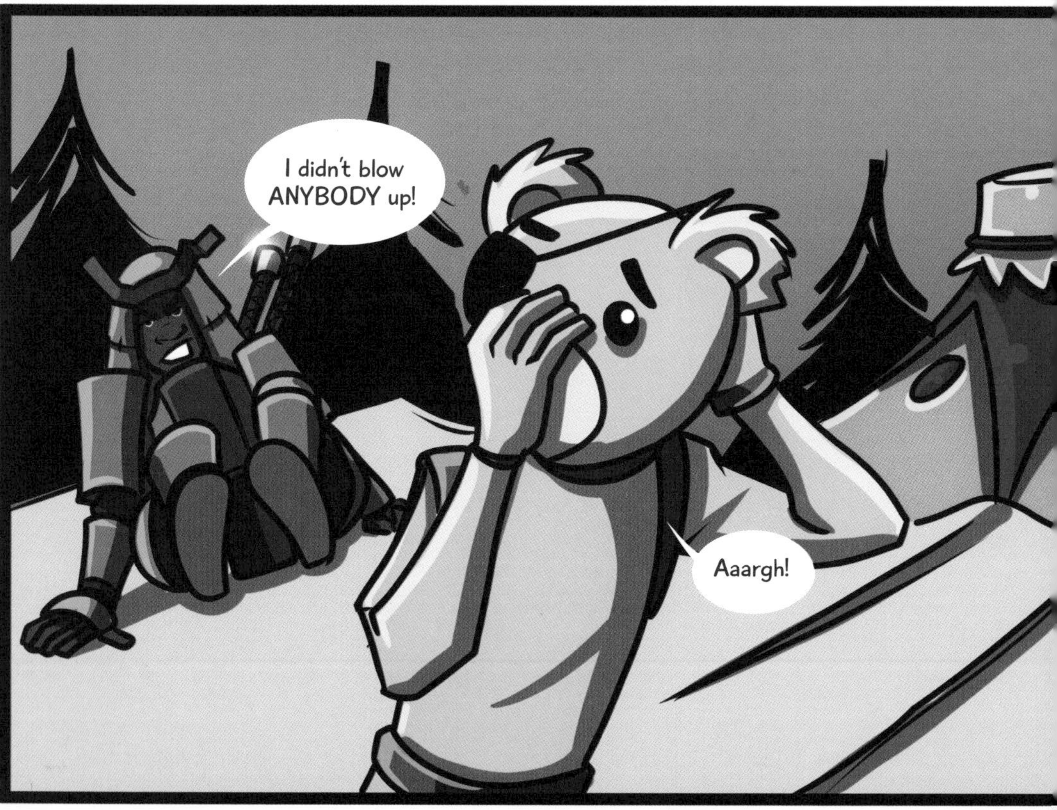
I didn't blow ANYBODY up!
Aaargh!

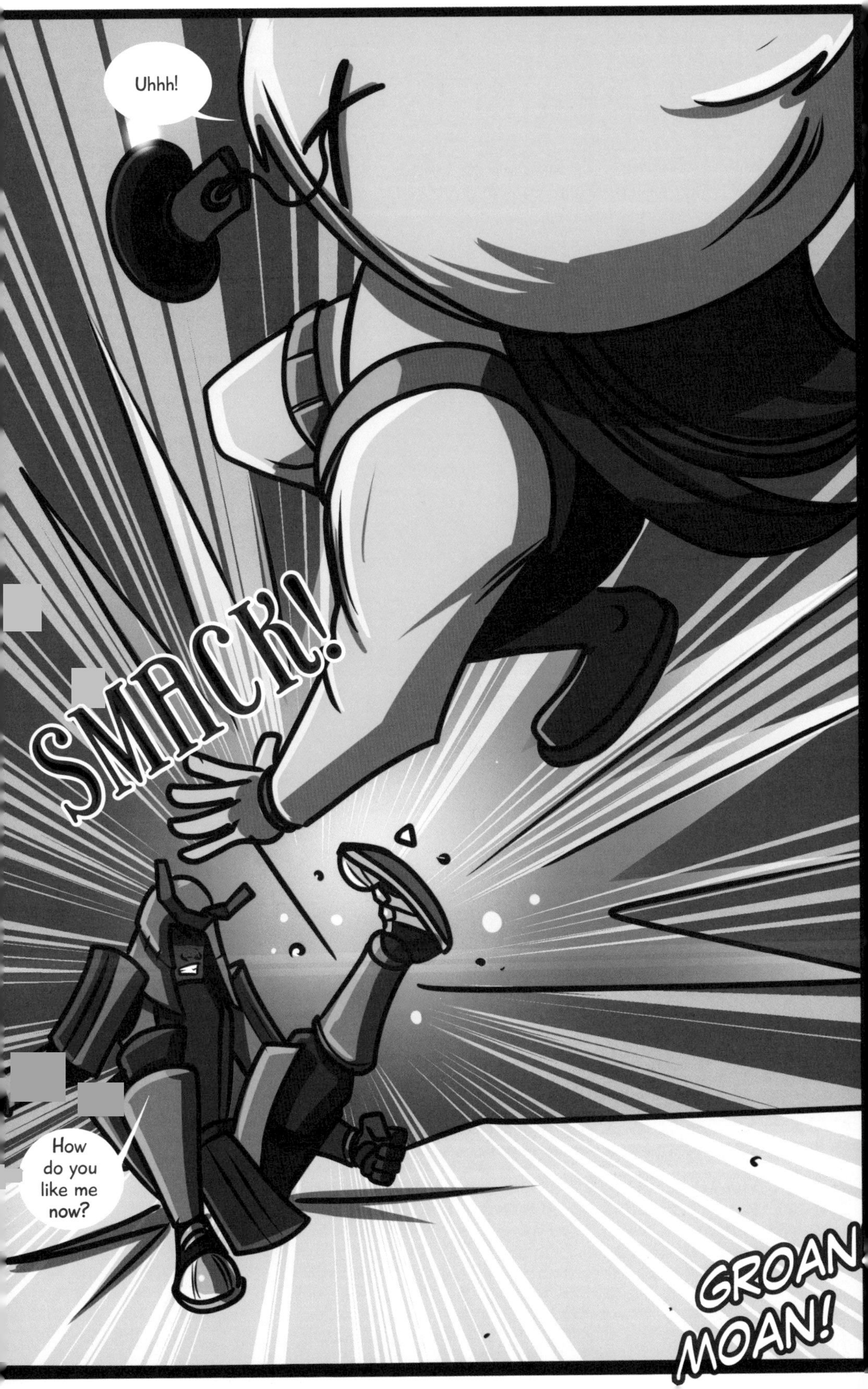
Uhhh!
SMACK!
How do you like me now?
GROAN MOAN!

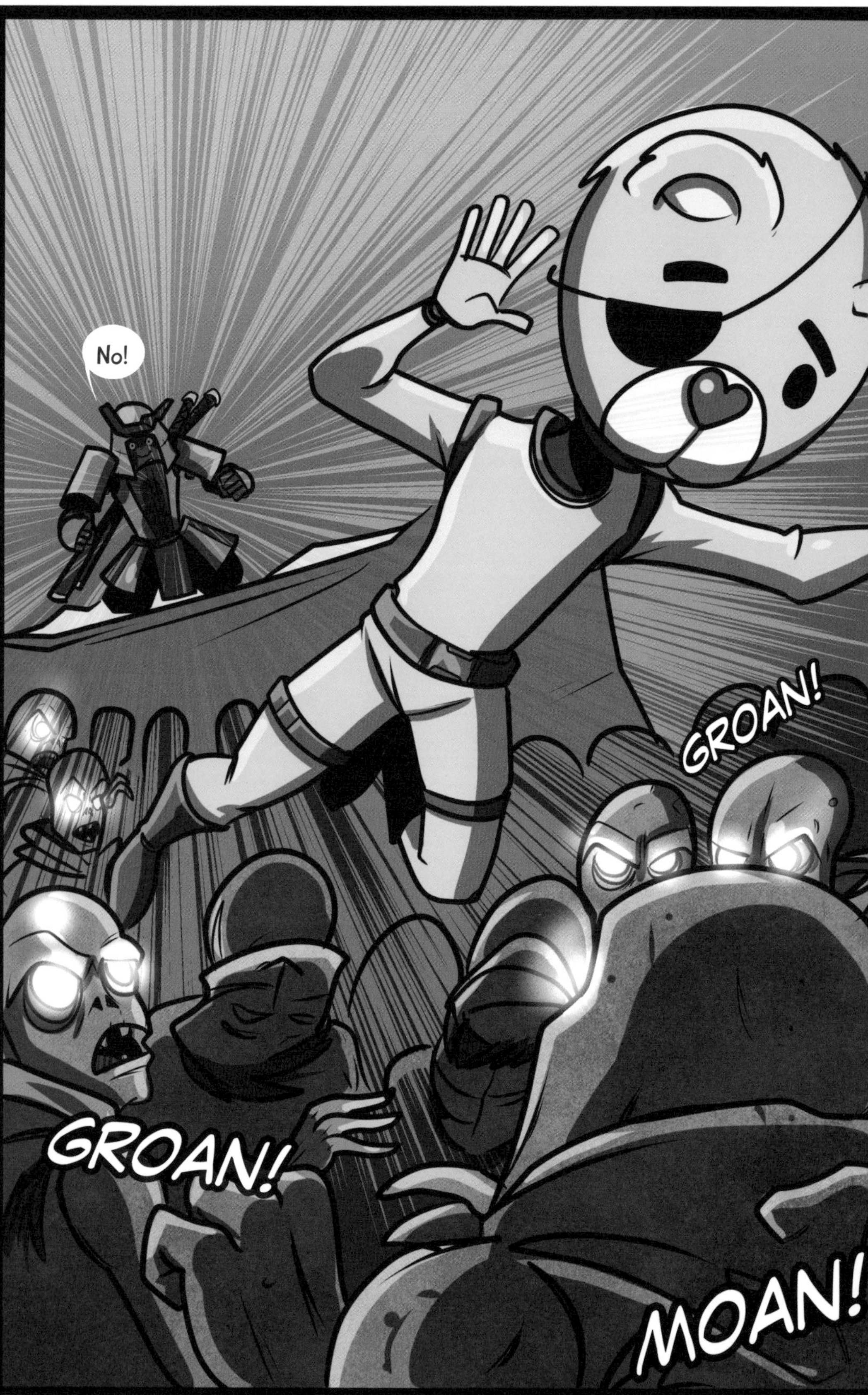
No!
GROAN!
GROAN!
MOAN!

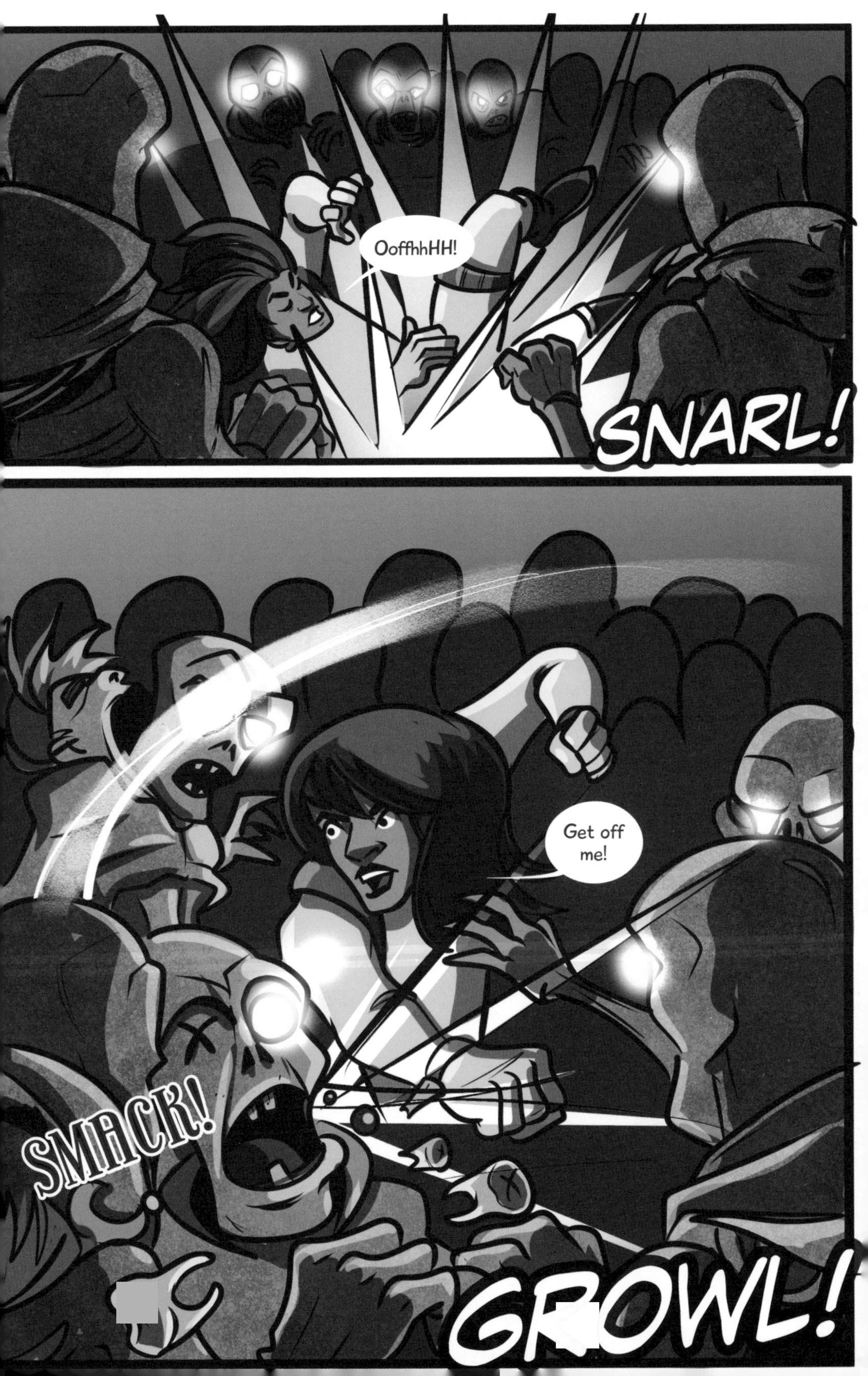
OoffhhHH!
SNARL!
Get off me!
SMACK!
GROWL!

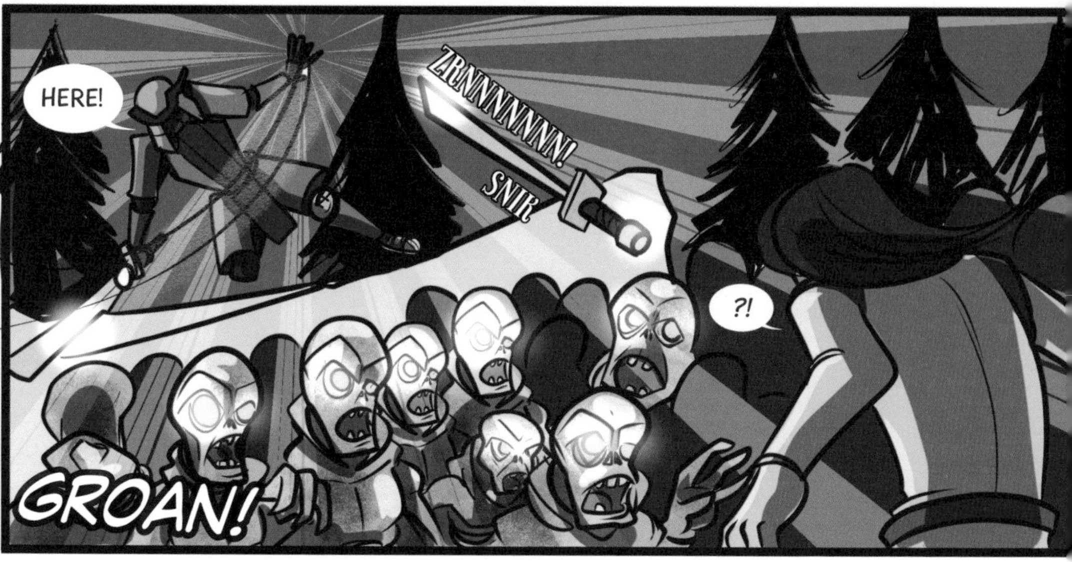
HERE!
ZRNNNNNNN!
SNIK
?!
GROAN!

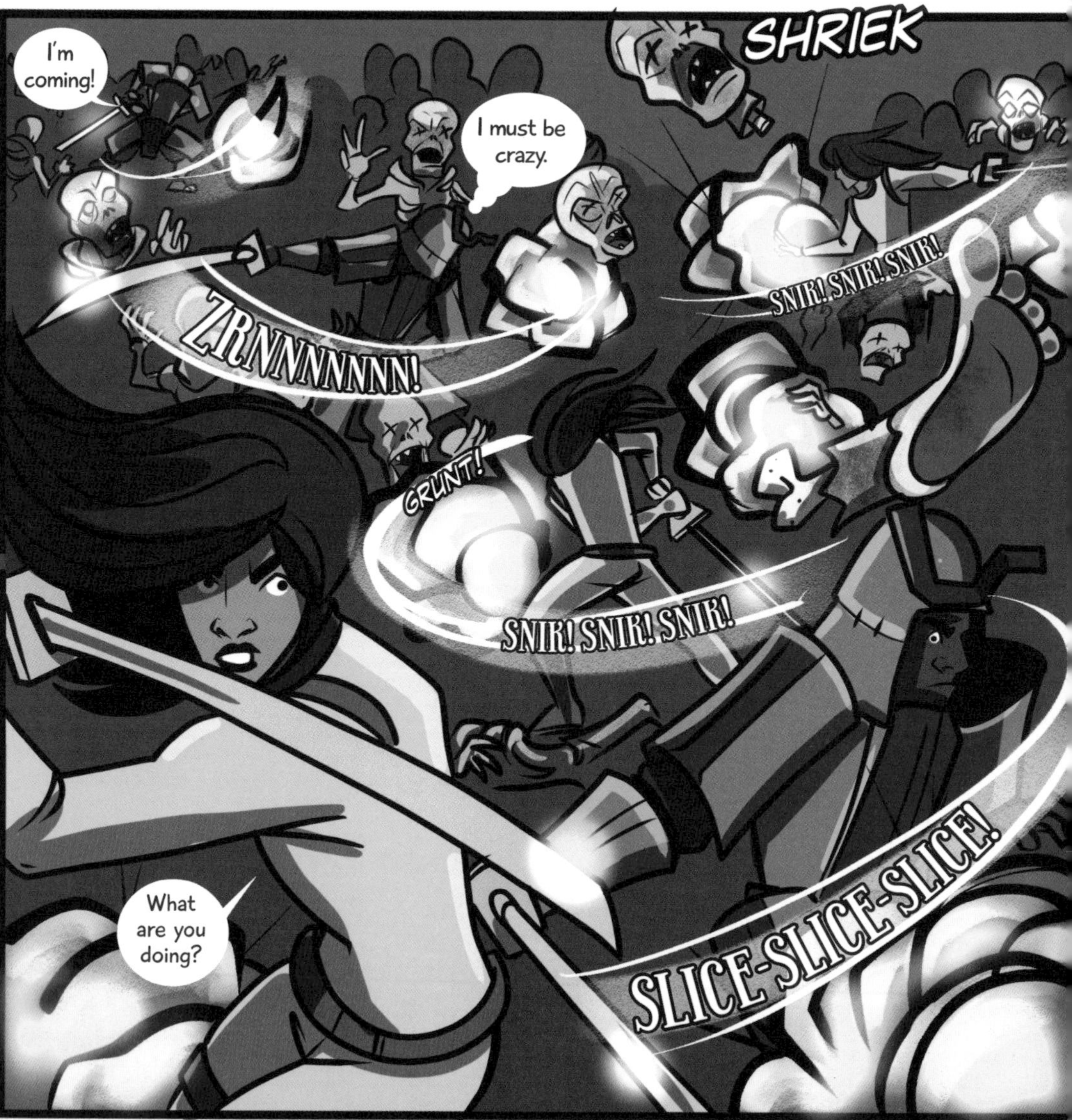
I'm coming!
I must be crazy.
SHRIEK
ZRNNNNNNN!
SNIK! SNIK! SNIK!
GRUNT!
SNIK! SNIK! SNIK!
What are you doing?
SLICE-SLICE-SLICE!

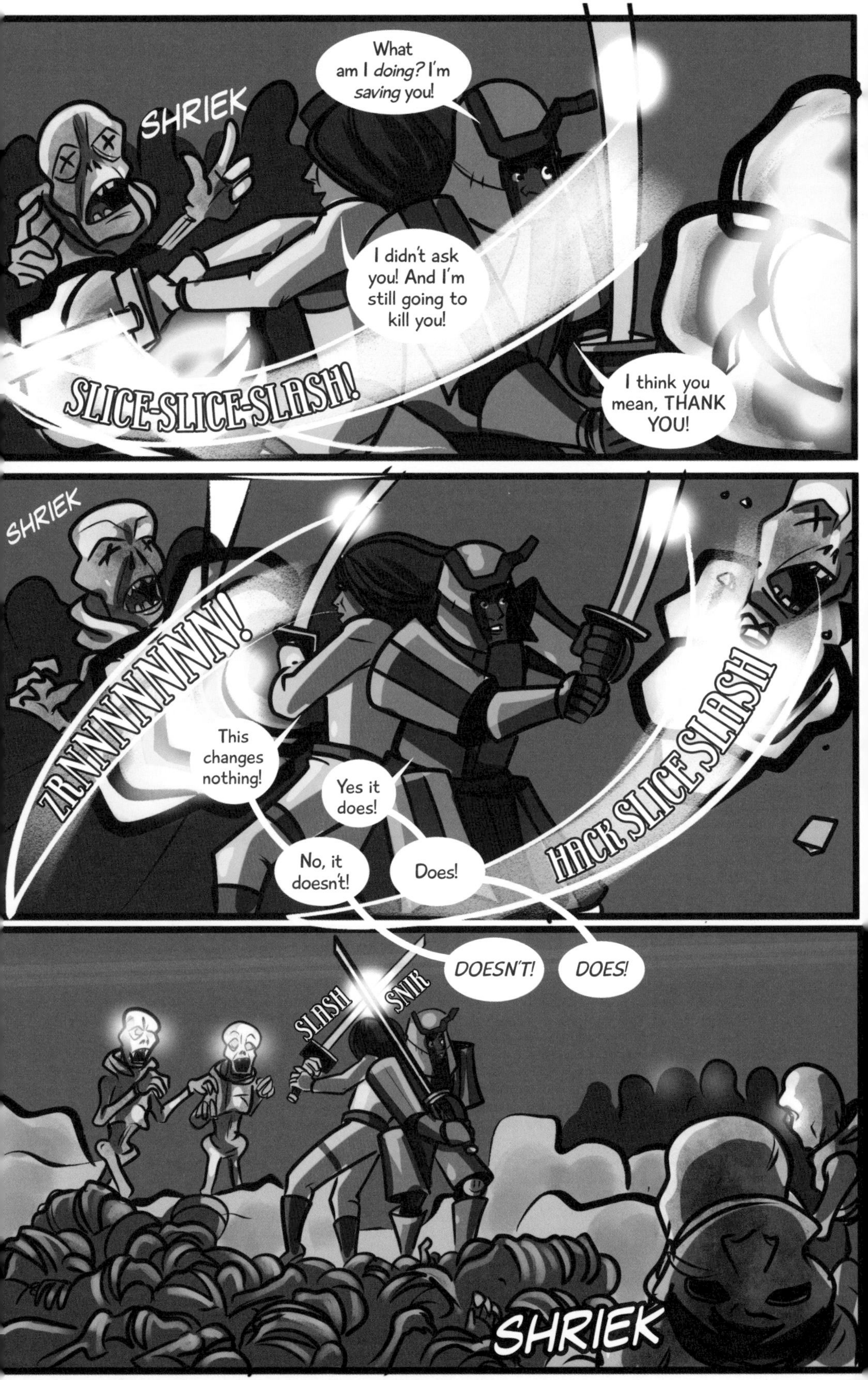
SHRIEK
What am I *doing?* I'm *saving* you!
I didn't ask you! And I'm still going to kill you!
I think you mean, THANK YOU!
SLICE-SLICE-SLASH!
SHRIEK
ZRNNNNNNNN!
HACK SLICE SLASH
This changes nothing!
Yes it does!
No, it doesn't!
Does!
DOESN'T!
DOES!
SLASH
SNIK
SHRIEK

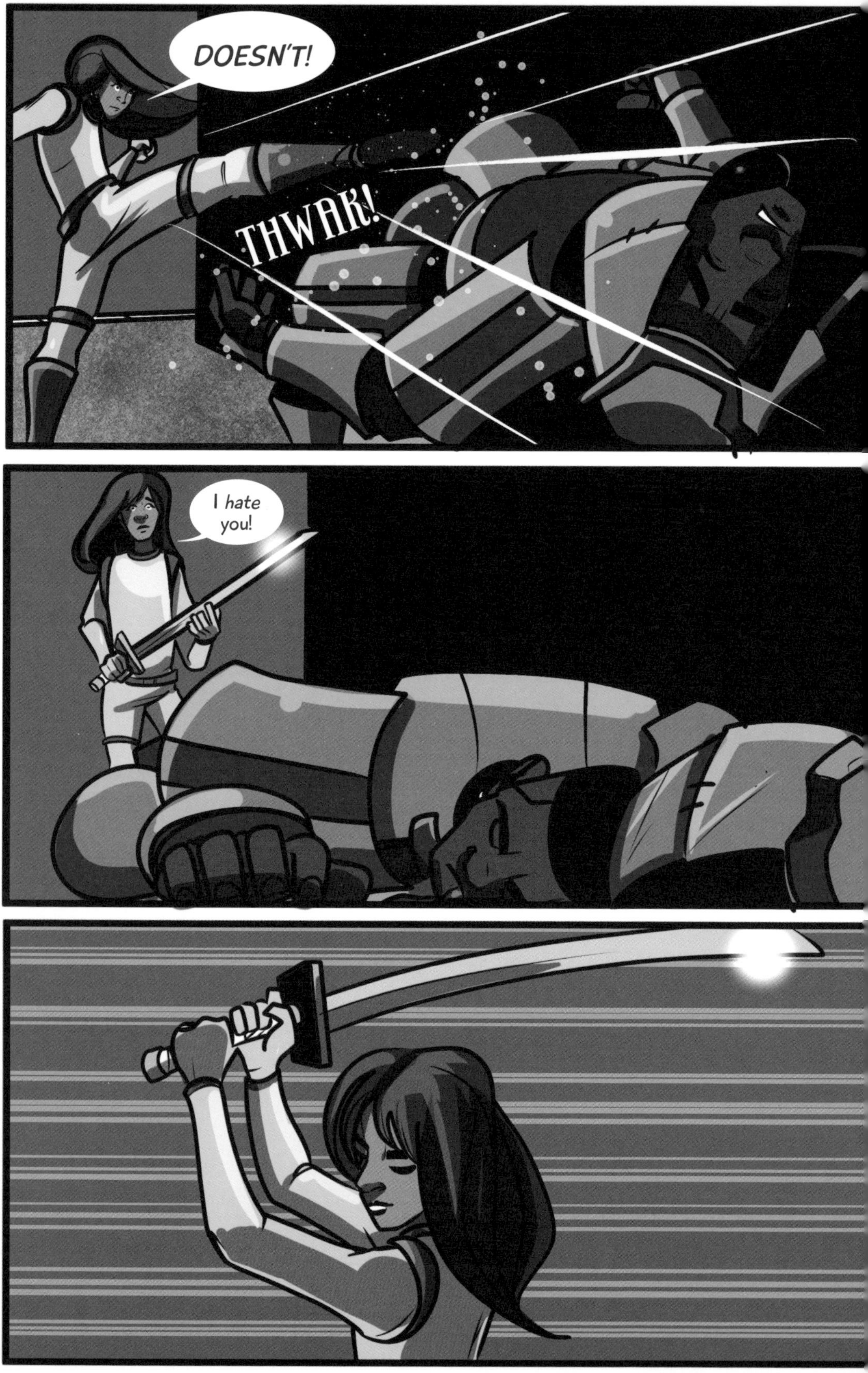
DOESN'T!
THWAK!
I hate you!

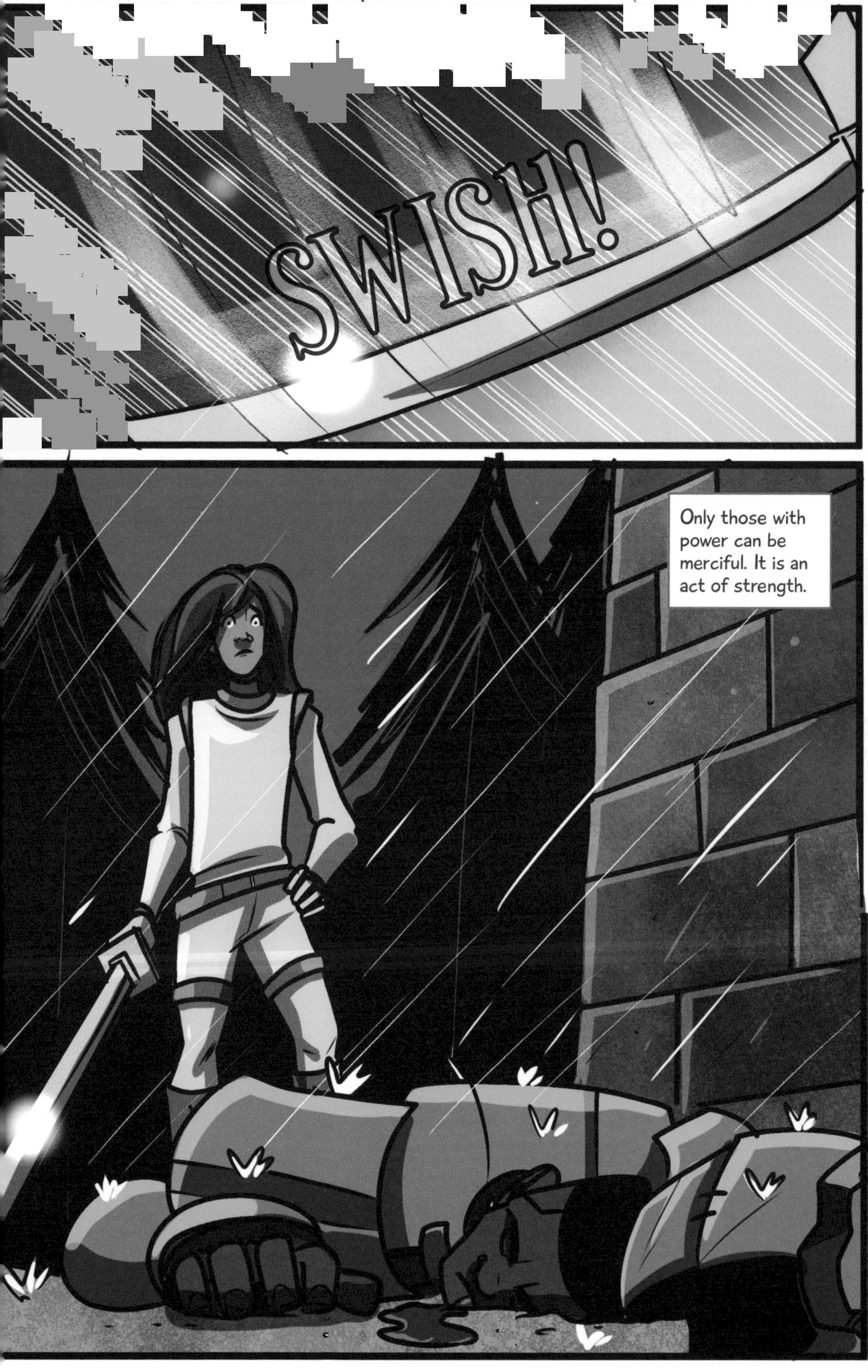
SWISH!
Only those with power can be merciful. It is an act of strength.

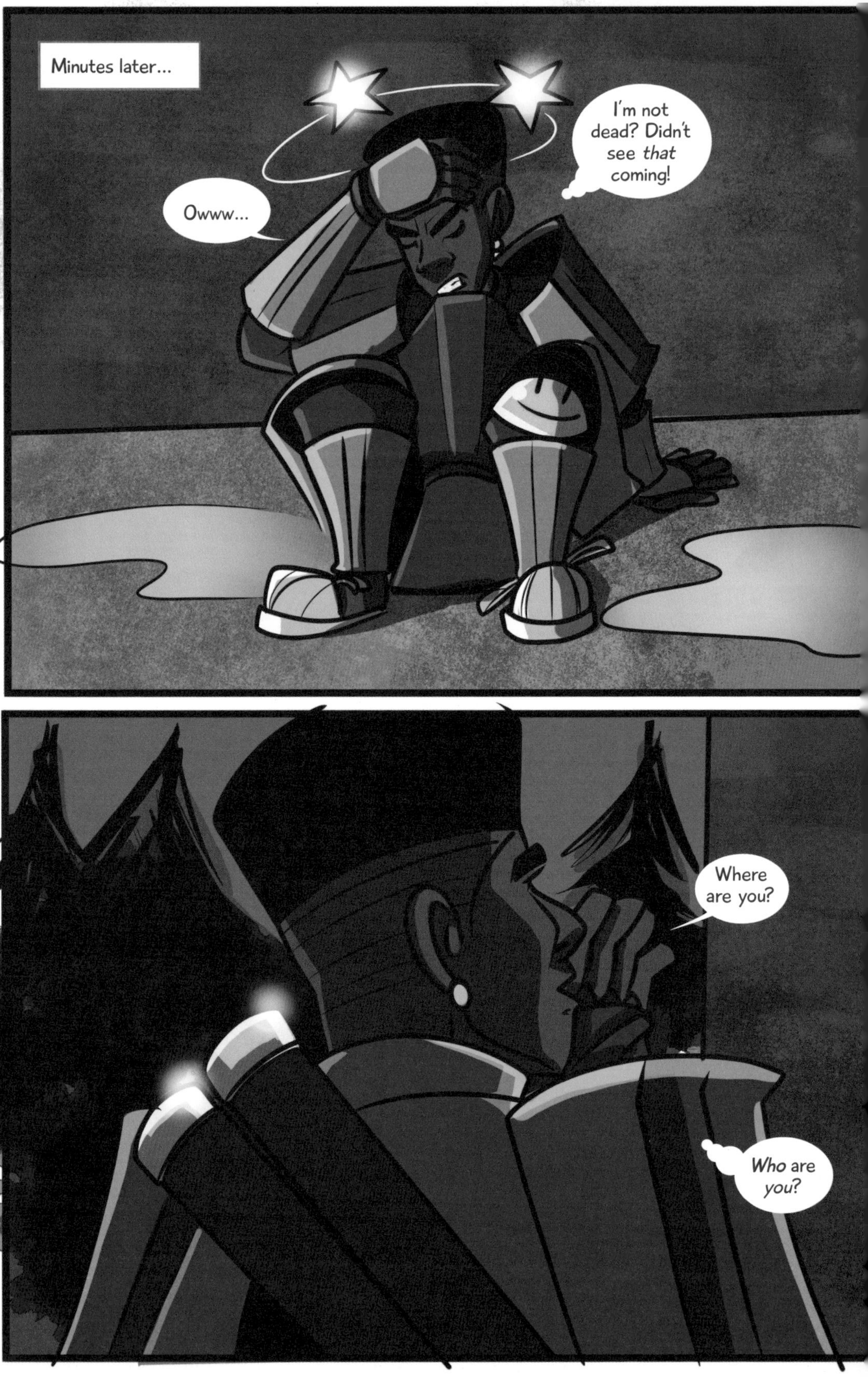
Minutes later...
Owww...
I'm not dead? Didn't see *that* coming!
Where are you?
Who are *you?*

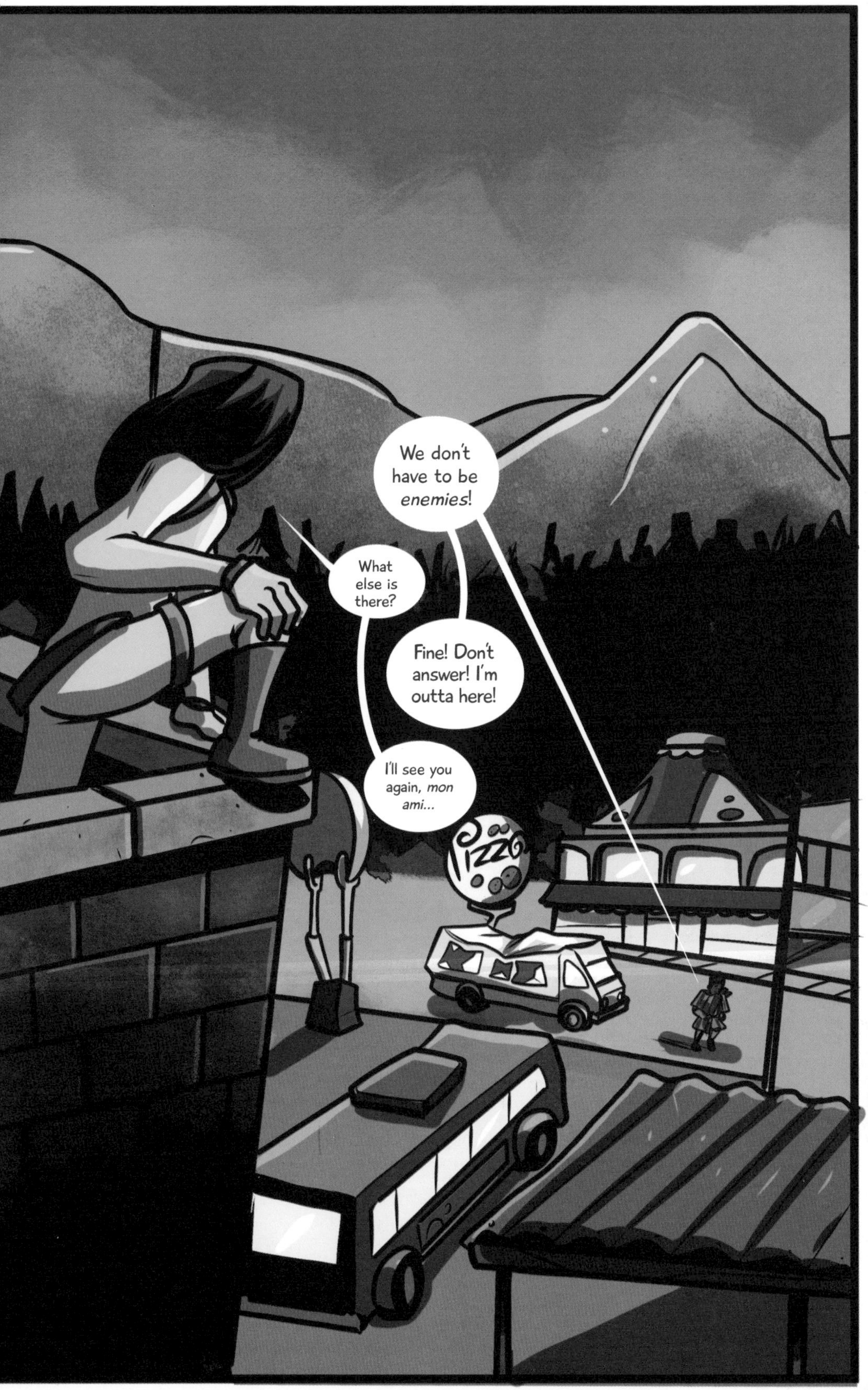
We don't have to be *enemies*!
What else is there?
Fine! Don't answer! I'm outta here!
I'll see you again, *mon ami*...

CHAPTER 11: A PROMI[redacted]E KEPT

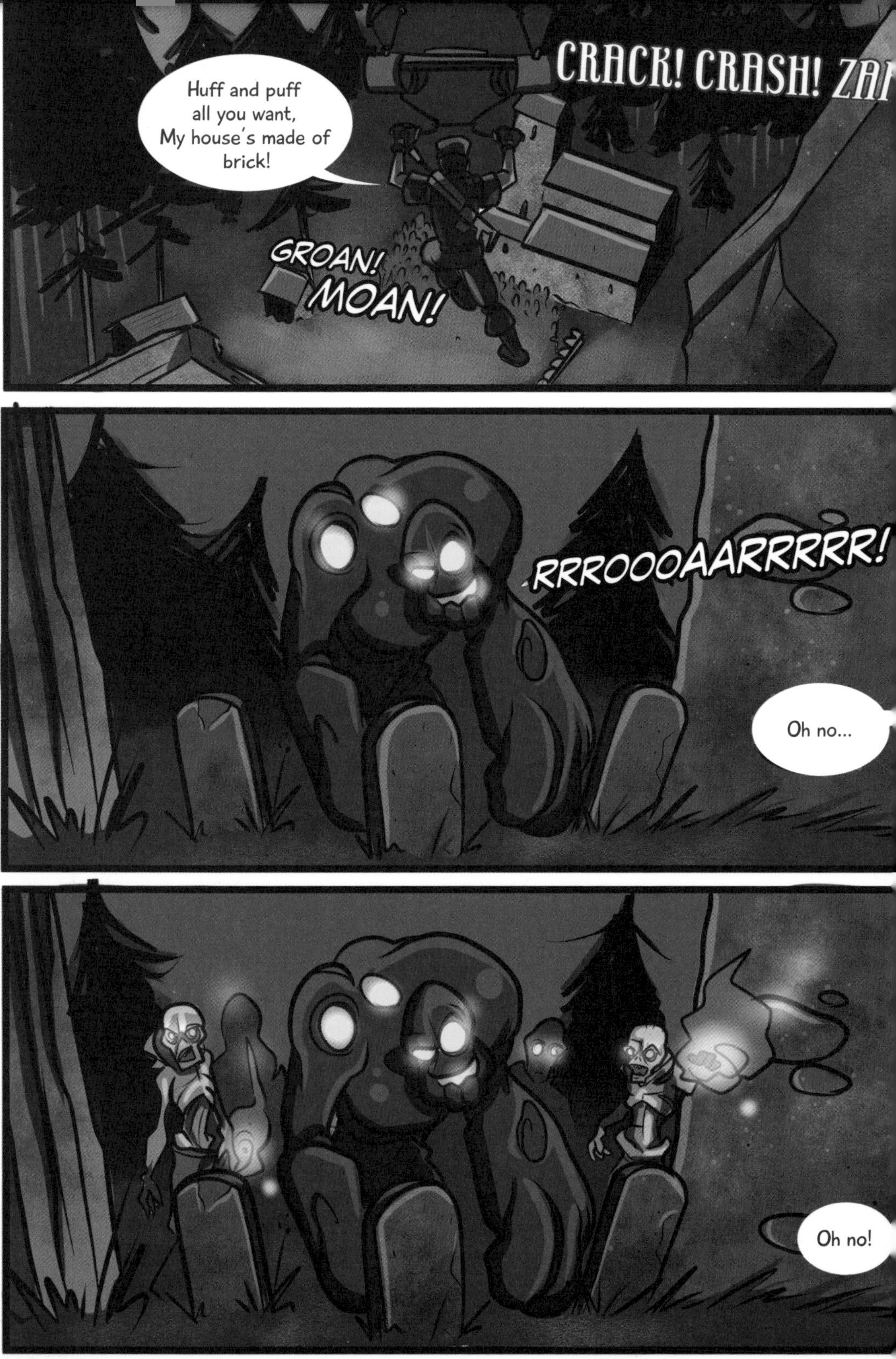
CRACK! CRASH!
Huff and puff all you want, My house's made of brick!
GROAN! MOAN!
RRROOOAARRRRR!
Oh no...
Oh no!

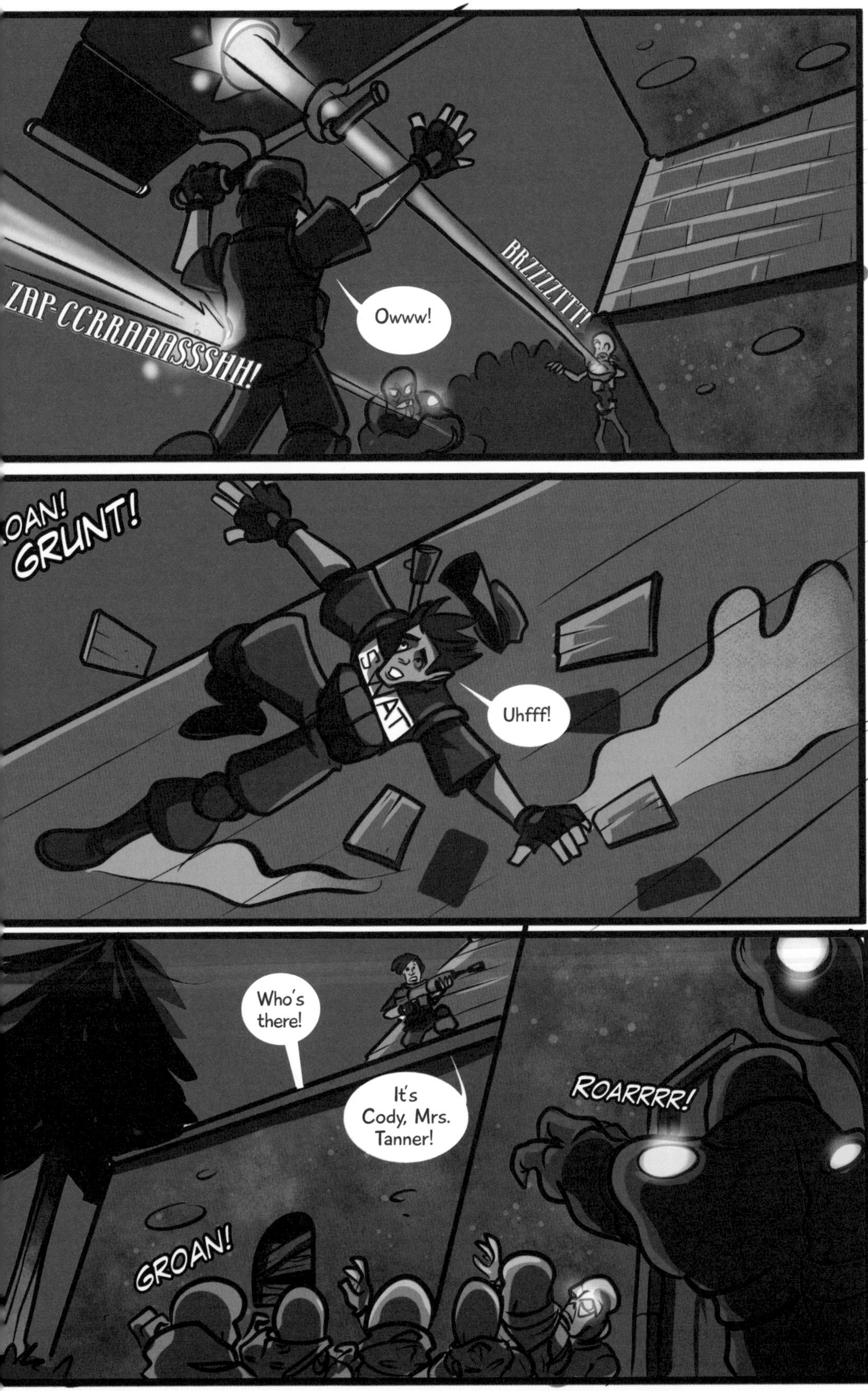
ZAP-CCRRAAAASSSHH!
BRZZZZTTT!
Owww!
OAN! GRUNT!
SWAT
Uhfff!
Who's there!
It's Cody, Mrs. Tanner!
ROARRRR!
GROAN!

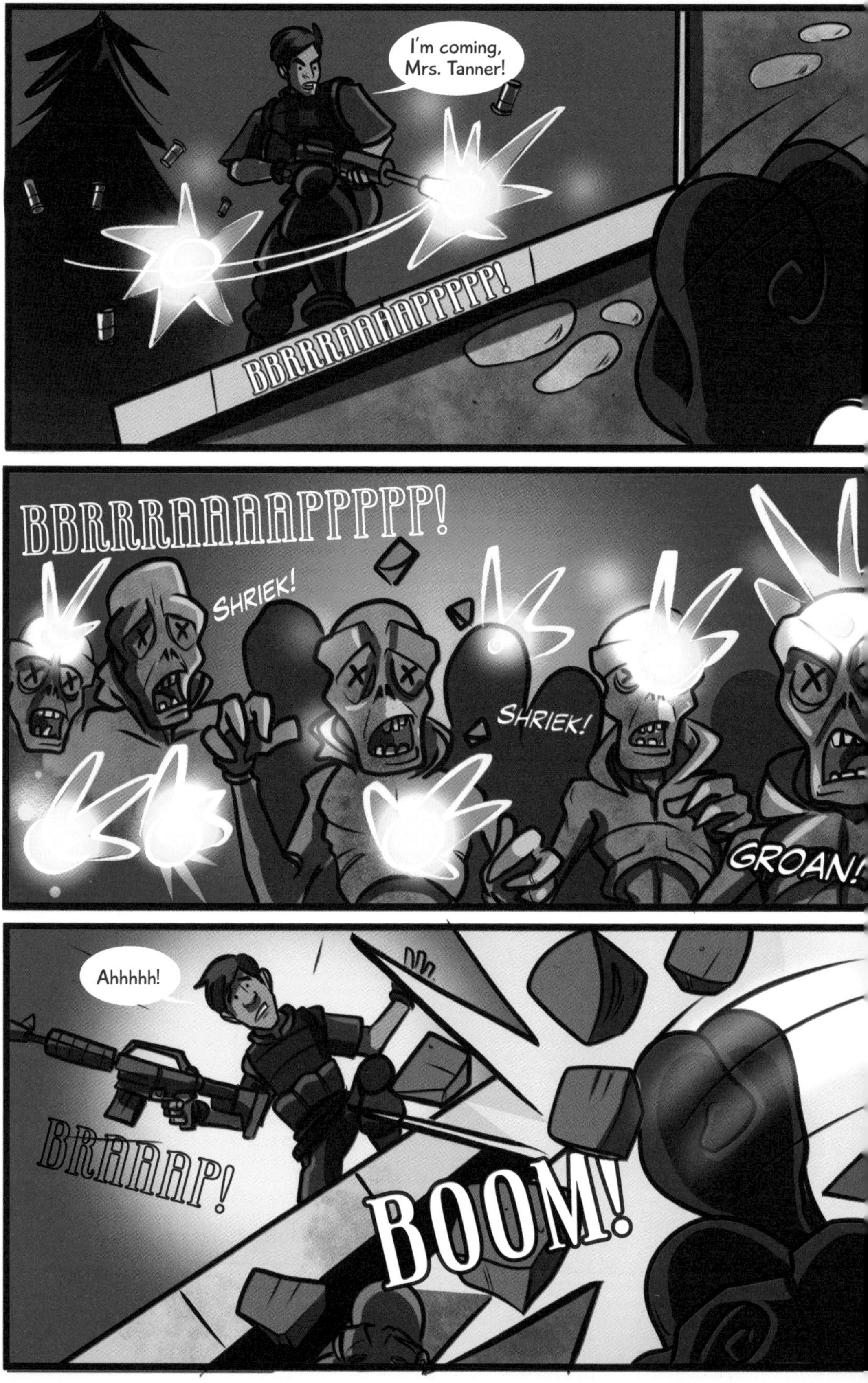

I'm coming, Mrs. Tanner!
BBRRRAAAAAPPPPPP!
BBRRRAAAAAPPPPPP!
SHRIEK!
SHRIEK!
GROAN!
Ahhhhh!
BRAAAAP!
BOOM!

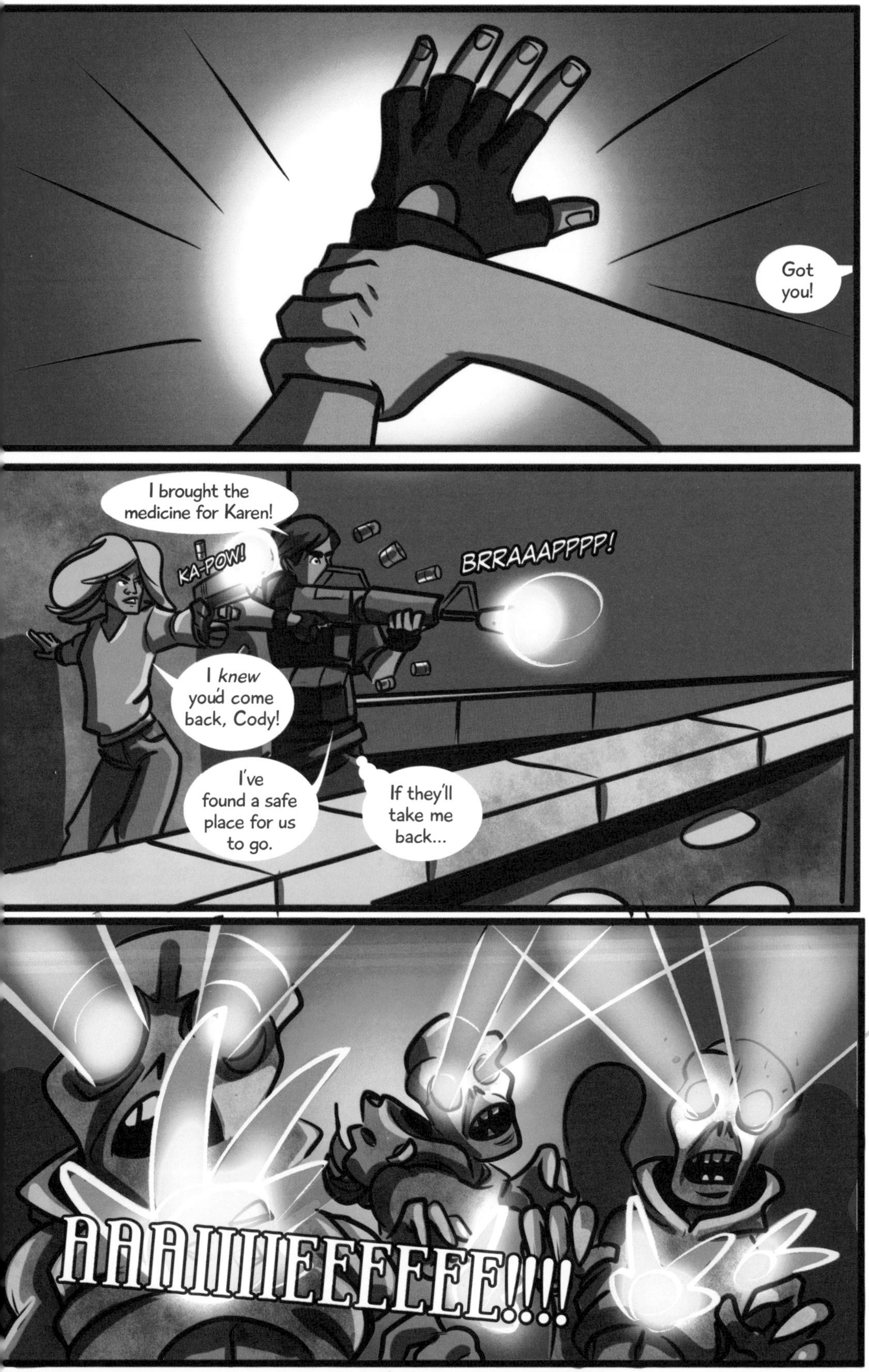
Got you!
I brought the medicine for Karen!
KA-POW!
BRRAAAPPPP!
I *knew* you'd come back, Cody!
I've found a safe place for us to go.
If they'll take me back...
AAAIIIIEEEEEE!!!!

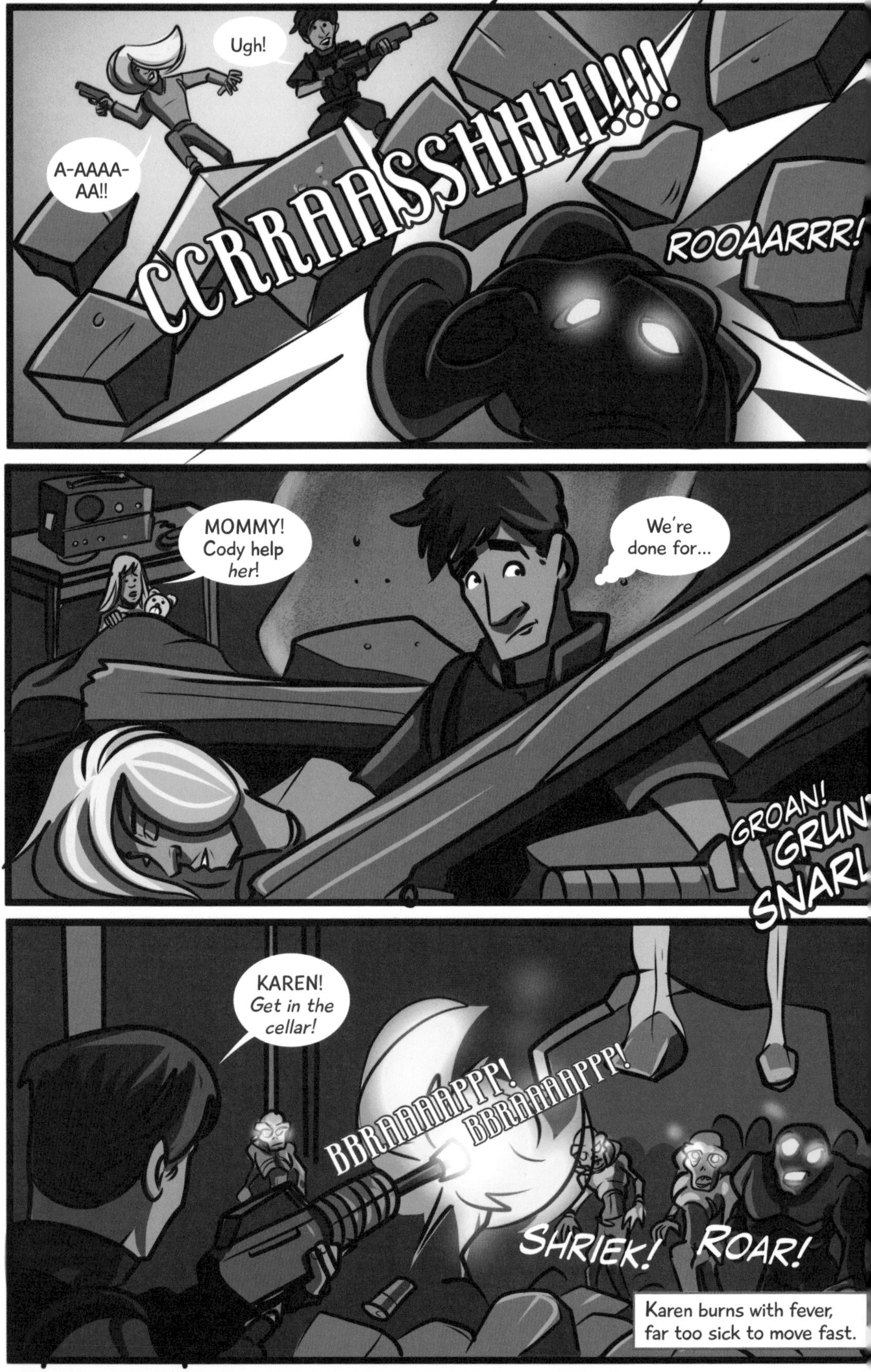
Ugh!
A-AAAA-AA!!
CCRRAASSHHH!!!!
ROOAARRR!
MOMMY! Cody help her!
We're done for...
GROAN!
GRUN
SNARL
KAREN! Get in the cellar!
BBRAAAAAPPP!
BBRAAAAAPPP!
SHRIEK!
ROAR!
Karen burns with fever, far too sick to move fast.

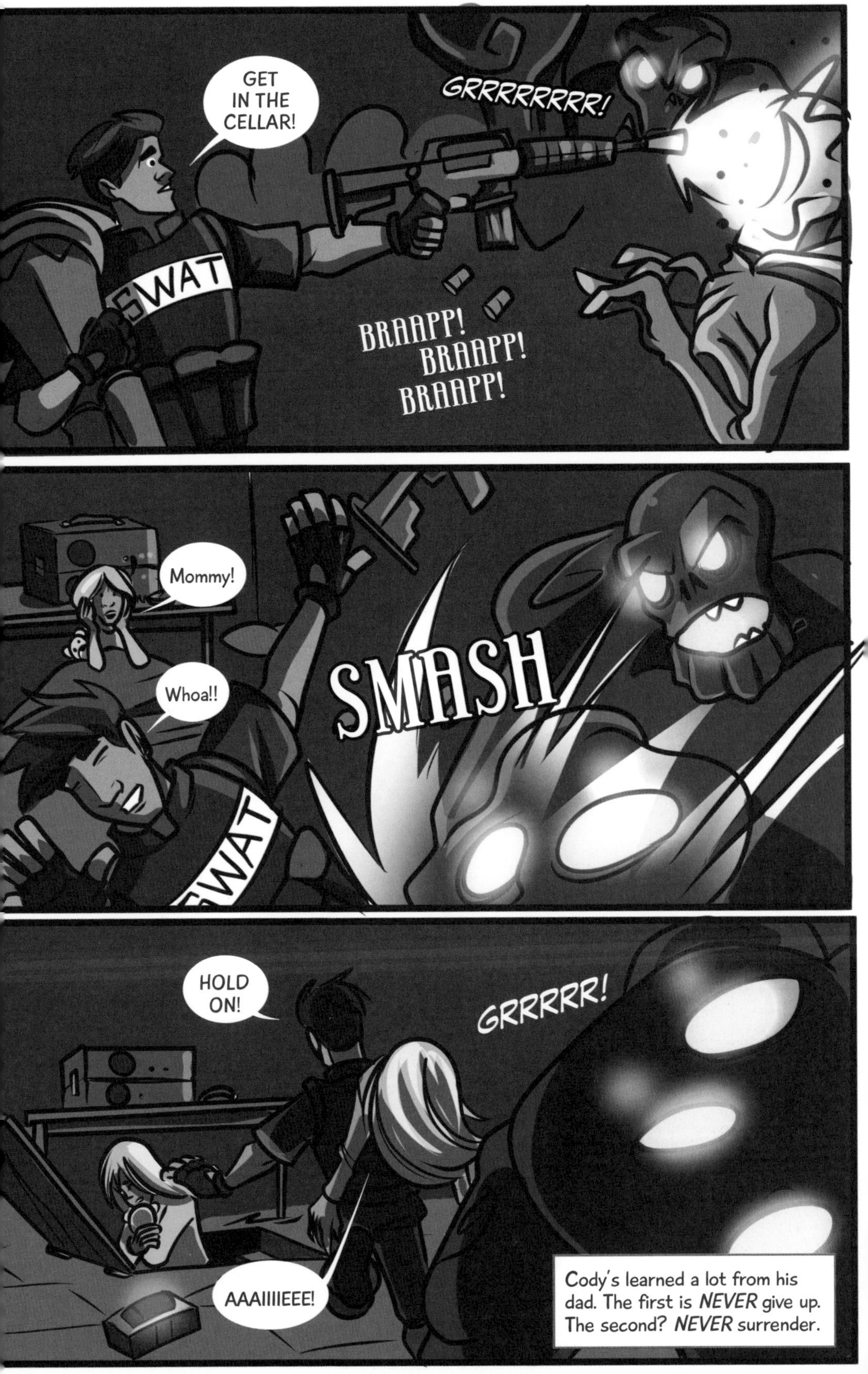
GET IN THE CELLAR!
GRRRRRRRR!
BRAAPP! BRAAPP! BRAAPP!
Mommy!
Whoa!!
SMASH
HOLD ON!
GRRRRR!
AAAIIIIEEE!
Cody's learned a lot from his dad. The first is *NEVER* give up. The second? *NEVER* surrender.

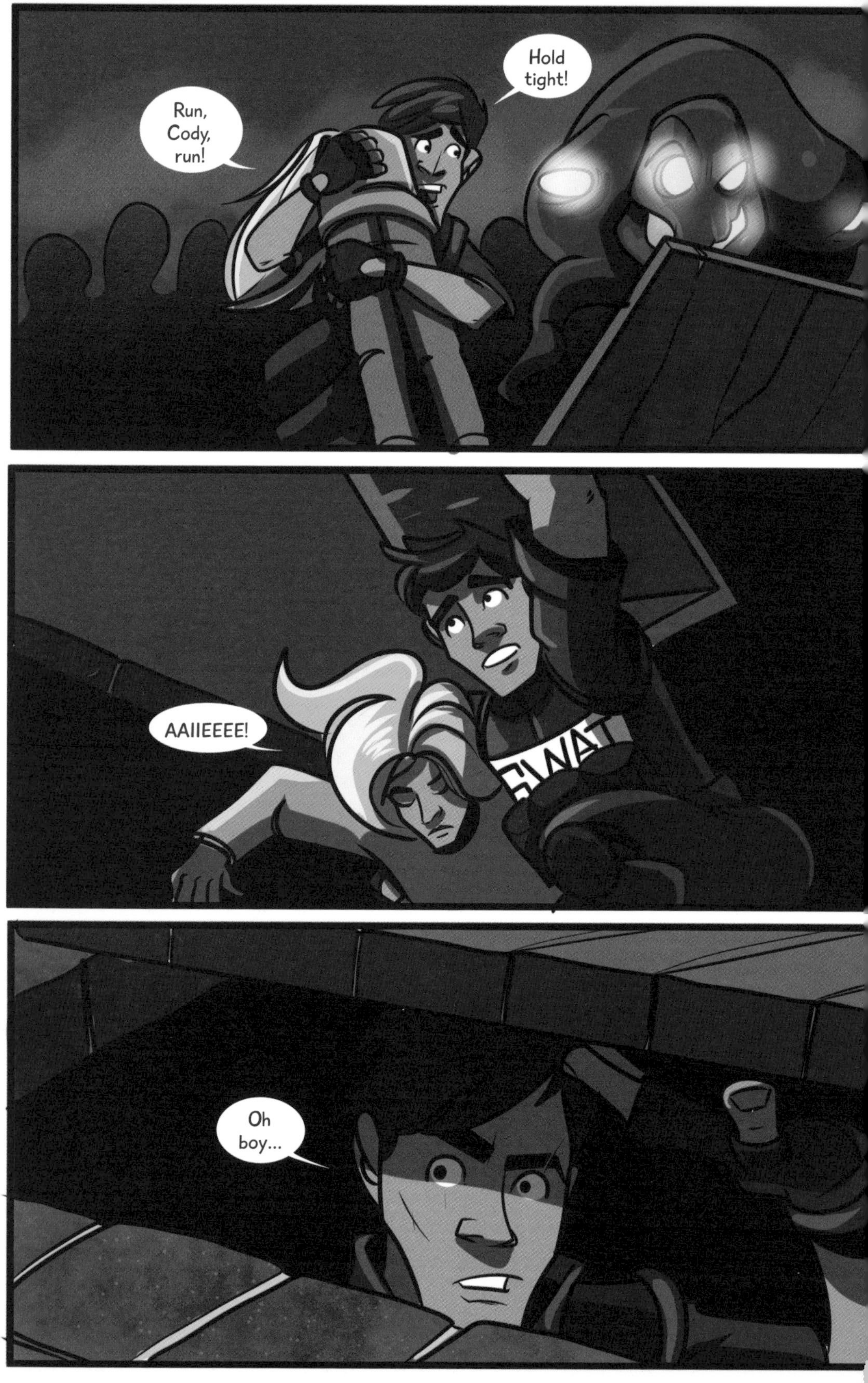
Run, Cody, run!
Hold tight!
AAIIEEEE!
SWAT
Oh boy...

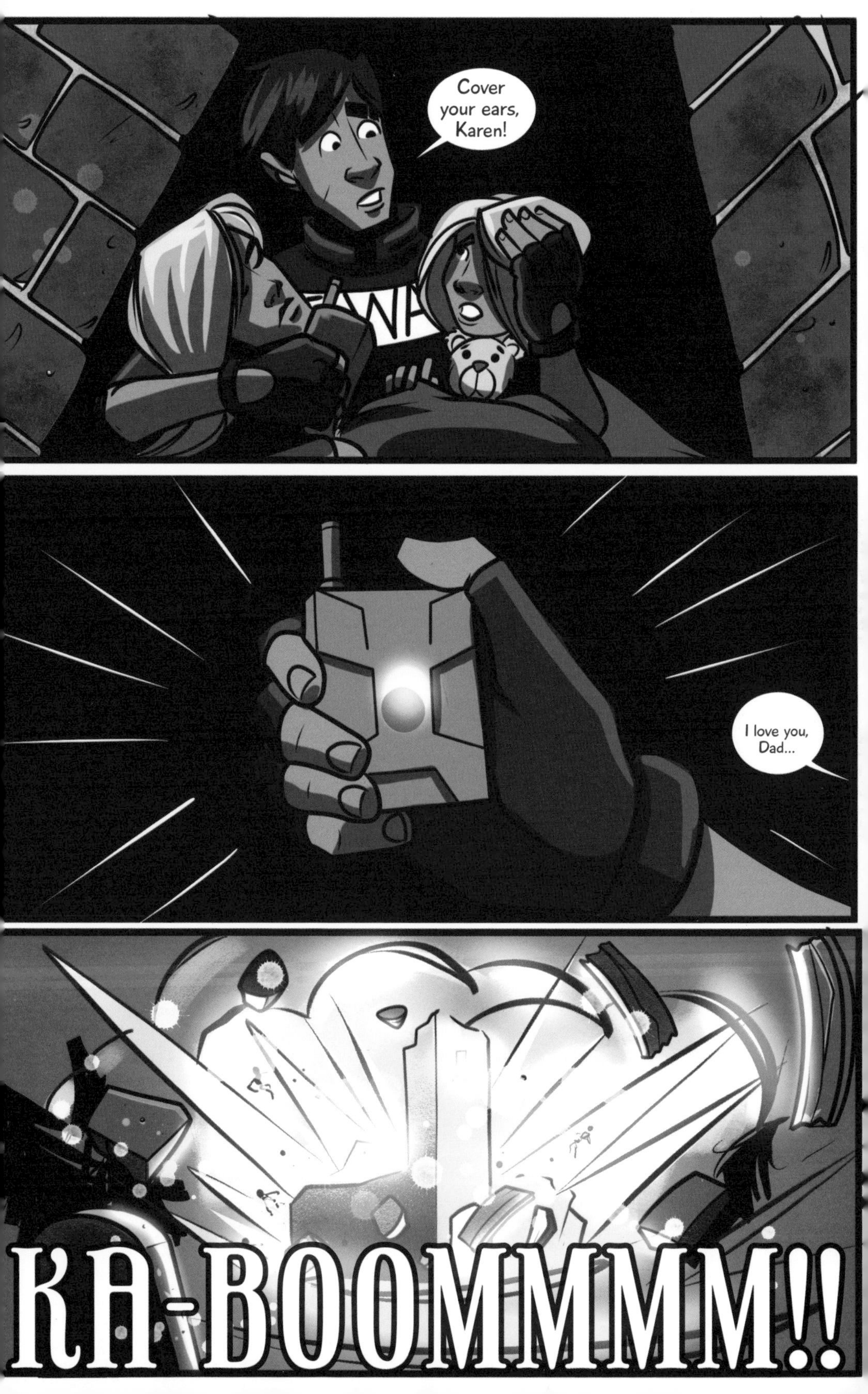
Cover your ears, Karen!
I love you, Dad...
KA-BOOMMMMM!!

CHAPTER 12: AGAINST ALL ODDS

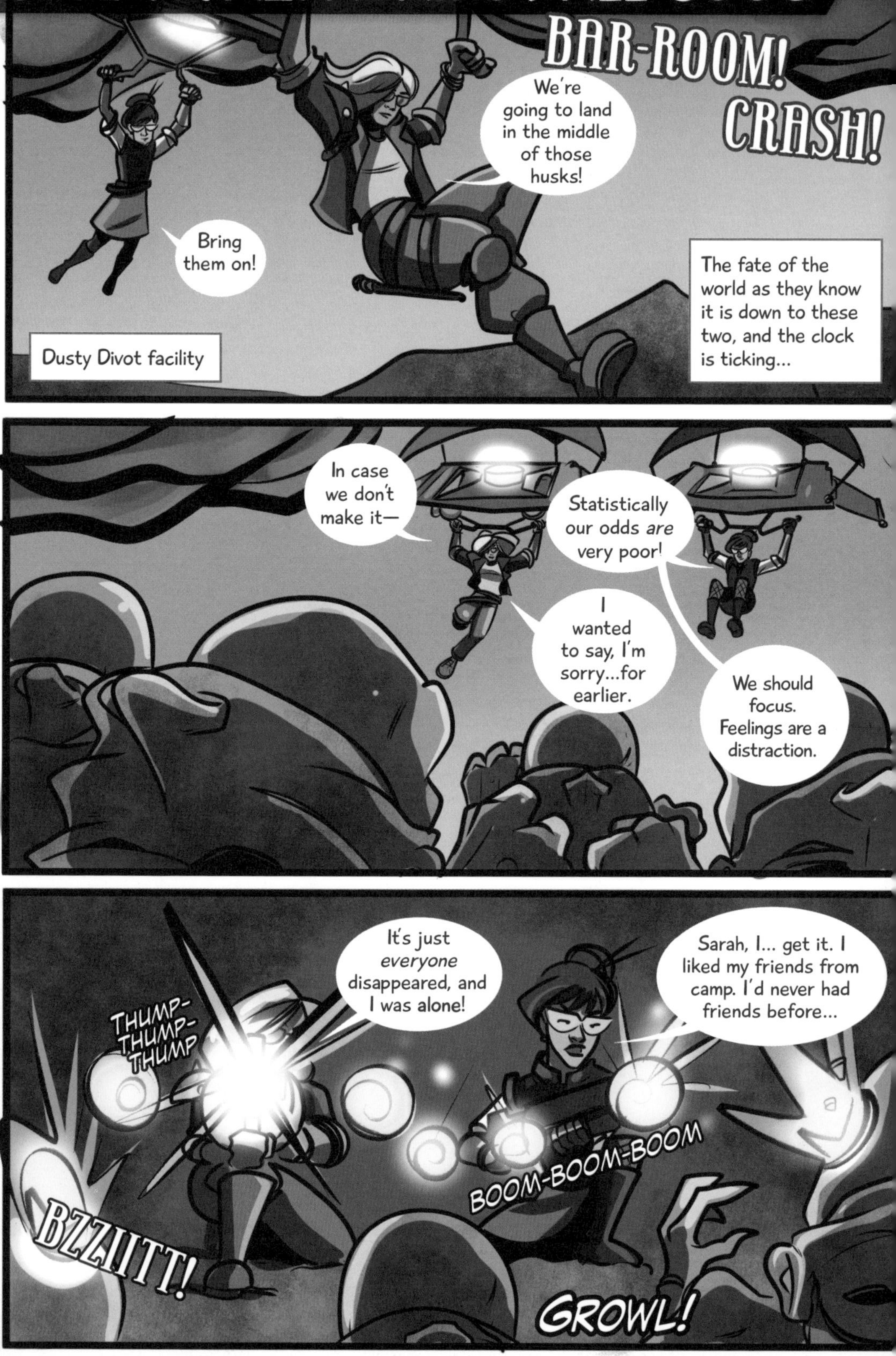
BAR-ROOM!
CRASH!
Dusty Divot facility
The fate of the world as they know it is down to these two, and the clock is ticking...
We're going to land in the middle of those husks!
Bring them on!
In case we don't make it—
Statistically our odds *are* very poor!
I wanted to say, I'm sorry...for earlier.
We should focus. Feelings are a distraction.
It's just *everyone* disappeared, and I was alone!
Sarah, I... get it. I liked my friends from camp. I'd never had friends before...
THUMP-THUMP-THUMP
BOOM-BOOM-BOOM
BZZIITT!
GROWL!

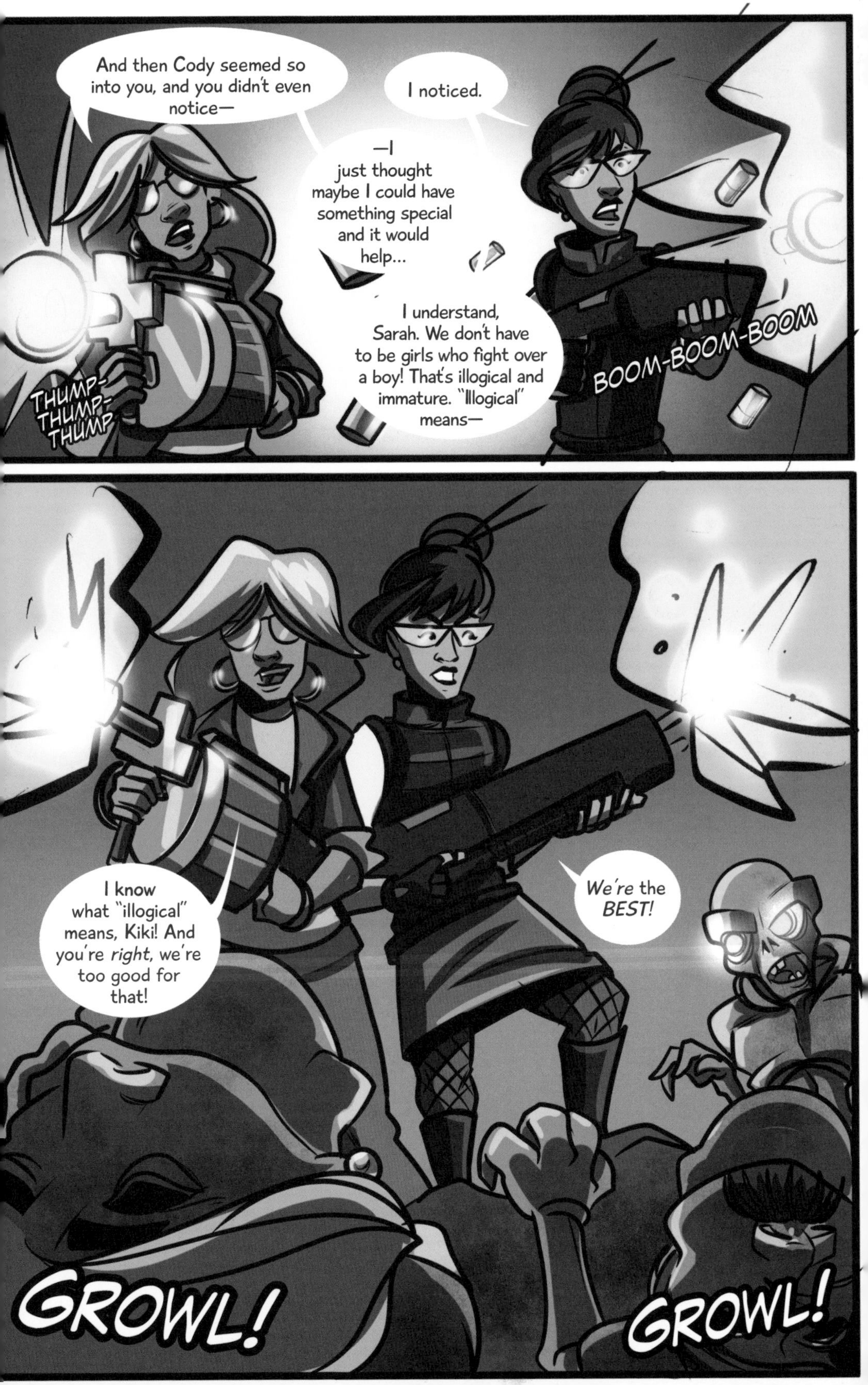

And then Cody seemed so into you, and you didn't even notice—
I noticed.
—I just thought maybe I could have something special and it would help...
I understand, Sarah. We don't have to be girls who fight over a boy! That's illogical and immature. "Illogical" means—
THUMP-THUMP-THUMP
BOOM-BOOM-BOOM
I know what "illogical" means, Kiki! And you're *right*, we're too good for that!
We're the *BEST!*
GROWL!
GROWL!

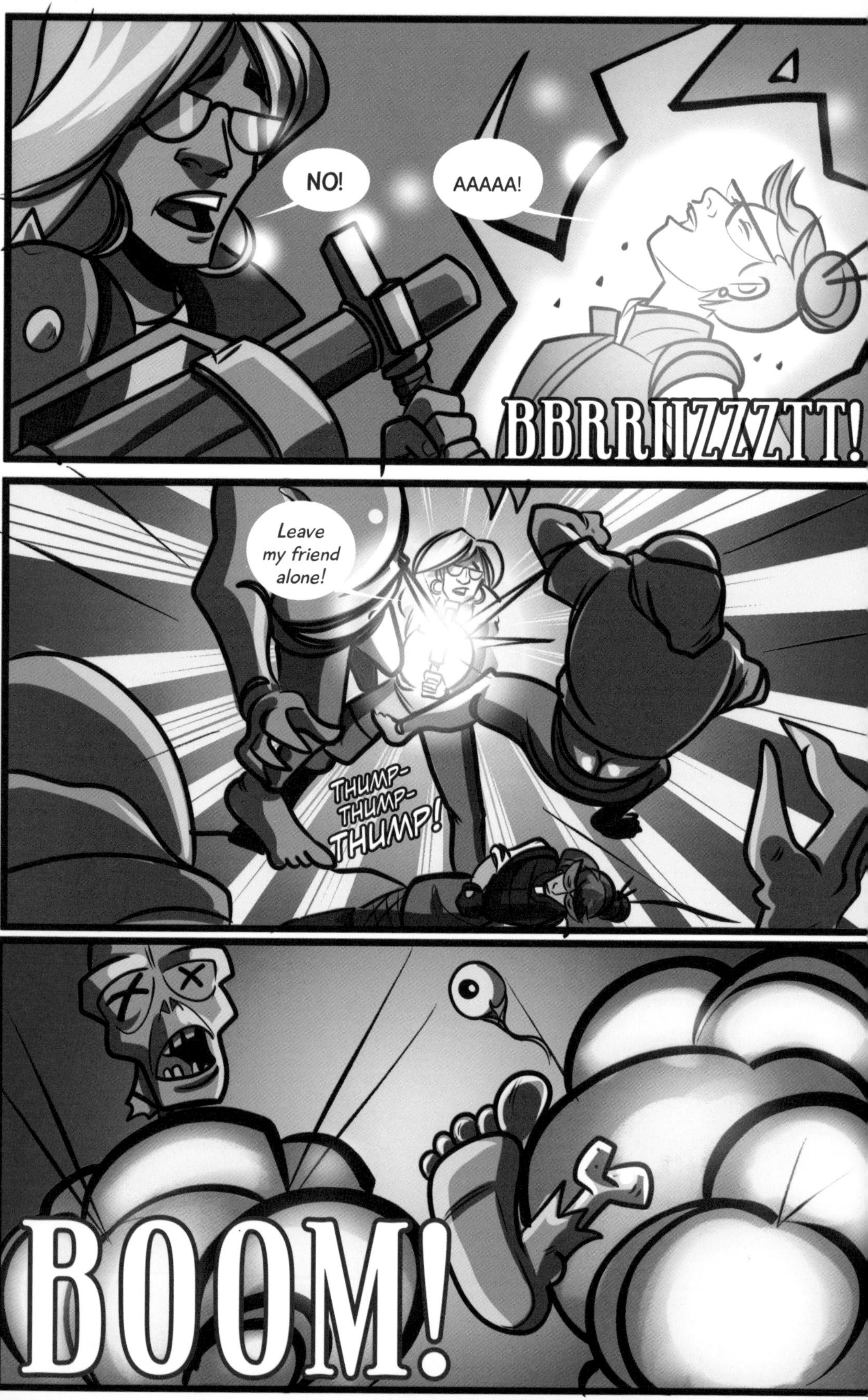
NO!
AAAAA!
BBRRIIZZZTT!
Leave my friend alone!
THUMP-THUMP-THUMP!
BOOM!

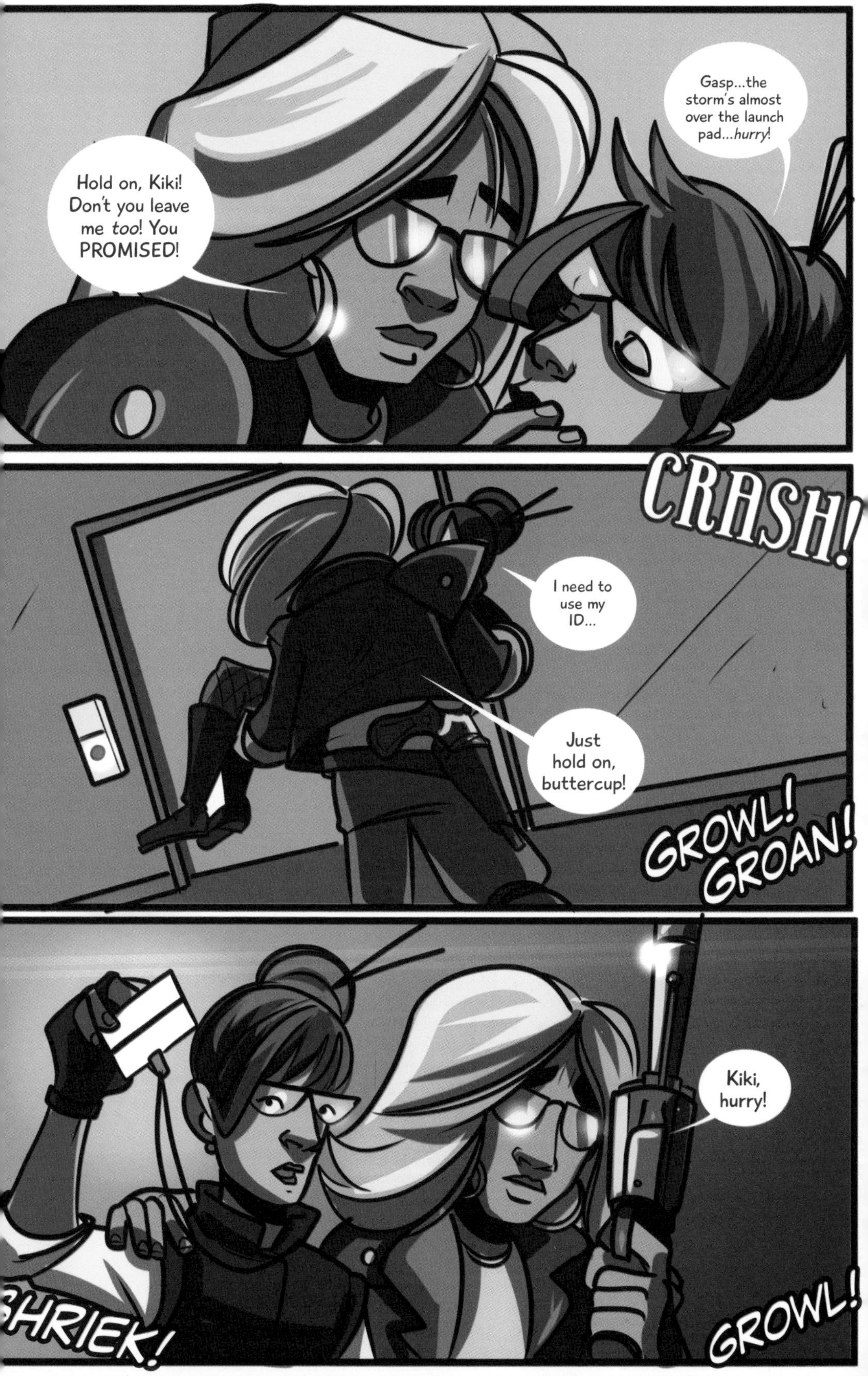
Gasp...the storm's almost over the launch pad...*hurry*!
Hold on, Kiki! Don't you leave me *too*! You PROMISED!
CRASH!
I need to use my ID...
Just hold on, buttercup!
GROWL! GROAN!
Kiki, hurry!
SHRIEK!
GROWL!

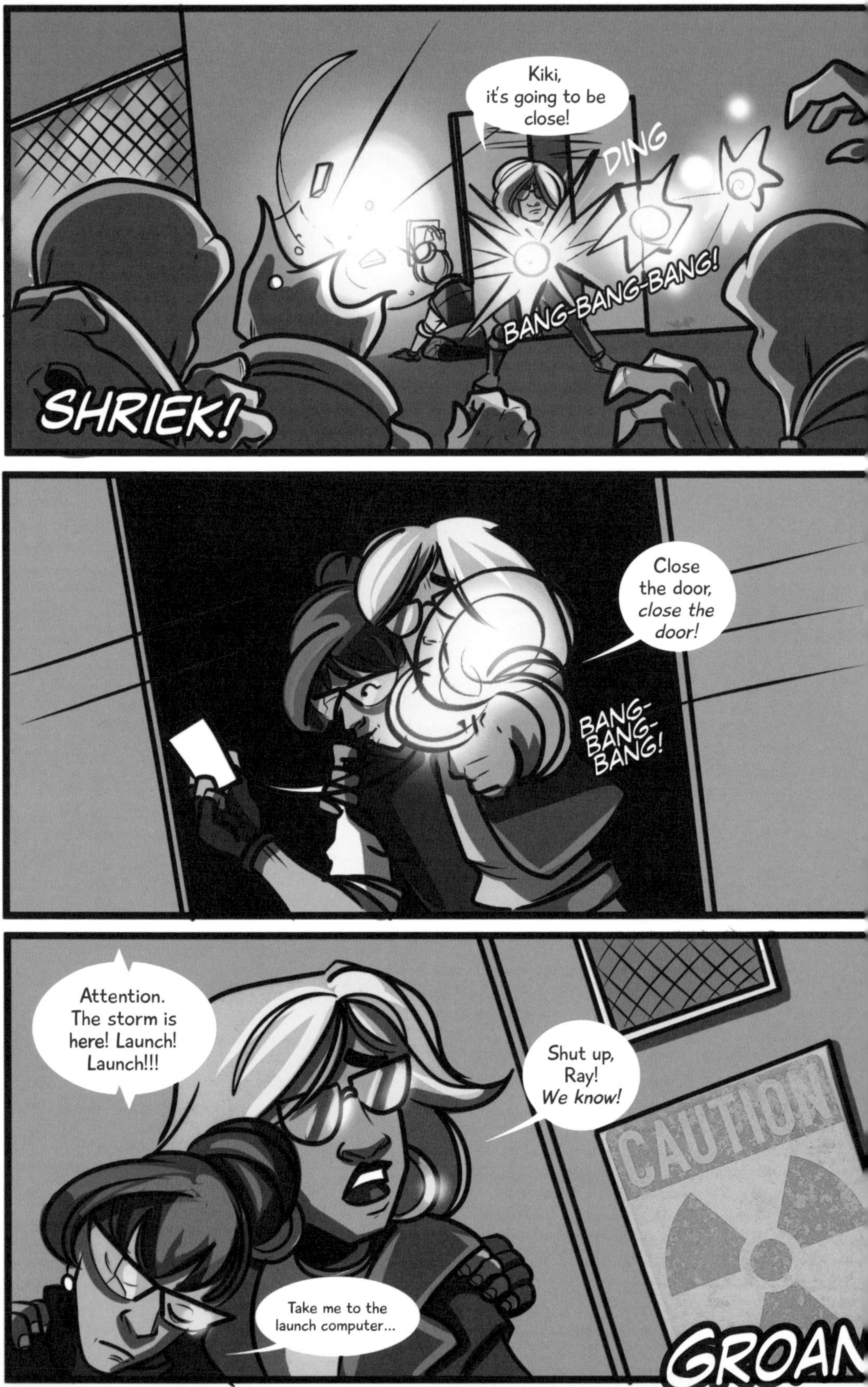
Kiki, it's going to be close!
DING
BANG-BANG-BANG!
SHRIEK!
Close the door, *close the door!*
BANG-BANG-BANG!
Attention. The storm is here! Launch! Launch!!!
Shut up, Ray! *We know!*
CAUTION
Take me to the launch computer...
GROAN

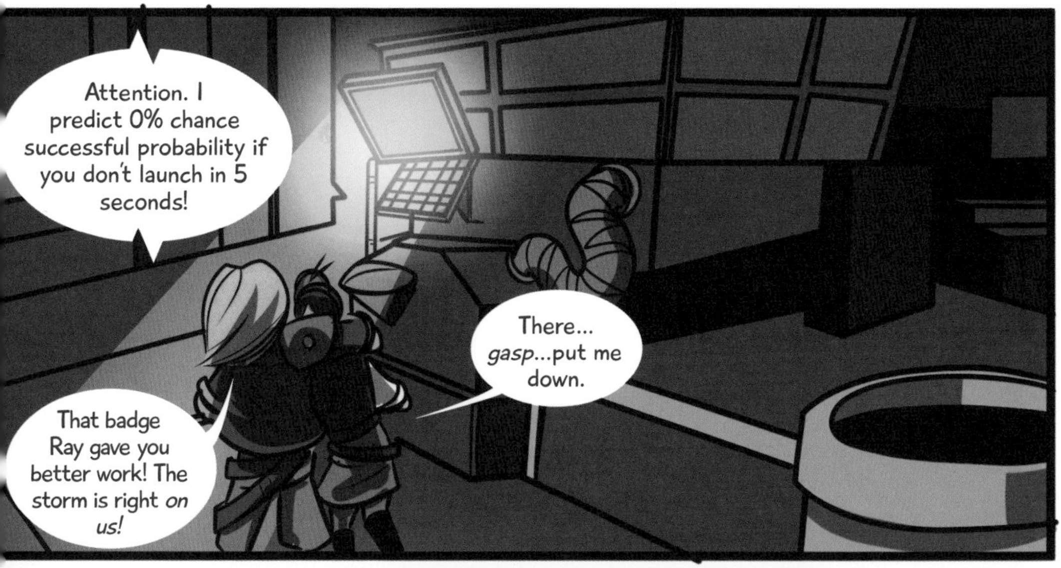
Attention. I predict 0% chance successful probability if you don't launch in 5 seconds!
There... *gasp*...put me down.
That badge Ray gave you better work! The storm is right *on* us!

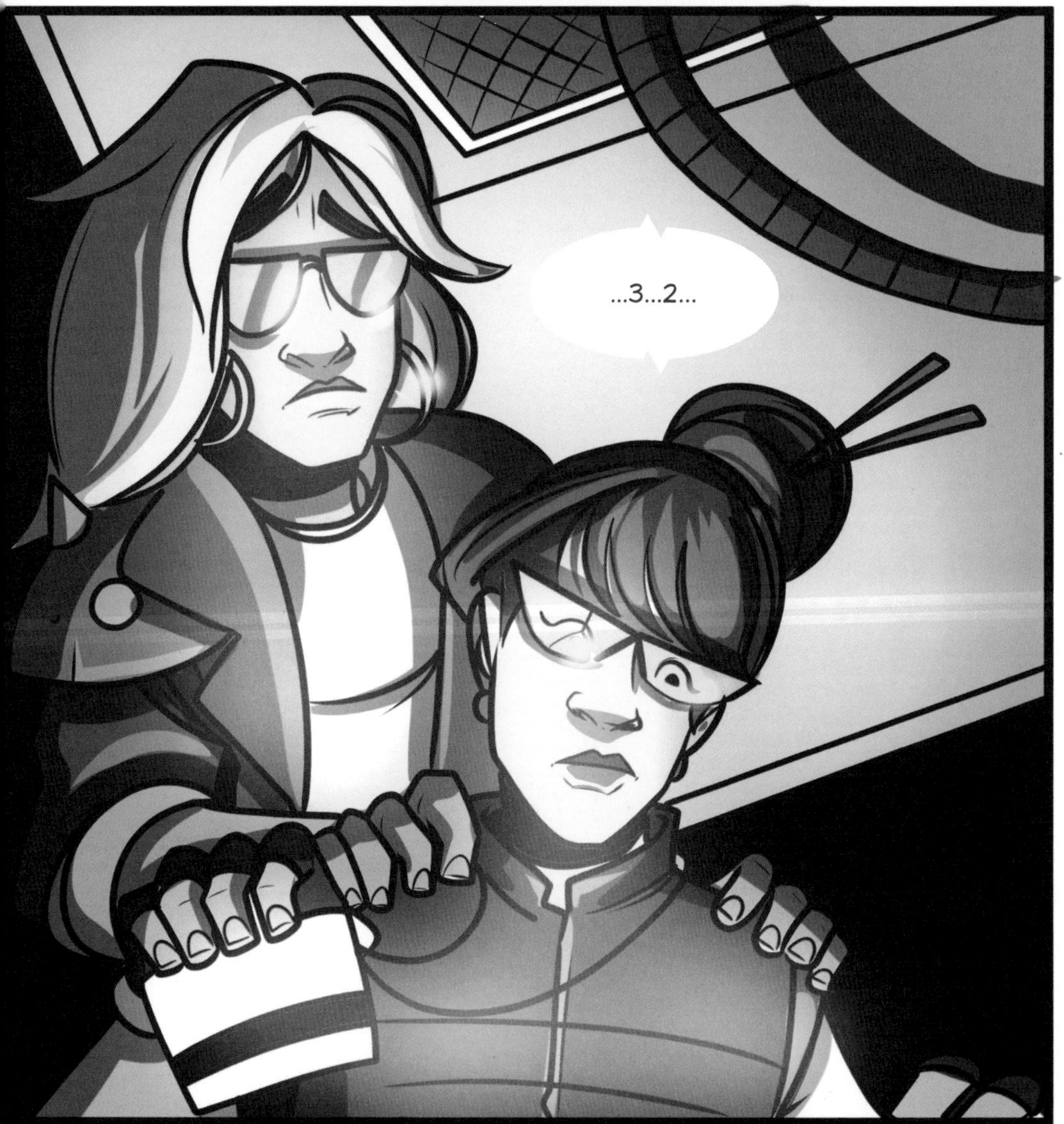
...3...2...

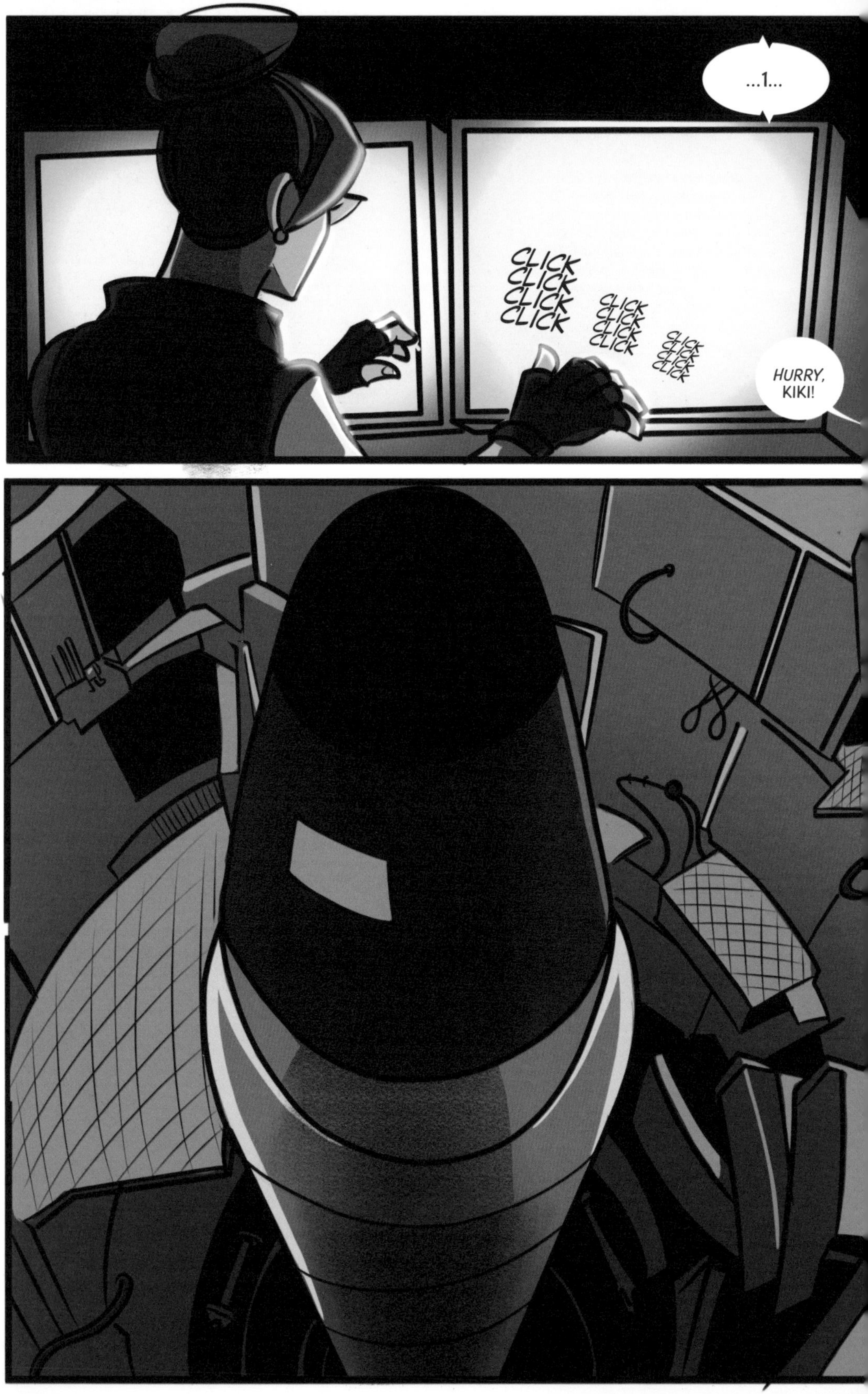
...1...
CLICK CLICK CLICK CLICK
CLICK CLICK CLICK CLICK
CLICK CLICK CLICK CLICK
HURRY, KIKI!

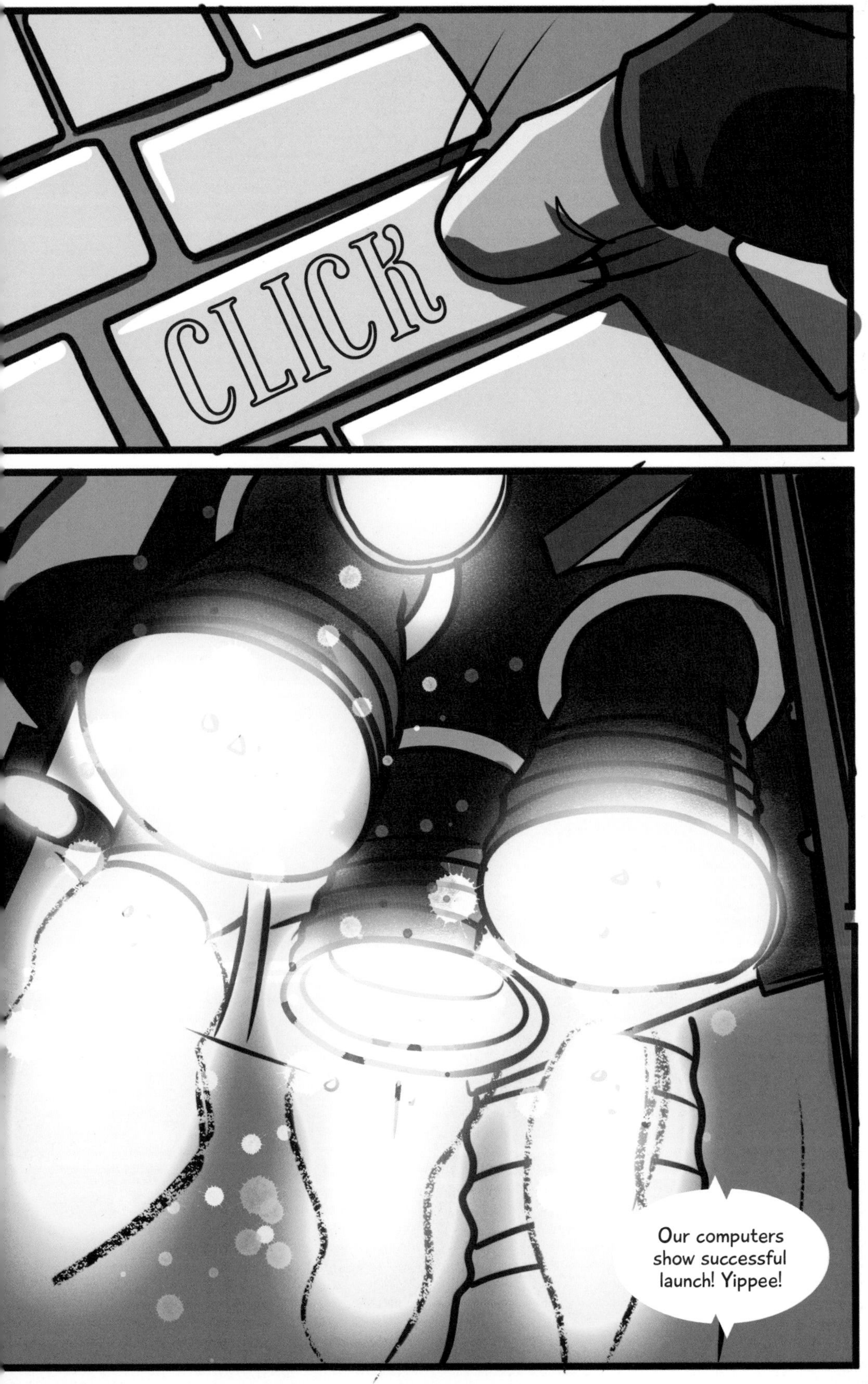
CLICK
Our computers show successful launch! Yippee!

Epilogue

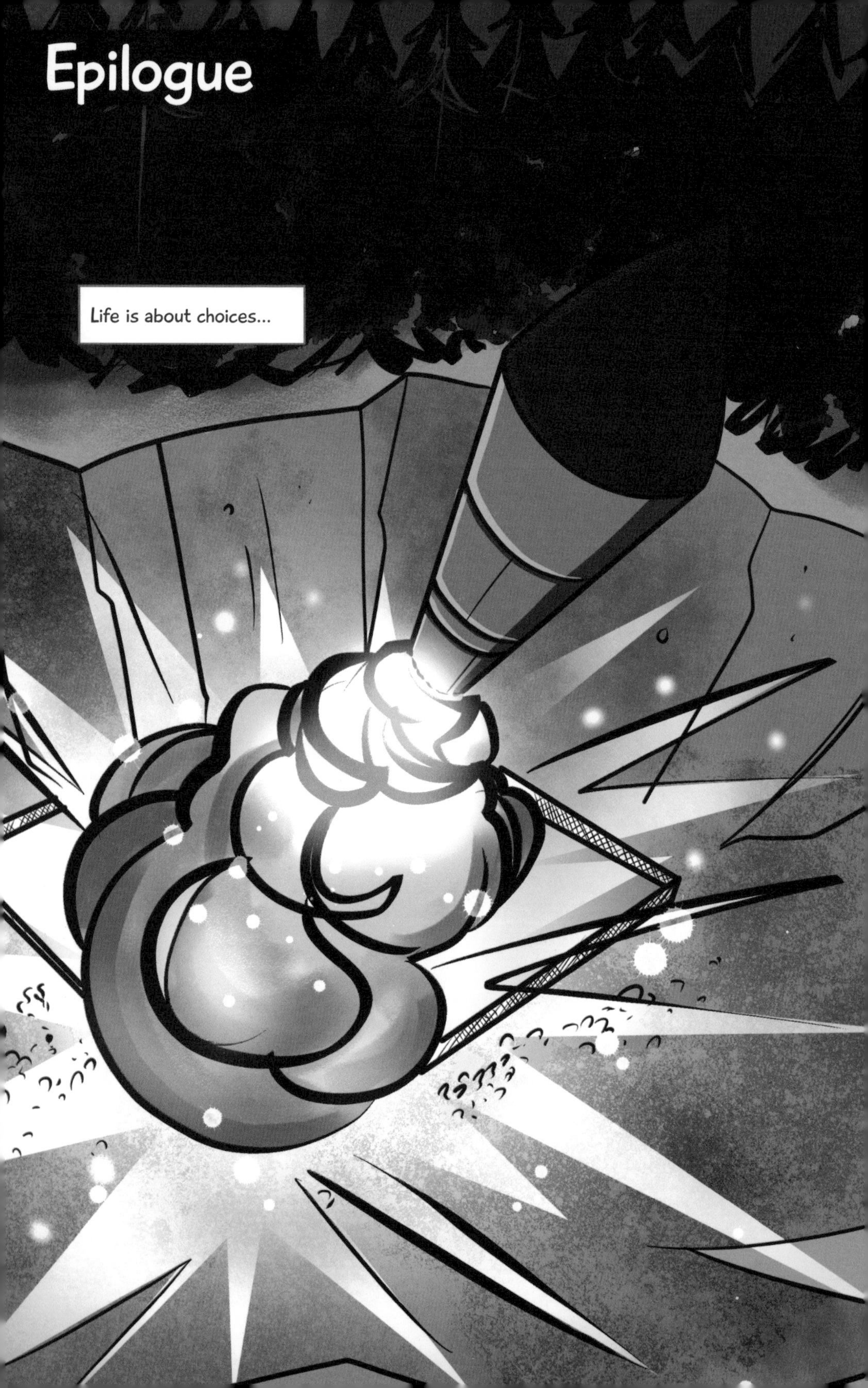
Life is about choices...

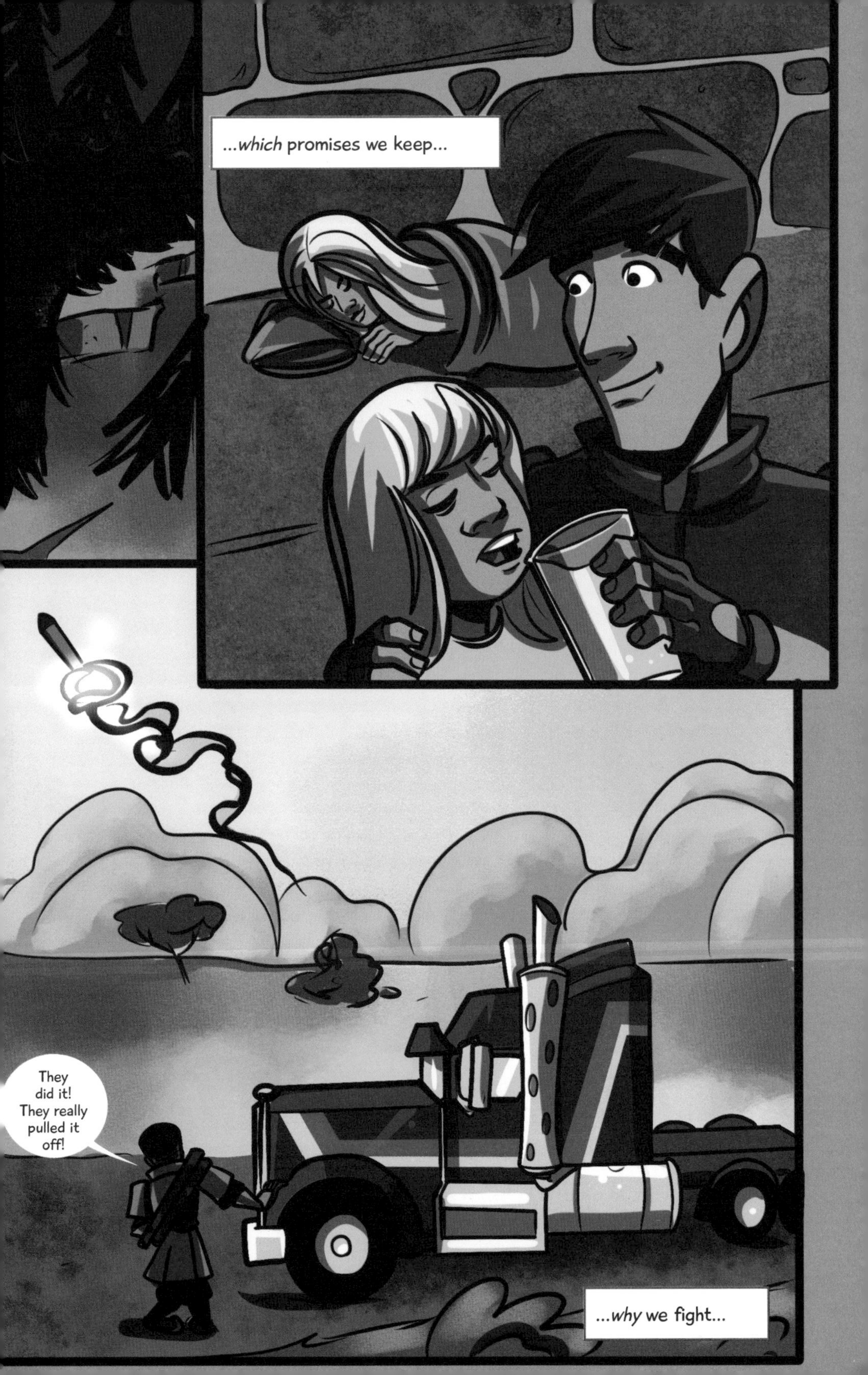

...*which* promises we keep...
They did it! They really pulled it off!
...*why* we fight...

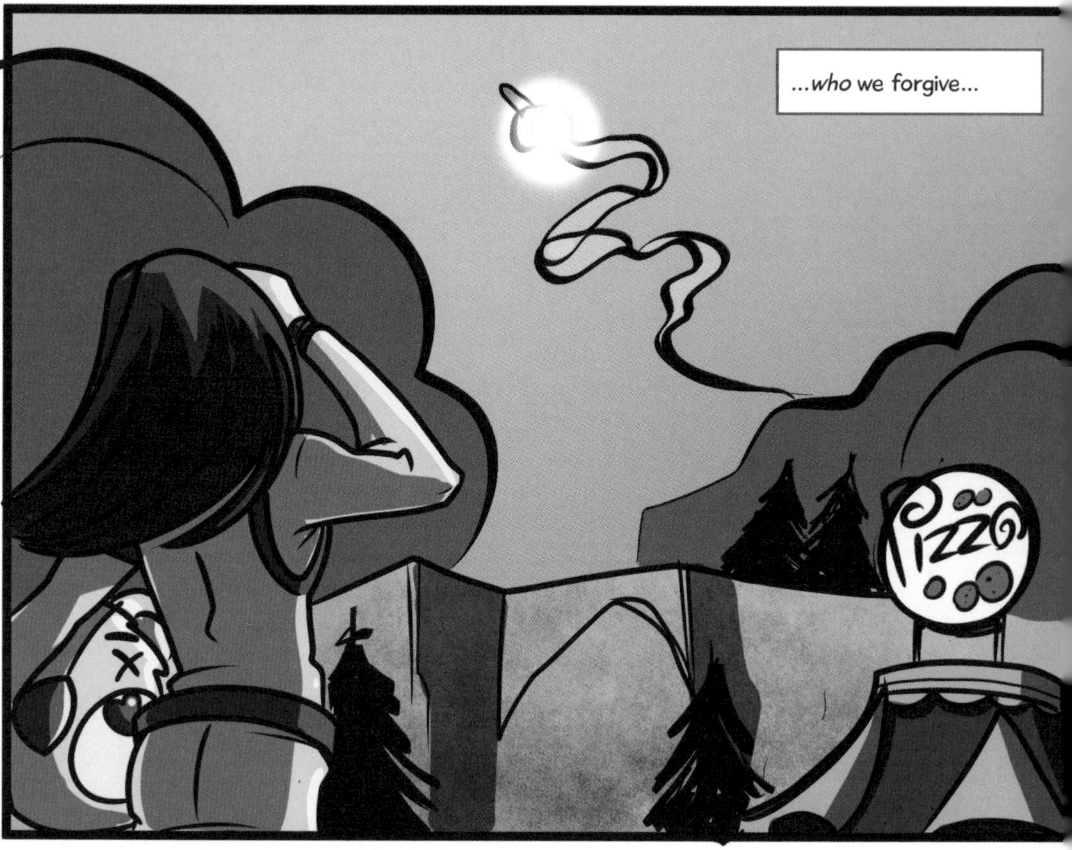
...*who* we forgive...

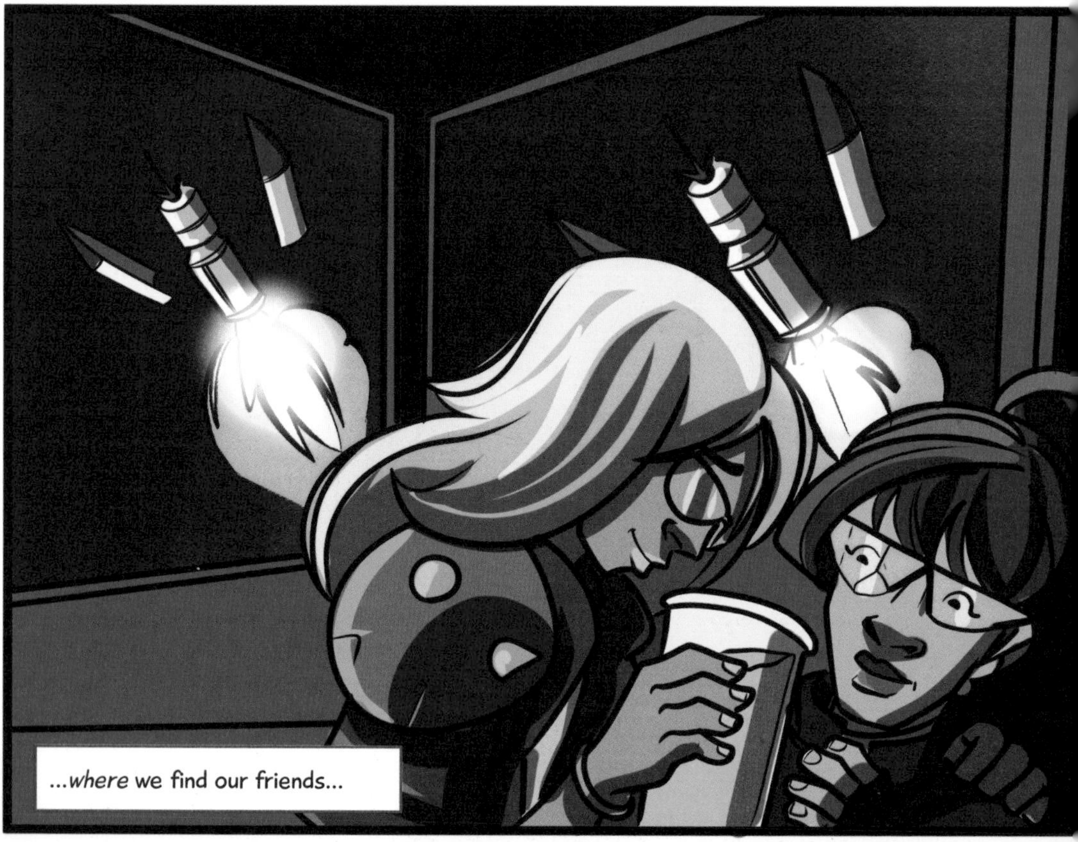
...*where* we find our friends...

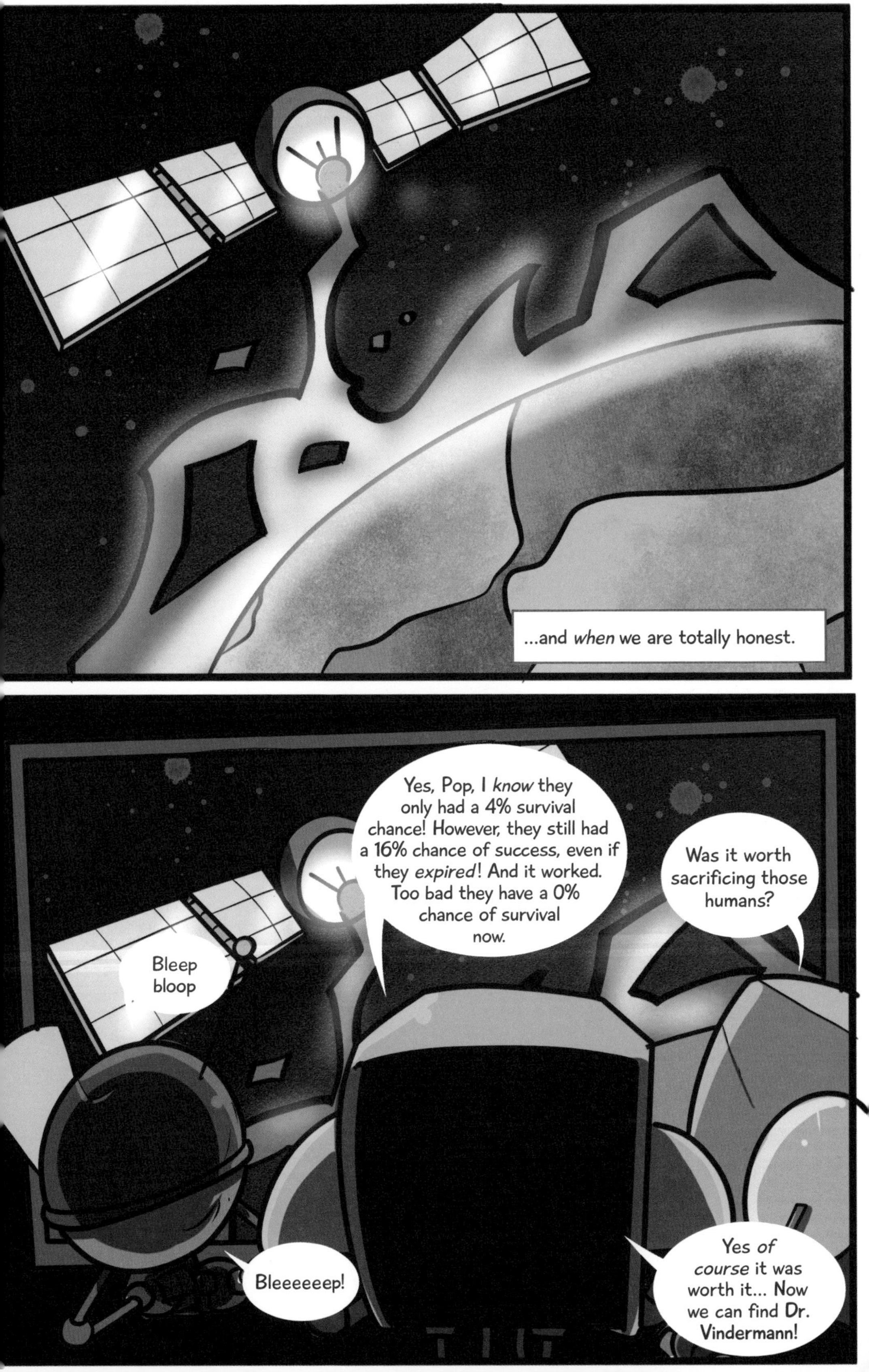
...and *when* we are totally honest.
Yes, Pop, I *know* they only had a 4% survival chance! However, they still had a 16% chance of success, even if they *expired*! And it worked. Too bad they have a 0% chance of survival now.
Was it worth sacrificing those humans?
Bleep bloop
Bleeeeeep!
Yes *of course* it was worth it... Now we can find Dr. Vindermann!

CHECK OUT THESE OTHER UNOFFICIAL FORTNITE SERIES

TRAPPED IN BATTLE ROYALE

by Devin Hunter

Follow Grey through these exciting adventures in Battle Royale!

TRAPPED IN BATTLE ROYALE
#1
CLASH AT FATAL FIELDS
AN UNOFFICIAL FORTNITE NOVEL
DEVIN HUNTER

TRAPPED IN BATTLE ROYALE
#2
BATTLE FOR LOOT LAKE
AN UNOFFICIAL FORTNITE NOVEL
DEVIN HUNTER

TRAPPED IN BATTLE ROYALE
#3
BETRAYAL AT SALTY SPRINGS
AN UNOFFICIAL FORTNITE NOVEL
DEVIN HUNTER

TRAPPED IN BATTLE ROYALE
#4
THE SQUAD OF LUCKY LANDING
AN UNOFFICIAL FORTNITE NOVEL
DEVIN HUNTER

TRAPPED IN BATTLE ROYALE
#5
FIGHT FOR DUSTY DIVOT
AN UNOFFICIAL FORTNITE NOVEL
DEVIN HUNTER

TRAPPED IN BATTLE ROYALE
#6
ATTACK FROM TILTED TOWERS
AN UNOFFICIAL FORTNITE NOVEL
DEVIN HUNTER

SKY PONY PRESS

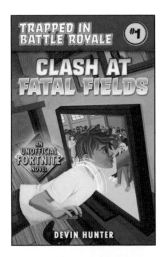

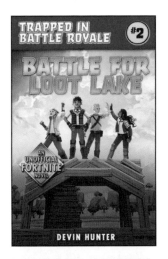

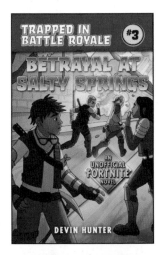

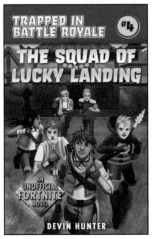

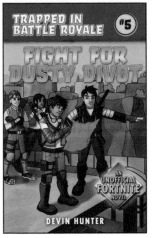

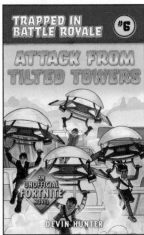

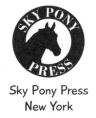

Sky Pony Press
New York

BATTLE ROYALE:
SECRETS OF THE ISLAND
by Cara J. Stevens

Tag along with The Impossibles
as they battle for victory!

BATTLE STORM
BATTLE ROYALE: SECRETS OF THE ISLAND
AN UNOFFICIAL FORTNITE NOVEL
CARA J. STEVENS

THE ALIEN CONSPIRACY
BATTLE ROYALE: SECRETS OF THE ISLAND
AN UNOFFICIAL FORTNITE NOVEL
CARA J. STEVENS

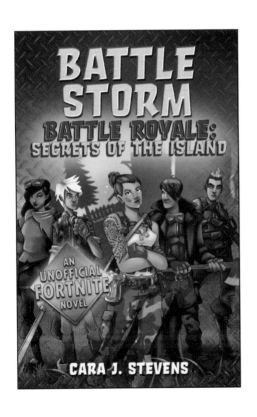

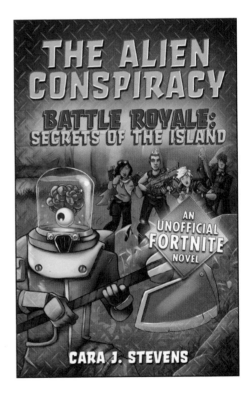

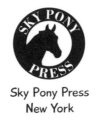

Sky Pony Press
New York